SPECIAL MESSAGE TO READERS

THE ULVERSCROFT FOUNDATION
(registered UK charity number 264873)
was established in 1972 to provide funds for
research, diagnosis and treatment of eye diseases.
Examples of major projects funded by
the Ulverscroft Foundation are:-

- The Children's Eye Unit at Moorfields Eye
  Hospital, London
- The Ulverscroft Children's Eye Unit at Great
  Ormond Street Hospital for Sick Children
- Funding research into eye diseases and
  treatment at the Department of Ophthalmology,
  University of Leicester
- The Ulverscroft Vision Research Group,
  Institute of Child Health
- Twin operating theatres at the Western
  Ophthalmic Hospital, London
- The Chair of Ophthalmology at the Royal
  Australian College of Ophthalmologists

You can help further the work of the Foundation
by making a donation or leaving a legacy.
Every contribution is gratefully received. If you
would like to help support the Foundation or
require further information, please contact:

THE ULVERSCROFT FOUNDATION
The Green, Bradgate Road, Anstey
Leicester LE7 7FU, England
Tel: (0116) 236 4325

website: www.foundation.ulverscroft.com

Dinah Jefferies was born in Malaya in 1948 and moved to England at the age of nine. She has worked in education, once lived in a 'rock 'n' roll' commune and, more recently, has been an exhibiting artist. For a while she was an au pair in Italy, and also spent five years in northern Andalucía, where she began to write. She spends her days writing, with time off to make tiaras and dinosaurs with her grandchildren. *The Separation* is her first book.

You can discover more about the author at www.dinahjefferies.com

THE SEPARATION

Malaya, 1955: Lydia Cartwright returns from visiting a sick friend to an empty house. The servants are gone. The phone is dead. Where is her husband, Alec? Her young daughters, Emma and Fleur? Fearful and desperate, she contacts the British District Officer and learns that Alec has been posted up-country. But why didn't he wait? Why did he leave no message? Lydia's search takes her on a hazardous journey through the war-torn jungle. Forced to turn to a man she'd vowed to leave in her past, she sacrifices everything to be reunited with her family. And while carrying her own secrets, Lydia will soon face a devastating betrayal which may be more than she can bear . . .

DINAH JEFFERIES

◆

THE SEPARATION

Complete and Unabridged

CHARNWOOD
Leicester

First published in Great Britain in 2014 by
Penguin Books Ltd
London

First Charnwood Edition
published 2015
by arrangement with
Penguin Books Ltd
London

A catalogue record for this book is available
from the British Library.

ISBN 978–1–4448–2565–7

Published by
F. A. Thorpe (Publishing)
Anstey, Leicestershire

Set by Words & Graphics Ltd.
Anstey, Leicestershire
Printed and bound in Great Britain by
T. J. International Ltd., Padstow, Cornwall

This book is printed on acid-free paper

118988538

For my mother and my daughter

Prologue

1931: Weston-super-Mare, England

The man smoothed down the lion's paws with a sponge he'd dipped in a bucket of water, then withdrew a knife from a leather pouch at his waist. He glanced up at the waiting crowd, before bending his head and carefully sharpening the creature's claws.

The young girl, squatting a foot away, reached out to touch the lion's mane with her fingertips.

'No!' the man shouted, as he pushed the child away. 'Not yet.'

Her head hung for a moment, but then she glanced back over her shoulder, smiled shyly at the woman who stood watching, and swivelled back to keep her eyes on the creature.

A gust of wind lifted a layer of sand and sent a thousand grains dancing and whirling. The man reacted quickly, dampening down the surface of the beast before more could be whisked away.

The watching woman shivered. Her red-gold hair was cut close to her head, with a Marcel wave to keep it neat, and she wore a pale blue dress with darker blue cornflowers at the modest hemline, with only a thin white cotton cardigan to protect her from the sudden chill.

Once he had satisfied himself that the animal was complete, the sculptor bowed, then walked round the crowd, an upturned hat in his hand.

The woman listened to the chink of coins and dipped into her purse.

The sound of horses' hooves rang on the cobbled road behind the esplanade, but it was not they who drew the woman's attention. Her eyes remained fixed on the little girl, now kneeling on the sand, and gathering handfuls that glistened silvery-gold in the pale sunlight.

As the milling crowd dispersed, instead of their murmurs, or the noise of screaming seagulls and the waves of the ocean, the tap of hammer on metal filled the air. The woman glanced back at what had once been the grand pier, its elegant wrought ironwork bent out of shape by fire. She caught the scent of cockles in vinegar.

'Are you hungry?' she asked the child.

The little girl shook her head. There was hesitance, an uncertainty that revealed itself in the child's slight blush.

'What about a liquorice stick?'

The woman knelt down beside the child and drew close. Close enough to smell the sweetness of her hair. She took a long slow breath, and exhaled through lips that trembled only slightly. She stood, shook sand from the hem of her floral skirt, and took hold of the girl's hand.

'Let's run, shall we?'

A look passed between them and they raced along the beach, kicking up sand and shells and stumbling and slipping until they reached the waiting nun.

At heart the nun was not unfeeling, and with a kindly look she touched the woman's shoulder.

Just a fleeting touch that ensured the exchange would be smooth, tears kept at bay, and emotion restrained. The child tipped back her head and turned her hazel eyes on the two women, then beyond them to where red and blue flags lined the sandy sweep of the bay.

For the woman, the day had begun with excitement and a sense of elation. Now it was almost over, she could not take her eyes from the child's sharp-angled, stick-thin body. She patted the little girl's auburn hair and fixed the moment in her memory.

But it would be different for the child. As *her* memory receded and blended into the past, she would doubt: wonder if the day, the lion, and the woman existed only in her mind. She would seek to capture details of a time that could not be recovered. There would be resonance — a dress, a smile. Only that. And the woman would continue to stifle her sorrow.

'Come along,' the nun said, and took the child's hand. 'We need to get on that tram, or we won't reach the railway station in time.'

The woman in the blue dress stepped away, then glanced back to look at the golden sand lion, aware the incoming tide would soon wash it away.

1

1955: Malaya

They couldn't see me beneath the house on stilts. But I spied on them. Our amah, and Fleur, my little sister. I heard sandals on the patio — flip-flop, flip-flop — and Fleur's sobs as she ran. Then the swish of her old pink rabbit, dragged by its ears over the pebbled path.

Amah's shrill Chinese voice came after. 'You come here now, Missy. You spoil rabbit. Carry him like that.'

'I don't care! I don't want to go,' Fleur shouted back. 'I like it here.'

'Me too,' I whispered, and sniffed a mix of dead lizards and daddy-long-legs. I didn't mind them.

Beyond my earthy hideout, past the end of the garden, was the long grass, where nobody dared go. But I wasn't scared of that either.

What I *was* scared of was leaving.

Later on, when the sky turned lavender, Daddy pointed out across the same view. Now, from an upstairs balcony, a Tiger beer in his hand, he looked past the lawns and over the hills. To England.

'It's never warm enough there in January,' he said, talking to himself and rubbing his jaw. 'With a raw wind that makes your cheekbones ache. Not like here. Nothing like here.'

5

'Daddy?'

I watched his bony face, the large Adam's apple and straight line of his mouth above. He swallowed, the apple rose and fell, and his eyes came back to me and Fleur, as if he'd just remembered us. He sort of smiled and gave us both a squeeze.

'Come on, you two. No need to look so miserable. We'll have a great life in England. You like swinging from trees, don't you, Em?'

I nodded. 'Well, yes, but — '

'What about you, Fleur?' he broke in. 'Plenty of streams to paddle in.'

Fleur's mouth remained turned down. I caught her eye and pulled a face; it sounded too much like the jungle to me.

'Come on,' Dad said. 'You're a big girl now, Emma. Nearly twelve. Set an example to your sister.'

'But, Daddy,' I tried to tell him.

He went to the door. 'Emma, it's settled. Sort out the books you want to take. That'll keep you busy. Just a few, mind. Come along, Fleur.'

'But, Dad.'

When he saw my tears, he paused. 'You'll love it, if that's what's bothering you. I promise.'

I felt very hot, and the thought of my mother made me catch my breath.

He opened the door.

'But, Dad,' I called after him, as he and Fleur went out. 'Aren't we going to wait for Mummy?'

6

2

Lydia dumped her dusty case. Out on the patio, her daughters' bikes lay abandoned beside the jacaranda tree.

'Emma, Fleur,' she called out. 'Mummy's home.'

She stepped from the patio to glance down the pebble path that led to the long grass. As the sky darkened, an enormous moth, from the fringes of the jungle, smacked her in the cheek. She brushed its black dust off, then ducked back inside to escape the oncoming rain.

'Alec?' she called again. 'I'm home.'

Her husband's clean-cut features came to mind, skin smelling strongly of soap from the Chinese market, light brown hair cut short back and sides. There was no reply.

She fought off a pang of disappointment in the too-silent house. She'd sent a telegram, just as he'd asked; so where were her family? It was too hot to have gone for a walk. Were they at the pool perhaps, or maybe Alec had taken the girls for tea at the club?

She climbed the stairs to her bedroom, glanced at a photo of Emma and Fleur on the bedside table, and felt such a surge of love. She had missed them.

After undressing, she ran her fingers through her shoulder-length auburn hair, and flicked on the fan. Tired from the journey, and a month looking after a sick friend, she really needed a bath. She pulled open the wardrobe doors, stopped short, frowned. Her breath caught — none of Alec's clothes were there. Throwing on her loosely woven kimono, she ran barefoot to her daughters' room.

Someone had left their wardrobe open, and she saw, straightaway, that it was practically empty. Just a few pairs of roughly folded shorts on the top shelf, and crumpled paper on the one beneath. Where were all of their clothes?

What if, she thought, but the sentence died in her throat. She steadied her breathing. That's what they want: the men in the jungle. To frighten us. She imagined what Alec would say: *Hold your head up. Don't let them win.* But what can you expect to feel, when they throw a grenade into a marketplace packed with people?

She spun round at the sound of a cry, and ran to the window. Her shoulders slumped. Just the flying foxes hanging in the tree.

With one hand on her heart, she slid her fingers under the crumpled lining paper in the wardrobe and pulled out one of Em's notebooks, hoping for a clue. She sat on the camphor wood chest, sniffed the comforting familiar smell, and clasped the notebook to her. She took a deep breath, then opened the notebook to read:

The matriarch is a fat lady with a flabby neck. Her name is Harriet Parrott. She has raisin eyes and a shiny buttery nose which she tries to hide with powder. She slides on little feet in Chinese slippers, but wears long skirts, so you can only just see them at the edges.

Harriet. Had they gone to Harriet?

She stopped abruptly, grasped the edge of the chest, reeling from a rush of heat and the panic that was rising in her. Too much was missing. A note. Of course. He must have left a note. Or a message with the servants.

She ran downstairs two at a time, missing her footing, diving into the downstairs rooms: living rooms, kitchen, scullery, the covered corridor to the servants' day quarters, and the storehouses. Just a couple of abandoned crates remained, everywhere was dark and empty, the servants gone. No amah's rocking chair, no cook's day bed, all the gardener's tools removed. She scanned the room — no note.

She listened to the rain and, biting a fingernail, racked her brain, hardly able to think for air so heavy it weighed her down. She pictured her journey back home, hours squashed against the jammed train window, a hand cupped over her nose. The pungent odour of vomit from a sickly Indian boy. The distant gunfire.

She doubled over, winded by their absence. Fought for breath. This couldn't be. She was tired. She wasn't thinking straight. There had to be a rational explanation. There had to be. Alec would have found a way to tell her if they'd had to leave. Wouldn't he?

She swivelled round and called their names, *'Emma, Fleur.'* She choked back a sob and pictured Fleur's dimpled chin, blue eyes, fair hair parted with a bow. Then, recalling the jungle mists that concealed desperate men, her worst fear overtook any remaining chance of rational hope. Sweat crawled under her kimono, her eyes began to smart and she covered her mouth with her palm.

With trembling hands she picked up the phone to dial Alec's boss. He'd know what had happened. He'd tell her what to do.

Then, she sat with the phone in her lap, sweat growing cold on her skin, flies humming overhead, the sound of the fan churning, click, click, click, and the flutter of a moth's wings beating the air. The line was dead.

3

In the taxi on our way to the port, I couldn't understand why Mum hadn't arrived home in time to come, even though Dad had said she would be back. On the last day at our house in Malacca, right up until the end, I'd hoped she would make it, kept rushing to the window to stare her home.

Dad was hopeless at domestic things, and as Mum wasn't there to organise the packing, I helped Amah do it. Fleur was only eight and would just get in the way.

First, I picked out the pink gingham party dress Mum made for me, and slipped it into the trunk. With a full skirt and little puffy sleeves, it was the only dress I loved. I had cried when I grew too big for it and Fleur got to wear it.

Dad came into our bedroom. 'You won't need party dresses,' he said.

'Don't they have parties in England?'

He sighed. 'Leave your Malayan clothes, that's all I mean. And we do need to get a move on.'

'What's going to happen to the things we're leaving. Shall I put them back in the wardrobe?'

'No need. Amah will take care of them.'

'How long are we going for then?'

My father cleared his throat but didn't speak.

I handed the dress to our amah, Mei-Lien, who added it to the growing pile of unwanted stuff.

11

'What about our Coronation clothes?'

I held up Fleur's white dress, decorated with red and blue braid, far too small now.

He shook his head, but I slipped my prized Coronation edition of *Dandy* behind my back. With a golden horse and six white horses printed on the cover, it was too good to leave.

'Where's Fleur?'

Amah pointed outside.

'Cartwheeling, I suppose,' Dad said. 'You two can manage on your own, can't you?'

I nodded.

He was about to go, but glanced across at my bed and paused. 'What's that you've got?'

'I've written to Mummy.' I picked up the envelope for him to see.

'Oh,' he said, with raised brows. 'What about?'

'Just how much I miss her, and that I'm looking forward to seeing her in England.'

'Okay. Give it to me.'

'I wanted to leave it on the hall table.'

He held out his hand. 'No need. I'll take care of it.'

'I wanted to do it myself.'

'Emma, I've said I'll take care of it.'

I had no choice.

'Good girl,' he said, and turned to leave.

'Daddy, before you go.' I picked up Fleur's rabbit. 'What about this? Shall I pack it, or will Fleur want to have it in the cabin?'

'For heaven's sake,' he said. 'I haven't time for minor details. Big changes are on their way, Emma, big changes.'

I frowned, not so sure. It seemed to me *big*

changes had already happened. More than three weeks before. That's when they started, as far as I could tell.

★　★　★

We'd been on our way home after a wedding. A rainy dark evening. At the party Mum had danced in a bright yellow dress, and high-heeled, crocodile-skin shoes. Mum is younger than Dad, and really beautiful, with lovely pale skin and hazel eyes. Dad didn't dance because of his wartime injury. But it didn't seem to stop him playing tennis. Once in the car, Mum rubbed her forehead with the tips of her fingers, and I knew *he* was angry.

'Slow down, Alec!' my mother yelled. 'I know you're upset, but you're going too fast. It's wet. For heaven's sake, look at the water.'

I peeked out of the window. We were in the foothills and the road was swimming with water.

From behind I saw the veins stand out in his neck, and I noticed one of Mum's lizard earrings drop as she reached across to grab the wheel. I tried to tell her, but the car whizzed off to the other side of the road. With his foot still on the accelerator, Dad tried to twist us back over to the right side of the road, but he raced forward round a bend, and had to slam on the brakes.

The car went over the edge with a loud bang, and wedged halfway into a storm ditch, beside a big clump of bamboo.

Mother's voice cracked. 'For Christ's sake, Alec. You're off your goddamn rocker. Look what you've bloody well done now.'

I knew we were in trouble because Mum didn't swear, except when she thought we couldn't hear, though I'd heard her swear when they'd both had too much to drink. I'd roll the sounds out, say them under my breath, daring to get a little bit louder each time and finding words to rhyme.

I heard Mum plead with my dad.

'Don't leave us here. What if there's a road block?' She sounded scared, but it didn't stop Father.

'Here. Use that if you need to,' he said, and threw a pistol on the driver's seat. 'Emma. Look after Fleur.'

As soon as he left to get help, the jungle crept closer, with leaves the size of frying pans, and in the branches, eyes that blinked at you. Mum turned round and stopped sobbing, as if she'd suddenly remembered us sitting there, with our bare legs sticking to hot leather seats. 'Emma, Fleur. Are you okay?'

'Yes, Mummy,' we both said, Fleur's voice more tearful than mine.

'It's all right, darlings. Daddy's just gone to get help.' Her eyes flicked over us. She was trying to make it sound all right, but I suspected it wasn't. I knew about terrorists in the jungle. They'd tie you to a tree, and chop off your head as soon as they clapped eyes on you. Then put it up on a pole. I squeezed my eyes shut, terrified of seeing a head grinning at me.

Mum started humming.

Soon it would be completely dark and the

stars would come out, then it'd be better. Though on the subject of terror, Mother didn't know that I'd seen even worse at the waxwork museum. Just past the shrunken heads, there was a *Children Prohibited* section. I didn't stay. Only long enough to see tiny waxwork models of white women and children, pinned to the ground, still alive, their painted red mouths wide open in a scream. Coming towards them, driven by a Jap, was an enormous steamroller, normally used to flatten tarmac roads. Only this time it was being used to flatten those people. When I got outside I was sick in a rubbish bin.

Japs were bad. Our parents said so. Though the people in the jungle now, the ones they called terrorists, they were Chinese. I didn't understand. Our amah, Mei-Lien, was Chinese and I loved her. Why was it that Japs were bad before, but now Chinese people, though only some? It didn't make sense.

Our car was stuck well off the main road and almost where the bandits were. But even deeper in the jungle lived the spirits who ate children. Our gardener, whose mouth was red from chewing betel nut, told us.

'If you ever get lost in the jungle, watch out for the *hantu hantuan*,' he said. He narrowed his eyes in a scary way, but it was confusing because he never told us what they looked like.

'Emma, can you move your arms and legs?' Mum asked.

I wriggled them to show I could.

'Fleur?'

Fleur tried and could move her arms and her

left leg; but when she moved the other, she cried out.

'It's probably bruised. Get her shoe off before it swells, Emma.'

I did it, though Fleur struggled. 'I don't like it. Where's Daddy?'

I told her she had to keep quiet and that Daddy had gone to get help. She sniffed a bit, made a few moany noises, and then stayed still.

It was evening time, but in the distance the sound of an explosion broke up the quiet.

'Mummy!' we both yelled.

'Shhh! It's nowhere near us.'

The sky started to turn brown, and white mist slid down from the mountaintop. But at least we weren't properly in the hills. Because *'Ada bukit, ada paya'* — where there are hills there are swamps. And they would swallow you whole.

Eventually Dad came back with an armoured truck that had been on its way back to Malacca. We had to get out while the soldiers pulled the car out of the storm ditch, and by the time we went to bed, it was much later than we'd ever been to bed before.

★ ★ ★

The next day, Mum didn't pick us up from school. Dad did. With an *I'm not in the mood for questions* face, he ignored us when we asked where Mummy was. Just said we were going away to England.

Back home, we rushed upstairs to see if Mum was there. She wasn't. I smelt the lemongrass

16

outside our bedroom window and thought of her big smile and wavy hair. She'd pin it up, with an orange bird of paradise flower, but by lunch it all came tumbling down. And she was always singing, even first thing.

'Come on, Em,' Fleur said. 'She's not here. Let's play outside.'

I shook my head.

Fleur went out to cartwheel, her ankle fine. She always made a fuss.

I brushed my hair. It's curlier than Mum's, and redder. Feral hair, Mum calls it. Then I felt under my pillow for my notebook. But as well as my notebook, an envelope came out, addressed to Fleur and me. What a funny place to leave a letter, I thought, as I tore it open.

Darlings, I read.

Suzanne phoned today. I am so sorry, but I have to go to help her. She's been diagnosed with a dreadful illness and just isn't able to cope on her own. Her husband, Eric, ought to be back from Borneo in a couple of weeks, so I shouldn't be awfully much longer than that. Take care of yourselves. Be good. Daddy and Mei-Lien know what to do about school. You can go on the bus. I know how you always want to. If you need any help, get Amah to call Cicely or Harriet Parrott. Their addresses are in the red book.

All my love, Mummy

I put it back under my pillow, and went out to hide under the house.

★ ★ ★

It was our last day, and more than three weeks since Mum had gone. Just before we left to go to the ship, Amah was still folding useful clothes into our trunk. Trousers, underwear, a sweater or two. I didn't really care. My pink gingham party dress sat on the pile of unwanted stuff, and *I* sat on the bed, thinking of the Holy Infant College, my school. Next to a row of palm trees, it was painted white, and there were add-on rooms, with no glass in the windows. Just bamboo shutters that got closed up when we went home.

I felt sad. We wouldn't be going to school there any more, but my biggest sadness was it looked like we'd be gone before Mum came home. Because if that happened, she'd come back to an empty house. I was pleased that, at least, she'd have my letter.

Mei-Lien picked up my school tunic. 'You want keep?'

I looked at it and shook my head. 'No point.'

'Daddy say we finish pack now. No daydream. Go now.'

I took the tunic, folded it neatly, and put it on top of the pile. I put Mum's note in the trunk, then slipped in a framed photo of her, hazel eyes all crinkled up. Last of all, I put Fleur's pink rabbit in. If she had it in the cabin with her, it might get lost, or even end up overboard.

Half an hour later, we drove off without Mum.

A lorry had come to take the trunks, and the taxi was taking Dad, Fleur, and me. As we left Malacca, I looked out at the sea, and wound down the window to smell the wild orchids. They were nice, but my mind was full of questions, and I had to pinch my skin really hard to stop the tears.

4

At the sprawling colonial residence, the Malay servant led Lydia through a large, glass-ceilinged hall, with a crystal chandelier. A framed picture of the queen faced you as you entered, the floor was tiled in black and silver chequered marble, and heavy furniture edged the pale green walls. The formality, intended to impress, made her heart pound.

Harriet Parrott's husband, George, was District Officer, or DO as they were generally referred to. Apart from the Commissioner, it was the highest position you could hold in the British Administration of Malaya, with a key role supporting Britain's armed forces. If he doesn't know, she thought, who will?

The hall led to a veranda, where she was asked to wait under the shade of a mature angsana tree. Glad of protection from the morning sun, she looked about and tried to steady her breath. At the front of the lawn, a crimson-bellied sun-bird flew over two bushes of fragrant golden hibiscus. In the distance, coconut palms stretched tall trunks to the sky.

This felt all wrong. It was time to take the children to school. She closed her eyes and saw herself drive there, but her head felt muddled. Something stopped her, like in a bad dream. A voice kept repeating, Where are the girls? Where are they? She saw the main school buildings in her mind's eye, and willed the girls to race across the gravel at the front, satchels flying.

An aroma of chilli-pepper reached her from the kitchens. She felt her throat close. Was it Friday today? She managed to swallow. Whatever day it was, there would be no drive to school, and once the heat descended, it was impossible to travel without a car. She looked out at the blue sky. The car. She hadn't checked the garage. Could it be that Alec's driver had taken them somewhere in an official car instead?

At the sound of footsteps, she turned to see a tall, heavy-bosomed woman approach: Harriet, poised and self-assured. Orange lips in a plump face full of powdered wrinkles, dyed black hair loosely piled on top of her head, and, famous for her citrus colours, she wore only silk. Today it was green and yellow. And though Em's description of her was less than flattering, Lydia could see why her daughter called her the matriarch.

'Lydia. Dear,' said Mrs Parrott, holding out her fleshy hand, nails lacquered in Chinese orange. She wore a half smile in sharp, black eyes.

Aware of the early hour, Lydia gulped, her skin flushing deeply. 'I'm so sorry — but the phone's down,' she said.

Mrs Parrott inclined her head, and settled herself into a wide rattan armchair. Lydia perched on the edge of her own and took a deep breath.

'Alec and the children aren't at home. Everything's gone.' Her voice rose as she raced through the words, and she held her hands together to stop them shaking. 'I came by taxi. Sorry it's so early. I don't know what to do. As Alec's boss, do you think George might?'

Harriet raised high pencil-drawn eyebrows. 'My dear. Have you no idea? Have you been to the police?'

Lydia shook her head, holding back tears. 'I should've gone last night, but I didn't dare leave the house. Stupid of me. I thought they might come back.'

'Maybe no need. I'm sure George will know. Thick as thieves, Alec and George.' She picked up the hand bell. 'You're lucky. He's working from home.'

Within minutes her thin-hipped houseboy, Noor, was sent off to bring the master to the salon. Immediately.

Lydia stared out of the window and prayed Harriet was right. She heard George's deep voice echoing off the walls of the corridor leading from his office. Even from where she sat, Lydia could tell he was annoyed.

'What's all this, Harriet? I am busy,' he said, exploding on to the patio, his large square frame filling the doorway.

Without missing a beat, Harriet indicated Lydia, sitting sideways to him.

'Lydia is desperate to know where Alec and the children are.'

Dressed in tropical linens, George came round to face Lydia, his heavy eyebrows meeting in the middle. He coughed, ran a hand through short salt and pepper hair and scratched his chin.

'Sorry. Didn't see you there.'

She stared up at the sweat shining on the skin above his top lip.

There was the slightest pause.

'I thought he'd have left instructions,' he said, puffing out red cheeks. 'Been posted north. Up at Ipoh. Bit of a rush job. The chap running financial admin up there kicked the bucket suddenly. Heart I think.'

She let out her breath, felt the room spin, put a hand to her chest. 'Oh my Lord. Thank you. That explains everything. Thank you so much, George. I knew there had to be an explanation. His note must be missing.'

'Alec went ahead a few days ago. Maybe he left instructions with the bank. You know, in case the house was reallocated before you got back.'

Harriet nodded. 'That makes sense.'

'Bad roads to Ipoh,' George said.

'How long will it take?'

'A couple of days by car, depending on land mines and what have you. Longer by bus, of course. By train could be best. Fantastic Moorish station at Ipoh.'

'I could phone Alec. Ask him to meet me there.'

'No phones or postal service working in the district. Lines all cut. Terrific chaos. Not as bad as getting to Penang, but still.' He dashed off, mumbling a few words to Harriet as he passed.

'Can you let me have the address?' Lydia called after him.

He looked back over his shoulder. 'Just the rest house up there. Larger than usual, fifty or so rooms I believe. Temporary, until they get allocated a house, but they should still be there. Best be careful, travelling alone in the Emergency.'

There was a silence as he headed for the door.

Harriet peered at her.

'I'm not going to give you the third degree, but you don't seem too good. A bit less Rita Hayworth than your usual look.'

Lydia dabbed the moisture from her hairline and slapped at the flies settling on her skin. At thirty-one, she was shapely and vivacious, and knew how to make a splash, but apart from the hair, the resemblance to the film star was slight.

'An old friend has polio. Suzanne Fleetwood. I've just got back. I hated having to leave the children for so much longer than I expected, almost a month actually, but her husband is in Borneo and she couldn't reach him. You know he's in intelligence.'

Harriet shot a look at George's disappearing back.

Lydia sighed. 'I know. Keep it under my hat. The awful thing is they're shipping her back to England in an iron lung.'

'A sad business. You will have been a great help to her. But you must feel better now, knowing where your family are?'

Lydia's eyes lit up. 'Oh yes. It's just I was so looking forward to seeing them again.'

'Have you had breakfast?'

She shook her head.

Harriet's lips tightened. 'Right. I propose to get something brought out. You know as well as I do that one must keep up one's strength in this God-awful climate, or one's done for. I should know.'

Lydia raised her brows.

'Oh, it was nothing in particular, but if you don't take care of yourself you'll go downhill damn fast. Now, will pancakes do you?'

⋆ ⋆ ⋆

With no wind to stir the air, Lydia felt damp beneath her clothes. She walked quickly, glancing up. Only distant specks of cloud littered the clear horizon, with not a sign of rain. She hopped on a local bus back to Malacca, and made her way through noisy streets, where, trapped within narrow alleyways, the air was already thickening with the smell of saltfish frying and open latrines. She fought the choking sensation in her throat.

At the bank, two ceiling fans ineffectively blew warm air. She waited in the queue, scalp prickling. At the Parrotts' she'd made light of it, but now she felt edgy about the journey ahead. She went through a list in her head. Bus timetable for a start, train times too, check the garage, pack. How far was Ipoh? All she could remember was that it was in the Kinta Valley. A hundred miles? No. More like two hundred. Two hundred miles of possibly mined roads. And, if she had to go by bus, it might take days.

In her haste, that morning, she hadn't pinned up her hair. Hands clasped behind her head, she lifted the heavy bulk off her neck and flicked the hairs that clung to her face. Most English women opted to crop their hair; she hadn't. Symbol of womanhood, Sister Patricia used to say, but the other women had the right idea; she'd get it chopped. She shuffled forward, flexing her shoulders to release the tension building there.

She thought of her girls, imagined herself in the car, waiting as they came out of school, waving and waving, tearing along the flower-lined paths that wound between squat buildings. At the makeshift stall opposite, lollipops stuck like flags into a board, sold for a couple of cents. The ones she allowed only on Fridays. It wasn't just the sugar that bothered her, it was the combined sale of sweets and gambling, for concealed round the end of just one or two was the prize of a one-dollar note.

She shook her head. She didn't want them learning that so young. You had to be so careful.

At last she reached the front of the queue. The young Malay, with soft wavy hair and dusky skin, smiled.

'I need to withdraw some money,' she said.

He inclined his head. 'Certainly, madam.'

'Cartwright. The name's Cartwright.'

He turned to face a bank of filing cabinets, and after a moment, withdrew a file.

'I think fifty dollars should do it.'

He flashed her a look, then bent back down to study the papers.

She frowned. 'Is there a problem?'

'According to this balance, there's only fifteen dollars left in the account.'

'But that's ridiculous,' she said, cheeks burning. 'We were nowhere near the red last month.'

The man's lips tightened. 'Mr Cartwright came in a few days ago and withdrew a large sum.'

'Did he say anything?'

'Something about a journey.'

'He didn't leave a letter for me?'

'I'm sorry. Just that from now on he'd be using a different bank. He left fifteen dollars, and instructed me to close the account after it was withdrawn.'

Lydia took a deep breath, and let it out very slowly through her mouth.

'So he left no other instructions?'

The man shook his head.

Finely balanced, she managed to keep hold of her temper. The important thing was to get to her girls. But fifteen dollars to get all the way to Ipoh? It wasn't the teller's fault, but what was going on?

5

Dad told us not to budge, but to wait beside some metal stairs on the deck, while he went down to talk to one of the ship's stewards about our cabins. I stood still and listened to the sounds.

'Shush,' I said to my sister as we leant against the damp rails and looked into the stairwell. 'Can't you hear them?'

Fleur pulled a face. 'No.'

I frowned. It wasn't difficult to hear footsteps that echoed in the salty gangways below.

'This ship is haunted,' I whispered, and made a scary face. My sister rolled her eyes and turned away.

'Sorry. Come on, Mealy Worm, let's run.'

Mum's favourite name was Emma. Her lizard earrings had the letters E and M engraved on the back. It was my name, but also Fleur's second name was Emilia, sometimes known as Floury Millie, or Mealy Worm by me.

We ran up and down the deck shouting to each other, and when we were out of breath we doubled over and held our sides. Then stood to watch the ocean, as the red sun dropped into the water, and the day was gobbled up. Spots of pink and yellow bobbed up and down in water as dark as liquorice, and the sound of sea birds carried all the way from the harbour to our deck.

'See the traders, sailing across in sampans,' I said.

'What's sampans?'

'Little boats, silly. Can't you see?'

We shrieked as they ducked out of the way of bigger boats to come alongside our ship, their reflected lantern lights wobbling in the water. Men stood up and shouted, then passed stuff up in large baskets. We got told off by the sailors, but not before we saw sparkly oriental slippers and strings of glittery beads. To Fleur and me, running up and down, the ship felt like fairyland — until we saw our father.

'I don't want to spoil your fun,' he said, as he marched over. 'But you can't run wild out here.'

'But, Daddy!'

'No buts, Emma.'

'We won't go too close,' Fleur pleaded.

'Nice try, sweetie, but no dice. Only with an adult, out here, especially at night. Never on your own. And I thought I told you to wait by the stairs.'

'Not fair,' I grumbled under my breath.

'I mean it, Emma. Anything could happen.'

I didn't say a word, but listened for ghostly voices behind the deck chairs, and imagined a shadowy figure creeping up to tip me over. And if not that, the sea would pull me from the deck and into the place where Orpheus danced with water sprites. I'd learnt about Orpheus at school.

'Emma?'

'Okay.'

We went inside with him, but I crossed my fingers behind my back. I couldn't help myself. I loved the ocean as the world turned purple and then darkest inky black.

In secret, I pretended it was an adventure, and waited until Fleur was asleep. Then I slipped out of the cabin, crept up the narrow metal staircase to the deck, and waited until nobody was about. I ran across to one of the lifeboats. It was quite high off the deck, but I found a crate someone had left behind, stood on it and hauled myself over, head first into the boat. I rolled on to my back and looked up at the sky. The air was still warm, and all the stars were out. The little boat shook if I moved, so I kept very still, just like the sea.

It reminded me of lying on the grass in our garden, and watching clouds fly over like puffs of sherbet lemon. I had to remember as much as I could, because I didn't know when we were coming back. When a little voice in my head said *if* you're coming back, I sat up and stared at the sea. I hugged myself and took a deep breath of salty air. I wanted to jump into the water and swim back to the place where Mummy was. But the quiet sea made me feel calm, and I stayed in the lifeboat until I got too cold.

★ ★ ★

We shared our dining table with Mr Oliver and his sister. Her name was Veronica, and his was Sidney. Veronica was tall and thin, nearly as tall as Dad, with soft swishy skirts, tight blonde pin curls and a quiet voice. She patted her hair to keep it tidy. Both of them had white skin, as if they'd lived hidden away from the Malayan sun, though her cheeks were pink, as pink as the tiny

30

glass beads that sat round her neck. She seemed to like us, especially Father, smiling with pretty blue eyes and giggling at his jokes.

Mr Oliver and Veronica were late for lunch, and we were alone at the table. While we waited, Dad told us she had a flat in London but used to live in a place called Cheltenham, not far from where we were going. He said hers was an unhappy story, and that we should be kind to her. She didn't have any children of her own, and her husband had been a schoolmaster, a man who'd died from a sickness called cholera.

'What's cholera,' I asked. 'Does it make your eyes pop out?'

He sighed heavily. 'No, Emma, it does not. It just makes you very tired and grey until you get worse.'

'And then you die.'

He nodded. 'Probably.'

In the background, Doris Day was singing one of my mum's favourites: 'Secret Love'. I felt sad when I thought of Mum's pretty oval face and her shining eyes. The hazel colour was speckled with green and blue like the tail of a peacock-pheasant, and one of her eyebrows was a bit higher than the other. I liked to sit and watch her try to make them level. She never could.

It was a Malay meal for lunch, with the sweet smell of kaffir lime leaves, which I loved. The pudding table wasn't great, but I still ate too much peach melba and had a tummy ache. I asked Daddy if I could leave the table and go to my cabin to lie down.

Veronica smiled at him. Tanned from being outdoors so much, Father was lined and kind of dry, and he wore round tortoiseshell specs. I noticed he'd made even more of an effort than usual to look smart.

'I'll look after Fleur if you like,' Veronica said, in a bubbly voice. 'Then Emma can have an undisturbed sleep and wake up feeling better.'

In the cabin, I lay on top of the blue candlewick bedspread, ears buzzing. I was on the bottom bunk, Fleur's, because I didn't want to climb a ladder with my stomach hurting. Our tiny cabin smelt stale and salty. You could hear the ship hum, and the waves thump against its sides. I shut my eyes and the noise of the engine quickly sent me to sleep.

A little later, a tap at the door woke me, and Mr Oliver came in. I suspected Dad must have sent him to see how I was, though I was surprised he came, and not his sister.

He sat on the edge of my bed, out of breath and puffing.

'Shove over a bit, love,' he said, with a grin.

His face was so close I could see broken red veins in his nose.

'Close your eyes, my dear,' he said, and started to stroke my forehead ever so softly. I forgot it was him and at first it was nice. It reminded me of Mummy. I drifted in a sickly sort of dream. I missed her so much and Dad wouldn't say when she was coming. But then I had a funny feeling in my tummy and my legs. Something didn't feel quite right, and I let out my breath when Mr Oliver left me on my own.

When we entered the Bay of Biscay, silver clouds rushed across the sky, and at lunch the boat was rolling. Mr Oliver squeezed in next to me, and beneath the table put a sweaty hand on my bare thigh. I didn't like it. I shuffled my body away from him, and pushed myself back in the seat. He winked at me and my cheeks burnt. Everyone was busy talking about the weather, so no one saw my face.

After lunch, I stayed on deck to watch the world turn black. Lucky for me, Mr Oliver wasn't a good sailor, and was first to disappear to his cabin. Then Fleur was sick, so Dad and Veronica took her down too. Dad told me to follow them, but it made me feel better being out on my own, so I stayed. It was for the best. The water leapt higher and higher, the deck shuddered and shook, and even some of the sailors were sick.

I found my sea legs, and shrieked as huge waves flew over the deck, knocking me from side to side. Birds screamed, the wind roared, and I forgot Mr Oliver's hot hand, even forgot that we'd left my mum behind. I stayed out to breathe great gulps of salty smelling air, and afterwards, ran my hand over the crusty handrails and licked the crystals from the tips of my fingers. They tasted as fishy and salty as they smelt.

★ ★ ★

The rest of our journey passed quickly, and on the last day I woke up before it was light. I climbed on a chair to look through the cabin porthole, and could just make out a long dark shape in the distance. My first sight of England. When the ship tied up later that morning, I scrambled up the stairs and on to the slippery deck. For a minute I looked at the pale sky. Then I closed my eyes, said a prayer for my beautiful mother, blew her a kiss across the sea, and asked her to get here soon.

At the Liverpool dock, crowds of people blocked the way, and there was an oily smell in the air. Men in cloth caps coiled ropes round heavy metal stops on the quay, and the air was full of the jangly sound of bells, wheels, newspaper sellers, and swinging crates that banged and thumped on the ground. Most of all it was people shouting. You had to jump out of the way, because nobody could see you through the mist. Smog, Dad called it.

I felt very small, and took a deep breath while I waited, as if the bright future Dad had promised would be there to meet me. It wasn't. It was smelly, cold and grey. I never knew what grey was until then, and wanted to slip my hand into Mummy's, for her to smile at me and say, 'Everything's going to be fine. You'll see.'

When he saw me looking upset, Dad did say it, but it wasn't the same.

We had to kiss Veronica and a green-looking Mr Oliver goodbye. I screwed up my face, and as soon as it was over, ran off down the edge of the

34

dock. It was a freezing February day, and the run warmed me up.

'Don't go too close,' Dad shouted.

I didn't go far. My feet hurt. Fleur and I usually played in flip-flops or barefoot, Dad laughing and calling us savages. Now we'd been forced into brown shoes with a strap and a button. And long itchy socks. We both complained loudly, though we showed off the red jackets that Mum had knitted ready for the next home leave. There'd only been one leave that I remembered, which had left me with a fuzzy idea of this place called England.

Thinking of Mum hurt my heart so much.

So far Dad had given no reason for her delay but I asked again at the dockside.

He took off his specs, wiped them on his sleeve, puffed out his cheeks and simply said, 'She's not here at the moment. I'm afraid that's all I can tell you.'

'But when is she coming?'

'Emma, I don't know.'

'You did leave her the letter I wrote?'

'Of course.'

Mum's probably held up, I thought. Maybe Dad won't say because he doesn't want to make a promise, and have to disappoint us, if he gets it wrong. But it didn't stop my imagination. And I saw my mother everywhere we went. Even in the big draughty waiting room where we waited for a porter, and where the smell of soot and smoke made your eyes smart. And though Mummy wasn't really there, I imagined a fine line that wound halfway round the world. It was the invisible thread that stretched from west to east and back again; one end was attached to my mother's heart and the other to mine. And, I knew, whatever might happen, that thread would never be broken.

6

Lydia looked back over her shoulder, as a jeep of khaki-clad Malay police armed with machine guns drove by. Since MNLA guerrillas had killed the British High Commissioner, Sir Henry Gurney, in 1951, nobody felt safe. She placed a hand on her throat, then tapped at the door of Cicely's Portuguese town house, a beautiful pale pink building with decorative arched windows and a colonnaded walkway beneath. Moments later she was shown through to an airy room at the back, painted pale blue, a through draught lending some relief from the scorching day.

She wheeled round as Cicely entered the room, hands outstretched, nails shimmering in icy pink to match her pale shift dress.

'Darling. What an unexpected pleasure,' Cicely said, her voice low, the vowels elongated.

An elegant beauty, with swinging platinum hair, a light tan and deep plum lips, she tucked her long limbs under with implicit boredom as she sat. One dyed calfskin shoe with a high, ultra-thin heel hung from her toe.

'I'm sorry . . . but I need your help. It's very awkward.' Lydia hesitated and straightened her back, trying to find a way to say it without arousing pity.

Cicely coolly raised one, expertly plucked, arched eyebrow. Neither of them was the kind of colonial wife absorbed by digestive disturbances or household tittle-tattle, and it had been inevitable they'd become friends, of sorts.

Lydia resisted the urge to tidy her hair and forced herself to speak. 'I'm sorry to have to ask this, but could you lend me some money?'

Her friend's sparkling eyes, somewhere between topaz and emerald green, flared with delight. 'Oh, darling, what on earth has happened?'

Lydia proceeded cautiously. Cicely wasn't malicious exactly, but was, so Alec had it, caught in a loveless marriage, and living with tales of her husband's affairs. There was a pause. Only the drone of the fan stirred the air, as Lydia wondered how much to reveal.

★ ★ ★

In the old Chinese quarter, they elbowed their way through the flowing current of people and dodged an army of bicycle-pulled rickshaws. Cicely led her through a backstreet market, where mah-jong players provided a clickety-clack chorus to bright blue birds singing in bamboo cages.

Cicely nodded and smiled, rubbing shoulders with Chinese shopkeepers and Malay street hawkers. She stopped beside a bucket of live deep-sea crabs, and came away with packets of food. Lydia's eyes widened, acutely aware of the sour sewer smell drifting across.

'You must try this, darling. Utterly delicious.' Cicely smiled, and stuffed a taste of banana leaf curry into Lydia's mouth. 'Come on, sweetie. It'll be all right. You worry too much. Though I can't think why Alec didn't leave enough money for you to follow him. What a shit.'

At the end of an alley, beside lurid posters advertising Lucky Strike cigarettes, Cicely stopped outside a shop with a dragon painted on a red hanging sign. She leant against the doorpost with willowy sex appeal, ignoring the rigid watchman who sat there with a shotgun on his lap.

'Here we are,' she said. Her narrow face spread in a wide grin, the single row of pearls at her neck gleaming.

Next door was a herbalist and snake charmer. He stood outside his shop, a burly Indian, chewing betel. Lydia eyed the snake baskets.

'Don't worry, darling.' Cicely laughed, and pushed open the door. 'The cobras always sleep until sundown.'

Inside the shop Lydia held her nose, but it reeked only of cheap incense and coconut oil. The Chinaman behind the counter wore an embroidered red gown, and what looked like a hostile stare. Lydia's eyes slid over to Cicely who, without flinching, emptied a bag of charm bracelets, gold earrings and half a dozen necklaces on to the counter.

Sweat broke out on Lydia's forehead, and she felt herself redden. 'But these are real gems.'

Cicely shrugged and squeezed her hand. 'Mainly Chinese tat. Honestly. Don't worry. Now, have you got photos of your scrumptious girls?'

Lydia bent her head, reached into her crammed bag and pulled out a purse. Inside were two small photos, one of Emma and one of

Fleur, taken in a booth at the zoo. She looked at Fleur gazing out with a slight squint and Alec's serious eyes, and then at Em's lopsided grin. The photo revealed her elder daughter's straight nose and angular face, but fell short of capturing laughing turquoise eyes, and sun shining through flaming curly hair. It can't show how tall she is for her age, nor how clever, she thought with pride.

'She's very grown up,' Cicely said.

'Who?'

'Emma, of course. Fleur's prettier, but hardly speaks.'

Lydia thought of her younger daughter and her heart skipped a beat. Since having pneumonia, Fleur was more withdrawn than ever. 'She speaks, but Em loves words. Even when she was only three, she pretended she could read.'

'Seems old for twelve.'

Lydia blinked rapidly. 'Nearly twelve.'

Cicely put a comforting hand on her shoulder. 'Right,' she said, picking up a locket on a silver chain from the counter. 'My present. Round your neck is always safest in this country. And look after the cash. Don't worry, you'll catch up with them soon enough. And that lean husband of yours.'

Lydia nodded, unable to identify the source of her unease. She didn't like being parted from her girls, ever, and the hazards of a separation during the Emergency were alarmingly clear. But was there something more than that?

'And then you'll long for a bit of peace and

quiet. I don't know how you do it. Being a mum, I mean.'

I love them, Lydia thought, that's how.

'And Jack. How do you feel about him?'

Lydia felt a flush spread up her chest to her face, and fought off the urge to unburden herself of her essentially unacknowledged feelings.

Cicely narrowed her eyes. 'Well, I couldn't be a mother. Now let's get that hair chopped.'

★　★　★

At last, a brief shower brought rain splattering from the gutters, not enough to really cool the sticky air, but enough to freshen her. She struggled to push aside wet purple bougainvillea, encroaching on the garage door. Everything grew so fast. The door squealed as she jerked it open, and she saw the solid shape of the Humber Hawk parked there. She glanced inside, relaxed a little. The keys were still in the ignition. At least Alec had left the car. She slid into the driver's seat to check the petrol gauge.

In her bedroom it didn't take long to roll up some practical clothes into a couple of holdalls. As she slipped out of her damp dress, the emptiness of the house jolted her. In the silence she sniffed the air. It lacked the usual smell of polish and now they were gone it didn't smell like home. She touched the silk of her Indian dresses, run up by herself in unexpected colour combinations: pink and orange, green and peacock blue, lacquer red with black. Her favourite dress style had an oriental touch, but she decided on a sensible navy dress, less likely to show the dirt. The Indian dresses she left, but packed two sequinned evening dresses, too good to leave behind.

She slipped Emma's notebook into the bag. How very much she craved the girls: the touch and smell of them. Her skin prickled with anticipation, but she resisted the desire to read the notebook. She'd be seeing her daughters soon enough.

Back in the hallway, something was odd. There were sounds of life. Maybe George was mistaken and Alec had come back for her after all. Her heart picked up. Maybe they'd been to the island and hadn't even gone up to Ipoh yet. She pictured the deep green island waters, the salty breezes and the lemon oil she smeared on the children's skin.

There was a sequence of sounds from the kitchen: a sniff, a smothered sob, and the sound of rapid Chinese. One of the servants then. She marched over to the kitchen and threw open the door, shading her eyes from the sun's low afternoon rays, as sharp as knives.

In the corner a slight girl with drawn features, black hair in a top knot, and frightened almond-shaped eyes, sat cross-legged on the floor. A young child, also with straight Chinese hair, sat on her lap, and hid his face in her chest. In baggy blue trousers, barefoot, with a beaded anklet on one leg, he looked undernourished. Lydia stared, sure she'd seen the girl leave their house once before.

'Mem.' The girl got up, a well of misery in her

eyes. 'I am Suyin. This my sister's boy.'

There's something familiar, Lydia thought, as she took in the girl's shiny tunic.

'What's the child's name?'

'Maznan Chang, Mem. He was at hospital. Cannot go home. Please, he go with you.'

Lydia glanced at her watch, but the girl, rigid and pale, pitched headfirst into her plea.

'The jungle not safe for him. They hurt him.'

The boy stood, and pulled up his shirt to reveal a red welt across his side. Lydia saw that besides being thin he was very dirty, and the injury was obviously recent.

'He help you, Mem. He speak Malay and Chinese.'

'He looks so young.'

'He is seven, small for age.'

The boy turned damp eyes on Lydia, and gave a wary smile. She was taken aback. Pretty like a girl, he had a flat face and full-nostrilled Malayan nose, but pale eyes, and skin with a touch of amber, lighter than most Malays. Only his hair looked Chinese. He smiled again, displaying a row of even teeth.

She sized things up, pushing aside the pinch of anxiety about the delay. An image of Emma flashed in her head and she heard her daughter's voice as if she was in the next room. *Hurry up, Mummy. Aren't you here yet?! I've got a new story to tell you.* She closed her eyes and felt her heart constrict.

'Mem?' the girl said, interrupting her.

'Why is he not safe?' Lydia asked.

'His mother. She run away to inside.' The girl

43

waited to see a reaction before pressing her point. 'She in jungle, Mem. If they don't come get him. The others take him next time.'

The penny dropped. The child's mother had run off to join the communist rebels.

'Which others?'

The girl looked embarrassed. 'The white people, red hairs. Please. Take this boy to resettlement village, or even Malay village. They take care of him.'

Lydia wavered. 'What about the police?'

The girl curled her lip and spat on the floor.

Lydia felt torn. She needed to catch up with her girls, get on before the day drew to a close. But then she imagined if it were them who were alone and dependent on a stranger for kindness. 'All right,' she said, making a snap decision. 'I'll take him. What's your address? And the name of the place to take him?'

She stared at the girl's pinched face. Then it came to her. 'You're the driver's daughter?'

The girl nodded.

'Can't your father have him?'

The girl shook her head and Lydia saw a look of anxiety in her eyes.

'Did your father drive my husband to Ipoh?'

The girl shook her head. 'My father sick.'

'Well, let me have your address, so I can let you know where the little boy is.'

The girl stepped forward, held the child by one hand and placed his other in Lydia's. She bent down and, again in rapid Chinese, spoke in his ear. He shook his head, hair wheeling out round his face. The girl straightened up, spun

44

round, raced through the door, picked up speed along the covered walkway, and melted into the long grass.

Lydia called out, but the girl had gone. She sighed and peered at the child. He almost had the eyes of a European child. Was he really in danger? A picture of the orphanage came up. The pitiless grey block on the outskirts of town. If the rumours of neglect were true, it was no place for this little one. The thought of her own girls there made her hold her breath.

He looked up, then counted his beads in Malay. '*Satu, dua, tiga, empat, lima.*'

She exhaled slowly. Poor little thing, she thought, what on earth am I supposed to do with you? You don't look like you fit in anywhere.

A noise from the direction of the garage caught her attention. Damn cats. She pulled the boy up, and planted a kiss on top of his head. She glanced at her watch again. Where had the time gone? They both needed a bath and something to eat. Then she'd put the child in Emma's bed, and try to catch some sleep herself, before an early start in the morning.

7

It turned into a morning of startling brilliance, the early mist melting away as soon as they left the house. The streets were still quiet, though a few knots of men in sarongs of orange and yellow stood gossiping outside tea shops. Further out, Malays whizzed by on bicycles, and finally, right at the outskirts, shiny-faced Tamil women workers sweated as they cut back the dark vegetation, their long-lobed ears swaying.

Lydia sang, glad to be on her way. She'd always had a good voice, and feeling confident, she put her foot down, tyres ringing on the tarmac road. She raised her voice to match. The boy, sitting in the seat beside her, giggled.

'My singing that bad?' she said, and glanced across at him.

He shook his head and smiled.

He'd eaten a filling breakfast at the roadside stall, she thought, and that was a good start.

As waving trees in a million shades of green flew past, she went over the journey in her head. It was about fifty-five miles to Seremban, so if they got past there, in three hours' time they'd stop for an early lunch, and stay out of the afternoon heat. Then push on until it started to get dark. It'd mean finding a cheap place to stay for the night. Rawang maybe, or Tanjung Malim. How many miles from there to Ipoh? She thought of Jack. Perhaps not Tanjung Malim. No point asking for trouble.

An hour and a half into the journey, the car shook and came to a sudden halt.

She got out, and peered down the road. Blue haze rose from the dust. She lifted the greasy bonnet of the old Humber Hawk, stared at the engine, and tried to recall the mechanical checks Alec had tried to instil in her. Maznan pointed at the oil slick on her palm. She puffed out her cheeks, the boy was right, she knew nothing about cars, and there was no point getting filthy.

She slammed the bonnet shut, wiped her hands on her dress, then bent down and slid her hand under the driver's seat, in search of a manual. There was no manual, but she felt something sharp. She pulled out her lost lizard earring and smiled. So that's where you got to. I'll take it as a good luck sign.

She folded her arms across her chest and glanced at the child. Now what? In the Emergency you never trusted a stranger. I could wait for a British police patrol, she thought, but not if I have to use all my cash staying somewhere and getting it fixed. Damn you, Alec, why couldn't you just delay for a couple of days?

She prepared to wait for a bus. She'd ring the police later, get them to pick up the car. With a sigh, she squatted like a native in the shadow of a fifty-foot clump of bamboo, the silent child by her side. A bright orange jungle butterfly landed on her knee. The boy giggled and reached out a hand, his ability to be enchanted reminding her of Em.

'Do you like butterflies?' she said.

He nodded.

The edges of the jungle were scented with wild ginger, cinnamon, and figs. High above, in tall trees that blotted out the sun, hornbills cried. Beautiful in a way, but, still, the whirring clicking life of the jungle's creatures unsettled her.

She took out Em's notebook, flicked the pages. The words for Doris Day's 'Secret Love', written in Emma's confident hand, stared out. She began to hum the tune, but faltered, and bit the skin round her thumbnail. She stood up, deliberated. It would be too much effort to carry two cases in the heat, so she kept the larger case, and chucked the other into the squat ferns at the roadside. She imagined a happier time when they'd be off for drinks at the club, the children safe in their beds. But who can be happy in this damn country, she thought, apart from men like Alec.

'What about when they get independence?' she'd asked him once, on their way to the annual sultan's ball.

'There'll always be scope for someone like me,' he said, dismissing her concerns. 'And there's no chance I'd ever go back to my parents' house, nor to England, for that matter.'

She peered at the tall razor sharp *lallang* grass that lined the road. She had no reason not to believe him. Alec was not in contact with his parents, and there had been an awful atmosphere at their home.

She and the boy walked a little.

There was no breeze, and even the feathery pink tops of the grass were completely still. Wary of fat vipers concealed in the grass, and the bigger snakes coiled in the trees, she kept to the road and heard the brain fever bird, its call rising to a maddening crescendo.

Maznan still hadn't spoken, except to count his beads. He only ever reached five, and said them over and over. *Satu, dua, tiga, empat, lima.*

She closed her eyes for a moment, sweat stinging the lids, and heard it before she saw it. A brightly painted yellow and red Bedford came roaring up the road. With a shout, she lurched towards it, hindered by the child who hopped beside her, jabbering in Malay, and 'helping' with the case. The driver slowed to a crawl, spread his arms out wide and shook his head. Her heart sank as thirty pairs of eyes stared through the open windows. The bus, stuffed with people, baggage, chickens and goats, was full.

The driver revved the engine. From the back an Indian woman with bulging eyes stood up, and pointed at Lydia and the boy, as if protesting. The driver shook his head again but she seemed to win. He shrugged, and beckoned Lydia forward as the bus burst into life.

Once on the bus, she clasped the child's hand, dragged her case, and they bumped their way along the aisle to the back seat. The Indian woman, a floral shawl over her head, shifted over. With a sigh of relief, Lydia sat on the metal bench; no upholstery for insects to inhabit.

The woman grinned, revealing red gums from chewing betel nut, and a couple of pink teeth. Lydia smiled self-consciously, the only white woman in a bus crammed with Malays, a scattering of Chinese in black baggy trousers, and Tamil workers wearing saris. She saw their eyes on her, and though she didn't understand what they were saying, she picked up their grumbles. She'd thought she had a decent command of Malay, but realised now this was true only if the person speaking enunciated carefully, and spoke directly to her. Here, they could say what they wanted, and no one cared if she was the mistress of a sizeable house with a sprinkling of servants.

She smiled vaguely at eyes that slowly turned away, then stared out of the window as the bus swayed from side to side through the tunnel of green.

Her eyes glazed over and an ache settled in her heart. She put an arm round the child and he leant against her. Until the moment her daughters crawled away with her heart, she hadn't known what love was, but now she would give anything to be with them.

A few moments later, there was a sound of rattling paper, and through heavy lids, she glimpsed the Indian woman offer Maznan a pastry. He wolfed it down and held out his hand for more. The woman grinned, pulled out two more cakes, handed one to the boy, and, nudging Lydia, gave her the other.

She savoured the sweet cinnamon and nutmeg, tried a few tentative words, but the woman stopped her. 'Speak English,' the woman said, passing her a flask of citrus-tasting tea and a small yellow pancake. 'Is good cake. Keep the Pontianak away.'

'The Pontianak?'

'Evil spirit of dead woman. Will come and take your child away. Cake protects him,' said the woman, pointing at Maznan.

'Oh no. He's not mine. Mine are up north with my husband. He's . . . ' And she stopped. The Indian woman smiled and indicated she was all ears.

'He's — ' she paused ' — the son of an acquaintance.'

The woman looked doubtful.

Lydia sighed, turned the boy's face towards her and stroked his smooth cheek.

'He's a good boy.'

Maznan smiled.

People were falling asleep, their snores and whistles oddly comforting.

Lydia's longing for her family was uppermost. Her girls. And Alec too. The first man she'd ever met at a party. She closed her eyes and thought of that night.

It had been a typical wartime bash. She'd spotted him leaning against the wall outside, a tall older man in uniform. He'd rubbed his leg, and turned his head as she approached. She'd been wearing a green striped dress, her waist pinched in. Only eighteen and feeling flattered.

'Do you smoke?' he said, and opened a tin of Woodbines.

She hesitated but took one.

She studied his face. He was too thin and every few moments he winced. 'Shouldn't you be sitting down?' she said.

He shrugged. 'Sick of sitting, to be honest.'

'RAF?'

He raised his eyebrows. 'Fairly obvious.'

'Why aren't you smoking Player's Airman then?' she said, with a flick of her hair.

So much had happened since. She'd become somebody for a start. A wife, a mother, now on her way to a third new beginning since coming to Malaya.

She looked out of the bus window again, squinted in the bright light, a dull heavy feeling in her head. The green waving trees spawned more green trees in unbroken monotony. One more time, she went back to the start of things with Alec, picked at it, as if searching for something.

They'd got together a second time, for Spam and lettuce sandwiches in the Fiddler's Arms. He'd offered coffee at his lodgings, where he covered the window with a blackout curtain on a pole, fag in hand, the lamp off, but even the glow from their cigarettes was banned. He brushed her neck by accident and she felt herself redden.

'Did you hear about the man who was fined ten shillings when he struck a match to look for his false teeth?' she joked to cover her nerves.

He didn't laugh, just held up the bottle of Camp coffee. On the label a turbaned Indian servant waits on an officer in a kilt who sits relaxed, sipping the brew.

When the prospect of Malaya arose, he described starlit tropical skies, drinking Pimms by night, and lazing on silver beaches laced with palms. They'd have to marry, of course.

She sighed. She'd happily swop all of that now, for some good old British weather. She was thinking how much she missed the seasons, when there was a bang and the bus lurched, bumping wide-eyed occupants against each other. A terrific thud followed, and they came to a jolting halt. Outside, shrill voices barked orders in Chinese. She held the boy close and checked to see if he was hurt. He looked up at her with enormous eyes, as if trying to work out if he could really trust her.

She patted his arm, and shifted round to the Indian woman.

'What happened?' she whispered.

The woman put a finger to her lips, and threw her floral shawl over Lydia's head.

'Insiders. Look down,' the woman said. 'Lean against me.'

Lydia hid the child inside the shawl and buried her own face. She remembered the blinding white light of the grenade thrown into the packed market place, and fear ran through her like a current. Communists. What did they want? Had they come to recruit people into the Min Yuen, their supply organisation, or was it something worse? She glanced up and saw the thin ragged rebels drag two Chinese from the front of the bus. Stories of terrorist atrocities flashed into her mind. She looked down, aware of the shock passing through the people sitting rigidly in front. The little boy started counting. *Satu, dua.*

Through the dusty window, she saw the road was deeper into the jungle now. The two Chinese men had been tied to a tall tree, and several more were made to get off the bus. As they reached the ground their hands were tied together. Shrieking like macaques who'd burnt their mouths on red-hot chilli, they were dragged a few yards, then pushed up the road and forced to run. The remainder stayed on the bus.

Lydia and the Indian woman exchanged looks. The Indian woman shrugged, her eyes uncertain. At the sound of gunfire, the little boy trembled; Lydia bit her lip and forced her eyes from the window. But for the echo of the gunshots, it was silent, and a single chilling thought rang in her head. She lifted her hand to her locket and held it tight.

Outside birds still sang. She dared risk a look, felt a flash of anger overtake the fear. This was not how she'd expected Malaya to be. Alec hadn't mentioned the endless battle against humming mosquitoes, nor the wet heat, which approached like a solid wall — nor the war they called an Emergency.

She noticed a man with a shaved head sitting very still near the front. She hadn't picked him out before, but now the bus was half empty, she could see a smooth brown head and shoulders, high above the rest. The man was dressed in a Malay tunic, the colours subdued, yet when he stood, she saw a sarong woven with silver and turquoise. His height set him apart. Not an ordinary Malay, he looked more worldly. Eurasian maybe? Out of the corner of her eye, she saw two insurgents start down the central isle and head her way. She faced them and held her breath. One ran his tongue across his teeth, lifting his lip in a sneer as he brushed past the tall man. The man twisted his head towards her, his face grave. With searching dark eyes, he focussed on their path towards her, tense, ready to spring it seemed. For an instant their eyes met.

The Indian woman put an arm round her and the child. But it did no good. All three were ordered off at gunpoint. For a moment Lydia's heart failed to beat, but the child stood immediately and held out his hand to her. She stumbled to her feet, her bottom numb from the metal seat. Through the window she caught sight of the ceiling of low black cloud sliding across the sky. She managed to climb off the bus, holding tight to the child.

8

I woke up to a frozen jungle, the windowpanes iced with giant white lotus blossoms. Cold seeped round the frames and under the door. I shivered and my breath rose in clouds. It made no difference if the window was closed or not, so I opened it, heard pigeons coo in the neighbour's garden, and stretched my neck to catch a glimpse of them on the ridge of the pigeon house.

Opposite, a field lined with brown ridges went all the way to the church, with a row of black trees behind. You could see the spire poke up above the other buildings. I called Fleur to come and look, but she'd already gone to find Dad.

Downstairs, Granddad Cartwright patted us on the back, and Gran wiped away her tears. Gran was small and round. She nodded and smiled a lot, had deep blue raisin eyes with crinkles at the sides, and wore a complicated thing on top of her blouse and skirt. It went over her shoulders and round the sides and did up with strings. She called it a pinny, and it made her kind of baggy looking. She wore slippers and had fine grey hair, pins falling out at funny angles. Not a bit smart like Mummy.

Granddad was old too, with a shock of white hair. He made a painful sounding wheeze as he moved and he had black hairs sprouting from his nostrils, and big brown liver spots on his hands.

They showed us round the house. It had brown flowery wallpaper, carpets the colour of sick, and so much furniture there wasn't any room to play. The kitchen was Gran's world, the only cheery room, and she beamed as she pointed out the brightly coloured pictures of chickens and pigs on the wallpaper. Granny was proud of the house, though there wasn't much to see. Just a square semi-detached, down a country lane in Rampton, Worcestershire. What it did have was an enormous garden, surrounding the three sides of the house that were not joined to the house next door. At the back, a wire fence separated the garden from the field.

In the only room with a fire, I asked Granny where the servants' quarters were. She clapped her hands together, wiped her eyes with her pinny, and dug Granddad in the chest.

'Goodness, ducks, the only servant you'll find here is me. Isn't that so, Eric?' Eric was Granddad, and he nodded and sat in the chair smoking his pipe.

Fleur nudged me and whispered behind her hand. 'We're not ducks, are we, Em? Why does she call us that?'

I shushed her, and my eyes fixed on a tin of boiled sweets on the shelf. Gran saw me look, gave us some, and kept giving us more, forgetting how many we'd had.

'Do you the world of good,' she said.

'What are you on about, Mother?' Dad said.

She made a gentle tutting sound.

'Too much sugar spoils kids' appetites.' He loosened his tie. 'And it's too hot in here. Don't you know coal smoke's bad for Fleur. She needs fresh air. Look, she's already coughing.'

Fleur gave an obliging cough.

'No need to get aerated,' Granddad protested.

Dad turned on him. 'You have no right to a say.'

'Now, now,' Gran said. 'You don't want to drag all that up again. Least said, soonest mended.'

Granddad looked away, but I noticed Dad's lips tighten and he stomped off.

Once he'd gone we sat on the doorstep, playing a game with Daddy's old tiddlywinks and eating sweet cigarettes, while keeping an eye on the street. I pretended I was smoking real cigarettes, until it got too much and I had to chew. We watched a boy come cycling up the street. His bike was too big and he had to stand to ride it. He wobbled a lot, because of wide baskets attached to each side, and a lovely smell of baking followed as he called at every house. When he stopped at ours, Fleur shouted for Granny.

I stared hard at him, wanting very much to like him. He was skinny, wore a cap on his head, and had teeth too big for his mouth. But he had smiley brown eyes, and a nose dotted with freckles. When he grinned you forgot about the teeth, because they fitted better.

★ ★ ★

The next day we started school. I didn't ask Father again, but I wished Mum was with us and couldn't wait for her to come. I wondered if she'd got back to our house in Malacca, and if she'd read my letter yet. It was always Mummy who had made everything okay. In my grandparents' house, she would have been the smile that said goodbye in the hallway. And at our school, I imagined her waiting outside and waving, while we ate iced buns and were forced to swallow freezing milk in miniature bottles.

At playtime there was a buzz when someone from my class overheard me say to Fleur the iced bun was stale. The baker's boy spun round with a furious face, and without his cap. I saw his hair was badly cropped, with a few tufts left on top.

'They're lovely, they are. Not stale,' he said.

'They are too. We had better ones in Malaya. Nyonya cakes, and lovely Chinese kuehs.' I thought of the sweet rice cakes, and my mouth watered.

'Oooh, Malaya, is it? Where's that when the cows come home?'

Hands on hips, I stood my ground, though I was shaking inside. 'In the east if you must know. And we didn't have horrible frozen milk either. We had freshly crushed sugar cane juice, or coconut milk.'

'Why don't you go back there then? We don't want you here. Stuck up, you are. You're not even English. You're an immigrunt.'

A little group of kids gathered round to chant in sing-song voices. 'Immigrunt. Immigrunt. Back to where you came from.'

Fleur burst into tears, but I grabbed a fistful of the boy's tufts, and yanked as I yelled in his face.

'I'm as bloody English as you are, tuft head!'

We landed on the ground, kicking and pulling at each other. The other children whistled and laughed, and shoved each other to get a better look. I got hold of his jumper and tugged. He grabbed my tunic and I heard it rip at the back. Oh no, I thought, Gran'll kill me.

'Fight. Fight,' the others shouted. 'Come on, Billy. You show 'er.'

We rolled around a bit, but the noise died down when the head teacher loomed over us, blocking the light. I looked into his pig-pink face, while his voice crashed into the silence.

'Emma Cartwright, you can't behave like a savage here,' he said. 'This is England.'

He came so close I saw red veins in the whites of his eyes.

The boy got a clip round the ear and a beetroot face, and I had five ruler smacks on the palm of my hand. I didn't cry and I wasn't scared. I was angry.

The girls were worse, sniggering behind their hands, skipping and chanting, or juggling balls, and not letting me join in. They gave me mean looks, then turned away and talked in loud voices. I blinked away tears and stuck my nose in the air, though I suppose with tanned skin and hair lightened by the sun, I was different. In any case, they hated me for it, talked over me in class, pushed me to the back of the queue at lunchtime, and at the end of the day they stood in my way, hands on hips. They were nicer to Fleur because she was really good at skipping.

* ★ ★

At home, Dad announced he'd had a letter from Veronica, and she wanted to come to tea one Saturday. I didn't know what Mum would think of that. I quite liked Veronica, but what if she brought her brother? I asked my father, but he told me not to be nosy. Father and she were friends, Gran said. Veronica had a flat in London, but she rented a cottage in a village called Drake Broughton, about fifteen miles from Cheltenham. She liked Cheltenham and might sell her London flat to buy one there. Gran looked very impressed, when she told us Veronica had *private means*.

When I was in bed that night, no longer safe beneath a mosquito net, I thought of Mummy. I imagined her sitting beside me like she used to, singing 'Baby It's Cold Outside'. It always sent me into laughing hiccups, because in Malaya it was so hot. It made more sense here.

Though I hadn't cried in the playground, I cried in bed after Fleur was asleep. Gran heard me and tiptoed in. She gave me a hug when I told her about being left out.

'Giving you the cold shoulder, is it?' She screwed up her eyes and her chubby cheeks went even rounder. 'I know, ducks,' she said, nodding and lifting up my wild hair. 'We'll make you look the same as them. With bells on. You'll see. Now sleep tight.'

'Is Mr Oliver coming to tea too?' I asked, before she left.

'He might be. He's staying with Veronica,

61

while he looks for a new position abroad.'

I crossed my fingers, hoping he'd find a job quickly, before he had a chance to come to tea.

9

Under the hot sun, Lydia couldn't bear to see the lifeless bodies still tied to the tree, their heads rolling forward like abandoned puppets. She turned away, but something about the horror drew her back, as if only by looking could she convince herself that what had happened was real. Maznan whimpered, and Lydia fought her instinct to pass out at the smell of blood. She pulled the boy closer to her, wrapped her arms round him and brushed away the flies settling on his skin. He buried his face in her dress, and she lifted her eyes to the sky to say a silent prayer.

The rebels approached. She took a step back when one of them cupped the child's chin in the palm of his hand. She attempted to pull the child back with her, but Maznan stood his ground, wiped his eyes, and stared at the man. She saw the man was small and gaunt, his eyes sunken, the deep lines on his face blackened with grime. She heard the drone of insects behind his head, then at either side of him. The sound moved closer. She felt dizzy, closed her eyes. Now, it was inside in her head. Buzzing. Buzzing. She opened her eyes, looked at the man's face again, cringed at the open hatred in his eyes.

He muttered to the other, and lifted his gun. She made out only one heavily accented word, 'English.' She held her breath, forced herself to stand tall, despite legs that threatened to buckle.

The other, a stockier-looking man, with puckered skin on his cheek, took a step towards her. Clearly the boss, he shook his head, and pushed her against a broad-trunked tree. Her breath caught — for a moment she considered resisting, but noticed the child give a slight shake to his head and appear to acquiesce. She followed his lead and squeezed his hand. While the stocky man roped them both to the tree, she tried to make out the expression on his face. It was blank. The thin man tied the Indian woman beside them. The stocky man stepped away.

Her muscles constricted, and her throat was so dry that she couldn't swallow. Would they kill the boy too? Would it be now? Should she beg for his life, for her life too, plead for her daughters' sake. But the Indian woman put a finger to her lips. As Lydia closed her eyes, memories flashed through her mind. Fair-haired, snub-nose Fleur, squinting up from the table. Em racing in with a banana spider in a jar.

The thin man lowered his rifle and moved close to Lydia, so close she smelt his sour breath. As she felt the cool tip of the rifle against her leg, she forced herself not to scream. He slowly lifted the hem of her dress with the rifle. She froze. With his other hand he touched the bare skin beneath her collar bone, slid a finger down between her breasts. She noticed Maznan was staring at the ground, and for a moment did the same, but glanced up as the stocky man returned. He waved the smaller man aside and grinned at her, then pushed her head back against the tree and held her by the throat, just beneath the chin. She felt his hand tighten, the fingers digging into her flesh. With his other hand he made a cutthroat movement across her neck. Her heart twisted, and she bit her lip so hard she tasted blood. Tears spilled down her cheeks as she finally pleaded to be spared.

But the man immediately spun away from her, and she gasped as he fired two shots at the front tyres of the bus. With hands on hips he rocked with laughter. Lydia watched the wide-eyed shock of the few remaining occupants as the bus tilted, then jerked them about as if they were at the funfair.

She caught the flash of colour as a pair of blue-crowned parrots flew past into the trees. Beyond them, a troupe of suddenly silent, long-nosed monkeys viewed the spectacle from high branches. What little remained of the clear morning was fast disappearing behind black clouds, and in the stinking air the world seemed to stand still. She gulped and closed her eyes. Naive she'd been. Reckless. Now everything was at stake, nothing mattered but her girls. Nothing.

She came back to the smell of blood and urine. To the unearthly cackle of hornbills, and the Chinese barking orders.

The boy spoke softly. 'Do not worry, Mem,' he said, in precise English. 'They will not kill us.'

She held her breath.

'And they have not set the bus on fire.' Tongue loosened by the shock, it was the most he'd said so far.

The boy was right. The men crossed the road, slashed the *lallang* between tall trees, and edged

65

back into the fringes of the jungle, glancing behind to jeer at the two corpses they dragged, heads bouncing on the ground. The remaining people climbed off the bus. Faces pale, eyes dark, they stepped over slippery trails of blood, speaking in whispers, and lifting their shoulders in bewilderment.

The Indian woman freed herself, then worked on releasing Lydia and the child. In answer to Lydia's puzzled expression she said, 'All show. These days they do not kill women and children. They need our help.'

'But the ones they killed?'

'Traitors.'

Maznan wandered off, and Lydia, trembling with relief, turned to see him hunched up and talking with a group of Malays from the bus. Without any warning she vomited into the bushes.

As she wiped her face with her skirt, the child ran across.

'This man knows the way to a village,' he said in a rush. He smiled at her, their shared ordeal uniting them. 'Come.'

A quick look at the Indian woman was rewarded with a grin. 'Go. He takes those others too.'

'What about you?'

The woman shrugged. 'God's will. Another bus tomorrow.'

The fear had been replaced by an overwhelming feeling of fatigue, and doubt fogged Lydia's mind. From force of habit, she glanced around for her girls, but of course, they had gone ahead.

Should she stay and wait for another bus, and whatever other dangers might lie in wait? Or should she just go with the child? It'd be too dangerous to remain on the road once night fell, especially if this was a curfew area. Maznan stood waiting, one hand outstretched.

'You look after me: I look after you,' he said with a shy grin.

'Deal,' she said, and took his hand.

At least he was talking, and now the terror was over, it seemed they were in it together.

As the straggly group veered off the road a little, the monkeys set off howling and screeching again. Lydia looked back over her shoulder for a moment, still uncertain, her scalp itching, and sweat pouring from her head. She smelt the sickly scent of wild climbing orchids, her tongue stuck to the roof of her mouth and her stomach turned over. She wiped her hairline, and tried to appear calm for the sake of the child, but there was no way of knowing if the man was leading them into a trap.

10

I liked to get up early to see the milkman. Gran said that before too long he'd have a van, and then I wouldn't see his horse and cart again. I pulled the lace curtains aside and peered out. He came a bit later on Saturdays, so I went out and lolled around on the doorstep, tapping my foot to 'You Belong to Me'. It was an old wartime song Mummy used to sing, and I'd join in on the bit about the jungle. I was always in trouble for lolling. Don't loll, Emma. Sit up straight.

It was April now, and the month before I had turned twelve. The morning was already light, with birds singing in the garden, and yellow streaks in the sky behind the black trees. I watched as the houses and church spire turned pink. Red sky in the morning: shepherd's warning. Perhaps it would rain. I caught sight of him turn into our road, in his smart white uniform and peaked cap. When he got to Gran's, he put two pints of milk on the step, called me his early bird, and gave me some coppers to spend on sweets.

After breakfast I headed for the barn, sloping like a panther. People said I walked like Mother. She was like a cat, nimble and stretchy. I was skinny and tall, but not with freckles like her. My best feature was my eyes, Mum said. Turquoise blue. Fleur was different, not a string bean like me. She liked to take her time, push her doll's pram up and down. Up and down. Up and down. Snub nose in the air. She sat up straight, and liked dresses too, more than shorts — like a good little girl, a pretty little girl, Dad said.

In Malaya Daddy took a lot of exercise. Tennis, rugby, even cricket. In England he didn't, and he nearly always wore a suit and tie, all in dark brown or grey. At the weekend, he wore a knitted Fair Isle waistcoat Gran made. He sighed when he saw me looking untidy. And that was practically always.

The wooden barn was set back from a side road, about twenty minutes from my grandparents' house, and in the grounds of a big house. Kingsland Hall. Though the barn was near, a wide stream crossed the grounds, and if you wanted to get to the hall, it was a long way round by road, and too far to walk. The barn had mice and maybe even rats too, but a few of the local kids still played in there. I tagged along, half accepted. We climbed the ladder, and, away from prying eyes, the boys showed us their bottoms in return for us showing private bits of ourselves.

Billy, the skinniest boy, and the one that I fought, took his trousers down right in front of my eyes and then weed in the corner where I could see. I sneaked a look, and blushed to see his little tassel poke up like a stick. He called me horrid names when I refused to join in. The others pointed at me, but I stuck out my chin. I wanted to be one of them, but nothing would make me do it.

When the other children left early, he sat beside me, smelling of mud and rotting wood. It wasn't so bad. He had nice conker-coloured eyes and a big grin, once you got used to the teeth, and now his hair was grown a bit, he had a short straight fringe and you could see it was blond.

He grinned at me, and got out a grubby pack of cards.

'Your hair's changed,' I said.

'Nits,' he said, not bothered. 'Mum chopped it off before. Sorry I said you're an immigrant. You're not. Just foreign. Want one of these?'

I nodded and he passed me a large purple gobstopper.

'Where do you live?' he said.

'At my gran's, but you're wrong, I *am* English.'

'All right. All right. Keep yer hair on.' He scratched his head. 'They call you *stuck up*, you know, the kids.'

'I know. And they call you *stink*.'

We both laughed.

'Tell me about that place. Where you come from. What's it like?'

'There's a rain storm every day and there are millions of animals in the jungle.'

'Monkeys?'

I nodded.

'Never saw a monkey for real. Got a picture though.'

He pulled out a dog-eared card and handed it to me. His face was all bright, but his fingernails, and the skin around them, were bitten raw.

'There's hundreds of monkeys in Malaya. All sizes. The little monkeys hang on their mothers' furry tummies, and howl like real babies.'

'Cor!'

We sat in silence, sucking the gobstoppers.

'Can you whistle?' he said.

'I can.' To show him, I took my gobstopper out, and then whistled a song Mum taught me about coins in a fountain. 'Mum says I whistle like a man.'

'Where is she? Your mum.'

I felt a lump in my throat and swallowed hard, not wanting him to see. 'She's coming soon.'

'Want to help me make a go-kart?'

'You bet.'

We climbed down the ladder. He charged over to the corner where he'd hidden some bits of old wood, a set of bent pram wheels, some rusty metal and a crate. He poked under the hay and brought out a hammer and some nails.

'Dad's,' he said, and we set to work, arguing about how to do it.

When it was nearly finished we stood back, covered in scratches and splinters, and inspected our kart. It didn't look pretty, but it worked, and we were happy.

I looked at my watch. Half past five. Veronica was due at four. I should have waited at home, watched television, but then I remembered there were no programmes in the day. Dad rarely spoke, except to tell me off, and despite what he said about fresh air, spent evenings stuck to Grand-dad's television set. Dad bought it for him, even though he and Granddad didn't see eye to eye.

I'll really catch it now, I thought.

'See you at school tomorrow,' he said with a grin.

'Yup,' I said, and turned red, pleased I'd made a proper friend.

I arrived home as the coal merchant was coming up the road. *Wilson's* it said on the side. Everyone was out on the pavement. A cold wind blew, and my eyes watered, as I watched Veronica with Dad and Fleur. Dad kissed Veronica on the cheek. She blushed, patted her pin curls down, and tied a headscarf over her hair, while her skirt swished round in the wind. Then Mr Oliver came out of the house.

'Ah, there she is,' he said, and grinned at me.

Dad spotted me. I'd hoped I could pretend to have been there all along, but the apple in his throat jumped, and his lips went thin. 'I'll speak to you later, young lady,' he said under his breath. 'Come to the car to see Sidney and Veronica off. At least you can manage that.'

I hung back, wanting to keep away from Mr Oliver, but just as we reached the car, Veronica called me over to where she stood beside him. 'I missed you, Emma. Let's have a day out soon. Just you and me.'

She smelt of lavender and starch, and wanted to hug me. When she put her arms round me I could tell she was lonely, but held back. She got into the car and waved a pink-gloved hand, while her brother put his hand on my bottom and patted it. I had to put up with it. There was nothing I could do. I'd have said something to Mum, but not Dad.

'Toodleoo. See you soon,' Mr Oliver said with a grin, and showed a mouthful of very white teeth and bright pink gums.

'Not if I can help it,' I whispered, and pulled a face at his meaty smell. Then, feeling my stomach rumble, I turned to Father and said, 'Can I have a scone now?'

He looked at me with angry eyes. 'Not ruddy likely. Upstairs to your room.'

I climbed the stairs one at a time, instead of bolting up, my heart thumping as he followed.

'Bend over,' he said, when we got to my room.

I bent over and stared at the threadbare carpet, wishing myself a million miles away. It was completely silent in the room. I thought he might smack me, but took a sharp breath when I heard him undo his belt.

I was trembling, but tried not to show any fear. Suddenly there was a sharp sting across the back of my thighs. The faded pattern of roses and leaves on the carpet leapt about and began to blur. I blinked away the tears, and dug a thumbnail into the fleshy part of my hand.

'Don't.' The sting came again. 'Let me.' Whack. 'Ever see you.' Whack. 'Disobey me like that again.'

I didn't cry then either, but when I stood up and saw his face turn red as a tomato, probably redder than my sore bottom, I looked straight at him and spoke in as clear a voice as I could. 'No, Daddy. Sorry, Daddy.'

I saw his jaw twitch but he didn't look at me.

'It's for your own good, Emma,' he said as he put on his belt. It seemed to take for ever as he fumbled it through the loops. When it was done he moved away, still not looking at me.

'It's for your own good,' he said again. 'You

can't do what you like in this life, and the sooner you stop playing silly buggers the better. Now stay in your room.'

He'd never really walloped me before, and though the buckle hurt, I smarted more from shock at what had happened than actual pain. He'd growled at me before, lost his temper and given me a clip. Like the time I spilled ink on my school uniform and tried to clean it with bleach. His face was scrunched up and red as he yelled at me. But it wasn't fair. It was an accident and I didn't know bleach would turn navy blue to pinky white. He said I'd bloody well have to wear it like that, and I screamed at him and said I would not. I lost my temper out of fright. I shouted that he couldn't make me and I'd rather die, and then picked up a vase from the coffee table and threw it on the floor.

That night, after the walloping, I lay awake in the dark, wishing for my mum. I listened to my father's snores through the bedroom wall. At heart I longed for Dad to love me, and it made me sad that sometimes he didn't even seem to like me much. He never smacked Fleur. She had a squint and looked like him, and it was usually me and Mum, and her and Dad.

I was lucky to have Gran, because we didn't have any relatives on our mother's side; Mum was brought up by nuns, and Mum never knew her mother. I once asked why she never wanted to find out who her mother was, but she only said, 'I've got you and Fleur now. That's all that really matters.'

But a voice hissed in my head — *If you matter*

so, why didn't she come with you?

Shut up. Shut up. Her friend was sick.

I closed my eyes, hoping so see Mum, but the picture was fuzzy and her face was gone. I brushed my tears away, and thinking of the pattern of roses and leaves on the carpet, went to sleep in a beautiful garden, where we once sucked the sweet nectar of needle flowers. Where Fleur knocked over iced lemon as she turned cartwheels on the lawn, and Mummy laughed and said she'd have to wear specs. It was the garden that led to the undergrowth, where gibbons howled and forest dwellers with squashed faces hunted for food. And where the long grass was, where nobody dared go because of the snakes.

11

Ahead of her Lydia heard the child rattle on in Malay. As she navigated the springy undergrowth beneath the vast umbrella of trees, a fluorescent bird cackled right above her head. She jumped, thinking of Em's spirits, cunning as crabs, who slip into your blood and make it go cold. She pulled herself together and fought off the cloud of insects whistling round her head. Haunted by her early romantic ideas of how life in Malaya was meant to be, she stood still.

Not an idyll at all, it was noisy, stinking, and frightening.

She glanced back to see black trees silhouetted against a yellow sky, and hearing a rustle above the drone of cicadas and crickets, saw the tall Eurasian man she'd picked out on the bus. With an easygoing Malay stride, he came up behind her; she tensed and looked ahead for the boy.

'Watch out for the *malu-malu*,' the man said, pointing at a carpet of pretty pink flowers. 'They have thorny stems.'

She nodded, noting his deep voice, slanted eyes and the well-shaped contours of a clever man. His was not an open Malay face, but a complicated face, more western in appearance.

The smell of wood smoke reached her, and there was Maznan, at the edge of the village, hopping on one foot, looking just like Mowgli from *The Jungle Book*: all knees, elbows, and a

76

whirling mop of hair. He grinned as she caught up and ruffled his hair.

They picked their way through the vegetable patches surrounding the kampong, and reached the thatched houses, built high on wooden stilts. Lydia carefully avoided the Malay jungle fowl pecking in the dust.

Maznan laughed. 'They are chickens.'

'I've never seen chickens three feet tall before.'

He shook his head, still grinning.

'What's *malu-malu* mean?' she said.

'It is a shy flower.' He lifted his arms, and with his hands made the shape of petals closing up.

She kept her distance from the grazing buffalo, but the simple domesticity was comforting and she realised it had been the right decision to come here. At least for the moment they were safe.

On the two narrow bridges that crossed the stream, children attempted to catch flickering fireflies, hopping and twirling, clapping their hands when they got close. It wasn't the way Alec depicted native villages. Rat-infested he said. Disease-ridden.

'The Malays are downright lazy,' he'd said, when she pointed out their serenity.

Alec invested a lot in the British Administration, in his job, the outdoor life, the club. George, Harriet, and their ilk, that's what Alec aspired to. They all thought the same. Who would have guessed I'd be here now, she thought, smelling coconut oil and listening to the sound of Malay throat singing and delicate jangly music.

Maznan ran on to speak with two men in burnt orange sarongs and waved at her, indicating she should follow. She hesitated. He skipped back and slipped his hand into hers. Is this the place I should leave him, she wondered, as he pulled her over to a hut.

A young woman with the typical soft eyes, round face and polished skin of the Malays, offered her tepid water in a wide bowl. 'Lela,' she said, introducing herself. Maznan indicated Lydia was to wash her hands and face, but instead she took the bowl, reached for the child and began to remove his shirt.

'No!' He pulled it back down.

'I just want to wash it, Maznan. Will you let me?'

He frowned, as if weighing up her words.

'Only wash it? Not take it?'

'No, darling. I won't take it away. I promise.'

He stopped struggling; allowed her to take off his shirt. She washed the wound on the side of his body, then scrubbed and rinsed the rest of him from top to bottom. From a second bowl, she washed the lingering trace of vomit from her own face and sponged her skirt.

The finest slice of a crescent moon stood out in the orange sky. As it grew darker, lanterns flickered right across the village. She guessed they'd be eating soon. Outside, by the fire, if she'd understood correctly. The boy confirmed it, grinning widely.

'Rice balls,' he said, licking his lips. 'Sticky ones.'

She smiled and lifted his chin. Children were the same the world over. She felt a surge of

78

longing for her girls. It took her by the shoulders and shook her to her boots. She imagined the sound of their laughter as they sang to each other in the bath. How much longer was it going to be?

In the dark, clusters of fireflies took off and flashed in synchrony, lighting tree after tree all along the riverbank, but she felt lost; more than missing a limb, as people said, she was missing her heart.

That night she lay on her makeshift bunk, blue moonlight slanting through the glassless window. As the little boy snuggled up, she put one arm round him to hold him safe, then travelled to her daughters in her mind. She made herself cry with images of them asleep in bed, protected by mosquito nets, but not by her.

She felt Maznan wipe her tears away with his fingers, then she sang him to sleep and sent a prayer to her girls, across miles and miles of inhospitable jungle.

The shadowy image of a woman in a pale blue dress with darker flowers at the hem drifted into her mind. She stood on a beach, the skirt rustling against her calves, and Lydia longed for the image to become clearer. It did not. It never did. But she clung to the memory, buried inside the long years she spent at St Joseph's. When she'd asked who the woman was, the nuns had changed the subject and she'd had to make do with her imagination. She allowed the picture to fade, and despite the suffocating Malayan heat, was surprised to sleep soundly, the peace of the village wiping the terror of the day away.

She woke as dawn lit the walls of the hut and the scent of ripe pineapples and mangos drifted in. She went outside, sniffed the air, and found leggy Maznan counting the number of times he leapt over the remains of the night's fire. She smiled at his squeals of make-believe fear, knowing the fire was cold. Even though it was early, the men, bent double, toiled on the vegetable plots, and women swept the bare earth round their huts.

'Maznan,' she called.

He turned his face, grinned, and ran across to lead her to see the goats. Together they saw a clearing where the small herd of beige goats was grazing.

'Eight,' he said. 'You can touch them.'

She tentatively held out her hand to one of the smaller ones.

He laughed. 'The babies do not bite.'

Lela came out with a stool for Maznan and one for herself. Lydia was astonished at the little boy's proficiency as he began to milk. Again she wondered if it was the right place to leave him. It was hard to know. The girl hadn't been clear.

'Mem.' He smiled encouragingly at her. 'You try?'

She shook her head and saw the disappointment in his eyes. 'Would you like to stay here?' she said.

'For how long, Mem?'

'You can call me by my name, Maznan. I'm Lydia.'

'Yes, Mem. And you can call me Maz.'

She sighed. 'I mean would you like to live here, Maz, until your aunt can fetch you?'

The boy looked up at her with watchful eyes. 'Not my aunt, Mem. I will go with you.'

Lydia stared at the child and shook her head. He'd triggered her pity back in Malacca and now a dozen thoughts fought for space.

Part Malay, part Chinese, the girl had asked her to take him to a Malay kampong or Chinese resettlement village. He had relatives in both, but she hadn't said which ones and there were so many. She couldn't drag him all the way to Ipoh, and despite the Emergency this was a happy village. She wondered if she should have left him with the police in the first place, but the image of her own children shut up in a cell banished the thought.

The boy was still looking at her, his pale eyes hopeful.

'But you need to stay with your people, child. I'm going to find my own family.'

He left the milking and came up close, planting his hand in her own, looking up with tears forming. 'Please. I have no family here.'

She watched the swallows that flew about the place, heard the birdsong, the sounds of goats and chickens, and the rumbling noises beyond. Across the embers the tall man stood in the shadows watching with dark unblinking eyes. She stared back. He gave her a nod. After he had caught up with her the afternoon before, they'd walked the remaining few yards to the village in strained silence, and since then she'd only seen him at supper. He continued to hold her eyes.

She was the first to look away. He came straight across, moving fluidly as if he had well-oiled joints, like an athlete. A runner. He offered a firm hand. 'My name is Adil,' he said.

She nodded, removed her tingling palm, and looked down at the ground. But not before she'd noticed his wide high cheekbones, strong nose, and cool sable eyes beneath well-formed brows.

'Why did they ambush the bus?' she asked, for something to say.

'Execution and extortion. Next they will burn the bus if the company doesn't 'subscribe'.'

'You know about these things?'

He shrugged.

Though he didn't seem particularly young, maybe forty, his forehead was unlined, and, as she'd noticed on the bus, his head was shaven and brown. Two lines ran from the sides of his nose to a full mouth. He was lean but wide-shouldered, and although he was quite dark-skinned, she was unable to distinguish his nationality.

'Where are you travelling on to?' he asked.

'Ipoh,' she found herself saying. 'I'm going to join my husband.'

He rubbed his chin. 'Ah well. We shall go together. It is a difficult journey. I am headed that way.'

Lydia hesitated, considering his words. She hoped George Parrott had got it right and Alec and the girls were still there. She didn't know exactly where she was now, and she didn't know this man. He was reserved, but there was nothing deferential, as she might have expected. He could be anybody.

'Oh. I'll probably travel on alone,' she finally blurted.

'I insist,' he said, adopting a friendly expression and smiling softly. 'You'll be much safer with me, Lydia. It is Lydia?'

'How did you know?'

He shrugged, and palm upwards, indicated Maz. 'I must have heard you tell the child. You are leaving him here?'

What was it to him? It seemed more of a statement than a question. She noted his calm confidence and her previous indecision was instantly resolved. She looked away as she spoke. 'No, he's coming with me.'

Maz hugged her legs as a cloud of iridescent yellow butterflies flew past. She saw him try to count them, but they were too fast, and too many. The man inclined his head with a look of indifference, but not before Lydia noticed his lips tighten.

She moved away and helped Maz into his dry shirt. He beamed prettily, displaying the row of even white teeth, and patted the shirt all over. She repacked her case, ditching two pairs of shoes and one of the evening dresses. The gritty dust stung her eyes, and her newly cropped hair felt damp with sweat. She flicked the droning creatures from her face, scratched the bites around her ankles and prayed the journey ahead wouldn't be too fraught. She fingered her locket and took a deep breath. Won't be long, my darlings, won't be long.

12

They left the village with just a nod to each
other, and barely spoke as they picked their way
along a tangled pathway. After an hour or so they
found a station of sorts: no more than a simple
telegraph booth and a small platform at the edge
of the jungle. Lydia slumped on to a metal
bench. Sticky, tired, and with angry bites on her
ankles, she would have given anything for a soak
in a bath. The child wrapped an arm around her
waist and slept with his head against her chest. A
few leaflets flapped about declaring death for
those who supplied insiders with food, and on
the hoardings two posters advertised Tiger Beer,
and the songs of Dinah Shore.

'You'll be looking forward to seeing your girls
again,' Adil said.

Lydia frowned. Had she told him about Emma
and Fleur? Maybe she had.

'Nothing more important than family.' He
reached into a pocket hidden in his sarong, and
pulled out an orange. 'Here. Share it with the
child.'

'Thank you,' she said. 'I love oranges and I am
thirsty.'

She peeled off the skin. The citrus scent was
mouth wateringly lovely, but when she saw the
longing in Maznan's eyes, she passed the entire
orange to him.

Adil said nothing.

Hearing a rattle, she glanced at the rails, and prayed the train would be cool inside. Then, as it passed, her shoulders sagged as she stared at the clouds of dust obscuring its rear.

Unused to being out in the late afternoon, she was melting in the heat, and hoped rain wouldn't be long. Adil didn't seem to suffer from humidity the way she did, and had carried her case all the way. He nodded slowly with pursed lips, his brows furrowing.

'It seems the line is undamaged, at least for part of the way,' he said. He looked about, then told her he had something to see to and headed for the booth.

While he was gone, she spotted an excitable little spider-hunter bird, angry because she'd sat right beneath its nest. But she was too hot to move, and when Adil came back, she made no attempt at conversation. She sniffed the salty, sticky smell coming from her armpits and cursed Alec. She felt a tap on the arm and glanced down at the child.

'I am still hungry, Mem,' he said, rubbing his tummy and looking at her with huge eyes.

She smiled for his sake. 'What's your favourite?'

'*Nasi Dagang*. My mother made.'

It was the first time he'd mentioned his mother. 'Whereabouts in the jungle is she, Maz? Do you know?'

He shrugged and hung his head.

'Did your mother buy you that shirt? Is that why you didn't want me to take it off?'

He sniffed.

She thought for a moment. 'Tell me about *Nasi Dagang*.'

'It is coconut rice, with fish.'

She searched her pockets. A mangy dog slunk by, eyeing them hopefully. She had no choice but to speak to Adil, though something about his reserve tied her tongue.

She lowered her voice. 'What can we do? There's nothing left.'

His eyes were watchful, intelligent. She became aware they were staring at each other and turned away.

'If a train comes, we can buy food. Some travel only to sell. You still have money?'

She nodded, then found her voice again. 'I thought nobody was allowed to travel with food, and isn't the money they make wasted on the price of their tickets.'

'They don't pay. Just jump on and off,' he said, still looking straight at her.

'Don't they get hurt?'

'They're only natives,' he said, with a straight face.

He was teasing her. She observed the weeds growing in dust at the edges of the concrete platform, and thought of another journey. The time she and Alec had smuggled two Siamese kittens through customs at Johore. Somehow it had been all right for *them* to break the rules.

She glanced at the man sitting beside her. She knew nothing about him, but in the minutes that followed, she became intensely aware of hairs beginning to show up on her bare legs. She shuffled them further back under the bench.

When a battered train came to a screeching halt, a distinct scent of ginger and tamarind mingled with smoky engine fumes, and the smell of rain in the air.

They climbed on, found seats, and from a thin-haired woman wearing baggy trousers, they bought guava, and curried rice patties. Lydia saw for herself, despite prohibition, the movement of unofficial food and livestock carried on. The woman had a rucksack full of food, and live chickens in a lidded basket.

'They find ways to dodge the security forces,' Adil said.

'But doesn't some of the food find its way to the rebels in the jungle?'

'You must not tell anyone,' he said, with raised eyebrows, his eyes framed by thick lashes.

The light fell on his face and she saw real warmth in his eyes. She looked down, but in less than a beat glanced up again. He'd moved, something about his eyes had changed, and the warmth was gone. She swallowed hard, didn't know how to react. She'd had no casual relationships with non whites before; they were either Alec's subordinates at work, or worked for her. And you could hardly call the annual dinner at the sultan's palace casual.

'Eat up,' he said. 'It might be our last for a while.'

As the train picked up speed, rippling oceans of dark green trees flashed by. There was no toilet, and when it slowed again, a flock of people made a dash for the bushes. She smothered a smile at the sight of men pissing in the rain, and in full view of the windows.

Maz slept between them, head against her arm as she rocked with the movement of the train. From time to time she glanced at the man's face, at the strong jaw in profile and his closed mouth. Once he opened his eyes and caught her looking. She swallowed her embarrassment and turned away.

After a bit, she was aware of other looks coming her way. A tall military man and his wife, heading down the aisle, stopped in front of her. He was over six foot, well built, and purple-nosed. Clearly a drinker.

He bent his head towards her with a puzzled look. 'Are you all right?'

'Yes thank you. Perfectly fine. I'm travelling up country.'

The woman folded her arms across her chest and pulled a face. 'But with your gardener, dear?'

Lydia felt embarrassed for Adil. 'I'm fine. Thank you for asking. Goodbye.'

'Well!' the woman said, red-faced. Her husband took her elbow, and pushed her down the aisle in front of him. She could be heard from the next carriage, still protesting.

Lydia sighed and caught Adil grinning.

'Trim the oleander bush, madam?'

She opened the window on the sweet smell of the jungle after rain, and a delicate scent of wild freesia blew into the carriage. She laughed and everything was all right again.

They were rising now. Half an hour later, with her forehead against the glass she stared out at a ravine with a river at the bottom. The sun slipped out from behind the clouds, to reveal, about halfway up the hill, the ruin of a palace.

'What's that,' she said, turning to Adil.

'I think it may be the Sultan of Selangor's palace, which means that is the Klang Valley.'

Lydia frowned. Her geography of England was sketchy, of Malaya she knew even less.

'We're not far from Kuala Lumpur.'

Lydia pictured the map hanging on Alec's office wall behind his desk. He'd pointed vaguely at this place or that, hardly caring if he enlightened her or not. Now it was hard to recall. She knew Johore Bahru, Malacca and the island of Singapore. All in the south. And right at the start, they'd had a short but peaceful holiday up at Kuala Terengganu on the east coast. They had been more or less happy then.

With only a rough idea of where Ipoh was, she had no head for detail, and all she remembered of the map were places she'd been.

'We're about halfway.' Adil said, and produced a stub of pencil and a tattered notebook. 'I'll show you.'

Lydia carefully picked up the sleeping child and swopped places with Maz.

Close up, she caught the spicy scent of cedar oil on Adil's skin.

'See, Penang, in the west, is almost opposite Kuantan, in the east.'

She nodded as the long shape of Malaya took form. 'And Ipoh?'

'Here,' he said, marking a cross. 'A little below Penang, and a bit more than halfway from Kuala Lumpur.'

Still such a long way, she thought. 'How far does this train take us?'

'Depends on the state of the tracks, but it's meant to go as far as Tanjung Malim.'

Her breath caught — 'I know it. A friend manages a plantation near there. Jack. Jack Harding.'

For a moment she allowed herself to think of Jack's wide grin. Pictured him striding about the plantation, saw his muscular legs, arms swinging, shoulders glistening with sweat. Something Jack had spoken of, soon after they met, came racing back to her. He'd looked her in the eye and, wringing enormous hands, said, 'God damn it, Lyddy. I don't want to die in the jungle.'

She'd kissed him hard on the mouth, couldn't help being drawn to his grin and energy as electric as tropical thunder.

'Don't worry, sweetheart,' she'd said. 'You won't. But why did you come here in the first place?'

'After Burma, I couldn't stand the thought of an ordinary life,' he'd said.

In his early forties, Jack came from a good family and was privately educated, but had turned his back on it all. Jack didn't care for the opinions of others. Let them think what they damn well like, he'd say, spreading his arms in a shrug. Handsome and fair, he stood out in a crowd, like a great golden god she once thought. She hardly dared admit that from the start she'd smelt a bad boy.

It was his image that stayed with her now, the memory soothing.

The rhythm and heat of the train made everyone drowsy. Maz, curled up against her, seemed to be asleep, but when she glanced down, his little hand reached out and tapped her thigh.

'Now my mother is in the inside, I do not see her,' he said.

She pulled him close. Poor little thing, she thought, as someone brushed her arm, while moving quickly past.

A Malay woman, her baby snug inside a cotton shawl tied to her chest, was in a rush to get to the door. At the opposite end of the corridor, an approaching ticket collector called out for tickets. As Lydia glanced back, she felt Adil jump to his feet.

'What's going on?' she asked.

He didn't answer, just pushed his way through the melee of standing passengers, and followed the woman. Lydia craned her neck to see. At the door, the woman stretched out an arm, and began to turn the handle. By now the entire carriage was aware and everyone turned to watch.

The door opened. Lydia gasped and stood up, a hand covering her mouth. The train had not slowed, was not approaching a station. But the woman, one arm round the baby, already had one foot out. She leant forward, ready to jump. Just in time, Adil caught her shawl, and dragged her back inside, then held her firmly by the arms.

Lydia saw the concern on his face, watched him shake his head, saw the woman bend her head as he spoke, and her tear-stained face when she looked up. He reached into his pocket and pulled out a wallet, pointed at the ticket collector, and handed the woman some coins and a five-dollar bill.

The collector shrugged as he reached their seats, and Adil paid for all their tickets.

'That was good of you,' Lydia said.

He frowned. 'The tickets?'

'That yes, thank you, but I meant the woman. How did you know she was going to jump? She might have been killed.'

'I've seen it before. It was nothing,' he said, dismissing her approval, as if embarrassed.

But Lydia was impressed, not just by his kindness, but also by his quick reaction.

Outside, the wind was blowing the dirt about in billowing clouds. As the train came to a halt at a tiny station, Lydia saw a small bus waiting. Doors slammed, birds scattered, and people lugged their packages in a mass of movement. A swarm of lucky ones headed for the bus. A priest, waiting in the crowd as they approached, turned to her with a smile, a pistol snug in its holster at his waist. Once the sight of it would have made her shudder, now everyone had a gun and she hardly raised an eyebrow. The dusty air, and how they'd breathe if the bus didn't take them, were far more of a worry.

Adil found them places halfway down.

She sighed and wiped away the line of sweat that constantly formed at her hairline. Maz noticed her dejection. 'I think you are beautiful, Mem,' he said.

Tears came to her eyes. Once she might have been, now she just felt tired and dirty.

There was a sound of rumbling. She craned her neck to look, and on the road, escorted by police, a dozen lorries were snaking by.

Adil glanced out. 'They're transporting Chinese settlers from the edges of the jungle to a new resettlement village.'

She listened to the wail of a loudspeaker as the wind blew their way.

'There's nothing left for the Chinese in Malaya,' he said. 'Only the camps or the horror of living on the inside.'

Lydia knew from Alec that the police and even the military were involved in the resettlement programme.

'Aren't most people turning in favour of the government?'

'Well, wouldn't you? It doesn't mean they support the British. They're just sick of the violence.'

Lydia's head ached and her shoulders felt rigid from the struggles of the day. She closed her eyes and slept, this time with Maz on her lap, but maintaining a small gap between her and the man. Troubled by dreams of her childhood at the convent, and the ever constant yearning for the mother she'd never known, she was deep in the past when the bus came to a sudden halt. Her eyes flicked open and the woman in the blue dress rapidly faded. The bus was at a standstill.

She shook herself awake and sighed deeply. What now? She wiped her cracked lips with the back of her hand, then licked them to bring back some moisture. It only made them sting even more.

Adil was stumbling up the aisle. People stood, stretched, murmured questions to each other. The boy hadn't stirred. In the growing darkness, streaks of silver patterned the deep blue skyline, but she couldn't see the road ahead. She waited, learning the Malayan way. Alec would have embarrassed her with his stiff-backed British insistence. Her patience was rewarded when Adil struggled back.

'The local police have stopped us. The bus has to turn around. It's road mines. They're not taking any chances.'

Lydia caved in a little. Why did everything have to be so damn hard?

'But my girls,' she said. 'I can't go back.'

'I've arranged a lift for you to your friend's plantation. One of the constables here was due to transfer there in the morning. He's agreed to take you, and will leave now instead.'

At the thought of seeing Jack, her heart skipped a beat. She imagined the blue hills and dark green valleys of the plantation, as he'd described them. The chirp of chi-chack lizards outside his bedroom window, the guttural song of bullfrogs. She shook her head. Jack wasn't why she was here.

'How do you know about Jack?'

'You mentioned him, remember? I checked with the police here at the block, and Bert is one of the officers who have been assigned to the estate. It will give you and the child a chance to rest, eat, sleep, clean up.' There was amusement in his eyes as they swept over her face and clothes. 'You don't want to meet your children looking like that, do you?'

In the fading light, she stared at her blistered feet, and legs covered in weeping sores. She smiled grimly. Everything itched. She hesitated. It was too much of a risk. As a wave of weariness washed over her, she wiped a hand across her forehead and wriggled her swollen fingers. She tried to twist her wedding ring.

'I can't go to Jack.'

He looked at her kindly. 'It's really your best chance. The bus won't come this way for another week.'

'What about you? Aren't you coming?'

'No. I will go back with the bus. It will turn round immediately.'

She sighed, surprised by a flash of disappointment.

'Can't I go back with you?'

He shook his head. 'A week's a long time. What would you do?'

She gave in. He was right. This way she'd reach Emma and Fleur sooner, but what would Alec say if he found out?

Adil carried her case, and holding on to Maz, shepherded them to the armoured police car, where a stocky British officer in green camouflage stood smoking beside a turbaned Sikh police sergeant.

Adil nodded at the man. 'This is Bert.'

With one hand, she shaded her eyes from his torch to see the man who'd be driving them. With the other she brushed away air full of flying ants. From what she could see, Bert had a friendly face, slicked back wavy hair and freckles like her own.

'No problem, anything to help a lady,' he said in a broad Yorkshire accent. 'I'd have been going in the morning anyway.'

She smiled faintly, surprised by how sad and homesick for England it made her feel.

Lydia settled Maz and climbed into the car. Just as she was about to close the door, she hesitated. Bert was in the driver's seat, key in the ignition, ready for the off.

'Sorry,' she said. 'Just a sec.' She got out and walked back to Adil.

'Who are you? I mean really. You've been so . . . so kind.' She touched his hand. His face was in shadow, but she saw his eyes glitter as he smiled. She saw real depth there, realised that his dignity and reserve reminded her of the old legends she'd read to the girls, about powerful native priests. Tranquil, like Adil, but warriors in their hearts.

'No problem. We live in dangerous times.'

They looked at each other just for a moment and she enjoyed the fleeting contact.

'Well, whoever you are, I wanted to thank you. For your kindness.'

'It was nothing. A friend. Think of me that way.'

★ ★ ★

Bert stuck to empty tarmac roads. As it grew darker, far into the trees they glimpsed the occasional brightness of kampong fires. At a high barbed-wire perimeter fence, they stopped. Bert shone his torch upwards, and Lydia saw two policemen staring down from a watchtower partially hidden in the trees, both armed with Bren guns. Bert flashed his credentials to a third man at the gate, who accompanied them to the house. In the distance great beams of light from even more watchtowers shone directly into the plantation.

The estate road itself was longer than Lydia expected, but when they arrived at a brightly lit two-storey building, surrounded by more barbed wire, her heart picked up speed. After unlocking another gate, the guard let them through. He walked round an azalea bush lit by a lamp rigged up on a post, then waited in the shadows.

The main house was square and imposing, circled by a veranda and what looked like a sizeable garden, with an annexe at the side. She'd never seen the estate before, their rendezvous taking place in hotels during the day, and more daringly once or twice at her own home.

Lydia wondered at the wisdom of this. What would Jack think of her turning up out of the blue? Better to have gone back with Adil, even if she'd had to wait a week.

In the hush of the entrance hall, she looked round, unsure, and breathing very slowly to calm her heart. It felt empty, barely lived in, apart from one pale blue Chinese rug in the middle of the floor. She took in sparse furnishings, dark woodwork and the masculine odour of tobacco and wax.

A slim Chinese girl, with unsmiling eyes and silky blue-black hair right down to her waist tripped across the smooth tiled floor. She had pale olive skin and delicate features, and something about the fluid way she walked was confidently sensual. Lydia felt hot and sweaty, but attempted a smile.

'Yes,' the girl said, in English. Her eyes flicked over them.

Bert looked a bit taken aback, but remained polite. 'Is Jack about please?'

'He may still be up. Who shall I say is here?'

'Bert Fletcher. I'm one of the additional Special Constables relocated to this estate. I was meant to arrive tomorrow.'

Lydia knew there'd been trouble at Jack's plantation. But she hadn't realised it meant Jack required Special Constables of his own.

'Just temporary, then I'll move on to the new resettlement village,' he said, turning to Lydia. 'We work in pairs.'

The girl left and Lydia stared as a pinkish-brown gecko crept across the wall. She tugged at her damp dress and absently brushed the flies from her face. Another gecko raced along to clutch hold of the first. She watched as the original one left its tail, which continued to squirm. It was a good omen and she was so absorbed in watching and trying to stop herself from crumpling she failed to see Jack's face as he entered the room. By the time she spun round at the sound of his steps, the moment had passed and she'd missed whatever his first reaction had been. He stood barefoot, muscular shoulders visible beneath a thin blue bathrobe, sleeves rolled up, hair damp. She watched his bright blue eyes, tried to gauge what he was feeling.

The Chinese girl stood silently behind him, her perfect tiny frame outlined against the light of the standard lamp behind.

'Lyddy,' he said, coming across to her. 'What on earth?'

Aware of scabby sores and dirty hair, Lydia suppressed the urge to cry and put on what she hoped was a brave face. As his eyes swept over her, he made no attempt to conceal surprise. Self-conscious despite the exhaustion, she smoothed her sweat dampened hair.

'This is Maznan,' she said, extracting the boy from her skirt, where he clung, limpet like. 'Maz for short. I'm sort of looking after him.'

Jack looked completely bewildered, brushed his dark blond hair from his eyes, swung round to the girl and spoke rapidly in Chinese.

The girl inclined her head and left the room.

'Lili will run a bath and sort out some food. You look done in.' He came up to her and held her by the shoulders. Suddenly his face lit up. 'Have you changed your mind? Is that why you're here?'

She felt herself tremble, shook her head and clenched her hands to hide the shaking.

He lifted her chin. 'What on earth has happened then?'

She bit her lip to stop the tears, but they fell anyway. She wanted him to sweep her up, take her to his bed, make everything all right. But she'd promised Alec. Made her choice.

He wiped the tears from her cheeks. 'Very well. I can see this isn't the time. I have to be up before dawn. Back by twelve. Then you can tell me. There are twin beds in the spare room.'

He nodded at Bert. 'The guard will show you where to go. See you tomorrow, Lyddy.' And with a light kiss on her forehead and a fleeting smile, he left.

13

The window had three sections, with metal criss-crossing the glass in diamond shapes. I stared out at the summer sky, turned pink by the sun, and felt homesick. I still smelt the dusty spot under the house in Malacca, where I crept to spy. Whenever I used to slide out, clothes and hair crawling, Mealy Worm stuck her snubby nose in the air and said, 'Poo. You stink.' She never went under the house. And Mum would say. 'Honestly, Emma. What have I told you? You'll get bitten to death.'

I ached to bursting for my mum's speckled eyes. I imagined her pinning up her hair, and laughing when it all came tumbling down. But could she still be laughing, without us? Without me? It was getting harder to find her in my dreams. When she did come, I was breathless with smelling her perfume and wanting her.

We'd been in England for six months, but memories of Malaya still beat inside me. I missed the beasts and ribbons of jungle scent that wound round the trees at the bottom of our garden and trailed us into town. If you were unlucky and one caught in your hair, it would wind right round, then pull you into the undergrowth by the neck. There weren't any ribbons of scent trailing from Worcestershire trees, though I looked, just in case.

It was still early and while my sister slept,

Gran and I got on with making a doll's house for Fleur's ninth birthday. She thought she was getting a plastic tea set, so we had to be quiet. Granddad hammered the bits of wood together while we were at school, and Gran and I painted and decorated it in her bedroom, to keep it away from Fleur. We'd already glued pieces of leftover orange wallpaper on to the walls, and stuck down bits of brown lino for the floors. Now, I was sewing one of the dolls. Gran sat in her apron and slippers, making a table and chairs out of matchboxes. She'd finished the table and was starting on the chairs, when there was a tap at the door.

'Are you in there?' Dad's voice.

I groaned.

His voice came again. 'Veronica and her brother are coming to lunch. They'll be here at eleven. That is in two hours' time. I expect you to be here, Emma. All the time. Take a leaf out of your sister's book. Understand?'

Unlike me, Fleur sat on his lap, sweet and dimply, and his face went soft as he smiled at her. Now she wasn't sickly, she looked even more like him, with the same cool blue eyes and quiet well-behaved hair. I heard the tick of the brown clock on the mantelpiece. I could choose not to answer, pretend not to be there. But he'd only come in and find me. Gran gave me a nudge.

'Yes, Daddy,' I called out, trying to make out I was smiling.

Veronica was okay. When her husband fell sick, Mr Oliver went out to help her with the special school there, and after the death had been kind

102

enough, Dad said, to accompany his sister back to England. Veronica was a bit sad, which I understood, but Dad smiled more when she was around.

Gran had to get on in the kitchen, so we stowed the doll's house away in her big wardrobe, and I got ready to slip out of the house to see Billy.

Fleur woke up just as I was putting my last layer on, and stood hands on hips. Fleur loved dolls so I had to stuff the one I was sewing under my pillow, just as she marched over to my bed. She said she knew I was up to something, and if I didn't share the secret, she'd tell. I was so cross I almost said, just for spite. But she was only little and it would be mean. And now she was going to have to wear specs too, so I tapped the side of my nose and said mind your own beeswax. She pouted a little, but when she saw I meant it, shrugged in a funny grown-up way.

'You're not going out?' she said.

'Just for a bit. Don't tell, will you?'

Fleur put her head to one side and looked at me with narrow eyes.

* * *

Billy and I had something in common: we loved to use our imaginations. For about a month we'd been working on new ways to be in the world, and we did it every Saturday at the barn. He didn't usually get there before ten, but when I climbed the ladder, I saw he was there already.

'Oh good,' he said with a toothy grin. 'I didn't

know if you were coming. Can you stay all morning?'

I groaned. 'I've got to be back by eleven.'

Billy was a joker and bad, like me. We slapped our hands together and said it together in loud voices, 'Bad like *meee*.' Then fell about laughing. It was my turn to come up with an answer to a problem that would save lives. If you couldn't think of anything, you had to take off a piece of clothing. To make sure it'd be okay, I wore a vest, a long sleeve cotton top, a jumper, a cardi, a pair of shorts, a pair of socks, and my skirt. All of it under my tight winter coat. It was August and I was sweltering.

Billy didn't have many clothes, and stood with skinny legs poking from baggy underpants, and wearing a holey vest passed down from his brother. It didn't quite cover his chest, and wasn't really fair, so I relented and gave him my coat. Billy's family was quite poor, mainly because his dad drank. That's what Granddad said. They had a cottage on the edge of the village. Occasionally the smell of wee lingered, though he said he had washed. Not well enough, I said with a sniff, sticking my nose in the air.

We began our imaginings, and immediately lost track of time.

'What about seeing with sound instead of light,' he said, stroking a pretend moustache, sticking out his chin and turning down the corners of his mouth, like a mad professor.

I laughed. 'You mean like bats?'

'Yeah! Blind as a bat.'

By the time I remembered, we were lying in

104

the hay in our underpants, slapping each other to stay warm.

'What time is it?' I yelled.

'Dunno.'

I looked at my watch. Oh no! Half past twelve. Lunch was always at twelve forty-five sharp. How could I have forgotten again?

I hopped about getting dressed, throwing my clothes on higgledy piggledy, while he looked me up and down.

'What?' I said.

'Straw in yer hair.'

I stepped back, ran my fingers through my hair, clambered down the ladder, tripped on the laces I'd left undone, landed in the dirt, and arrived home filthy. I came in by the back door in the hope I could get away with it. Say I'd been doing something in the garden. Dad, Gran, and Veronica stood together in the kitchen, and the table was laid with a new checked oilcloth. Veronica was looking very pretty with baby pink lipstick, and wearing a cotton dress with a full skirt that swished as she came over. Dad's face looked rigid, his mouth a thin hard line, his Malayan tan faded to yellowy grey.

Gran ran a hand over her untidy hair, put her face in a big smile so that her bright eyes had crinkles all round, and said, 'Ah, the chimney sweep has arrived.'

I stared at the brown lino floor.

'What did I tell you, Emma?' Dad said.

I risked a proper look at his face. I should've kept quiet but I couldn't help myself. Keep talking, make them smile, I thought.

'I was busy teaching Billy about monkeys. He wanted to know what they liked to eat. I said leg of lamb. He didn't believe it, but it's true, isn't it . . . Mum said she left one on the side and they nicked it. So they must like leg of lamb.'

I caught Gran's smile, which she hid behind a hand, but from the look of Dad's clenched jaw, I knew I was only making it worse.

'That is enough, Emma,' he said, in a sharp voice, the Adam's apple rising and falling as he spoke.

'Keep your shirt on, Son,' Gran said. 'She didn't mean anything by it. She's just a bit of a scallywag. No harm done.'

Veronica smiled and said hello.

I turned my back on her without speaking. Gran started picking the straw out of my hair.

'Well, she hasn't missed lunch,' she said. 'Though what you've got all those clothes on for I don't know. You'd better get them off and give your face and hands a scrub, ducks.'

I imagined the looks going on over my head. So far there was no sign of Veronica's brother. I breathed more easily, but then Granddad came in from the lounge and I saw Mr Oliver follow behind.

* * *

After lunch, Dad arranged to drop Gran and Granddad down at the doctor's Saturday afternoon surgery, then go for a drive with Veronica and Fleur. Granddad had palpitations and this was the only way Gran could get him to

106

go. The doctor was on call seven days a week, and would have come to see Granddad, but Gran said the fresh air would help. I was to be sent to my room in disgrace, punishment for coming back late and being rude to Veronica. I don't know why I was rude to her. I wanted to say sorry, but the words stuck in my throat and just wouldn't come out. I was cutting off my nose to spite my face, Mum would have said.

'But who'll look after Emma?' Gran asked.

'Oh, that's not a problem,' Mr Oliver said. He gave me a wink.

My heart wobbled. I wanted to shout, 'No. Don't leave me with him!' But whatever I said, they'd think I was making it up. I went upstairs, opened my window ever so quietly, and wondered if I could jump out. They were still talking on the doorstep.

'Don't know what's got into her,' I heard Dad say. 'She was always a difficult child but now it's much worse. I blame her mother for letting her run wild.'

I imagined my father throwing his hands in the air and rolling his eyes, shaking his head with a worried face, smiling charmingly at Veronica, to sort of suggest his helplessness.

From outside I heard Veronica say, 'Don't be too hard on her. She's missing her mother.' It made me feel doubly bad for turning my back on her.

I squeezed my eyes shut and thought of Malaya, of the deepest places where I'd never been, but imagined in the middle of the night when I woke from a dream.

Our gardener used to say beware the lure of the dusk, when demons would come out to play in the shadows of the long grass. They called to children with sweet dainties made of coconut and threads of spun sugar and only came out if somebody was lost. You had to be careful not to be lost, and if you went further and further, trying to find your way, they tempted you with sweet limes and sugar trees. And if you followed them, even once, you'd never be seen again.

Yet despite all of that, it felt safer there than it did here in Worcestershire, being left alone in a house with Mr Oliver.

14

Lydia woke to a room exploding with sunlight, a cup of cold tea on the bedside table. The girl must have come in to open the window. Lili. Wasn't that her name? She sat straight up, stretched her arms out wide and yawned, feeling energy in her blood for the first time in days. She'd talk to Jack today. She could hardly wait. After all, talking didn't count, did it?

An ice-cold shower, a book from the bookshelf and breakfast on the veranda.

On a small wooden table, next to a bowl filled with mangosteens, a jug of coffee and a plate of toast sat beside a copy of the *Malay Mail*. Until Jack got back she decided to enjoy the peace. Even though the sun had not reached its full strength, warmth rose from the land in waves, and the air was tinged with the smell of charcoal. Tall round-headed rubber trees towered close by with shiny, dark leaves, and incisions made into their bark. There the strange sweet smell of latex took over. This was Jack's world, and she breathed deeply.

A large patch of springy grass grew in front of a wooden platform, enclosing the house on three sides. On the furthest side, a covered corridor led to the servants' quarters, and from beyond the rubber trees strong jungle scents drifted over.

Leaving her book and taking a second cup of bitter coffee, she explored the outside of the house. It was a large rambling building, brick and wood built, with fancy ochre roof tiles and brown shutters. If not for the Emergency it would be beautiful. Was beautiful.

This was where Jack had been when he wasn't with her. For the whole year of their affair, this had been his place. And though she'd imagined it a million times, she'd never seen it. But now, as if to make up for that, she saw him in the shadow of every tree, heard him in every rustle. Despite everything she'd promised Alec, and even though she'd been the one to end it, she could barely admit to herself how much she longed to see Jack again.

At the back of the house, a number of fruit trees grew clear of the rubber plantation. Bananas, papayas and chakka fruit. And from behind a tall tree, the sun lit dozens of fluorescent parrots as they flew off one by one.

She stepped back in through tall French windows and found herself in a large wood-panelled office. No rugs, no pictures, just one lamp on Jack's metal desk and a single comfy-looking chair. Choosing the further of two lacquered doors, she opened it silently and entered another hallway with pale painted walls. This room had two brown doors, both ajar. Peering in, she discovered one led to a badly lit corridor, the other to Jack's bedroom. She padded into the latter.

It was cool and dark. The windows were wide open for air to pass through the wire mosquito mesh, but with the slatted shutters and the door to the veranda firmly closed to keep out the sun.

110

She inhaled deeply, smelling Jack's leathery after-shave, his cigarettes and his sweat. She hesitated. There was something else. Something faintly exotic.

She looked round: took in a neat pile of freshly laundered clothes and the deeply polished floor. This was not the Jack she knew; undomesticated, he was a man who only felt alive when there was a thrill to be had.

She headed for the soapy-smelling bathroom. This was too good a chance to peep into Jack's hidden world. His toiletries sat on a glass shelf above a slightly discoloured wash-hand basin, with a magnifying shaving mirror to the right and a small tin bathroom cabinet to the left. Jack's damp towel was draped over the edge of the bath, and the showerhead dripped intermittently. She picked up the towel and held it to her face. It smelt smoky: coal tar soap, she thought. She washed her hands in his basin and splashed her face. The water came out cool, though flecked with rust. She dried her hands and face with his towel, her scent mixing with his. She folded the towel the way it had been and turned to face the cabinet on the wall. She really shouldn't, she told herself. But her hand lifted up and turned the cabinet key.

Inside, along with Jack's toothbrush and toothpaste, was a jar of Pond's cold cream, a lipstick and a tiny glass vial of scent.

She folded her arms across her middle, the breath knocked right out of her, and sat abruptly on the edge of the bath. A voice in the back of her head told her not to be silly. He must have had other women. Alec said he had. And Cicely insinuated as much, even when Lydia was seeing him. But it was Jack who'd begged her. Leave, he'd said. Live with me. It was he who kissed her and pleaded for her not to end it.

She knew that it was stipulated in his four-year contract that he couldn't marry or live with anyone on his first tour, but when she'd raised it, he said there were ways. He'd been saving money to buy his way out of the contract. They'd take the girls; go back to England. In the end she couldn't do it; Alec saw to that.

Her heart was racing. Who was the woman? Well, for a start her things may have been sitting there from before she herself had met Jack. She picked up the tube of lipstick, a make she didn't recognise, and wound it down. Pale pink. Blossom it said on the back. The scent only had two Chinese characters on its label, which she didn't understand at all. She dabbed a touch on her wrist. Jasmine? No. Without a doubt, it was the unidentified fragrance in Jack's bedroom. Her heart sank. The woman was recent after all. She looked at her watch. Nearly twelve. He mustn't find her there. She pulled herself together, escaped by the door to the veranda and shuffled into her seat at the front of the house.

With a hand on her heart, she forced herself to smile as Maz ran across and clattered into the seat beside her. He chattered and pointed at drifts of butterflies, impossible to count, and they both listened to the high-pitched trill of a flower pecker. Though she felt hurt, there was no point fretting, after all she'd be leaving soon to go to her family. And by the time Jack strode back, her breathing was calmer and her face composed.

'You seem better.' He grunted as he flung himself into an armchair and pushed the wave of blond hair from tired eyes.

'One of the great unwashed. I must have given you a fright. I didn't start off that way, you know. In fact I looked rather nice.' She grinned. Her navy dress, piped with white, was now in the bin, ruined beyond repair.

He laughed. 'You always look good to me. Though I prefer your hair long. Is that what they call a pixie cut?'

She ran her hands through her shorn locks. 'Not quite. It's easier like this.'

He ate rapidly as if on red alert, curry soup with noodles, followed by chicken satay.

'What's that?' Maz said.

'A magpie robin. Why don't you see if you can find him?'

While Maz went off in search of the bird, she was able to tell the whole story, only feeling a lump in her throat when she spoke of the girls.

'And you're sure they're in Ipoh?' Jack asked.

'At the rest house, George said. Is it okay if we stay for a couple of days?' She gestured at Maz sloping between the nearby trees and pocketing the prettiest stones.

'Stay a bit longer. I'm going up to Ipoh next weekend. I can give you a lift in the truck. In fact the Company office is right next door to the Government Building, so I can take you straight there. It's where Alec is based, right?'

She nodded her thanks. 'It's nice, your house,'

she said, waving her arm around.

'Not bad. Used to be the owner's. My boss didn't want it so I was next in line. The Japanese occupied it during the war. Left it in a terrible state.'

She didn't mention the perfume in his bathroom and searched for something else to say, but the fragrant vial hung between them, and she struggled for words.

'How are things here?' she eventually said.

'Not so good. A few tappers were threatened. Then we found one strung up yesterday, hacked to death with a *parang*. The Chinese bandits don't waste bullets on their own.' He raised an eyebrow. 'Save them for us. And last night an estate truck was burnt.'

'Dead?'

He let out a slow breath. 'No, but yesterday was a hell of a day. Probably why I was so bushed when you got here.'

She shrugged. 'It doesn't matter.'

'After lunch I usually take a snooze. Best way to escape the afternoon heat.'

He got up, stretched, loosened the muscles in his arms, then stood behind her chair. He began massaging her shoulders. She was sweaty and tried to suppress her response, but couldn't help arching her back. With one hand he stroked her neck, the other slid to the curve of her breast. She touched the blond hairs that curled at his wrist. A strong, wide wrist. She turned his palm over, saw it was pale against his tan. Did it matter very much?

'God, Lyd. They're like rock. Your shoulders.'

114

He came round in front of her and bent down to look at her. A tremor ran through her. She opened her mouth and leant back. He held her chin so she had to look straight into his eyes and then covered her mouth with his own.

'Come on,' he said, as he pulled away. 'I know what you need.'

'But the child?' she said, as Maz turned up at her side.

Maz pulled a face. 'I did not see the bird.'

Jack chucked him under the chin. 'There's always next time. Now, young man. Off to bed with you.'

Lydia led Maz to his room, and once he was settled, closed the door.

Before they went to Jack's bedroom, he opened a door into a shuttered room. 'I should have said last night, but if there's an attack, grab the boy and both of you get in here. There's water and tinned food in that cupboard.'

She looked at the walls piled high with sandbags. 'But how will I know?'

'You'll know. If it's dark, the sentries raise a heck of an alarm by banging on empty tin drums. All the lights in the house go off and you mustn't speak.'

'Heavens!'

'Don't worry. You won't be here long. Can you handle a gun?'

She shook her head and hummed a tune that kept repeating. Alec got irritable when she hummed, but the more nervous she became, the more she couldn't help it.

'What's that song?' Jack asked. 'I know it.'

115

' 'Stranger in Paradise'.'

He laughed. 'Aren't we all . . . ? By the way the phone's on the wall in the hall. There might be a telephone call while you're here'

'I'd call the offices in Ipoh to speak to Alec, but George said the lines had been cut.'

'He's right. The local police headquarters test our line here daily. Make sure it's not been cut too. There's a special code, so it's probably best if you don't answer. They'll call back anyway. And don't ever open the door after dark.'

She thought of the yarns she'd heard of Penunggu pranksters: poltergeists who ring doorbells or phone you up in the middle of the night. She grinned. 'Anything else I should know?'

'No. Just watch out for the giant millipedes, poisonous scorpions, and deadly, biting vipers!'

He laughed and grabbed her by the waist, driving her back against the wall. 'Here, or in the bed?'

A wave of guilt gripped her. She paused, thought of Alec, held her breath. But the heat of the moment won. She brushed the guilt aside, and with a broad grin, broke free. Her feet thudded as she arrived in the relative cool of his bedroom, where she quickly undid the buttons of her shirtwaister, leaving it in a green stripy pool on the floor. Jack was already beneath the thin cotton sheet, his blond hair sticking up in the breeze from a fan. Eyes closed, hands clasped behind his head, he gave her his come and get me smile. She slipped in beside him and smelt musk on his warm skin. She tingled and put a palm to his chest. She felt the thump, looked at him, and saw his bright blue eyes stare right into her. She felt a shiver of longing.

'Do you like it that way?' he said, watching her closely as his large hands slowly began to move over her inner thighs.

She felt the rough skin of them, and the heat of him along her entire body. Oh God, what was she doing? This couldn't happen. She had to make it stop. She'd promised Alec. But she needed the contact with Jack so much, needed *him* so much. She knew she shouldn't, but couldn't stop. Somehow he'd settled in her flesh, and now she wanted him so much, it made her eyes water. She bit her lip.

He looked puzzled, scratching his chin. 'Don't cry. Hey, Lyddy, you know I love you.'

He wiped away the salty tears, licked his fingers and used them to trace the soft skin of her throat.

'Sex is all about the woman,' he said with a grin. 'Not many men know that.'

She laughed.

In the sweltering afternoon, he explored the skin at the back of her knees and the place behind her ears, stroked the moist curls at the nape of her neck. Kissed her eyelids.

She looked past his shoulder at the late, flat light on the patchy walls, on the door, on the folds of their clothes. With Alec, three drinks and she could fake it. With Jack it was different. She took a deep breath and fell head first into the animal smell of him, and though she didn't voice it, knew that danger made the heat even stronger.

'Damn it, Lydia, you're so bloody fuckable,' he said, and they rocked together, bodies burning.

Afterwards she scratched the sores at her ankle and watched him shave. The room filled with the scent of coal tar as the cut-throat blade slid against his skin. She laughed at his facial contortions: nose to the right, nose to the left.

'What's so funny?'

'You.'

'You should see yourself put on lipstick.'

One hand on his hip, he minced to the mirror, formed his mouth into a wide-open O shape and mimed the lipstick going on. Then he came back to stroke her cheek and plant kisses down the side of her neck.

'Jesus, Lyd. I've missed you.'

'Have you?'

'What kind of a question's that?'

Back in bed she pulled the sheet up. Had he missed her? She remembered the perfume bottle, and felt the ache of separation.

After Jack went back to work Lydia stayed there to sleep, only rising when a breeze rattled through the trees, and sent a draught of cool air into the room. She showered, towelled her hair, then went out into the greenish evening with Maz. They walked in the shade of the nearest rubber trees, their silky branches reaching upwards to the light. Long before Lydia heard hastily retreating footsteps crack the twigs and leaves, Maz cocked his head. It was enough to remind her of ever-present dangers.

'We'd better go back,' she said. 'At least to the veranda.'

The air spun with screaming insects, and Jack appeared in his dusty clothes and jungle boots. His face lit up when he saw them, and they began walking back together. He stopped, bent down, and then scooped something up with his hands. Opening his palm, he showed Maz a delicate red and green moth, its wings outstretched.

'Why does it not fly?' Maz said, his eyes glowing with interest.

He shrugged. 'It's dead, I'm afraid. Come on, or we'll be eaten alive.'

The light was fading fast and screeching monkeys echoed all round. They got back just in time to watch the sun setting orange in the west.

'Look, Maz,' Jack said. 'Before the light goes completely.'

Maz giggled as Jack pointed out a large, untidy nest under the veranda, loosely made from dried leaves, twigs, and moss. 'It's a magpie robin nest. But the birds have flown.'

Lydia looked up at the sky. 'Sunsets here are beautiful,' she said. 'But over so quickly.'

He put an arm round her and squeezed her shoulder, then, looking worn out, leant against the railings, shoulders hunched.

There was the rasp of a door opening behind them. Lili walked over and bent to speak to Jack, her features unfathomable. The girl stood poised, waiting. He took a step away from Lydia and replied in Chinese. There was a restrained outburst as the girl narrowed her eyes, then, with what looked like a sharp expression, left. There was something unsettling about the look and

Lydia went to Jack, frowning slightly when he didn't explain.

'She never smiles,' she said, sitting again.

He sat opposite, tanned thighs spread apart. 'No. Not at the moment. I guess you're right,' he said, and looked at her blankly, the skin around his eyes pinched.

The silence stretched and went on too long.

She made a point of looking at her watch. 'Maz should be in bed. I'll just sort him out.'

Jack seemed relieved.

In the bedroom she saw pebbles laid in a line all round both their beds.

'Fifty-seven,' Maz said. 'For protection.'

She longed to cuddle her own daughters, but hugged him in their place. He held her hand and covered it with kisses.

Back outside she caught the citrus scent of pomelo flowers on a sudden breeze.

'Tell me about your work,' she said, pulling a chair closer to Jack. 'Tell me about the plantation. What you do, day to day.'

'Heck, it isn't what I expected, I can tell you that. Falling in streams, hacking through *lallang* grass as high as our shoulders. I guess it keeps me fit.'

Lydia closed her eyes.

'There's an art to rubber tapping,' Jack said. 'The cut has to be just right or the tree bleeds and dies.' He sighed. 'And I can't tell you how grim it is to see dozens of good trees burning. They set them alight and there's very little we can do.'

He was interrupted by the sound of a motor

bike, then someone calling his name from the front of the house.

He stood up, stretched, and, flexing the muscles in his arms, went round the veranda to his office at the back. It was nearly dark. The still time in the tropics when the sounds of day have gone, and the world waits for the noises of night to begin. She fanned away the mosquitoes with her hands, and a sensation of being out of place ran through her. She was so far away from her real life. Her real self. The minutes inched by. She heard a flutter of wings and the scream of an unknown animal, then jumped as a flight of bats swooped over her head.

She heard Jack say, 'Christ!' After that, his voice became a murmur, and she listened to the increasingly subdued tone as he spoke.

15

I lay on my bed and tried to read, hoping that Mr Oliver was snoozing and wouldn't move until the others came back. I already knew *Heidi* and *Black Beauty*. Now it was time for *Treasure Island*, one of very few books in the house. I was shocked when Gran said they handed them in during the war at a book drive. The paper was needed for ration books. Dad promised we could have comics delivered instead. I asked for *Eagle* but he said it was for boys, and *Girl* landed on the doorstep.

Boring.

Something really exciting had happened though. On Friday a letter with a Malayan postmark lay on the hall table waiting for Dad. Mum must have got home and read my letter, I thought, and wished she'd written to me as well as Dad. He was out at the time, but all day long I went back to it, picked it up, held it to my lips, sure it was from Mum, telling us when she'd be coming. It was typed so I couldn't tell from the handwriting, but who else would be writing to Dad? I wanted to find out, but now I was in trouble again, it wasn't a good time to ask Dad.

In the pale summery light of England, I longed to play under the hot Malayan sun, until it whizzed into the sea at night. I had missed my mum terribly and was so excited as I thought of all the places we'd go. The barn, the little alleyway behind the church where all the cats lived. The long walk round the village.

I tried not to think of Mr Oliver, and spent ages counting the faded roses on the carpet and the number of squiggly lines on the wallpaper. Spare bits of both had decorated the doll's house we were making for Fleur. Granny had even made some artificial flowers and a little tree to stick on the side of the house.

I looked out at the field opposite, dotted with black and white cows now, and the same long line of dark trees at the very end. I thought about making a dash for it as the sun lit up the garden and the roofs of the village turned silver. I could keep a look out from over there, and hide until I saw the car come back.

But even though it was summer, the sun disappeared and it quickly became a grey watery day. I was hungry. I'd hardly eaten any lunch, and would give anything for a jam sandwich. There were Catherine wheels and walnut whips for tea, and Gran had made a Dundee cake, but I didn't dare tiptoe down the stairs. If Mr Oliver was asleep, I didn't want to risk waking him. I peered out of the window again, in case I could catch sight of the car coming back early. But only saw the Worcestershire fish 'n' chip van, with 'Meals on Wheels' printed on the side.

I took out my exercise book, sat cross-legged on the floor, and made myself concentrate on my latest story. It was about a death in Spain and was set in a seventeenth-century monastery. I couldn't wait to show it to Mum. The chief monk had died in a beautiful crypt, having taken poison. Everyone would know what he'd done, because he left a note saying he was going to take his own life as he could no longer live with himself. Though I hadn't worked out why, it would be something dramatic. Suicide was a terrible sin, and the young monk who found the note decided to destroy it, in order to protect his master.

I was trying to figure out how he was going to get rid of it, but the smell of fish 'n' chips from a hatch at the side of the van distracted me. I got up and looked out again, and saw the fish man in his white chef's outfit, with a tall white hat. My mouth watered. It was only by chance that my eyes flicked back across the room, and I saw Mr Oliver blocking the door. I hadn't heard him come up the stairs, but, with a sharp breath in, I ran to my bed, shuffled my bottom right back against the wall, then held a pillow across my lap. He came over, his face smooth and white. My stomach turned over and I wanted to pee.

'Hello,' he said, and closed the door.

I told myself to run while I had the chance, but my body wouldn't obey. I don't know why, but I couldn't move.

His left eyebrow raised and he gave me a funny look. I saw the little flecks of white on his lapels when he sat on my bed. He cupped my chin with his hand, squeezed and sort of pulled my face a little way towards him.

'Please go,' I said.

'But I've been looking forward to seeing you,' he said, and started to stroke my forehead. 'You liked this, didn't you?'

I wriggled away.

'Now there's nothing to be frightened of, is there?' His eyes narrowed, and he let go of my chin.

I thought for a minute he was going to go. But then he held me by my arms. 'It'll be easier, dear, if you keep nice and still.'

He pushed me down by my shoulders.

I wanted to shout, but all that came out was a squeak. I struggled, tried to roll out of the side of the bed. He held me firmly and with one hand threw off the pillow. With the other, he kept a grip on me.

'Let me go. Please. I promise not to tell,' I begged.

'Don't be silly, dear. Of course you won't tell.'

He pulled up my skirt a little way, and put his hand just above the left knee on the inside of my thigh. I was so frightened, I thought I was going to wet the bed. The same fear I'd had before. But worse. Much worse. I tried to push him off again.

And even though tears filled my eyes, he shook his head and smiled.

I longed for my mother. I could see her so clearly it hurt. Mummy. Mummy. Mummy. Where are you? My pulse was banging in my ears, and in my mind I was out of the door and running to her. I knew about people leaving their bodies and how if you concentrated hard enough you could do it. I tried but it didn't work.

I looked at the wallpaper and started to count the flowers there, but all I could think of was my mum. As his fingers poked at my skin, my head filled with roaring and my chest hurt so much, I

125

couldn't breathe. He was strong, but if I waited until he was distracted and relaxed his hold. Maybe then. A wind whistled under the door. It was the only way. In that moment I didn't care about any punishment. In my bedside table, that's where they were. We were playing with them yesterday, Fleur and me. I shifted towards the edge of the bed.

'So you have decided you like it after all,' he said, mistaking my movement towards him as obedience, his fingers running just inside my knicker elastic.

A wave of sickness came in my throat, but I forced myself to wait.

His eyes were closed and a panting kind of breathing began. He removed the hand that had been holding me down, his left hand, and wiped his forehead with the back of his hand. Now, I thought. Do it now. I slipped one arm out ever so carefully so as not to warn him, then whipped open the drawer. I clutched hold of the dart and with all the strength that I had, jabbed it into his neck.

His hand stayed at the edge of my knickers, not moving now, but his eyes opened wide and he turned scarlet. For a moment I thought his eyes would burst right out.

Then his head jerked sideways. He took his hand from me and put it to his neck. The dart was stuck. He lifted bloody fingers to look at them, puffed out his cheeks and started to cough and splutter. His started to speak, spat out the words through clenched teeth. 'You — little — bitch.'

Then he lashed out.

I wasn't scared of the blood, and dodged the blow. He took another swing at me. I dived out of the bed, charged down the stairs and ran.

I ran past the abandoned farm sheds where the boys played war and pirate ships: too scary when it got dark. Past the woods where Robin Hood plotted with Maid Marion. Too creepy. I went on running and when the stitch doubled me over, held my side, my breath coming in gasps. By the time I reached the barn, the light was almost gone.

I climbed the ladder and sat on the wooden boards, my head down between my knees. After the sickness passed, I hid under the hay, pulled it all around me, to keep the world out. I didn't even care about the rats. I imagined what was happening at home. Veronica's shock. The blood. Dad's anger. Mr Oliver would lie, tell them he did nothing, tell them I attacked him for no reason. And if I told them the truth, they'd believe him, not me. I was the one with an explosive temper. But what if he was dead? What if I had killed him? I trembled at the thought.

Billy will come in the morning, I thought, help me get away, hide me first, then help me get away. I'd go to Liverpool, stow away, find my mum. I was proud I hadn't passed out at the sight of blood, though Mum would have.

Oh, Mum.

When the loneliness came rolling in, I felt as if I'd fallen down a deep hole that I'd never get out of, and I wept for my mother like never before.

16

Jack's face revealed little. He remained hands on hips, looking awkward, shifting slightly from foot to foot, in scuffed, open-toed house sandals.

She stood. 'It's bad news, isn't it.'

'Not great. That was a police messenger. They think the government offices in Ipoh are going to be targeted. All staff and paperwork are moving to the rest house. It'll be cramped, but they can't ignore the threat.'

'My girls will be okay?'

He nodded. 'Sure. But my meeting's been cancelled. The boss won't go near the office until the all-clear.'

Her face fell.

'No, I didn't mean that. I'll still take you, Lyddy. No problem. Just that we'll go straight to the rest house and not into town to the offices. And it'll have to be quite a bit sooner. Tomorrow in fact.'

He looked forlorn but her heart leapt. She didn't want to hurt him and felt torn, but she was going to be with her girls, and very soon. She took a deep breath and let it out slowly. Tomorrow. She opened her locket and lingered over their faces. She'd missed them so much. Tears welled up as she turned to him again.

'Thank you. Thank you so much. Sorry to be a bother.'

'You're never that,' he said.

She took the hand he held out, kissed his

fingertips, searched his face. Felt a surge of longing, but looked down and let go of his hand.

'Nothing has changed, has it?' he said, then pulled up a rattan armchair and collapsed into it.

'I'm sorry. You know I have to give it a go with Alec. For the sake of the girls.' She bit her lip. 'Maybe one day.'

'One day I may be gone.'

'Oh, Jack.' She went to stand behind him. He leant the back of his head against her stomach. She wrapped her arms round his middle, kissed the side of his neck, bit his ear.

He sat very still.

She ran her fingers through the hairs on his chest.

'Well, at least the rest house was fairly empty,' he said, too brightly. 'So there's enough space for the influx. Everyone's there. They're having a knees-up tonight to cheer everyone up. Should be quite a bash.'

'We still have tonight,' Lydia said. She came round to kneel, put a hand on his groin and looked into his eyes. Buried there she saw deep-seated hurt, too far for her to reach, and, she felt certain, not purely of her making. She tried to connect.

'Best not,' he said, removing her hand. 'Early start in the morning.'

How times have changed, she thought, and couldn't help but feel sad, remembering the thrill when they first met.

Funnily enough, just like Alec, she'd met him at a party. He came through the door, grinned at some other acquaintance, but then caught her eye as he scanned the room. She'd been at her best, in a black cheongsam with orange and gold flowers and a high split up the side, the black contrasting brilliantly with her pale skin. She'd had too much gin and flushed when he came across, Cicely by his side.

'Look after him, darling. I need to mingle.' And Cicely had winked at them both.

Alec was there too, huddled in a group of smoking, drinking men, his back resolutely turned. In another room, she and Jack danced for much of the night, ignoring the risks involved. As she waited in the hall for Alec as the party was wrapping up, Jack had come over, pushed a strand of her hair behind her left ear, bitten the lobe, then slipped a warm palm inside the slit of her skirt.

From then on, the heady mix of his sweat and the scent of her Shalimar brought the memory to life. He'd whispered something and she shivered from the warmth of his breath on her neck. Blotches came out on her chest. Too much to drink. Cigarettes. Desire. And with added risk, she was hooked.

'Where? When?' he asked.

'In the park,' she said, spotting Alec from the corner of her eye. 'There's a tea room. Nine-thirty tomorrow morning.'

'A morning girl eh?'

'Not really. It comes from having two kids to drop off at school.'

With a shake of her head, she let the memory go. Things had changed. Back then, to be so close, but not touching, would have been unthinkable.

Now, as it began to thunder, Jack went to sleep in his own bedroom, and Lydia joined Maz in the spare room.

'Will you tell me a story?' Maz said, and snuggled under the sheet. 'Please.'

'Do you know the one about the crocodile who ate a clock?'

His eyes widened. 'Did it kill him?'

'It didn't. But it did scare Captain Hook.'

'Who was he?'

'Captain Hook was a pirate.'

Maz gave a sigh of enjoyment.

Once she'd told the tale of Peter Pan, Lydia felt the thundery air press down on her, and found it hard to drop off. The jungle night erupted with screeching cicadas outside her bedroom window, and in the distance, the desolate howl of wild dogs. She pulled the thin cotton sheet up to her nose. The sounds outside distorted, merged with others, became a booming, heaving, night-time racket. Wide awake, she heard the flapping wings of birds, the hum of the generator, and the bleak hooting Emma always said was lonely ghost birds.

She ached for her girls. It was for the best they were leaving, and as for her one night with Jack, she forced herself to stuff down her guilt. It had been only once after all.

* * *

The next morning they set off before dawn in the makeshift armoured car, Jack lifting Maznan from his bed, eyes still firmly closed. He gently

131

laid the child on the back seat and across Lydia's lap. A Malay policeman sat in the front. Though Maz slept soundly, Lydia had not slept a wink. On the plantation road the tall trees came into sight in the half light, and passing the squat workers' building, she took in the bleakness. Nobody spoke.

She kicked off her shoes, hoping to relax. But Jack's closeness, and the musky coal tar smell of him kept her tense.

'Bear up, Lyd,' he said, twisting his head to her as he drove along the boundary of the plantation. 'Sleep if you can. It's a fair way yet.'

She wanted to slip into their old ease, but there was a distance between them, and with the policeman there, her tongue was tied. In any case what more was there to say? She closed her eyes, and behind the lids her daughters played. She held out her arms for them, sniffed the talc on their skin and the apple fragrance of their hair. Fleur holding on and Emma spinning away and pulling her hand, impatience straining every muscle. *Come on, Mummy, hurry up.*

She slipped into the bumpy rhythm of the car and slept deeply, only vaguely awakened once, by a slow down and flashlights at a police road-block, and the dawn chorus in the forest.

After a couple of hours, when daylight unveiled a pale pink sky with plump round morning clouds, the abrupt halting of the car broke through her dreams. She felt sweat at the back of her neck and opened her eyes. They'd been waved down and Jack was outside gesturing at a Malay officer. At the sharp exchange of voices, she sprang to attention. She saw Jack hang his head for an instant and the two men walk heavily towards the car.

A chill ran up her spine. 'Jack,' she called from the window.

He cleared his throat and looked her full in the face. His blue eyes had turned the colour of muddy water and his face had a strange raw look.

'Jack?'

The immediate woods were quiet. But it was a throbbing quiet, and from beyond the rest house came the hum of the jungle. She climbed out and stood barefoot on the tarmac. She covered her nose from a sharp smell of burning, eyes darting round for the source. Over to the right a plume of grey smoke rose in the pale morning sky.

She began to run. Jack too, the officer coming up behind.

'Madam,' he called. 'Madam, you can't. The site is out of bounds, dangerous. There's nothing left.' The man caught up with her and grasped her arm, the smell of saltfish on his breath.

She shrugged him off, unaware of Maz's light footsteps following her.

Jack grabbed Maznan's hand. He bent to speak to the child. 'Stay with this man. Okay. Stay here.'

'You will come back?' Maz asked.

'We'll come back.'

Lydia ran on. 'Why didn't you see the smoke?'

'I did, but there was no way of knowing what it was.'

In the woods they ran through tunnels of green, stumbling over snaking roots and colliding with low-hanging branches. At each dead end, they turned back, through mushrooming smoke trapped under the great canopy of trees, and tried again, until they found the driveway and the signpost for the *Governmental Rest House*. They ran up the drive to a large colonial building, dark with soot, its roof collapsed, smoke still rising through the black rafters and a stink of combustion coming from inside. A constable guarded the entrance.

Feet planted in ash, Lydia froze. Her vision blurred and her teeth chattered as if it were an English winter.

'For Christ's sake, Jack. Ask him if the girls got out.'

The officer overheard her. 'I'm sorry, but they found no survivors, madam.'

She looked again at the remains of the building. She felt distanced, as if she was somewhere on the outside looking in. She blinked rapidly, sank to her knees, and gathered a handful of gritty ash. Jack came to squat beside her and attempted to wipe her dirt-smudged face.

'Get off. Get the fuck off.'

She felt her stomach turn over. She heard Maz sob somewhere behind them, and turned towards him with a confused look. Jack tried to cradle her. She came to life, jerked into action, pushed Jack off, and ran past the startled officer, into the charred building.

Millions of particles of white dust danced in

unexpected shafts of light. Further in, the smell caught in her throat. Rafters still smouldered and there seemed to be no oxygen in the air. She stood still, twisting her head from side to side, hearing the thud of blood in her ears and a strange hissing sound. Which way? She began to run. What if they'd hidden in a cupboard, or a bathroom? They might still be there. Might still be safe. She struggled through the building looking for their hiding place. Skeletal metal and broken glass blocked her path. She ducked and dived, her own safety irrelevant. She stopped only to gasp for breath, the voices of her children in her head. *Mummy! Mummy!* She didn't feel her feet seared by burning embers.

Jack was calling from somewhere inside the building. An idea surfaced. They might have run outside and hidden in the woods, might still be there, frightened, waiting. She followed a source of light and crawled out. On all fours, she shouted into the trees, but the harder she looked the more moving shadows she saw.

'Emma, Fleur. Where are you? It's Mummy.'

Jack fell out of another back exit, found her and tried to lead her away. 'Lyd, there's nothing we can do.'

Still on hands and knees, she panted like a dog and fought him off. Her throat closed as she opened her mouth, unaware of her own silent scream, hands flapping at the air and her eyes huge with shock. The trees blurred. Rooted to the spot she heard beating wings, Jack speaking, and another man's voice in the distance. In her mind's eye she saw the yellow flames move through the building, hissing, crackling. Saw the heavy black smoke slip under their doorway followed by curling flames. Saw the looks of terror in her daughters' eyes. Breathed their agony and smelt her own babies' burning flesh. *Mummy! Mummy!* Her mind went flat and empty, her legs gave way and she sat back on the ground cross-legged, skirt bunched up.

Beside her, a child's teddy bear with melted plastic eyes gazed up, its fur black with soot. She held it, rocked it in her arms, and through swollen stinging eyes, looked past the roof at the sudden brilliance of a sharp Malayan sky. Her last image was of the ground racing up as she bent forward, then she slipped backwards into the sky.

17

I imagined Mr Oliver lying dead on the bedroom floor, and longed for Billy to come. I had a wee in the corner, then comforted myself by thinking of him. He usually appeared and disappeared quickly, all part of his ambition to be a magician. He was building up the props he needed, bit by bit, and had already got a top hat and a pack of cards. I'd promised to help him make a black cape with silver stars and a purple lining. Mum had taught me how to use a needle and thread and it couldn't be all that hard.

Billy's ambition was something I understood. I practised stories on him and in return, he tried magic tricks on me. I gulped back a sob. It would take more than a magic trick to get me out of the fix I was in.

It got dark, the damp mouldy smell of the barn filling up the air. I closed my eyes and tried to imagine the barn bursting with shiny leaves and ferns, and bright blue birds flying through the air. But all I could think of was Mr Oliver's furious face and his bloody neck and hands.

When I woke I didn't remember where I was, until the memory of what happened punched me in the stomach. I was thirsty but there was nothing to drink, so I curled up in a corner of the barn instead, and buried my head in my hands until I heard the voices of Father and Veronica. Then I made myself tiptoe to the edge and peered over to make certain it was them. Three faces stared up. They must have forced Billy to tell, because he was at the bottom of the ladder too, red faced, the corners of his mouth held down in a scowl.

I backed down the ladder and stood itching and scratching at the bottom. Billy hung his head, wouldn't look at me, just sniffed and wiped his nose on his holey jumper. I glanced at Dad. With a stiff look about the face, his hands were bunched in fists. I was so scared I peed myself and felt warmth spread down my inside thigh. My father saw the dark stain appear on my skirt, and his mouth became a hard straight line.

Veronica knelt down, curls untidy, face as white as ash and her eyes pink. She spoke gently. 'Emma. Tell us what happened. Why did you do it?'

If Mum was like fire, she was like water, gentle and sweet, but I couldn't speak.

My father took over. 'For heaven's sake, child, cat got your tongue? Whatever possessed you to stab Mr Oliver?'

I hung my head.

'Well, all I can say is, you're lucky Sidney hasn't gone to the police.'

At least he's not dead, I thought.

'Don't think you're getting off scot-free,' Dad said, and took me by the elbow.

Back home, he marched me up to my bedroom, then locked the door. It wasn't fair. Mr Oliver should be the one in trouble, not me. I opened my mouth to say, but the thought of saying the words made me feel sick.

'You'll stay in your room,' Dad called out from the landing, and slammed his fist against the door.

I tensed, afraid of what might happen next. Was it my fault? Had I done something to make it happen?

After a bit, Veronica brought up a tray of Bournvita and two Cadbury's orange sandwich biscuits. My eyes filled with tears.

She leant close and patted my leg. 'Don't cry. Sidney isn't badly hurt. It looks worse than it is. Bit like your dad — bark worse than his bite. It'll be all right.'

I noticed her narrow wrist bones and small white hands. She'd changed into a dress with yellow flowers and sort of fixed her hair, but the pins were loose and the lines on her face showed. I felt an ache in my throat. I wanted to ask her how it would be all right, but didn't dare. I knew she was being kind — more than I deserved — but it could never be all right ever again.

★ ★ ★

They moved Fleur's bed out of the room. I was to sleep alone. Gran crept up while Dad was out, unlocked the door ever so quietly and padded into the room, her finger to her lips. Then she sat on the bed beside me and gave me a cuddle. A beam of sunlight shone on her, and I saw how old and worn she was, her face a mass of wrinkles bunching up. I hung my head. She was so small and it was all my fault.

'Emma, my duck. Tell me what happened?'

She'd spoken very quietly and I felt tears welling again. I wanted to say, but the words just stuck.

Gran handed me two bars of Cadbury's. 'Make them last, my love. And be sure not to tell your dad.'

'What's going to happen, Gran?'

She nodded and tightened the strings of her apron. Somehow the tighter it went the more baggy looking she was.

'They're looking for a boarding school for you.'

My face fell. 'Dad and Granddad?'

'No, dear. Your father and Veronica. Very concerned for your welfare, she is. Lucky for you she's not a bit cross about her brother.'

I frowned. What did that mean? Did she know what her brother was like? If she suspected him, maybe things wouldn't be so bad for me.

I sniffed and looked in Gran's deep blue eyes. 'Why does he hate me?'

'Who, dear?'

'Dad. Why does he hate me?'

Gran looked flustered and stood up to smooth out her apron. She sighed and I thought she was going to cry.

'It's not you, dear, but there are things you don't understand.'

'What things?'

'Maybe when you're older, sweetheart . . . now, ducks, you must eat humble pie for a bit. Your father has a lot of worries and he's doing his best. Never forget that. Make sure not to cheek him and everything will turn out all right. I promise.

140

But, Em, dear, you must learn to curb that temper. Do you promise?'

I hung my head, but her words made me think. Was my father as bad as I made out, or, like a baddy in one of my stories, had I invented a character for him? Was it me who was wrong and not him at all? And how did anyone ever know who was really right? That question bothered me more than I can say.

'Well, the proof of the pudding . . . ' Gran said, and looked at me with a funny expression, then kissed me on the forehead. 'Good girl. Now remember, not a word. I'll put the radio on in the kitchen, so you don't feel too lonely. It's *Music While You Work* now, but maybe Lonnie Donegan will be on *Pick of the Pops*.'

I smiled wanly. 'Or Bill Hayley.'

'That's the spirit. I'll turn it up so you can hear. All right, ducks?'

'Can Fleur come up and play snakes and ladders?'

'Oh, Fleur's going, my dear, for a little while, staying with Veronica while your father sorts things out. She's taking her to the optician on Tuesday.'

My heart sank. What about her birthday? Fleur and I weren't especially close but we were sisters and I supposed I loved her. It had never occurred to me before that Mr Oliver might do to her what he'd done to me. Surely Father would notice if anything was wrong? He hadn't noticed with me, but Fleur was his favourite and I sometimes even wondered if Fleur missed Mum.

141

Before Gran went downstairs I asked her if Mum was ever going to come.

'I don't know, dear. Only what you know. Just what your dad says.'

'But why would she take so long?'

Gran shrugged, said she couldn't remember, and even Dad didn't know. I groaned and stretched out on my bed.

Gran called Fleur up.

'I'll leave you two to say goodbye,' she said, when Fleur came in, and left the door ajar.

I looked up at Fleur who stood just inside the door, shuffling her feet. I asked if she missed Mum. She said she had Veronica and Granny, so what was the point. Her answer bothered me.

'Mealy, don't you love Mummy? Don't you long for the long grass?'

Fleur wasn't speaking. I had to wait. I'd learnt to wait. First, when she was small and couldn't catch up, then when she was slow to learn to talk. Now I waited because it took her time to say what she meant.

'I do, Em. I do.'

'But you don't cry.'

She bit her lip.

I stood up and stared at her. 'But don't you remember the island, Fleur?'

She shook her head.

'But you must. How can you forget?' I saw the silvery coastline of our island holidays. 'You must remember when jellyfish stung Mummy? And how we had to watch where we put our feet.'

Fleur hung her head and wouldn't look up.

'You remember the coconut trees, don't you?

142

And how you were scared of the breakers.'

'I wasn't scared,' she said in a small voice.

'So you do remember! I knew you did. When Dad and I ran in and out, you made sandcastles and Mum swam nude.'

'Shut up, Emma. Stop it. Stop going on about Mummy.' She ran from the room and slammed the door.

I didn't go after her, even though I heard her sobbing in the bathroom, and it was me who'd made her cry.

After a while, I decided I wanted all my favourite things with me, if I was to be sent away. I got out my box of treasures and built a pile. My notebook, for observations, some old black beads of Mum's, a lovely purple and orange marble and my bristle hair brush. I had to brush my hair a hundred times each day. Most precious was my fountain pen, and bottle of Quink. At school we used a horrid wooden pen. It had a scratchy metal nib with a slit at the end. You had to dip it into a little inkwell in the desk every few words and it dripped, so all my work ended up covered in blots.

I sat cross-legged on the floor and poked at my stuff, tears prickling the back of my lids. There was a sound in the hall. Dad. I threw everything in, dumped the box in the wardrobe, and noticed a pink rabbit ear sticking out from where it had got lost beneath a tartan blanket. I pulled the rabbit out to give to Fleur to take to Veronica's, and made an effort to hold my face like a well-behaved little girl.

18

Lydia had no recollection of her stay in hospital. No memory of waiting for her smoke burnt lungs to heal, no memory of the journey up to the rest house, nor her wild dart through the embers of the building. When Jack tried to speak about the children, she turned her face to the wall. For a week he fed her, forcing her to swallow, and when she couldn't sleep, he read to her. She heard the sounds but couldn't understand the words. Instead she stared into a past where her children lived and breathed, where they smiled and laughed and argued in the way they did.

Mummy, come and see. Mummy, watch us. We're dancing.

In an atmosphere of artificial calm they dressed her cuts and burns, then sedated her. When they opened the shutters for the first time, she lay blinking, blinded by the light. Under the midday sun she dreamt of escape, deep into the trees, where she could fall into one of the dark streams and feel the water close over her head.

She heard Jack murmuring to a doctor. 'Clearly an intense heat, signs of flashes, and traces of accelerants placed right round the building, which means multiple points of origin.' She listened as his words carried on. 'Fire investigation now complete. Terrorist activity, aided by wind direction. No identifiable bodies.'

'Stop!' she shouted. 'Stop!' She pulled up her

knees, covered her ears with her hands and rocked back and forth. Two nurses, one on either side, tried to force her back down. She freed her right arm and lashed out, but a nurse managed to slide a needle into her thigh. On the other side of the room Jack gulped back sobs, tears pouring down his cheeks. One by one the lights went out. What was the matter with Jack, she wondered, as she slipped inside the walls of a cold underwater world, which she shared with silver fish and overgrown terrapins.

★ ★ ★

On the morning she woke from dreams of palm trees and white sands, she heard tapping feet in the corridor outside her room, and heavy rain thundering on the roof. She wanted to shut her eyes and for them all to be gone, stretch out on white hospital sheets and for that to be an end to it. When they came in, she shook to discover she'd been wandering and spinning for weeks. Though time had inched past, it appeared to have gone in a flash. She looked up from her hospital pillows and saw a row of yellow flowers on the windowsill. A man with concerned eyes stood beside her bed.

'Can I go home now?' she asked, and took a sip of lukewarm tea.

The man nodded. 'Mr Harding's here to collect you. The burns are healing and your lungs will be right as rain in a few weeks.'

She caught her breath. 'Harding?'

The man nodded.

'Oh, you mean Jack.'

As soon as Jack came into the room with a look of worry behind his smile, her tears welled up.

'Tell me it isn't true,' she said. 'Please, Jack.'

She watched him swallow.

'Lydia — '

'I have to know for certain. Can you go to Ipoh? Or phone George? He'll know. Ask him. Please, Jack.'

'I've already done both. I'm so sorry, but the children were there. George had it firsthand. Alec had not been allocated a house, and there's been no further record of them anywhere else.'

'Maybe they went to Borneo?'

'Lydia, Alec and the girls were at the rest house. George says there's no doubt whatsoever. They died in the fire.'

★　★　★

On their way to the plantation the heavy rain turned into clammy, warm mist, and she was aware of a deep nostalgia for England and steady English rain. Her daughters' images ran through her mind, sometimes fast, sometimes slow. She had no control of her emotions. Grief clawed at her chest, unrelenting, sent tears dripping down her cheeks, and was followed by hollow wordless fury. She stared straight ahead, not caring to go on living in a world in which it was possible for her children to die. One day you have a family and then you don't. How could that be? She thought of Em's stories, and slammed her fists into her eyes.

Maz slept on his own in the spare room. She chose to sleep with Jack: sleep, nothing more, though she feared them in her sleep, feared them waking from graves they had not lain in and turning accusing eyes on her. Jack held her hot sweating body when she cried out in defence. I didn't know, I'm sorry, I'm sorry. By day she remained curled up in bed, longing for oblivion, her face buried in the pillow to soak up the tears. How do people survive, she thought, how do they exist?

It was the physical pain that forced her to move. She showered with slow deliberate movements, her body stiff, doubled up like an old lady. She rubbed the steam from Jack's shaving mirror, examined the fragile woman who looked back at her, poked the waxy skin, stared at the eyes sunk back in their sockets. Where had she gone? Nothing about her looked the same, but for the one eyebrow higher than the other. She raised and lowered it, then spun round hearing their voices, did not imagine it, heard them clearly inside of her. It's all right, darlings, Mummy's here. But it wasn't all right, and Mummy had not been there.

She shaved her legs with Jack's razor, selected a cool linen skirt and emerald blouse and went outside to wait for breakfast. The sun was blazing in a bright blue sky. She breathed in and out slowly, aware for the first time that she was hungry.

An Indian woman in a bright sari came out, carrying a tray.

'Where's Lili?' Lydia asked.

147

The woman shrugged. 'My name is Channa.'

Lydia slowly chewed dry rice biscuits and oversweetened mango jam, felt she couldn't drink, but then held up her cup for more coffee. Maz sat opposite, watching silently.

She looked at him, noticed he'd grown taller and his hair was wild. He was so alive. How was it possible for Emma and Fleur to be dead? How could they be when he was still alive? When *she* was still alive. She could not stop the memories. The morning she'd left to go to Suzanne replayed in her mind. If there'd just been a sign. If she hadn't taken Suzanne's call. If she'd got to Ipoh in time. If she had only said something more than just goodbye.

Heat flooded her veins. None of it made sense. Somebody had to pay, somebody more than the faceless Chinese insurgents who had set fire to the rest house, somebody she could look in the eyes and scream at.

The burst of rage took her by surprise. Her fingers resting at the edge of the breakfast table suddenly stiffened, she closed her eyes, and with a shout she pushed the entire table over. As it tipped, coffee cup, plate, jam and biscuits slid off. She heard the crash and splatter on the veranda floor, heard Maz yelp and leap out of the way. She hung her head, kept her eyes closed, longed for her girls with the kind of longing that led nowhere, that could only bounce back at her and drive her crazy. When she opened her eyes, there was nothing. Just the day, the dust, the damp smell of the trees, and jam.

Channa came out with a broom and dustpan.

'Sorry,' Lydia said, and the woman looked at her with wide-set slanting eyes, but did not speak.

She listened to the creaks of the rubber trees and creatures stirring in the nearby branches. Tales the gardener used to tell the girls slipped in and out of her mind, and the way the children shrieked with delight when he did. *Mummy. Mummy.*

Maz looked at her with enormous sad eyes. She held out a hand to him and he let her squeeze his hand. They smiled at each other, and briefly, it was how it had been before. She knew it wasn't fair on Maz, and worried that he must have run wild while she was in hospital. He went back to the kitchen and she heard him chattering with Channa's son, Burhan. Hopefully he'd be happy counting stones or searching for butterflies with his friend.

The days stretched ahead. An image of a smart European woman she knew in Malacca came to mind. What was her name? Ah yes, Cicely. She'd sent a card. So sorry not to come, she'd said, but I'm just off travelling in Australia. Lydia didn't want her anyway. Didn't want anyone. It had been Cicely who warned her off Jack right at the start. An image of Jack naked flashed in her mind. Probably jealous. Gin and tonic, tinkle of ice, slice of lemon; a discreet before lunch drinker. It gave her an idea. A way for memories to be erased.

The drinks cabinet revealed an unopened bottle but no tonic. She hurried to the sombre kitchen.

'Tonic?' She held up the bottle and shook it. 'For the gin?'

No reply. The woman shrugged. Lydia pulled open the door of the fridge. A tall American refrigerator run on kerosene. Plenty of beer. She tried the small larder off the sooty kitchen, wrinkled her nose at the odour of overripe pineapple, but spied boxes piled in the corner. Careless of potentially deadly spiders carried in the spiralling dust, she pulled out two cases of beer and one containing soft drinks, then dragged it to the lounge.

The first few hits of gin lessened the ache in her heart and limbs, and dulled the flashes of rage. This was the answer. She wanted a cigarette. Jack had given up some time before, but there was bound to be a packet hidden away in the back of a drawer. She hadn't smoked since Emma was born, but once the idea arose, she became fixated.

In Jack's bedroom there weren't many hiding places, only a chest of drawers and the tall single wardrobe. She pulled open the top drawer. Vests, boxers and socks. Nothing else. The second drawer revealed little more than shorts and shirts. The third drawer various miscellaneous items. Odd bits of fancy dress. Bow tie. A pack of cards, Scrabble. Reading glasses. She'd never seen Jack read much, only a paper or magazine, though the bookshelves were groaning with the weight of books.

The fourth drawer stuck a little. She knelt, pulled hard, and the whole thing tipped out, spilling a pile of Chinese clothes on the floor.

She fingered the delicate cheongsams, loose flowing black trousers, pretty white tops, and smelt the same fragrance she'd found in the bathroom cabinet, gently infused through every item. She lifted a silky green cheongsam with a hint of black lace at the thigh and stood before Jack's small mirror. She could only see part of herself at a time, but whatever part of her she could see, top, bottom or middle, it was clear the woman was diminutive. She looked inside the little high collar. At the back embroidered in gold, the word *Lili* stared boldly out. Oh my God. What an idiot she was. Lili had never once smiled, had never shown that gentle consideration so typical of the Chinese girls. Lili glowed with self-assurance, or so it had seemed to Lydia, and this was the reason why.

Lydia knew stories of the old colonial days when lone planters maintained what was once called a *keep*. A girl to look after them, to cook, clean, and warm their lonely beds, and occasionally their hearts. Why hadn't he told her? She gave up her search for cigarettes and dashed back to the lounge. She picked up the bottle, unlocked the gate and ran from the house.

She passed the track and veered off into the darkness, fought her way through bushes of giant ferns, and dodged the catapulting branches of mischievous monkeys. Bright birds flitted through the spreading trees, and streams of sweat began to snake from her head down her neck and under her blouse. Her life was bottoming out, as if she was existing out of time, numb to the danger of forest scorpions hidden under fallen branches, or pit vipers in the grass.

She came to a wide stream and ran straight through, tore off her soaked blouse and went on. She swung the bottle, drank fast as if it was water, until her head throbbed, the breath squeezed out of her lungs, and the rage inside her exploded. With all her strength she threw the half empty bottle against the trunk of a rubber tree. The smash was briefly satisfying, but not enough. A thousand smashed bottles would not be enough. Not caring which way to turn, she stumbled along sodden marshy pathways, still unable to block out the random act of terror that had destroyed her girls.

In a small clearing, flashing sunlight blinded her. She heard a rough metallic chirp and a crimson sunbird wheeled across the patch of sky. Lili floated by, cool, nymph like, her skin as clear as alabaster. Lydia touched her own fiery cheeks and closed her eyes. When she opened them again, the girl was gone. Through the watery green air, another shaft of light exploded. Now it was Emma fading in and out of the trees, and sucking a lollipop with an impish grin, dressed as a Chinese girl for the Christmas fancy dress ball. She heard their laughter and smiled fondly.

When Jack stumbled upon her on his way back for lunch, she was melting at the side of the road, the air thick with gorging mosquitoes. She stared with blank eyes, then vomited over his shoes. He picked glass out of her feet and with a lit cigarette burnt off the leeches on her legs before carrying her home. She retched repeatedly, but better that sickness than the one that

152

ripped her heart to shreds.

While Jack slept, she lay down in the cool of the garden, stared at the half face of the moon, saw Emma calling from the shadows and wished she might go to her. She felt herself slipping far away beneath the surface of life, where nothing could reach her, where there was no love, no pain, and there was no point in hoping.

In the morning Jack found her there, stone cold on the ground, Maz kneeling beside her, in one of Jack's old tee shirts. Jack stood her up, slapped her face, and dragged her inside. He gave Maz a hug and told him to go and ask Channa in the kitchen for some coffee and biscuits. As soon as it arrived, he forced bitter coffee down Lydia's throat, then rubbed and slapped her hands to find some warmth. She passed out.

When she woke the light had changed, the room filled with the dusky pink of a setting sun. She felt pain in her legs and feet.

'Promise you'll never do that again,' he said.

'What am I going to do?'

'You and Maz are going to stay here with me. For as long as it takes. Then we'll see.'

'I haven't got anything.'

'You've got me.'

'No. I mean I haven't got money.'

'Lydia, for heaven's sake. I've got my salary. You don't need to think about that now. Get well. That's what's important.'

She nodded.

'I know you don't believe it now, but it will get better.'

She screwed up her face and shook her head. 'It's the lack of meaning.'

Jack stared at her. 'Sweetheart, I know, but you are going to have to find your own meaning now.'

Despite his kindness, she felt a familiar surge of heat. 'How can you say that? Emma and Fleur were my meaning.'

'There has to be something else, Lyddy.' He spoke gently, stroked her cheek, looked at her with eyes as blue as the bright Malayan sky.

She pushed his hand away. 'More than my children? Are you crazy?'

'There's still Maz and me,' he said, his voice so soft she needed to strain to hear.

'I don't know, Jack. I want to phone George again. Ask him if there's anything new.'

He pressed his lips together, let out his breath. 'Okay, if that's what you want.'

But both of them knew that once she faced the loss, she'd either sink or swim. She hoped Jack was wise enough to know she wasn't ready to say in which direction.

Maz sidled up, with eyes so swollen it was clear he'd been sobbing his heart out. She picked him up and hugged him to her. 'I'm sorry, darling. It's just your children aren't supposed to die before you.'

She stroked his hair, and over the top of his head, noticed tears in Jack's eyes too.

After Jack went to deal with one of the tappers, taking Maz with him, she went to phone George.

When she explained what she wanted, he sighed.

'Look, Lydia, I'm sorry, but there's no point clutching at straws. Alec and the girls perished in that fire, and the file is closed. And by the way, old girl, no need to concern yourself about the paperwork. I can deal with that, and if I need you for anything I'll get in touch.'

'Thank you.'

'Not that there was any estate. As you know, Alec didn't own a property in England or over here, and he hadn't even had time to open a new bank account up at Ipoh. So, unfortunately for you, all his cash must have gone up in flames. The police, here in Malacca, have your car. Shall I arrange to have it sold?'

'Please. I'm going to need the money. But George, how can you be sure they were there?'

'The facts are the facts. No sightings of them since, and as I told you already, everything tells us they were there. Alec had not been allocated a house yet. Now come on, chin up, old thing. In due course we'll be able to start the job of obtaining death certificates, but with no actual bodies it can be a lengthy process. Sorry to be blunt.'

Lydia swallowed, only able to mutter her thanks. She put down the phone, then sat outside and opened Em's notebook for the first time since the fire, and read.

★　★　★

One of the angels sits on my bed. She has wavy red hair, pale skin, and a white gown. No wings. Not even folded up. There is only air behind her. *Jack came to our house today. I wish he wouldn't. He's bigger than my dad and I'm scared they'll have a fight. I liked him at first. We were in the street buying our new flip-flops. Mine had a bright orange flower in the middle. Jack came over and put a hand on Mum's shoulder. Then he gave Fleur and me a lollipop. I prayed to the angel to make him stay away, but he came again. That was the night I saw them in the bed.*

She shut the book and watched a large moth spiral upwards into the lantern. She stared at it until her eyes stung. Sitting on the veranda in the moist warm air, watching faint clouds swim like one of her children's watercolours, she couldn't bear to read any more. She had known. Emma had known.

19

It was a cold September day, fields lost in white mist, so thick that as we approached the school, the building was completely hidden. I wished it would stay that way. Disappear for ever. My father drove up a driveway lined with oak trees that gradually showed themselves, their leaves bright red and gold.

Autumn was something Fleur and I had never seen. On my last day at home, my sister had raced about the lawn with a broom, chasing the leaves as the wind whizzed them along the wire fence where the nettles grew. There was a bright orange beech tree at the bottom of the garden. Ours was the only garden in the row with a big tree like that. Granddad had fixed a swing to it at the start of summer and Fleur swung for hours.

The night before, Gran had helped me pack my case. Two changes of clothes the list said, school uniform and a casual outfit, my slippers, pyjamas, my notebooks and pen. There was also Mum's folded note, and the one framed photo of her that I'd managed to take from our house in Malacca. They weren't on the list, so they had to be my special secret. Gran hugged me close when we finished. Her skin smelt of lily of the valley and I saw tears in her eyes.

Penridge Hall was a large Victorian building on three floors. Gran said it was used as a hospital during the war and now it was a boarding school, especially for 'problem' children, and partly run by nuns. That's what I was now. A problem.

I tried to stop myself as Father parked his Morris Oxford. I tried to hold back, knowing it'd do no good, but in the end, I clutched hold of his jacket, and the words burst out anyway.

'Don't make me. I'll be good, I swear. Please, Dad.'

He brushed my hand off, but softened a little. 'It's for the best, Emma. You can't expect not to be punished after attacking Mr Oliver.'

'But I didn't do anything wrong all summer. I promise I'll never do anything like that again.'

His jaw tightened, and the skin round his eyes turned white. 'We've been through that. It's too late for promises. I asked you why you did it, and you could not answer me. You are not to be trusted. Hopefully they'll bring you to your senses here. Now, out you pop, and don't scowl, Emma. It's most unbecoming.'

I stuck out my chin and ignored the row of staring eyes that gazed down from an upstairs window, though the fear inside me made my hands go clammy. As we walked past the cropped lawn and up the front steps into a square hall, I felt I was being gobbled up. The cloudy glass door swung behind us, and a woman stood waiting, her hands clasped round a little terrier.

'Headmistress,' my father said, and held out his hand. He'd obviously met her before.

'I've called for Sister Ruth,' she said.

'How kind.'

She spoke in a horrid neighing voice. I kept my

158

head lowered but looked up through my lashes. She was a funny-shaped lady, with square black hair, and patches of red skin on her face. Behind metal-framed specs, her eyes watched me.

I stuck out my hand to stroke the dog.

She glowered at me. 'Do not touch the hound. Sister knows all about you, and I've given her explicit orders to keep a strict eye.'

I hung my head.

'And the head will report to me on a monthly basis and we'll see how you get on,' Dad added.

'Does that mean I'll be able to come home again?' I felt a flutter in my stomach and held my breath.

'We'll see.'

Father handed the headmistress my case. He shuffled from foot to foot. He seemed embarrassed to be there and kept looking at the door. Then he pasted a smile on his face, nodded at the woman, and left. I blinked rapidly, trying not to cry. No kiss on the cheek. No hug. Nothing to make me feel better. The headmistress told me to wait, swung round on her heels, and went into an office.

I found the courage to lift my face properly and look about the hall. Three ladies were having a good old gossip in one corner. They had baggy tweed skirts, navy cardigans, loose white blouses, and fat ankles spreading over tight lace-up shoes. And a girl was standing with a placard round her neck declaring she was lazy. After I'd read it, I glanced at her face. She winked and I winked back.

When an ear-piercing bell rang, the ladies left.

'Who were they?' I dared ask the girl with the placard. 'Someone's aunties?'

'English, French and Music.'

'Teachers?' I gasped, accustomed to the smart teachers at the Holy Infant College.

The bell rang again, the hall emptied, and the girl was gone. I shut my eyes. Had my father never done anything really bad? Couldn't he understand at all?

★　★　★

The first night in the cold greasy building, I wore all my clothes at once. They kept the windows open at night, and chill seeped into my bones. With just a narrow cellular blanket and a thin eiderdown for cover, I shivered in my metal-framed bed. When I couldn't sleep, thoughts of my mum warmed me, like a full bowl of porridge with Lyle's golden syrup. I couldn't believe it was nine months since I'd last seen Malaya *and* my mother. I thought of our house and garden there. The purple bougainvillea, the pale orchids, and the creeping lizards. It was never chilly, nothing like here.

The school was almost as cold in the day as it was at night. The radiators made a clunking noise, but none of the rooms warmed up. The girls huddled in little groups, mostly ignoring me, except for two mean ones who snatched, and then hid, my satchel for a whole day. On Saturday, after one of the longest weeks of my life, a bar of Cadbury's chocola e arrived in the post from Granny. She'd eve. taped a two

160

shilling coin to the back. Many of the girls came from far away, and were as likely to have been sent from India as to come from Worcestershire. Not all of them were lucky enough to be sent chocolate, so I offered to share mine with the placard girl. I was glad I did, because she looked at me with her hands on her hips and grinned.

'I'm Susan Edwards,' she said.

My new friend had very frizzy brown hair, quite a large nose, and deep-set brown eyes.

We sat and shared the chocolate on the step outside.

'How do you get used to it?' I asked.

'You just do,' she said.

'What about the food?'

She shrugged. 'Awful. No getting away from that.'

She was right. The smell of boiled cabbage crept everywhere. That day we'd had lamb and potato stew with gristly meat and a layer of grease floating on top, and then tart, with grated coconut and jam on soggy pastry.

'You just have to find a way to have a laugh,' she said. 'I'm adopted. What about you?'

'Sometimes I wish I was.'

She laughed. 'Like that, is it?'

I made a face.

★   ★   ★

Dad didn't come, though he wrote stiff letters, signing himself *Your Father* with no hint that I was missed. He never mentioned the letter from Malaya, and Mr Oliver was not spoken of either, as if he'd simply stopped existing, though I often thought of the stream of blood trickling down his neck. The letters put into words Father's approval or disapproval, depending on which nun or teacher had reported. But there was one letter that was different from the rest.

It was a cool clear day when it arrived and I'd been hoping to play outside at lunchtime, but they told me to read it in the office, and a secretary brought me Ovaltine and one of her own jammy dodgers. Because of the biscuit, I knew the letter had to be important. I worried for a moment and didn't dare open it, but the secretary was hovering over me, so I had to just get on and do it. Inside was just a single sheet of blue Basildon Bond and I nibbled the biscuit as I read that my granddad had gone. At first I didn't understand, but when I did, what went through my mind was that I felt really sorry for my dad. They'd never got on, and now with Granddad dead, it was too late to make it better.

I thought of Granddad's old man's face, covered in liver spots, his shock of white hair, and the hairs sprouting at his nostrils. I was quite upset and didn't feel very well. The secretary was called away, so they sent for Sister Ruth, the pale nun who looked after me. She had gentle grey eyes in quite a plain face, but when she smiled she was beautiful. She didn't go on like the other teachers. She was kind, and that gave you the feeling she cared, and really was on your side.

They took me to sickbay and the next day when I woke up, she was leaning over me, light streaming in from the tall windows behind her. 'What's the matter with me?' I said, terrified I was dying.

'It's the flu.'

'I never had this in Malaya,' I croaked.

'No, it's a particularly British illness. The weather doesn't help,' she said with a smile. 'Sit up a minute. I'll sort out your pillows, then give you a wash.'

The hard soap they allowed us for strip washes morning and evening only made me feel worse, but I put up with it for her sake.

'You'll feel better for it,' she said. 'I promise.'

She had a terrible cough herself. It shook her body and took away her colour.

'Have you got it too?' I asked.

She shook her head.

'Why can't I stop shivering?'

She covered me with an extra blanket then sat down. 'What was Malaya like? I've often wondered what it would be like to be a missionary in the East.'

I gulped, feeling my eyes dampen.

'Would you like to tell me about your mother?' Sister Ruth wrung out a flannel in tepid water and ever so gently put it on my forehead, then sat quietly, hands clasped together in her lap.

I wondered why she was asking about Mum, and thought about what I ought to say. But then I felt pleased she'd asked, because I never got the chance to talk to anyone about Mum.

'She's beautiful, and her name is Lydia.' I thought for a moment. 'She's always singing, and she makes brilliant fancy dress costumes. At least she did. My little sister, Fleur, was Miss Muffet, and I was a snowman.'

'That must have been fun.'

'Yes. I won a prize. And Mum and Dad won too, for Peter Pan and Captain Hook. She learnt to sew at the convent. But it was sad for Mum to be there.'

'Why was that?'

'Because she never knew her own mother, only her name. Emma. I'm named after her.'

She looked at me and smiled. 'Do you know what happened to her mother?'

'No. Mum was actually born in the convent you see. She was at school there and the nuns brought her up.'

'Do you know which convent it was?'

'I'm not sure. It might have been St Joseph's. Or was it St Peter's?' My face must have been glum because Sister Ruth kissed me on the cheek.

'If it is the same place, there is a St Joseph's not so very far from here. Though they run Christian retreats, not a school. Now I think that's enough talking. You need to rest.'

I looked in her eyes and knew that in Sister Ruth I had a friend.

She became my registration teacher and, when well, taught us Religious Education and History. When ill, she appeared thin and nervous with bright red spots on both cheeks, and light shone in her eyes. If Sister Ruth was ill, Mrs Wiseman took over. She was a dwarfish Welsh lady with black eyes, straight salt and pepper hair and a stubbly chin. She had a red nose, and an accent

164

so strong it took me weeks to understand it. But now with Susan Edwards and Sister Ruth on my side, I was happy that at least I wasn't completely alone. They weren't Mum, but nobody was.

20

Lili had been like a mystical flower. Even sober how could Lydia compete, and today she was sober. While she waited for Jack, she heard laughter, and went to the window. Channa was pushing Maz on the swing that Jack had fixed to the strongest branch in the garden. She pushed gently at first, and Lydia suspected it wouldn't be enough to satisfy Maz.

'Higher, Channa. Higher,' he shrieked.

Channa ignored his pleas. But he went on shouting. 'Higher. Higher.'

She gave in, pushed him higher, and he squealed with excitement. 'More. More.'

'No more,' she said, and stood back.

Annoyed, he tugged at the ropes, pushed back his legs to lever himself higher, and with a yell, slid from the seat.

'Don't let the swing come back and hit him on the head,' Lydia shouted.

Channa ran round to keep him down on the ground. 'Crawl out slow,' she said, and held out a hand to catch the swing.

He crawled out and sat on the ground, nursing his knee.

Channa squatted beside him. 'Just little cut,' she said, and kissed it better.

When Maz got up, he wandered round the garden with a basket. Lydia watched him select small stones and pebbles. He glanced across at her.

'For protection,' he said, with a small smile, and started to line the stones up in a circle round the tree. 'Nasty swing cannot get me now.'

★ ★ ★

When Jack came in late, he stood in the doorway, hands on hips, and swayed. Something about the overpowering smell of gin on his breath brought back the night she had come clean and confessed the affair to Alec.

They'd been sitting covered in strong insect repellent, out on the covered veranda. She could smell it now, along with the gin, and the slight breeze full of dust. In the distance they could hear the tapping of the tok-tok bird and the rumble of the sea. She'd been twisting her hair in a topknot, while struggling to find a way to speak. Alec was relaxed and wore his tartan dressing gown. He was talking about his Indian assistant, and how he was unreliable since his demotion. In a lull she took a breath.

'Alec, I have something to tell you.'

There was a pause. He avoided eye contact and she sensed he wasn't going to make this easy.

'I'm so sorry, but I've been seeing some-one — '

'You think I didn't know?' he broke in. 'You must think me very stupid.'

'How?'

'I heard you on the phone. It isn't me you call sweetheart.'

He hissed Jack's name.

'I love him, Alec. I'm sorry.'

His smug look vanished, and the distress in his eyes silenced her. Aware she'd disappointed him, her cheeks burnt. No more words.

The long pause was broken by his intake of breath. 'Sex isn't love, Lydia. You've seen enough planters legless in the bars.'

'Alec.'

'And their tarts, *'all fur coat and no knickers'*.'

She flinched at the coarse RAF slang. He crunched an ice cube between his teeth, and a vein began to throb in his neck.

'Stench of the whorehouse. Jack's no different.'

She felt her heart race. It wasn't true.

'You fucked up, Lydia. Face it.'

Her breath caught — the place went quiet.

'Obviously, I'd want you to go on seeing the girls,' she said.

'You imagine I'll let you go to a rubber planter.'

She bristled. 'You have no choice.'

'Is that so? It might have been a life before the war, but now when guerrillas kill, they rope a man up then slice him open with a *parang*. Is that what you want?'

She felt sick. She'd seen the gardener use one to slash the long grass.

He rubbed his jaw with his finger, a muscle there starting to twitch. When he spoke, his chin jutted out. 'In any case, with your mucky little affair you'd never get custody.'

'Jack will look after us. We'll go back to England.'

'Risk breaking his contract?'

'He's saving to buy his way out.'

Alec paused. 'In any case, you'd never get custody.'

'I'll get a job.'

'With no education, no experience of work. No home. No visible means of support. And at fault. Take off the rose-coloured specs.'

'I'm sorry. I didn't set out to hurt you. It just happened.'

'No, Lydia,' he snapped, his Adam's apple rising and falling. 'These things do not just happen. You made a choice.'

'I've tried to be honest with you. You know how we've been. You can't be happy.'

'Happiness! This isn't about happiness, Lydia. It's about duty.'

She'd hoped to appeal to his heart, but saw, as he turned away to grip the railings, it was impossible. Alec never spoke of feelings. When he turned back his knuckles were white.

She listened to the sounds of the night. 'Well, are you happy?' she asked.

Unblinking, gazing at her with steel hard eyes, he ignored her question and just curled his lip.

'Here's another choice for you,' he said. 'You stay, or, if you decide to leave, you leave without Emma and Fleur. The choice is yours.'

She held back tears. He couldn't, could he?

'And make no mistake, Lydia.' He paused to wipe his glasses with a handkerchief. 'Make no mistake, I will see to it that you never set eyes on either of your daughters again.'

Stunned into silence, she wrapped her arms

around her middle, as if protecting herself from a punch. Then she swallowed hard and straightened her back.

'You can't do that.'

'Yes, Lydia, I think you'll find I can. Why don't you have another gin while you decide.'

Rattled by his tone of voice, she felt a flash of anger, picked up the bottle of gin and hurled it at the veranda railings. For a while neither spoke.

He sniffed at the overpowering smell of gin. 'So am I to take it that you'll stay?'

She looked past his weary face. There was no choice and Alec knew it. Connected to her children in the way that mothers are, he knew she'd never leave them. With a twist of her heart she thought of Jack. His golden skin, his vitality. Not expecting to fall in love, she hadn't imagined her heart would jump just at the sight of him. She didn't even care if Alec was right. Didn't care if Jack screwed around. Didn't care if he'd been stringing her along.

She leant her head against the back of the chair. 'You never talk to me, Alec. I never know what you're thinking.'

'So it was about talking, was it? That's what you did with Jack.'

She sat bolt upright, knew she shouldn't say it but couldn't help herself. 'No, Alec, for once in my life I had a bloody good fuck.'

They locked eyes.

'No dice, Lydia. I'm not carrying the can for this. You knew what you were taking on when you married me.'

'You needed me then.'

170

'Is it so hard to go on? I still need you.'

'To look after the girls.'

He shrugged and turned away. 'We were happy once, Lydia. But you're impulsive. It gets you into trouble.'

She studied Alec's back. He had his sport and self-admiration. He'd get over the dent to his pride. He came back to her and held out a hand, but she dropped her eyes, too angry to look up.

'You'd better pull yourself together,' he said. 'I don't want the children upset. We have a wedding to attend in the morning.'

★ ★ ★

She realised that Jack was still standing in the doorway, eyeing her cautiously, his cheeks flushed. For days the argument with Alec had played out in her mind. It was all her fault. Everything. If she hadn't had the affair with Jack. If she hadn't taken Suzanne's call. She had no one to blame but herself.

She glared at Jack. 'I thought you had more balls than that.'

He gave her an uneasy look. 'Lydia?'

'Alec was right. You can't tell the difference, can you?' She looked at the shadow the single lamp cast on his face. He was too thin. Had become too thin.

'What the hell are you on about?'

She reddened but carried on, looking at his bewildered face. 'Between love and sex.'

He frowned. 'So now this is my fault.'

'How could you not tell me?'

171

Understanding spread across his face. 'Oh, that's it — Lili. What would have been the point? You were going back to Alec, old darling. We had no future. You made that clear.'

'What about when you were with me. Was it me you really wanted? Or her?'

'Lydia please.' He shook his head. 'I cared for Lili. People do things. Make mistakes.'

She went across to stand in front of his chair. How Alec would have gloated if he'd known Jack had another woman all along. He stood and reached out his arms to her. Instead of accepting him she slapped his face.

He rubbed his jaw. 'Why are you trying to needle me? This is not my fault.'

He was right. Her children were dead and it was her punishment. 'I thought you were the only person in the world who knew me. I thought we were meant to be together.'

'We still can be. For heaven's sake, come here.'

She stayed where she was, battling the shadows, 'Did you find her in a knocking shop?'

He spread his hands out, palms uppermost, and shrugged.

Almost unaware of Jack lifting her and carrying her to his bed, she longed for an end. He laid her down, then sat on the edge holding his head in his broad hands. When he looked up, she watched a streak of moonlight fall across his hollow cheeks. She held out her hand and traced the contours with her fingertips. What a bitch she was, not to even consider Jack's feelings.

He slipped off her dress, then helped her into bed.

She felt such a mix of anger and shame at being alive; she lay awake, conjuring her daughters' faces, imagining it was all a ghastly mistake, that they were not dead at all. It grew in her mind, the doubt, and in the end, she nudged Jack awake.

He rubbed his eyes, sat up, and frowned. 'Lyddy, you need to sleep. We both do. What's the time?'

'Can you go to Ipoh again? Ask for proof that the girls and Alec were there.'

He sighed. 'Lydia, you've got to stop this. You know what George said. They were there. Nobody has seen or heard from Alec since then. The Administration couldn't compile a list of people killed in the fire, because the records went up in smoke, and you know there were no survivors.'

Lydia shook her head. 'I just can't believe it. Tell me exactly what they said.'

'You want me to be blunt?'

'Yes.'

'They said any remains had been taken by animals in the night.'

She covered her mouth with her hand.

'And even George said it was a wild goose chase.'

She hung her head, trembled at the memory of Emma's raucous laugh, Fleur's snub nose and dimpled chin, and allowed herself to weep. Am I mad, she thought, mad with grief? Or is it just that I don't know who I am any more?

In the morning they made love. For an hour she moulded herself to him and lost herself in

173

the sensation. She felt his skin and tingled as if it were the first time and when he entered her, she shuddered in shock and relief. For an hour she eased herself into a return of feeling that wasn't grief. With all her heart she wanted to discover how to be happy with Jack. He'd come to bed without showering, and she ran her fingers through his hair, finding the sticky threads of latex there. 'Thank you, Jack,' she said. 'I'll try.'

That afternoon, she watched swollen black clouds billow down the mountain side. The sound of children's voices reached her. Maz was outside playing chase with Burhan. When the storm came, she called them both in. She read a story in English, in an overbright voice, while Maz sat, cross-legged, on the floor beside her chair. Every so often she ruffled his hair, but he'd grown still around her, no longer commented on everything he saw, and when he counted, he did so quietly. The other boy fidgeted and went out to be with his mother.

Maz got up too. 'I will go with him, Mem.'

Though she wanted to regain Maz's confidence, visions of her girls still tormented her, and with a stab of conscience, she realised she'd forgotten how to listen to the little boy.

Only when the gale had howled itself out and the air was still again did her daughters' little figures begin to fade, no longer leaving parts of themselves behind. The sun appeared and it was over. For now. But the chance to heal hung like a thread. Fine, elusive. And as Lydia attempted to begin the slow process of mending her broken life, Maz came back to join her: pointed at a sunbird piercing through the base of a flower, its metallic blue-black forehead glinting as it hovered to sip the nectar. She smiled at the child. She would try harder. She would.

21

In Malaya, first thing in the morning, strong animal smells crept in from the jungle. Here it was burnt porridge. In Malaya we climbed the rain tree, and hid from the demons that sucked light from the world. Here I wrote lines, but imagined myself on my way home in Malacca, avoiding the frighteners who lurked in cracks, and bit off your toes if you trod on them. I no longer asked Dad when Mum was coming, and he always changed the subject when I asked who the Malayan letter had been from, or said it was none of my business. I gave up asking because it only made him cross, but decided to keep my eyes peeled in case another one arrived.

I was over thirteen and a half now, and in the year I'd been at the school, I'd written lines a dozen times. Usually for Mrs Wiseman. Though that wasn't much compared with Susan, who held the record. We were still best friends, though we argued like crazy.

I must pay more attention in class and not look out of the window. I must pay more attention . . . I was in lunchtime detention again. This time I'd been thrown out of domestic science for chucking flour in Susan's frizzy hair. She didn't care, and I hated cookery anyway. Without thinking I drew a little face at the bottom. Oh no! Mrs Wiseman would make me do it all again. Though most of the other teachers were fine, she didn't like me. My pencil had a hard eraser at one end, so I rubbed to remove the smiley face. When the girls came in, surprise made my hand slip, and I rubbed a hole right through.

There were three, all older than me, but I knew only one. Not her again, I thought. Her name was Rebecca, and she was one of the girls who had hidden my satchel when I first arrived. She had legs like tree trunks and was one of the few fairly local girls, like me. The rumour was that she'd given a teacher at primary school a black eye. Whatever she'd done, she had it in for me.

While she grabbed my paper, one of her friends grasped a handful of my hair, tipped up the chair and pulled me backwards. The other one held me down, and I kicked out at her.

'Let me go you cow!' I shouted, as I caught her on the shin.

She laughed a spiteful laugh, tipped the chair back even further, then let go of it for a moment, and caught it again, just as I let out a yelp.

'Ha!' she said. 'Got you.'

I carried on kicking, until I saw Rebecca scribble on my paper. I managed to push the girl off me, and tried to grab the paper back, but Rebecca easily dodged me.

'Don't do that,' I pleaded. 'My dad will kill me.'

'Hard luck, and if you tell, we'll get you again,' one of the other two said.

'Not so brave now, are you? Without Susan.' She laughed. 'Anyway, she's only your friend because nobody else likes her.'

The end of lunchtime bell stopped it. They shoved the desks about, whooped and punched the air, slammed the door, then pelted from the room. I still heard their voices and thundering footsteps, even from the furthest corridor. I felt dizzy, imagined myself on the sea again, everything booming and rolling from side to side.

I pulled myself together and stared at what was left of my work. Oh no! Pictures of quite well-drawn private parts leapt across my paper. If I hadn't been so frightened, I'd have laughed. Instead my head buzzed. I didn't know what to do. The only thing was to rip up the paper and start again. I looked around the room. There weren't any extra sheets. What was worse: paper ripped into a zillion bits or these rude drawings? I began tearing and worked quickly. Bits of bottoms, bosoms and a penis or two fluttered to the floor like confetti.

The door swung open.

Dwarfish Mrs Wiseman walked in with a sour look. My heart stopped, though her anger was nothing compared with my father's rage.

Hands clasped at her waist, her black eyes widened. 'What do you think you're doing? Give that to me.'

I broke out in a sweat as I held out the last of the paper.

She snatched the pieces from my hands, and I swear I saw hairs sprout from her chin.

I quickly ran through my options. 'I . . . I . . . I thought the handwriting wasn't good enough,'

I said. 'I was going to start again.'

'That is a barefaced lie. There are drawings on this paper.'

Her eyelids flickered, she stepped back and the pieces slipped to the floor. Her short body swayed, straight hair bobbing as her head went up and down, jowls wobbling. Every bit of her seemed to move separately from the rest. For a moment I thought she was having a fit, and any second would start foaming at the mouth, and I'd be able to gather up the bits, and get out. But she wrung her hands, and in an accent so strong it sounded as if she was choking, squawked at me. 'Go to your dormitory. Get out! I'll deal with you later.'

I darted from the room. They'd send for Father. I could explain, tell, but if I did that those girls would come again. And anyway, after this my father would never let me leave the school.

Instead of making for the dorm, I raced along a corridor to the other end of the building, and through a door marked *Private*. In the storeroom I grabbed a packet of Rich Tea biscuits. In a shadowy alcove near the back door, I hid. I held my breath when I heard one of the maids coming. Was she going outside for a quick fag? Oh, please no. She'd walk right in front of me and see. Please make her go into the storeroom.

Another of the kitchen staff called out to her. She stopped and turned on her heels, hesitating for a moment. 'I was going for another slab of butter.'

'More like a sneaky fag. Come along. Back to work.'

The moment the kitchen door closed behind them, I let out my breath and slipped outside.

I needed to cross the grounds, without being seen from any classroom window overlooking that side. As the gardens were in full view of dozens of pairs of bored eyes, all scanning the horizon for possible gossip, it wasn't easy. Especially as their most likely subject for chatter was the new gardener. He was gorgeous, with tightly curling dark hair, and the look of a gypsy. The older girls drooled over him, but the rumours were he'd been seen going to the cinema with the French mademoiselle, and they were arm in arm. All of us younger girls were out to see if we could catch them at it: something to taunt the older girls with. I checked the lawns — luckily he wasn't working on this side. My best bet was to wait for the bell at the end of the lesson, then make a dash for it.

My idea was to make for the woods, where Susan and I found hiding places when we wanted to get out of cross-country. There were hollow trees and great stacks of branches we'd piled up. If I could reach one of those, I'd be able to hide while I decided what to do.

The only way was to the left, where rose bushes lined a path leading to the woods at the back of the school. They provided little cover but it was my only chance.

A man's voice stopped me. I swivelled round and hid the biscuits in a fold of my tunic. For once I was glad of its baggy fit. It was just the baker, on his way to his van.

I heard the bell go and needed to run, but he

180

held out a tempting iced bun. 'Yes, please,' I said. 'I'll save it for later. Thanks.' And I ran like a maniac without glancing back.

In the woods, I found a place beneath a large oak, and wolfed my bun, deciding to save the biscuits for later instead. I had no plan.

★ ★ ★

When it got dark, people with torches tramped between the trees, calling out my name. After they went, the trees swayed about. I thought of men shooting crocodiles and diving for crayfish. I imagined the jungle, and the bandits who hid under leaves, just like me. I thought of Malacca and the smell of fried fish, and our old gardener burying bowls of rice for the spirits of the earth. More than anything I wanted Mum, but I covered myself with even more leaves and branches, and listened to the wind.

Protected by oaks and elms, and smelling of mould and damp, the scratching of unknown creatures reminded me of the *hantu hantuan*. I had never before been so frightened of the dark. I curled up small, and longed for a mug of hot chocolate and some scrambled eggs on toast.

Stow away and return to Malaya, that's what I'd do. Find my mother. But I was only a child; what could I do? Veronica might be friendly but she could hardly put me on a ship heading back to a country at war. I stifled a sob. It isn't fair, I thought, I haven't done anything wrong.

★ ★ ★

The next morning, Dad, the headmistress and two policemen stomped through the woods. Wet through, I was actually glad that they'd come.

'Come out, Emma, we know you're there.' My dad's voice, firm and controlled, though I knew, underneath, he'd be twitching with anger.

'Come out, dear. You're not in trouble. Better to come out now,' said one of the policemen, in a kinder voice.

'Emma Cartwright, show yourself immediately.' That was the headmistress.

I hesitated, but when I judged the policemen to be nearest, I shook the leaves and branches off and stepped out. On jelly legs, I called, 'I'm here.'

Then I felt my legs give way, and after that I don't know what happened.

★ ★ ★

In sickbay once again, I woke up to see my father sitting across the room, looking thin and stern. I heard the doctor talking to him in a quiet voice, about blood pressure.

'Dangerously low. Any history of heart problems in the family?'

'My father died from a stroke,' my dad replied.

'What about other grandparents?'

Through my eyelashes, I saw him purse his lips and shake his head.

'My wife was brought up at St Joseph's. Didn't know her parents.'

I wanted to talk to them, but my lips stuck together. I drifted a bit as they went on murmuring. Questions, answers and scribbling. A nurse moved about, carrying things and tidying up.

'Can we have your wife's current address?' the doctor asked.

I heard Dad take a sharp breath and pause, before he spoke in a very low voice.

'I'm afraid Emma's mother abandoned her family. Now she's missing, presumed dead.'

The ceiling raced towards me, and I felt myself fall backwards. I could only see a circle of light from the window. The light pulsed in and out, yellow with an orange rim, all the time growing smaller and smaller, until it was just a pinpoint. The room went black. I was pulled down into a dark well, but with my arms reaching out for help, I fought against it, desperate to find the light from the window again. For a moment it came, then I heard my own voice screaming. 'Mummy. Mummy. Help me.'

But my voice and I were far away. In Malaya, at the island, running in and out of the sea, as Mummy sat with ice-cold beer bottles in her armpits, to numb the jellyfish stings. The sand was white and fine, soft, soft sand, and the water warm like a bath. It was clear as day and felt like real life.

I was shocked when I came round to find I wasn't there. I swung my head from side to side, trying to make sense. Where had I been? What had happened? I saw two bags of fluid attached to thin tubes going into my arms. And then as the fluid went down, and was replaced by more, I remembered. *Mummy. Mummy. Mummy.* Tears poured down my cheeks, and I knew my heart was broken.

22

September 1956. And on the day hope returned, over eighteen months had passed since the terrors of the fire. Lydia stood in the centre of the sitting room, unsuspecting, looked out of the window and took a step towards it. First, the idea of eating popped into her mind. She swivelled round, and caught sight of a grey lizard flash across the ceiling. She watched it disappear into a jagged crack, then absentmindedly picked up a mango from the coffee table. She ran her palm over the smooth grain of the table, then felt the mango for ripeness. It was soft beneath her thumb but still firm underneath. Perfect.

In the bedroom, she put the mango down and opened the bottom drawer of the chest. Lili's clothes were gone, of course. Her own plain blouses and skirts lay quietly folded there. She missed her old clothes, the delicate raw Indian silks, the bright satins, the harem jackets. Her chest tightened at a memory. She and the girls buying fabric. She remembered fingering the satin, pink and patterned with fiery dragons. It reminded her of Cicely too, her old friend from Malacca, who had the same material, but in lilac.

The day before, Cicely, now back from travels in Australia, had arrived out of the blue. Cool as ever, dressed in a turquoise linen dress, with a rope of silver hanging from her neck, she'd said she was just dropping by on her way to Penang.

When Lydia asked why she was going there, she just shrugged her shoulders and wouldn't be drawn, but did offer to pay another visit on her way back south. Lydia had muttered some kind of excuse.

'Well, darling,' Cicely said, taking the hint, 'if you need anything at all, a place to stay, money, shoulder to cry on, I'll be in Malacca.'

'I'm all right for now. Jack's been very generous. Anyway, I still owe you for the jewellery you pawned.'

'Oh, forget that, sweetie. And the offer is there if anything changes.'

Lydia smiled at the thought of her friend. She couldn't really explain why she didn't want to spend time with her, except that Cicely was so much part of her old life. Then, she dressed in her only pretty skirt, a simple printed cotton, put on some red lipstick and went out to the veranda in the drizzle.

There was a slight wind, and Maz was there, watching a troupe of monkeys appear and disappear. She felt the blood rush to her head and leant on the wooden handrail. She closed her eyes, but the colours of the rubber trees still swirled. When the dizziness passed, she wiped away the moss that appeared on the chairs overnight, and sat looking out into the trees. So many paths threaded through them, it was a wonder Jack found his way home.

Maz was first to hear a whistle, as Jack walked across the grass. 'Jack!' he shouted and ran towards him.

Jack held up his palm to stop Maz. 'I wouldn't

come too close,' he said.

Maz took a step back as Jack came closer, and Lydia reeled at the overpowering stink of piss. She pulled a face.

'What on earth?'

'You'll never believe it,' Jack said.

She raised her brows. He wore a crumpled khaki shirt with the sleeves rolled up, hands on hips, a wide grin on his face. Not drunk then.

'We stopped off on our way back from Ipoh to clear up some burnt trees.'

'And?'

'Well, it seemed like rain, but the rumpus above made us look up. And then I saw the little blighters.'

'What?'

'A dozen long-tailed macaque monkeys, yammering away, and running up and down the branches, only stopping to piss on top of us.'

She smiled.

'It's good to see you smile, Lyddy. Sorry, no news.'

Lydia shrugged. Even though he believed there was no point, Jack had been to the government offices in Ipoh again, asking for details of the fire. But the destruction had been total and anyone who might have known was dead and gone. Added to that, there was no record of Alec's work in Ipoh. His entire department had gone up in flames.

That afternoon she made friends with Jack's house, spending silent, measured time in every room. She listened to noises that came from somewhere else, the village maybe, and there was an hour of calm, a simple kind of grace. Maz followed at a distance. When she spoke to him, his eyes were pale and watchful. He caught at her heart, and while she stood in Jack's wood panelled office, the idea came to her. She quickly gathered paper, pencils, pens and called Maz.

In the sitting room, she shifted the bowl of mangos to one side, knelt on the floor, and laid out pencils and paper on the coffee table. In faint, easy-to-trace letters, she began to write the alphabet. She called him again, but he hung back just outside the door. She went on writing, slowly, laboriously.

'Maz,' she tried once more. 'Come. I'll show you how to write. Wouldn't you like to learn?'

He shook his head but carried on watching.

She concentrated on the task and as she reached *k* she heard a shuffle. She didn't look up. When he sidled close, she held up a darker, blacker pencil for him. He shook his head, but sat beside her, skinny elbows wrapped round skinny knees. She started to trace over her earlier letters herself. When she reached *m* he reached for the pencil.

'M is for Maz,' she said. 'And milk and marble and mule.'

He traced the *m* carefully, and without glancing up said, 'M is for mother.'

Lydia bit her lip. 'It is, my little one. It is.'

★ ★ ★

Maz was a quick learner and Lydia took the task seriously. Without children's books or proper learning materials she went over the alphabet, encouraged him to copy basic words, and drew pictures of animals and objects to illustrate the words. A monkey that looked like a dog. A king cobra with two heads. A long-quilled Malay porcupine with a smile on its face. They laughed over the strange creatures that grew there, and his chatter returned.

She encouraged him to draw pictures of his life: his mother, his aunt and his old home. Then she labelled them and little by little the lessons sank in, but also something else happened.

He drew the shape of a hut with seven stick figures inside. She smiled and asked him to explain.

'This one is my mother, this my uncle, this my aunt and these four are my cousins.' Then he drew another picture alongside it, almost identical but missing a figure.

'Look Maz, you've left one out,' she said.

He hung his head.

'Maz?'

Silence.

'Do you want to tell me who is missing?'

He looked up at her, eyes swimming with tears. 'It is my uncle, Mem. He was killed.'

She pulled him to her and held him tight, and the little boy sobbed. She got out a clean hankie and wiped his eyes. It was clear he'd loved his uncle.

'I lived with my aunt and cousins.'

'Why did your mother go to the jungle?'

But the child wouldn't say what made her go. Maybe he doesn't know, she thought.

'Shall we go on reading?' she asked.

He nodded and Lydia patted his head. Though a part of her remained broken, she knew the boy was helping her turn a corner in the twisting road to recovery. I look out for you. You look out for me. Wasn't that what he'd once said?

★   ★   ★

The next day, Jack staggered in, a large cardboard box in his arms. He looked handsome and pleased with himself. He landed it on the coffee table, then put out a hand to catch a record and some sheet music sliding off the top. He pressed them to her and pulled out a Black Box record player.

'It's not new. But it should work.'

Within minutes he attached a plug, put the record on the turntable, and flicked the switch. Nothing happened. His face fell, and he tried another plug. The voice of Frank Sinatra filled the room. Lydia grinned and clapped her hands. Jack caught hold of her and slipped his arm round her waist. With his cheek to her ear they waltzed round, laughing and tripping over shoes, magazines and teacups. For a moment all her old hopes came flying back. She started to hum the tune, 'Three Coins in a Fountain', and he joined in.

'Bloody hell, Jack. You're tone deaf.' She poked him in the chest, and for a time life felt like it used to. She imagined herself back at the club on New Year's Eve, high heels, slinky black dress with slits up both sides, far too many cocktails and her eye on Jack with his broad shoulders and big hands. An innocent life, in a way, with not the slightest hint of what lay waiting.

'That's not all I've got,' Jack said, interrupting her thoughts.

He disappeared into the hall for a moment, then came back carrying an old Singer sewing machine.

'Say thank you nicely to Uncle Jack.'

She gave him a swipe. 'Heaven knows where you got it!'

'There's fabric too.'

She flushed bright red, embarrassed by her lack of cash and thinking of Cicely's offer of money. When she explained, he smiled as if they were an old married couple.

'You don't need Cicely's help. Anything mine is yours, Lydia. Anyway it's not as if you're out spending money every day, is it?'

Then he revealed where he was stockpiling his early release money.

'I used to keep it in the desk, but see, it's under this loose floorboard under the rug. In case you ever need any.'

He rolled back the rug, tipped up the floorboard and pulled out several thick wads of ten-dollar notes, held together with rubber bands.

'Heavens. That's a lot.'

He nodded. 'Quite a tidy sum. I said I was working on buying my way out.'

'I should have taken you more seriously.' She kissed him on the nose. 'Thank you.'

She watched a vein throbbing in his neck. What would she have done without him? What could she have done? He'd looked after her all this time, financially, emotionally, and in so many other ways. They were living an isolated life, with only occasional visitors, though Jack sometimes suggested outings to Ipoh, or to another plantation run by a couple he knew. She felt no desire to make small talk with people she didn't know, though maybe Jack needed to get out. He was a good man, and she'd learnt to wait for his occasional dark mood to pass.

'Why not come to the market in Ipoh?' he said. 'You can get anything there. It'd do you good. It's safe enough.'

She stared at him and sighed.

'Sorry. I know grief takes time.'

She bit her lip. She didn't want it to take time. She didn't want it at all. She was getting through it one day at a time, the pain of their absence long since settled in the pit of her stomach. She dreaded that soon their absence would feel normal. Sometimes when she woke and felt them there, it shocked her that there was only air, and all that remained of them was Em's notebook and the photos in her locket. She forced herself to think of something else.

'I learnt how to make vegetable curry,' she said, speaking too brightly.

Jack nodded, his eyes closed.

'You're tired. Let's have a good long sleep after lunch?' She touched him lightly on the arm.

'Tell you what,' he said, opening his eyes. 'Let's go swimming this evening.'

She tipped her head to one side and smiled. This was something new.

★ ★ ★

There were so many tangled paths through the trees, and as she and Maz followed Jack to the pool, she realised she'd never find it on her own, though Maz would. Once Maz travelled a path, he always found it again. She wondered if he did it by counting trees, or was it just something males did better?

When she glimpsed the glitter of water through the trees, she saw it ran from a source higher up, was piped down, and then out through a wooden spout into a deepish pool, screened by trees and giant ferns. Curtains of orange and purple butterflies hung in the air, and the water reflected a million shades of green. In the translucent pool, a few dark shapes lay at the bottom and at the edge of the water. Jack saw her look doubtful.

'Don't worry. They're only soft-shelled water turtles. They don't bite.' He removed his clothes, and jumped in, stark naked.

'Come on,' he called.

Maz was next and flew into the water with a piercing shriek.

'Come on, Lyd,' Jack shouted. 'What you waiting for?'

She hesitated, then threw off her sweaty clothing and slipped in too, hair flowing out behind her.

'Gracious!' she yelled, splashing Jack, who

192

ducked her under. Maz shook with laughter, jumped up and down in the water, and pointed at them both, a stream of rapid Malay firing out.

'This is fantastic, isn't it?' Jack shouted, showing off his physical prowess by turning somersaults in the water.

Limbs and hands flapped and floundered as they tussled. She slipped and lost her footing. He kissed her lightly on the forehead when she came up for air, swam round, then pulled her back by the hair. She fell into his arms and Maz swam round in circles, squealing and splashing, chasing butterflies. It was a physical release, the chill of the water cooling their burning skin.

This is the nearest thing to peace, she thought, and spluttered as she went under again. Maz giggled, and chased trails of bubbles, as Jack ducked her mercilessly, touching her breasts under the water, where Maz couldn't see.

Afterwards they climbed out, shouting to each other, shaking water from their hair and blinking it from their eyelashes. They sat, back to back, in a little clearing by the side of the pool and Jack lit a cigarette. She couldn't remember when he'd started smoking again.

She thought of the shining waters of her family's old uninhabited island holidays, the turquoise seas, the dolphins and the palm-fringed shore. She closed her eyes for a moment to enjoy the tranquillity, but had a funny feeling she was being watched. She suspected monkeys, but when a long tongue went shooting past Jack's left shoulder, he yelled and leapt in the air. She turned to see a flash of slit nostrils and a lumbering pale-coloured creature. Maz rolled over, white teeth gleaming, laughing and clutching his sides until he cried.

'It's biawak,' he said. 'A biawak.'

Hearing Maz, the water monitor slipped away into the pool.

'I never saw you move so fast,' she teased.

Jack pulled a face. 'Yes. Very funny I'm sure.'

The drizzle had gone and dappled light fell on Jack's face. He let Maz go ahead, holding Lydia back by her elbow. Way out in front, they heard Maz sing a throaty Malay song, the green of the evening turned pink, and suddenly the air was filled with hundreds of tiny black and white butterflies, floating like fragments of rice paper tissue.

'It's going to be okay, you know.' He held out his arms to her and they stood under the great canopy of trees, hugging and rocking as river frogs croaked round them.

23

My homecomings were never easy, but this would be much harder than usual. Because of Mum, and because I'd been ill, they allowed me time off, and in my relief at getting away from Penridge Hall, I'd almost forgotten my sister. But then, remembering how we used to stop at the shop in Malacca that sold mirrors and feathers, and drums and flutes, I cried. I pictured Mummy, and Fleur and me, as we bought crepe paper, and made wings of wire. Mum let us wear party dresses, and we danced like fairies for Daddy. Though I soon got bored of that, and went to hide under the house to spy on Amah. Now that nothing would ever be the same again, I wanted those days back, and it felt like the whole world had ended.

Gran met us at the door and squeezed me so tight I couldn't breathe. She had broken veins in her cheeks, and was more round shouldered than before. Behind her, I saw Fleur hang back with a cautious smile, her eyes framed by new, pink, plastic-rimmed glasses. Gran wiped her eyes with the back of her hand and let me go. Fleur hugged me limply. She had her own room and I was to go in with Gran.

'Since your grandfather passed I have no use for the other bed,' Gran said, with a sad look at the place where Granddad used to sleep. 'Your dad moved it to the window. It's yours now, duck.'

I frowned. 'But I thought he was buying our own house.'

'Things aren't going so well for your father just now. Money's tight.'

'If I came home for good, he wouldn't have to pay my school fees.'

'Oh no, dear. Your dad's not . . . '

'Not what, Gran?'

She covered her mouth with her hand, and stood abruptly.

'Dear me. Here I am chatting on, and still with the lunch to see to.'

'But Gran?'

'My memory is something awful these days. The long and the short of it is, I had to go for a test last week.'

'How did you get on?'

She poked me in the ribs and laughed. 'No worries, my duck. I passed with knobs on. Doesn't everybody know that Winston Churchill's the prime minister.'

Trouble is, I don't know if she was joking and knew it was Anthony Eden, or if she really thought it was Winston Churchill. I didn't like to ask. She remembered enough to say that Veronica and my father were seeing a lot of each other.

'I think it might be more than a flash in the pan,' she said.

I hung my head.

'I'm so sorry, love. About your mum.'

I didn't know what to say, just muttered, and she patted my back and said, 'There, there. Why don't you brush your hair and tidy up and I'll make you a lovely gooseberry jam sandwich.'

Fleur had Dad and now Veronica, and could be bought with liquorice allsorts. But I needed my mother, and felt ashamed by the flash of anger I felt towards her. It wasn't fair. How could she have abandoned us? How could she be dead?

I went through the act of brushing my hair, dragging the bristles through. In Malaya I had complained once that I didn't think brushing made much difference. 'Nevertheless,' Mum said in a sharp voice, and she took the brush and roughly pulled it through my hair. It was the day of the wedding, the same day we had the accident, and she'd been in a funny mood.

Fleur had watched, mouth open. 'What about mine?'

'Yours is easy,' Mum said. And with one or two strokes with a fine comb, Fleur's hair was tidy, a neat parting on the right, and a clip in the shape of a bow on the left.

'Can I have a clip too?' I asked.

'No use putting a clip in your hair, Em. We'd never find it again. And for goodness sake stop lolling about.' She laughed and I felt stupidly hurt.

I can't bear it, I thought, my mind burning up with questions that went round and round. What's actually happened to Mum? Doesn't anybody know? I decided to ask Fleur if she'd heard anything, so went to her room and stood inside the door. She was sitting on her bed colouring in a map of Great Britain, putting a frill of blue round the edge to show it was sea.

'The sea's not like that, Mealy,' I said, thinking of the way the sky fell into an indigo ocean at night.

She looked up coolly. 'Don't call me that. It's babyish. And go away. I'm busy. This has got to be done by open day.'

'Did you miss me?'

'A bit,' she said.

I hung about, but apart from some loud obvious sighs, she ignored me. I left the room. No point asking her. I wasn't even sure if she'd tell me. Could it be that sisters were as likely to mistrust each other as anyone else? It made me sad to think like that, but I wanted a sister more like me, who'd talk and tell me it'd be okay, and that Mummy was not dead. Not dead at all. Or at the very least would know how it had happened.

★ ★ ★

I didn't have to wait long for a chance to see if I could find out more. Gran and Dad were down at the primary school with Fleur. It was a bright afternoon for an open day, with cakes and teas, so I knew I'd have enough time.

Dad's room wasn't locked, but like a good spy, I made sure I heard their voices disappear as they went off down the road.

The furniture in there was: one dark walnut wardrobe, a matching dressing table and chair, a double bed and two bedside tables. A band of sunlight fell across the floor showing up the threadbare patches in the carpet. I looked in the bedside tables. Only job application forms and letters of refusal there. That's what Gran means about things not going so well, I thought, and turned to the wardrobe. Suits, shirts, a coat, black and tan shoes lined up in military order, cardboard boxes piled on top. I dragged the chair over and climbed up. All sealed. That left under the mattress, and the dressing table.

The mattress was lumpy and heavy to lift, but as I slid my hand under I could tell there was nothing there. I pulled open the first drawer of the dressing table. Shoe cleaning stuff tumbled on to the floor: a cloth, two brushes, one soft, one hard, a spray and four pots of different coloured polish. Dad kept everything tickety-boo, as he would say. I pulled a face, realising I didn't know the order he kept things in, so crossed my fingers and put it all back as I thought he might. Now for the bottom drawer. It must be there. Only if I saw it with my own eyes would I believe it. I scoured the contents: a calendar, an address book, a bottle of fake tan lotion, and, at the bottom, a book. With a grin I turned the bottle of tan over. My dad liked to have a tan. I lifted out the book: *A Gardener's Year* was the title. Must be one of Granddad's. Dad didn't garden. As I flicked through, a thin blue airmail envelope slipped to the floor. I hesitated, then picked it up, turned it over, and saw a Malayan postmark. I lifted the flap and opened out the letter. My heart nearly stopped. There was no address, but the date on the envelope showed it had been posted over a year ago, before I stuck the dart in Mr Oliver's neck. This had to be the letter I'd thought was from Mum way back then.

Dear Alec,

All taken care of. Nothing to worry about this end. I trust we're quits now, old boy.

Yours,
George.

I'd been holding my breath and let it out slowly. What did this mean? Nothing about what had been taken care of. This was strange. Was this about my mother? Or was this nothing to do with her at all? There was no other letter telling Dad that she was missing, presumed dead, nor that she'd abandoned us. I must have sat there for an hour, thinking and driving myself mad, imagining the worst. My mind kept going back to the waxwork tunnel, at the museum in Malacca. Had somebody shrivelled my mother's head? Every time I thought of that, I wanted to die, and almost missed the sound of them chatting as they came up the path.

'Well, she's doing very well, isn't she?' I heard Gran say. 'She'll do well at big school, when the time comes.'

My heart gave a thump. I slipped the letter back in the book, put it into the drawer, and tiptoed out of Dad's room to my bed, where I sat with my arms folded across my stomach.

Later on in the kitchen, fighting to control my voice, I asked Father if I could see Mother's death certificate. He turned stern eyes on me. 'There isn't one. She is *presumed* dead, Emma.'

'Then how do you know?' I said, a spark of hope returning.

'Because we were told.'

'But by who?'

'Whom, Emma.'

'By whom?'

Dad got up to leave. 'George Parrott had the details.'

I doggedly followed him outside. 'Write to him. Ask him.'

'Emma, I do not take my orders from you. George Parrott has informed me and that's an end to it. Now, I'm busy.'

I didn't let myself weaken and ignored the irritation in his eyes. 'When did he write? Show me the letter!'

He took a sharp breath and I noticed him struggle with himself. Then he smiled as if to say: what a silly girl, making a fuss. It was a smile meant to make me feel foolish.

'Now then, Emma. Have I got this right? Don't you believe what your father is telling you?'

I knew I was digging a hole for myself but couldn't help it. 'I just want you to write to him. What's wrong with that?'

'I received the letter a month ago. Now, young lady, if you know what's good for you, not another word.' He turned his back on me and shut the shed door.

Was my dad lying to me? There had been no sign of a letter like that in his room, nothing from George Parrott about Mum being presumed dead. Though I suppose if one had arrived, Dad could have just thrown it away.

Would he have done that though? I wasn't very happy and I felt as if I'd had no questions answered at all.

I went upstairs, sat on my bed again and opened the notebook I hid under my pillow so Gran didn't see. Sometimes I felt the world was too unfair, so when things got really bad I wrote stories. I loved the way you could make up anything you wanted. Whatever else, I would be a writer when I grew up. When I imagined stories in my head, I could pretend to be anyone I wanted to be.

I lost myself in a tale about grey-eyed statues that came to life and used their stony hands to throttle people. One of them was just about to get Dad when I heard him come back in. Veronica was there and they were talking. I overheard him say Gran needed to go into an old people's home, and that the local authority would be offering a place before too long. When Veronica came up to say hello I was almost crying. She came across, put an arm round my shoulder and stroked my cheek. I moved away.

'How are you getting on at boarding school?'

'Okay,' I sniffed.

'No promises, but if you make a really good effort, I think there's a chance your father might let you come back to live at home.'

I glared at her. 'He said school told him I wasn't ready.'

'I know, but things can change . . . I'm so sorry, Emma. I can never replace your mother, but if you let me I'll do my best.'

I didn't trust myself to speak.

'I know,' she said, 'I'll pick you up from school one day and we'll have a whole day out in Cheltenham. The works. Tea at the Oriental Café on the Promenade, a picture at the Gaumont. What do you say?'

I thought about it. Did this mean she was on my side? Or did it mean she really was trying to take Mum's place, and only pretending she wasn't?

'Why would you want to do that?'

'I haven't forgotten what it's like to be young you know.'

I glanced at her pale powdery cheek, frosted pink nails, tight pin curls, and wondered if that was true. It must take ages to get those curls so exact I thought, and ran my fingers through my own unruly hair. Still red, still wild.

'Tell you what. I'll show you my old school if you like. Wellington College for Girls in Pittville Circus. Oh my gosh, we had so much fun hiding in the warren of corridors there. I remember it had a battery of tall windows staring out on to the street. Thirteen altogether. Or was it fourteen? We used to love those front classrooms the best.'

She smiled, kissed me on the forehead with cool lips and winked. 'And I'll show you where we used to hang around for the boys at the Grammar School.'

When she left I went to the window and flung it wide open, then rubbed the lipstick off my forehead. Outside the world shone in the evening light, the trees, the church spire, even the field, but inside I felt strange and uncertain. If I were to be friends with Veronica, did that mean I'd be betraying my mum?

24

On their way back from the pool some weeks later, Jack encouraged Maz to run on, while he slowed down. The sky was golden and the air smelt sweet. For once you could forget the blanket of flies that lay over the stinking swamps, and the thorns as big as butcher's hooks waiting to tear your flesh. Lydia felt a new kind of peace. She loved the heat after the cold of the pool, and the burning sensuality. Loved the touch of Jack's body as they picked their way along the track.

He stopped and cupped her face in his hands, before kissing her forehead and then her lips.

'The child,' she said.

'He can't see. Probably at the house by now.'

She let him kiss her again, and they walked slowly on, holding hands.

As they reached the house, Maz flew out with overbright eyes. 'Channa let me in,' he said. A stream of words poured from him as he jumped up and down.

Jack laughed. 'What's the matter, Maz? Ants in your pants?'

Lydia caught him in her arms and Maz pointed at the back door.

'Wait here,' Jack said. 'Probably nothing, but just in case.'

She pulled Maz to her. The words stopped. He made little sniffing sounds instead and buried his face in her skirt. When a bird screeched in a nearby tree, she jumped.

Jack came out again. 'You'd better come and see.'

Inside, Lydia's hand flew to her chest. Broken china littered the floor. Books and clothes were dumped in heaps, and an underskirt hung over a lampshade. She felt a flash of anger at uninvited hands touching her things, picked up a broken teapot and threw it at the waste paper basket. She had the satisfaction of the teapot crashing.

'What were they looking for?' she asked.

He shook his head, squared his shoulders and got out his revolver.

'Tell me, Jack. I'm not made of glass.'

He scratched his jaw. 'Search me. They didn't find the cash under the floor, and apart from that and a few estate lists, there's not a lot here. Nothing that would merit this.'

★　★　★

Jack alerted the police, fixed a hole in the barbed wire fence, and replaced the back door lock where the intruders had broken in. The three of them ate supper in silence, then after rushing their usually drawn out bedtime story, and although Maz complained, she put him to bed early.

On the veranda, the insect repellent they burnt at night let off a faintly antiseptic odour, the bitter smell of it mixing with that of latex and rotting foliage. She watched giant moths circle the one lantern they placed at a distance from their chairs. Other than that it was dim, and the

205

whistling noise of night birds in the trees unsettled her.

'The house will be surrounded by fresh barbed wire in a couple of days,' Jack said. 'The old wire won't last. I'm afraid until then, security isn't great, even with the extra guards.'

Her shoulders slumped. She usually enjoyed a cool drink in the evening, especially after a trip to the pool, when her skin tingled from sun and cold water. Tonight nothing felt right. Her skin prickled and she felt the familiar red patches appear on her chest. Jack absentmindedly rubbed his arms, looking troubled.

Over a second Tiger beer he opened up. 'Thing is, Lyd, it isn't just the break in. I've had this.'

He reached into his back pocket, drew out a letter and handed it over. She scanned it twice. It was from Jim Dobson, Jack's manager. She read the words aloud.

It has come to my notice you are keeping a European woman and a native child at the house. It is my duty to remind you of your contract. I understand the special circumstances, but advise making alternative arrangements, at least for the child. Accordingly, I recommend a Scottish couple living not far from Penang. They run a school for local displaced children and can probably be persuaded to take him.

Her heart sank, as Jack puffed out his cheeks and sighed.

'Jim's a good type. He wouldn't recommend this if he didn't rate the couple. But it does mean I have to take notice. I could lose my job, and as I haven't saved enough yet, the penalties would be high. On the bright side, the sea at Penang's great. We could visit.'

Lydia looked up at the ink black sky, and remembered being at the seaside with a woman in a blue dress, the woman she always believed might have been her mother. She wasn't about to let just an occasional visit to the sea be the only contact Maz would have with her.

She looked Jack in the eye. 'So you're saying I can stay, but he has to go.'

Jack cleared his throat, the muscles of his broad neck standing out. 'You know the score. No wives, no kids. Not on the first tour.'

'He can't go. He needs me.'

'I have to get back to Jim tomorrow. I've already had this letter three weeks.'

'You should have said.'

'You're attached to the child. You know, things were getting better. I didn't want to — ' He shrugged.

★ ★ ★

Lydia was accustomed to Jack sleeping with a gun beside the bed, but that night it looked ominous. On the whole things had been quiet, but now she keenly felt the danger they might all be in. The police promised Jack extra guards, and Lydia hoped they'd already installed themselves at the plantation perimeter.

Despite a restless sleep, she didn't hear Jack get up, yet in the middle of the night she woke, and found him gone. She threw on her robe, and picked her way over the still-littered floor of the living room.

He was hunched up on the sofa. Gold reading glasses hung from the tip of his nose, gun on his lap, the book he'd been reading upturned at his feet. He peered over the top of the specs, and smiled a lopsided smile.

'Honestly, Jack. What the blazes is going on? You stink of whisky.'

'We can't go on like this.'

She frowned. His eyes were feverish.

He looked around the room and balled one fist hard into his open hand. 'Let's just clear off. Damn the blasted contract.'

'Clear off where?'

He flashed her a sad grin. 'I've had it, Lyd. The mosquitoes, the heat, the swamps. Most of all the bloody rubber trees. Let's just make a run for it. We can take the kid. Say he's ours.'

'Oh sure!'

'Why not? You said yourself he doesn't fit in anywhere, not Chinese, not Malay, not white.'

She noticed his drawn face, paler than usual. He looked suddenly beaten.

He picked up the gun and held it to his head. 'Bang,' he said. 'Bang, bang, bang!' And dropped the gun on the table.

She went to him, cradled his head. 'Oh, Jack.'

He carried on looking at the place where he'd dropped the gun.

She spoke softly. 'You said it yourself. Aren't

things a little better now? I mean with us.'

There was a long silence. If Jack was depressed, his was usually a more reserved kind of sorrow.

In the end he shrugged. 'It's just the drink. You know I'd do anything for you, Lyddy.'

He picked up his gun, lifted her too, and carried her to bed. While he fell asleep quickly, she lay awake, curled herself round him and listened to him breathe.

★ ★ ★

After Jack set off for early muster, she cleared up, and jumped each time the house creaked. In the living room she flicked through the book Jack had been reading: *A Survival Guide*. On the hall floor she found an English recipe book, earmarked oxtail stew and steamed pudding. It'd be good for Jack to have a reminder of home, something to cheer him up.

She made pancakes with cinnamon and sugar, then strolled across to wake Maz. We'll eat on the veranda and watch the lizards, she thought, then glanced through the hall window before opening his door. A heavy mist still circled.

She walked into Maz's room.

The window was wide open, the bed empty. She felt her heart thump. This wasn't like Maz. He always closed the shutters, understood they did it so their rooms wouldn't overheat. She closed them herself, and went through the house, calling his name. There was no sign of him.

On the veranda, hearing branches snap she spun round, but saw nothing. All round the place, she sensed the presence of the jungle.

She hurried along the covered corridor. In her day room, Channa sat cross-legged on the floor, eyes closed.

'Is Maznan with you?' Lydia asked. 'I can't find him.'

The woman looked into Lydia's face, her deep brown eyes calm and centred. She shook her head and got up. 'I help look.'

'Do you think it could be serious? You know. After the break in last night.'

Channa put a hand on her arm. 'He probably close by. I look round the back.'

Lydia nodded. She continued to call Maz. He'd been told often enough not to go far, but what if he had? What if he was lost, unable to find his way home?

Channa came round from the back.

Lydia took an eager step towards her. 'Anything?'

The woman held out a hand and opened her palm.

With a sharp intake of breath, Lydia took Maz's beads from her.

'They were on path,' Channa said. 'Near break in wire.'

'Could he have run away?' Lydia said, and began to peer through the fence surrounding the house.

'Boy happy here. No run away.'

She's right, Lydia thought, he feels at home here. He wouldn't go alone.

Channa put a hand on her shoulder and squeezed. The women exchanged looks. It seemed both knew what the other was thinking, though Lydia couldn't bring herself to say the words. Channa shook her head, and Lydia swallowed the lump in her throat. An image of Maz's smiling face came to her, the two of them writing letters and laughing at their animal drawings.

'The insurgents,' she eventually said.

Channa shrugged, but Lydia caught the look in the woman's eyes, saw that was what she believed.

'What shall we do?' she asked.

'Go back in,' Channa said. 'Wait.'

'I'll call the police.'

They went in. There was no point trying to find Maz without a guide. The plantation went on for miles, and to an untrained eye, it all looked the same. Endlessly, endlessly the same.

On the phone to the local police, she explained the situation as calmly as she was able, and managed to hold back her tears. But as she gave the man Maz's full name, her eyes filled and the tears spilled over. She put a hand to her temple, felt herself sway as the memory of finding the deserted house engulfed her. Malacca: her children gone. Her throat constricted. Not again. Surely, not again. It couldn't happen twice.

'Is he your son, madam?' the officer asked.

'No — I'm looking after him.' Lydia choked on the words.

He paused. 'Take a moment, madam.' After a moment's silence he spoke again. 'Is he English, like you? Maznan Chang is not an English name'

211

'No. Half Malay, half Chinese.'

The man made a sucking noise through his teeth. 'We'll do what we can.'

She put the phone down, and walked round the garden again, still hoping to catch sight of the child. A butterfly landed on her knee and she felt the lump in her throat come back.

By the time Jack returned for lunch, she was sitting on the veranda rocking back and forth.

'Hey, Lyddy. What on earth?'

She stopped rocking. 'Maz is missing.'

He sighed heavily. 'That's all we need.'

'Could your driver have taken him to the village?'

Jack collapsed into the chair and leant back. 'Channa's his wife. Surely she'd know if Tenuk had taken him.'

'But if she didn't know?'

'I guess we'll find out when Tenuk gets back.'

She stood up and stared at him. 'Don't you care?'

He sighed. 'I care.'

'You have a very funny way of showing it!'

After she'd hurled the accusation at him, she left the veranda, slamming the door behind her, then sat on the edge of the bath, blaming herself. She should never have brought Maz here. The worried faces of her daughters flashed in her mind, crystal clear, as if they stood in the room, Emma looking upset, Fleur chewing her fingers. Their faces receded and tears spilled down her face.

Jack came in and held out a hand. 'I'm sorry.'

She trembled as he took her hand. 'Oh God,

Jack! I can't stand it. What have they done with him?'

'We'll find him. I promise.'

He held her tight for a moment, then told her to stay put and went to search, taking two of his assistants.

She wiped her face and stared at the mirror.

★ ★ ★

The afternoon passed. Dusk. Wind snatched at leaves, and dirt spiralled in gusts. She paced the veranda, the spaces between the trees already darkening. She rubbed her temple and thought of the swamps and the vicious biting insects there. What if the rebels really did have Maz? What if they forced him to wade, chest high, in water and mud? She thought of stark camps hidden away, and the bandits who used birdcalls to signal each other — and wire to choke a person to death.

A crash startled her. She imagined their thin dark faces, with nothing to eat but bowls of cold rice. How would Maz survive?

She shifted tense muscles and told herself she was letting her imagination run away with her. Maybe he was with his mother. She peered deeper into the trees, but it had grown too black to see. Nothing looked familiar once darkness fell. The jungle waited, huge and black, crawling with hostile life. And Lydia knew, unless a full moon lit the tunnels of trees, or until the stars came out, the blackness was a time for throats to be slit soundlessly, and children to be stolen.

25

The idea of the new villages was to isolate the terrorists from their supporters. Lydia knew that, but was still shocked by sharp bamboo spikes, embedded in a moat surrounding three, parallel, chain wire fences and, at intervals, huge observation towers.

She glanced at Jack. In a white, freshly laundered shirt he looked handsome, but out of place.

'The police will let us know if they get any leads,' he said. 'But I reckon this place is our best bet. Unless he's in the jungle.'

Once through security, they began to search.

Lydia held her nose. 'It smells awful.'

'It's latrines,' Jack said. 'There's no running water.'

The place was bigger than she'd thought, noisy, and packed with people. For a moment her heart sank. 'This'll be like looking for a needle in a haystack. How many people are there?'

'A couple of thousand.'

'What do they do here?'

'Some are my tappers.'

'And the rest?'

He shrugged. 'The rest are a problem.'

Lydia brushed off the mosquitoes from her arms, and looked at the chilling rows of drab huts, none of them bigger than a garden shed.

'It looks like a concentration camp,' she said.

A bell clanged and a loudspeaker bellowed an announcement. The crowd thickened, and the noise stepped up a level. People began making their way to a raised platform, at one end of a bare open area. It was six o'clock and growing dark.

Her heart lifted. 'Look! Over there.'

A small, brown-skinned boy hung back in the shadow of a hut.

'Maz?' she called and stepped towards him. 'Is it you?'

The boy came out of the darkness, a ragged, dark-eyed child.

She sighed. 'I suppose it was a bit too much to hope for.'

Jack put an arm round her.

'What if he's hurt? Is there a doctor?'

Jack shook his head. 'Shall we hang on here? If Maz is anywhere, he'll likely be watching.'

'Not if he's held captive, he won't.'

'Let's just scan the crowd in case, and put the word round after. Try not to make it too obvious that you're looking.'

She tried to ignore the stale smell of sweating bodies as they followed the horde gathering at the stage. Jack slipped them into a gap near the front, where lanterns covered with green and orange saris were hung for jungle atmosphere. A beaten gong signalled the start.

Chinese dancers, in traditional dress and elaborate headgear, came out from behind a makeshift curtain. Lydia looked past the performers, head swivelling, eyes scanning the crowd. There were dozens of children that might have been Maz. She'd start to smile, think she'd spotted him, become excited, but every time it was not.

The Assistant DO stepped out to introduce the play.

'It's a piece of propaganda from our side,' Jack said. 'To persuade young girls to stop idolising the insurgents.'

Right now Lydia didn't care. All she cared about was finding Maz.

The play began.

'Smile. Try to act normally,' Jack whispered.

Lydia wasn't listening. Blood pounded in her ears. She'd seen someone. Not Maz, but in the crowd on the other side of the stage, Lili stood squashed between two rough-looking men. No longer dressed smartly, she seemed unwell. Shocked by the girl's thin face, Lydia tugged on Jack's elbow and turned to him.

'There — it's Lili. She looks awful.'

When she glanced back, the girl had gone.

'I don't think it would have been her,' he said. 'Lili knows how to take care of herself. I'm sure she's okay. Come on, let's go. Maz isn't here.'

'Where next?'

'Search the outer areas. Then work back to the centre.'

After elbowing their way out, they passed a square metal container, rather like a large hut, and heavily padlocked. Dozens of birds were scavenging in the dust.

'It's a food silo,' he said, seeing her frown. 'The police control the supply.'

They carried on towards the end of the camp,

216

where a ripe stench of swamp reached them from beyond the moat. Here the paths between the huts were muddy, the insect-laden air heavy, and no children ran about. Lydia looked past the wire and into the jungle's dark green depths. She felt its silence even more than its noise, couldn't bear to think of Maz out there.

'Not much hope here,' Jack said.

She shook her head, and crossed her fingers that he'd be here somewhere.

They retraced their steps and stopped at a coffee house. 'Wait here,' he said. 'I'll ask the owner.'

Dozens of leaflets flapped in the dust. She picked one up, and stared at pictures of fat ex-terrorists, showing off in front of their starving comrades. The Chinese letters stamped across the top were no doubt a call to surrender. She sat to wait for Jack, watched a bunch of children run along the narrow path. Could Maz be one of them? She called his name. None turned. Instead, a man came up, smelling of strong tobacco. He held out his hand, his face too close, reached in the pocket of his loose black trousers. Lydia drew back, afraid he was about to pull a knife. But all he held in his hand was a worn cloth purse.

She searched in her bag for coins, and put ten cents on the table. She felt uneasy. It was nearing dusk and paraffin lanterns shining from the huts made the place look friendlier, but her heart still thumped.

Jack came out with cups of coffee.

'I'm glad you're back. Any news?'

'No. But look. It's Bert.'

He pointed at a man keeping an eye on the crowd on the other side of the narrow street, while two soldiers went from hut to hut, and occasionally dragged people out.

'They're looking for anything illegal, to stop stuff getting out. If they do find something, the owner will be detained for eighteen months.'

'Without trial?' Lydia said.

He nodded. 'I'm afraid so.'

They went over to Bert and she asked him about Maz.

The policeman shook his head. 'The local Malay cops told me about a missing child. Sorry, I've not heard anything. Come on. I'll look with you, then see you back to the exit.'

They turned into a shop a hundred yards down. It was dark inside with two pools of light from Kerosene lamps. Jack questioned the shopkeeper and asked him to keep an eye out for the boy.

They continued to ask at each shop and coffee house for another half hour, then Bert led them past the smell of the swamp again and back to security, where a crowd seemed to be heading. Lydia felt her skin prickle. A baby screamed, and a row of beggars lined the rubbish-strewn street. Jack held Lydia's elbow and barged his way through the crowd.

All the time, she searched for Maz.

She missed his trusting pale eyes, his sweet face, the way he counted and chased butterflies. Couldn't bear that he was lost somewhere in this alien world. She prayed again that his mother had taken him, but not to be with the rebels in the jungle. She glanced up. Even against the darkening sky, the jungle still stood out, black, hump-backed, and ragged. Birds of prey circled overhead. She wanted to cry.

Shrill voices reached them from a group clustered at the exit. She felt an undercurrent of fear. Jack stiffened and she craned her neck to see. Her mouth fell open and she grabbed Jack's arm.

Two corpses had been thrown in the mud inside the enclosure, stripped naked and riddled with bullet holes. In the gloom Lydia stared at their broken emaciated bodies and lifeless eyes. Somebody's son, somebody's brother. She heard the sound of counting, and looked round to see a row of old women in black, pointing out the number of holes to each other and shaking their heads.

'It's a great deterrent,' Bert said, viewing the bodies.

Lydia let go of Jack's arm and stepped back. 'So on the one hand we entertain them and on the other we scare them half to death.'

'That's pretty much it,' Jack said.

'But they're people, Jack.'

'Probably the same ones who burnt down the rest house,' Bert said, stony faced. 'They want to frighten us, make us feel so unsafe we give in.'

At a loss for words, Lydia stopped listening. The smell, the sights, the noise were too much. She felt herself sway, noticed Jack scowl, then hold out a hand to steady her.

'Don't fool yourself,' he said. 'They call it an

Emergency for the insurance, but mark my words it's war. And everyone's on the make.'

'Well, heaven help us,' she said.

Jack snorted. 'Heaven. I don't think so.'

The floodlights at the gate came on, and a tall man let them through and across the moat, his shaven head and upright stature a reminder of Adil, the man she'd met on her train journey. For a moment she even thought it was Adil. Wished it might be him, come to help them with his knowledge of how things worked in this country. Help them find Maz. But, of course, it was not, and as they passed she saw the resemblance was only slight. They were on their own. Though Jack would do his best, there would be no help to find a little half-caste boy. Not from the police, not from anyone.

26

My mother's disappearance was an unbearable hurt I kept hidden almost all the time at boarding school. She might be missing but I didn't believe she was dead. At night I returned to Malaya, to pounding rain that splashed a yard up in the air as it hit the pavement, and monsoon drains swimming with dirty overflowing water. I heard my mother's voice, woke drenched in sweat and shaking from the loss, terrified she had never loved me.

By day, Susan Edwards and I poked fun at teachers *and* pupils. It was our only way to survive. She told me her mother had come home from India, pregnant, and had given birth in a hostel for unmarried mums, in Birmingham. The social found a family who wanted a little girl, but even after they adopted her, Susan didn't fit in, and this had resulted in banishment to Penridge Hall.

'Who's paying your fees?' I asked her, during an unofficial break in a trudge through the countryside. Cross-country trekking they called it.

'The local authority. There was nowhere else to put me. Rebecca's the same, though she won't admit it. I overheard the head telling a teacher no one will have her. She's actually funded by a charity for disturbed children, and it was either here or borstal.'

I was surprised. Susan nodded and pulled a face, but it made me wonder.

'Gran said Dad's stony broke,' I said. 'And she almost let slip that it isn't him paying for me. At least I think she did.'

'Why not just ask him?'

'You don't know my dad.'

'We could find out,' Susan said lightly.

'How?'

She tapped the side of her nose.

'I did attack that man. Would that make a difference?'

'I'd have thought you'd get borstal for that.'

'He didn't press charges. His sister's Dad's girlfriend.'

'It could be the education authority, or a charity, like Rebecca.'

I frowned. 'But I thought her parents were rich?'

'So she says!'

We were standing under the canopy of a wide horse chestnut, the best tree for conkers in the autumn. I looked at the view of washed-out fields and smudgy clouds.

'If the school want us to go trekking, they should take us to Malaya,' I said, and stuck out my chin. 'In the jungle.'

'Oh, shut up about Malaya. What do you think?' She peered ahead. 'We can dive off in a minute, and head back the quick way, through the woods.'

I thought of the night I'd spent there alone. 'I don't know.'

'Or we can go down the back lane. Go on, Em. It might be your dad or it might be the council. Don't you want to know who's paying? It'll be a laugh. There's nobody in the office now. And at least we'll get out of the bloody drizzle.'

I loved the way she swore, dark eyes shining, and she was right, the dull grey sky was hardest to bear. And on Wednesdays, straight after lunch, the whole school went on a hike across the countryside, all the teachers too.

We climbed over a fallen-down piece of fencing, jumped the ditch at the edge of the road, crossed a meadow where the long grass was cool on our legs, and immediately were in the back lane. Half an hour later, we approached the school buildings, and the only place to climb into the grounds from the back lane, unseen.

Inside the building we skulked round corridors, hung back in alcoves, and hissed at each other like secret agents.

'I'll wait here and watch the corridor. You just go and check the office really is unlocked,' she said.

We had to stop ourselves getting the giggles as I padded to the headmistress's room, turned the handle, and pushed the door open. Inside it was stacked floor to ceiling with files. I beckoned Susan over.

Her face fell. 'Blimey. There are hundreds. We'll never find yours in a million years.'

'We'd better start then,' I said. 'But remember, put each one back exactly as you find it.'

'I'd rather mess them all up,' she said with a laugh, and marched round the room yanking open random drawers. She picked out a magazine from the waste paper basket.

'Ooh get her! She reads *Woman and Home*.' She held out a picture of a woman with neatly set hair, wearing a pinny, with a fixed smile on her face.

I snatched it and read the words in a posh clipped voice: *'For every woman, happiness and fulfilment lie in the kitchen and nursery, the most rewarding and satisfying places for a woman to be. With an eight-page pull out of knitting patterns and a sensitive story by Lucilla Smythe-Watkins.'*

Susan stuck out her tongue.

I grabbed a chair and almost fell into a bowl of dog food. We hardly ever saw the terrier. From the chair I was able to scan the top files close up, and saw there wasn't any need to move them. You just needed to crick your neck and bend your head sideways. Each one had a sticky label on the spine, with a name and year of arrival clearly typed.

'Aren't they in alphabetical order?'

I stared at them. 'Some are. I'll keep going up here. You look down there.'

'But they go back for years. And they're all different colours.'

As the sun came out and threw a pattern of leaves on an open newspaper on the head's desk, Susan picked her way through more magazines piled up on a chair beside it.

'Get her! There's one here with Marilyn Monroe on the front.'

'I thought we were looking for my file.'

'The star who shines,' she read, *'the truth behind the dream.'*

'Oh my God, I think I've found it!' I pulled out a file with my name in bold letters across the front and side.

The head's voice carried up from below the window.

Susan froze.

'You go,' I said.

Susan shot me a grateful smile over her shoulder and dashed out. Seconds later I heard another pair of footsteps tapping along the corridor and a shrill neighing voice call out.

'What are you doing in this corridor, girl?'

'I felt sick, Miss,' Susan said, in a loud voice, so that I'd know.

'Did you ask permission to leave the walk?'

'No, Miss. I'm going to be sick, Miss.'

'Well, hurry along to sickbay. Though I can't imagine why you came this way.'

I quickly scanned the room. What if she brings the terrier too? He'll be sure to growl.

Behind the desk, two sash windows overlooked the playing fields, with floor-length curtains blocking out some of the daylight. I had no choice. There was nowhere else. I slid between the semi-drawn curtain and the window, clutched the file to my chest, and hoped the twilight wouldn't make the headmistress close them and therefore catch me there. I held my breath, scared that with eyes in the back of her head, she would be able to see right through the curtain.

She turned on a lamp and golden light filled the room. Thank goodness, no dog. She sat at her desk only a yard from me, pushed the newspaper aside and started to write. It went on for about an hour, though I daren't risk a peek at my watch. The walkers laughed and joked as they arrived back, and a car accelerated in the distance. I heard the mistresses' voices hurrying them along, sounding grumpy from the walk. They'd be doing evening register soon. I was dying to spend a penny, and my foot had gone to sleep. It went on and on, the curtains smelling so badly of chalk dust, I struggled not to sneeze. When the phone rang, I crossed my fingers and sucked in my breath.

'Hello. Miss Watson. Penridge Hall.'

Oh, please let it mean she has to go.

She swung in her creaky swivel chair, talked for a few minutes then got up and yawned. As she cleared the desk, it felt like an age. Finally she switched off the light, and only then walked out of the office, locking the door from the other side. Oh no! That was it. I'd be found. In the morning. All I could think was I'd have to go to the loo in the waste bin. Then I realised the office was only one floor up, and beneath it, to the left, stood the bicycle sheds. Could the other window be directly over the sheds? It was a sash window and a bit stiff, but I pushed hard, and opened it enough to look out sideways at the blue-black sky. I crossed my fingers, looked down, and with a sigh of relief, saw one end of a bicycle shed directly below.

27

In the six months following Maz's disappearance, Lydia swung between hope that he was with his mother, and fear that he was not. Not knowing for certain was hardest to cope with. But all her calls to the District Officer's office, to the police, to anyone she could think of, had turned up no leads. Jack looked for him in Ipoh, and all the nearby villages, but Maz had simply vanished.

Lydia felt low. The suffocating iron-grey sky didn't help. It was the afternoon and there was more terrorist trouble on the plantation. Jack, on the phone to his boss, was having a hard time persuading Jim to allow her to stay longer. His thick blond hair all over the place, he ran fingers through to flatten it, and sighed. Some of Jack's Malay police had been found to be corrupt too, and that wasn't helping.

Jim was amenable, but Lydia knew he wouldn't care for the disruption her presence might cause to the smooth running of the estate. It took time for an assistant manager like Jack to find his feet, cope with the loneliness, understand the harsh complexities of plantation life, and earn trust. It was physically tough too. He had to be strong, have the resilience to stumble through squelching undergrowth, hacking his way through thick grass, and dealing with hostile tappers every day. And that was without the constant threat posed by Chinese rebels. If danger was present, as it usually was, Jack had no choice but to ignore it.

Lydia looked up as he put down the phone. He shrugged. 'He'll let me know.'

She thought of all the times she'd shut him out and felt guilty. He had a good heart, but had never expected any of this when they met. She looked over at him. Now they only had each other, Jack talked of their future with shining eyes.

'Come to bed,' he said. 'It's too hot for anything else.'

It was tender gentle lovemaking they had now. They fell back on the pillows, his tanned arm resting across her middle. She ran a palm over the fair hairs on his arm, a silver bangle on her wrist glinting in the light. Sunlight streamed through the shutters as he repeatedly tickled her ribs, until tears of laughter ran down her cheeks. They listened to a magpie robin sing outside the window, then he hung an orange and gold sari over the shutter. Pink light washed over the room.

'I like your hair long like this,' he said, and pulled out one of the growing number of silver threads.

'Ouch!'

He pushed the damp mass of hair away from her face, then brought her hand to his mouth and kissed her palm. 'I like them,' he said and held the hair to the light where it shone silvery pink.

She frowned.

'For goodness sake, there are hardly any.'

They lapsed into a peaceful silence. He traced the blue veins of her inner wrist. 'Tell me about the girls again.'

Her heart lifted. She had no fear of their silent presence now, called for it even, replayed over and over the days they were born, fat solid little babies. Christmases, special occasions. Now the worst was over, their deaths had become a part of her, but it was the daily routine of their lives that was in the process of becoming lost. Their first words, their huge pupils and burning cheeks when they were sick. The funny little looks, the laughter. Now, fearful of forgetting, it raised her spirits to talk of them, and Jack knew it, his arms encircling her as she spoke. She shaped her back against him, his face so close she felt his breath on the nape of her neck.

'Emma always read lying on her stomach, waving her left foot in the air. We had this big old camphor wood chest. I kept all the old fancy dress costumes in there, and they used to fight over whose turn it was to wear the Peter Pan crocodile outfit.'

She longed for the old, jam-packed days. For Fleur to hold out a hand and say, 'I love you, Mummy.' For Emma to run in covered in mud and spiders. But her girls would have been older now, Emma nearly fourteen, Fleur ten. She tried to picture how they'd look but it hurt too much. She thought about Jack instead. He was strong and handsome, and she was grateful that he'd taken her in. She loved the blond hair that fell over his eyes, and his big hands as he brushed it aside.

He held her tight, as tight as if he was part of her, then drew back, moisture in his eyes. He reached under the bed and scattered some fresh petals over the sheets.

She laughed. 'What's this, you handsome devil? A new seduction technique?'

'We could marry. When my tour's up.'

'On the level?'

There was a silence between them for a moment.

'Don't we need Alec's death certificate? George did say he'd sort that out, but I still haven't heard.'

'You can remind him,' Jack said. 'But in principle. What do you say?'

She kissed him hard on the mouth, her heart thumping with pleasure. 'I say, yes.'

'Well then, Mrs Plantation Officer, I have something for you.'

A wide grin signalled his intention, and after the sighs and the moans were done, he lay smoking, eyes fixed on the ceiling.

'My sex fiend,' she said, and rested her chin on his shoulder.

He flexed his muscles and laughed. 'I have a question for you.'

'Another?'

'Where do you want to live?'

'In Malaya?'

'In the world.'

She raised her eyebrows. 'I don't know. I haven't thought. What about you?'

'Australia. Perth, I was thinking. There's money to be made out there. A mate of mine is setting up a copper mine. Wants a partner.'

'What's it like?'

'Don't really know. Hills, of course. Sea.'

'By the sea?'

'Yeah. We could have a boat.'

She laughed and snuggled up. 'It sounds great, Jack.'

An idea struck her and she felt hope rise suddenly. If they married she could have another baby. Together they'd make a new life. Whatever was still broken inside her would mend. The loss of her girls was a scar for ever, so total that for a long time there had been no comprehending a life without them. Yet here she was. She had survived. And could it be that at some point, the thought of them might not dominate every day?

★ ★ ★

In the intensity of the afternoon, when the urge to sleep had taken over, they were woken by the phone. Jack went into the hall to pick up.

'Yes, absolutely, I'll drive down immediately,' she heard him say.

He came back in and grinned. 'That was Bert. You'll never believe it, but someone has found Maznan.'

She gasped and sat bolt upright. 'Oh, Jack. Really?'

'Better get moving. I have to go now before the curfew, though the line was terribly distorted, I could hardly make out a word. And there's some kind of trouble with one of the tappers. But can you credit it? We're going to collect Maznan, after all this time!'

231

'Get Tenuk to drive you.'

'Well, he's not really on duty now.'

'Still.'

Jack went under the covered walkway to the servants' day quarters, but came back frowning.

'Nobody there.'

She raised her brows. 'Odd, but never mind, I'll come. I'd really like to.'

'We'll take the van,' he said. 'The car's low on petrol.'

She dressed, thrilled to soon be seeing the boy again, in a way Jack didn't understand. How could he know the unbearable bittersweet hold a child has on your heart. How you'd lay down your life in a heartbeat. How, when they die, it's as much as you can do to take another breath.

Outside, she heard the usual chorus of frogs, and looked up as lumpy clouds, edged with light, rolled down from the top of the hills. She waited while Jack brought round the small van. The side windows were armoured with big sheets of steel, and there were only narrow slits to look through. It was safer than the car, though Jack rarely went out without his driver, Tenuk, or one or two Special Constables. If the SCs weren't available he took the Malay *mata-mata*, especially when they used the heavy truck to convey workers. Jack said he didn't know whom he trusted the least, the Malay police or the Chinese rebels. But this time they were only going as far as the village.

Lydia had missed the times when she had breakfasted on the veranda with Maz, missed watching the shadowy trees, and listening to the day birds, before the baking sun sent them indoors. She hugged herself. It was all going to be okay now. She felt a sense of elation. Someone had found Maz. They just had to collect him and he'd be safe again, she and Jack would be married, *and* they'd have a baby. All of them live together. It crossed her mind she didn't know if Jack wanted children.

She started to climb in the front of the van.

'No, Lyd. Hop in the back. Safer to stick to the rules.'

She groaned, but full of hope, complied.

'I wonder why Channa's not there,' she said, leaning forward and speaking into the gap in a loud voice. 'She'd usually be resting before making supper.'

'She might be visiting relatives. She sometimes goes on her bicycle after lunch. But what great news,' Jack shouted back. Steel, partially dividing the front from the back, made it hard to hear.

Feeling a rush of excitement, and longing to see Maz, she hugged herself. 'I'm so happy. Did Bert say any more?'

'No. There was something going on.'

It was neither the time nor the place, but she couldn't stop herself. He didn't hear at first, so she shouted the second time.

'What do you think about having a baby?'

The van jerked and Lydia held her breath. What if it wasn't what he wanted? He wanted a boat, cricket, rugby. He might not want to be a father. Men had adventures. Women had children. That was just the way of things.

'Bloody Ada, Lydia. That's enough to give a

man a heart attack.' He paused. 'Let's get Maz back first, then see what the future brings.'

'Maybe we could adopt him.'

He drove on for a while in silence and Lydia, smiling at the thought of seeing Maz, felt full of energy. She'd make him a little pageboy suit. She wouldn't wear white, but they'd get married the moment this first tour ended, not long now, and straightaway try for a baby. For the first time the future looked really bright, and the world, wide open, waited for them. They could make a new life in Perth, or anywhere they chose. Her mind travelled off in a stream of imagining. Their life together. Maz, and the child they'd have together. A little brother or sister for him. Their garden with a big lawn, apple trees and a swing for them both.

She was shaken from her thoughts by a terrific din. The van swerved to the right and ended up wedged nose down in a storm ditch.

'Get right down, Lydia,' Jack hissed and pushed his head through the gap in the metal that separated them.

'What's happened?'

'Don't know.' He blew a kiss, and passed through his spare revolver.

She took it with trembling hands.

'Point this through the slits and don't hesitate to use it. And whatever happens don't get out.'

Her heart thumped. 'What about you?'

'I've got to look.'

'No, Jack!'

She heard him struggle with the door as he got out, then the sound of shrill Chinese voices. She peered through the slit in the steel at the side of the van, but round at the front, Jack was out of her sight. In the split second before the shot was fired, she was certain she saw Lili standing back from the road, half hidden behind a rubber tree. She saw the girl gasp and cover her open mouth with her hand, her eyes wide with shock.

Lydia's mind spun with a thousand images. Jack safe, Jack with her. Married. Happy. A baby. Their baby. She barely registered the second shot. Everything went unnaturally quiet. With her fingers on the trigger of Jack's gun, her body froze, though her heart raced in terror as the silence grew. She felt sick, violently sick, as if her entire body wanted to drive out the truth behind that shot.

This could not be happening. Not Jack. Not after losing the girls. She closed her eyes and all she could see was the look on Lili's face.

In the back of the van she doubled over and began to shiver. She clenched her fists and shoved them into her eye sockets, refusing to believe it, pleading with God, for the warmth of his body and the light in his bright blue eyes to still be there. His slow wicked smile when he wanted sex, his big hands. His throaty laugh. She heard the sound of whining mosquitoes, saw the jungle snakes and scorpions in her mind's eye. Her body was rigid with shock, but she had to move. Get out. See Jack. Be with him.

She reached across and tried the back door. Locked.

Of course, it only opened from the outside. She stood up and crawled head first through the narrow gap into the front of the van. When she straightened up, she caught sight of his blood, so much blood pooling on the tarmac, the air thick with the sweet salty odour of it. With one hand covering her mouth, she pushed open the door, now hanging at an angle, squeezed down into, and then climbed out of, the storm ditch. She ran, falling to her knees where Jack lay face down on the road. It began to rain, the water washing his life away in a stream along the road.

She gently rolled his body over to look at his face. His lips were white, his eyes vacant. Dead eyes. Not even a hint of accusation there. So quickly. It had happened so quickly. She remembered the warmth of his lips against hers, his smile, the way he tickled her. Tears sprang and slid down her cheeks.

Oh, Jack.

The rain stopped, leaving the sound of drips, and steam rising into the air. In the lengthening shadows, she got up to pee, squatted in tangled undergrowth, not taking her eyes from him for a second. Didn't care if they shot her too. She deserved it. She blamed herself. If she hadn't pestered him about Maz, and if he'd been able to concentrate on his job, this would never have happened. She didn't notice the night descend. But when it came fully, she welcomed the curtain of darkness that separated them from the rest of the world. She lay on the road beside him, wrapped herself round him one last time, held him, kept him safe, her clothes soaking up his blood.

* * *

It was a glittering dawn when they found her. Four of them. Two police constables in khaki, Bert and another SC in an armoured lorry. She looked up and glimpsed silver birds swooping in the dawn sky, behind Bert's head. His fingertips reached out and touched her hands. He lifted her off the ground. Bert with the strong Northern accent and purposeful walk. How incongruous the British are in a Malay jungle, she thought.

He rubbed her hands to warm them. 'Come on now, Lyd,' he said. 'There's nowt we can do for Jack.'

She felt Jack's loss physically, as if a kick in the guts had knocked the stuffing from her. She flinched at Bert's touch and folded over, her throat burning with grief. One arm tight across her midriff, she held herself together. When he led her to his car, she turned towards him, but for a moment couldn't look him in the face.

'We were on our way to see you,' she mumbled.

Bert looked puzzled.

She straightened up and stood in front of him with angry eyes. 'You called Jack. Told him someone had found Maz. You must remember. You called him. Said to go to the village.'

'No.'

She clutched his shirt and shouted. 'You must remember.'

He gently removed her hands, then held her by the shoulders.

'Lydia, I never called Jack.'

237

The sound of the shot echoed in her head. He was wrong. He must be wrong.

'There's nothing we can do,' he said. 'I'm afraid Jack's been a victim of some kind of trap. I'm so sorry.'

Her legs were trembling so much she felt they might buckle, but Bert's words clinched it. She slowly shook her head. He was wrong; there *was* something she could do. She'd find out who had betrayed Jack, work out who'd really phoned him. Find out who knew he'd be on the road without police protection, whatever it took. And she'd start by finding Lili.

She turned her back when the other two constables walked over to Jack, couldn't bear to see their struggle as they lifted his stiff body, or see them shake their heads at yet another waste of life.

★ ★ ★

The funeral took place the next day. The cloudburst had blown over, and it was a hot blue day. There were few formalities, as you couldn't delay in the sweltering Malayan heat. A small group, eyes turned from the hole in the ground, gave each other uncertain smiles. Holding a wilting bunch of yellow canna lilies, she nodded at Bert and another officer, at one or two mates of Jack's she didn't know, Jack's boss, Jim, and a beautiful Chinese woman, who scattered rose petals on the ground. The woman didn't speak to anyone, but muttered to herself, her eyes expressionless.

They held a short service outside. The grass, damp from the recent rain, shone in the sunlight, and wind lifted particles of earth from around the grave. How cruelly life goes on, she thought, and stared at the ground as Jim read out a poem.

Do not stand at my grave and weep
I am not there — I do not sleep.
I am in the morning hush.
I am in the graceful rush
Of beautiful birds in circling flight.
I am in the star shine of the night.
Do not stand at my grave and cry —
I did not die.

It was fitting. Jack believed in the natural world, not God, nor an afterlife in heaven or hell. 'Hell's this bloody place,' he'd say with a groan.

The coffin was lowered into the ground. She'd chosen a decorated one, and paid for it with a little of the money Jack had hidden under the floorboards, though he'd have called it a waste. The rest of the money she'd use to live on until it ran out. She thought of his words when he'd shown it to her. In case you need it, he'd said. There was a snapping, crashing sound from the depths of the trees, then, just for a moment, as if suddenly suspended, the world stilled. She felt a dull ache behind her eyes as she crumpled some dry earth from the plantation garden on top of the coffin and tossed the lilies on top. Right beside her feet, displaced by the grave, a nest of ants was swarming. Motionless, she smelt the earth and the lilies, shocked by the sight of the coffin, and frozen into silence by thoughts of the place where his living heart used to be. Then she took a deep breath and listened as the noises of the jungle came back: the rattles and thumps, the hum, the buzz.

Bert gently led her to where someone had brought chilli chicken drumsticks and honeyed dates, which they ate with their fingers, sitting cross-legged on the ground. After the priest left, they drank gin from the bottle and each in turn remembered Jack. The gravediggers came to fill in the grave, so they retreated further into the shade of the trees to watch. In the distance a lone dog barked. A sad, forlorn sound. When the light started to dim, someone produced a small lantern and Lydia gazed at orange moths hovering in its light, a gentle breeze cooling the air.

After a while Bert turned to her. 'Better be off. Is Jim taking you back with him?'

'He's taking me to Jack's to pick up my things, then tomorrow I'm heading south.'

'You okay for cash?'

She nodded, and over his shoulders, in between the trees, saw a figure move. For a moment her heart filled with a raw, angry feeling. 'Wasn't that Lili?' she said.

'Sorry, didn't see. By the way, do you know where Jack's other gun is? We couldn't account for it.'

'I gave it to Jim,' she said.

Just as he was getting into his car, she remembered the Chinese woman who hadn't joined them for the graveside booze-up. Flushed from the gin, she asked Bert about her.

He turned his palms up and shrugged. 'Old flame of Jack's, I should think. Does it matter now?'

She shook her head. Nothing mattered now.

Fragments of sound came on the breeze, the drone of insects, a car engine revving, the moans of the jungle. For a moment the world glistened in the long low light. She thought of Jack's large shadow and their once secret laughter. So long ago and before all this. She thought of his back, his strong shoulders, and how she'd curled herself to him, so deeply loved it was as if they were breathing one another. Her heart raced, almost tripping itself up, as she turned round to look at the mound of earth that covered him. 'Goodbye, my love,' she whispered, no longer holding back her tears. 'Forgive me.'

Worn out words, but all she could manage.

28

I avoided the homework monitor and stared at the file. It was thick and I hardly dared peek inside the sepia cover. Nosy people find out things they'd rather not know. That's what Gran always said. In any case, it was probably the local authority paying, so that wouldn't be a surprise, but a thought flashed in my mind. Was there a chance it might be Veronica? The door swung open.

Susan sprang across the room with a wide grin. 'How did you get away?'

'I jumped.'

'Crikey!' She gave me a dig in the ribs. 'You haven't opened it yet, have you?'

I shook my head.

She grinned. 'Give it here.'

I passed it over and looked on as she flipped open the front cover, scanned the first page, flicked on a bit, then stopped, her smile fading. She covered her mouth with her hand.

'What?'

Without a word she closed the file and passed it back to me.

The front pages gave name, address, age, parents' details. The next page stopped me. I glanced up at Susan, then flicked through, as page followed page. Notes from teachers. Copies of letters sent to my father describing my academic progress, and complaining of only a few minor incidents of disobedience. They said that while there was still some room for improvement in attitude, I was generally doing well, and that it was time I went home, because they'd done all they could. They recommended I'd do better now in my home environment.

'But he told me they said I wasn't ready,' I blurted out.

Susan's nostrils flared. 'That's mean.'

I turned another page, and there a letter from my father explained that my mother was missing. But not to say anything to me. He'd decide when the time was right. Better I stayed at boarding school, for stability.

I gulped. 'If I hadn't overheard, was he ever going to tell me?'

Susan patted my back.

'Dad wants to make space for Veronica. That's why he wants me to stay here.'

I hated the thought of that and stood up, pressing my cheek against the dormitory wall to feel the coolness. 'And he wants Gran to go into an old people's home.'

The idea of Gran away from the house she had lived in for so long was too sad. And she wasn't that bad. I saw Veronica's glowing white face. Perhaps she really was behind it, giving Dad the money for my school, quietly urging him to get rid of Gran.

'Dad wants to make space,' I said again.

'What?'

My mouth twisted. I'd spoken quietly, almost to myself, forgetting Susan. 'He only wants Veronica and Fleur. He's getting rid of everybody else.'

'Do you really think so?' Susan said.

'I don't know.'

'Can you see any bills?'

'Not yet.'

I was puzzled. If Gran was right, my father couldn't afford the fees. But if the local authority was paying, wouldn't they cough up only for as long as was necessary.

Susan looked curious. 'Come on, Em. Let's see what else there is.' She took the folder and flipped over a few more pages, then stared at the ones at the back.

'What?'

She put the folder into my hands. Her voice faltered. 'Em, they're all from some solicitor.'

I flicked through a series of letters stapled to the bills. Term by term, all said the same thing. *Please find the enclosed cheque, covering the payment of fees for Miss Emma Cartwright, on behalf of our client.* All of them sent by a Mr N. Johnson, of Johnson, Price & Co. of Kidderminster.

'I don't understand. Who's the client?'

'It doesn't say.'

'What if I write to the solicitor?'

'They won't say. If the name's not there, it'll be confidential.'

We sat on the bed in the few remaining moments of silence, until the dorm doors flew open at the other end of the room, and girls began to file in. As soon as they did, Susan put herself in front of me, legs planted wide apart.

'Hey what happened to you two?' one of them said. Some of the others made jokey comments, but then with a snort of annoyance, Rebecca said, 'You sneaky devils. How did you get up here early? You're up to something, aren't you?'

I felt myself turn red, glad I'd slipped the file beneath the covers of my bed, and hoping no one had seen.

29

The station air smelt strongly of metal and sweat, the noise of people, trains and traders overpowering. Despite that, Lydia felt her resolve stiffen, and with some difficulty tracked down a call box. She dialled Cicely's number, took a sharp breath when her friend answered, and kept her voice level. For a moment Cicely's cool, offhand voice almost derailed her, but she pressed the receiver against her cheek, took another breath and came out with it.

'I have nowhere to go.'

She heard Cicely's sharp breath in. 'So it's true. Where are you now?'

'Here. At the station.'

'Stay right there.'

Lydia wiped the beads of sweat from her forehead, thankful that Jack, with uncanny prescience, had shown her the hoard of money he'd kept under the floorboard. She still needed to get a job, but there was enough to keep her afloat for a few months. And at least she'd made it south in one piece. This time, the journey had not involved ambushes, derailing, or diversions: everything had been surprisingly normal. So much so that she had to pinch herself, as a reminder that Jack and the girls were gone, and she wasn't simply travelling back home to Alec.

Lydia was sipping an iced lemon by the time Cicely arrived, looking crisp and smart. She brushed cool lips over Lydia's cheek. 'You can tell me all about it on the way.'

★ ★ ★

Cicely threw open the door to her town house and looked about. It was a wonderful old merchant's house, in a well-heeled part of town.

'Good. No sign of Ralph. Men never know what's really going on. Darling, you look a fright. I think a bath for you and then something to eat.'

'I always thought men were the ones who *did* know what was going on,' Lydia said.

Cicely laughed and waggled a pointed finger at her. 'You have a lot to learn, my girl.'

They walked across the quiet hall.

Cicely reached over and took Lydia's hand. 'Darling. You already know how sorry I am about Emma and Fleur. But now Jack too. It must have been utterly ghastly, but at least he died like he lived.'

Lydia's stomach turned over. 'Someone tricked him on to the road that afternoon.'

Cicely stared. 'Any idea who?'

Lili's face flashed in her mind, but Lydia chose just to shrug. 'Also a little boy I was looking after vanished. I need to make sure he's safe.' She leant back against the wall. 'Harriet Parrott might be the place to start. You know, with George's contacts. Would you help me?'

'I'll ring and tell her you'll be there tomorrow at twelve sharp. Now you stay with me as long as you need. Okay?' A wide smile lit Cicely's face. 'That's what friends are for, after all.'

Lydia followed her to the exquisite guest suite on the top floor.

'Will this suit you, madam?' Cicely said. 'No need to come down. I'll have food sent up.'

After Cicely left, Lydia dropped her bag, and looked out at the distant Straits of Malacca. Rain blurred the view, blending the colours in watery blues and lilacs. She felt her shoulders relax, hadn't realised how tense they'd been. Her room overlooked a courtyard garden, a water garden with giant lily pads and a fountain. She wandered round the guest suite. Decorated in pale pink and gold, it couldn't have been further from Jack's place. Here she had a bedroom, a bathroom, and her own sitting room. And right now a sanctuary was what she needed.

Whenever thoughts of Jack's murder threatened to defeat her, she was learning to place a palm over her heart and take deep breaths. It calmed her, and gradually the thumping rush of panic would fade. Then, to stop herself from becoming dead inside, and although it made her cry, she'd think of the good times, and the love they'd shared. Anything to resist the image of his dead body as it lay on the tarmac. To think about that would finish her.

★ ★ ★

She was woken by a vast, sun-bleached sky, not revealing any hint of an oncoming downpour, just the kind of day she liked best.

In the bathroom she shrank from a startling, well-lit mirror. Painted lilies curled the corners

248

and lean palms stretched up the sides. Indian she thought. Her shoulders sagged at the sight of the full-length reflection of her skinny self, with sore puffy eyes and blotchy skin. Remembering the nascent feeling of hope for the future — her pretty skirt, the lipstick — just before Jack was shot, she winced, and threw her treasured bottle of Shalimar in the bin. The scent was too painful now. She splashed her face with cold water and ran her fingers through damp hair. There was a clack of high heels on the floor outside her room, and Cicely entered, trailing a whiff of Chanel No. 5, and carrying a silver-inlaid ebony tray.

Lydia strode into the room completely naked and stretched her arms out wide. 'Look at me. Just look!'

'Hideous, I know.' Cicely laughed. 'There's plenty we can do about that. I've made an appointment for you. The hairdresser at eight and then we're going shopping, but first we need to make a plan.' She plumped herself down on a pale chintz sofa in the window and patted the cushion beside her.

'I was thinking of Jack.'

Cicely pulled a face. 'I know darling. It was rotten luck.' She pointed across the room. 'There's a gown you can use over there.'

Lydia paused to put it on. Silk, of course. 'He asked me to marry him, you know.' She felt a tightening in her throat, as if she might choke on tears that were never far.

Cool as a cucumber, dressed in an ice blue suit and flaunting what looked like an emerald necklace, Cicely shook her head. 'Darling, you have to forget Jack now.'

Lydia sighed, sweat forming at her hairline. 'That is a great deal easier said than done.'

'The best way is to think about other things, make plans. If you don't, the despair will drag you down.'

There was a pause.

'What's your secret?' Lydia said, to change the subject. 'You don't suffer in this climate.'

'Water. I shower a lot,' Cicely said and laughed.

'I'll never get used to heat like this, water or not.'

She thought of the pool. The fun she'd had with Jack and Maz. The wonderful cool of the water on a boiling day, such a brilliant way to cope with the heat. Then the man she'd met on the train popped into her mind. Adil. She remembered their journey together, so long ago. The blood rushed to her cheeks. That had been before everything went so terribly wrong. Before Emma and Fleur. Before Jack.

'Penny for them?' Cicely said.

Lydia wasn't sure why, but found she didn't really want to reveal her innermost thoughts to Cecily. 'Oh, nothing really,' she said. 'Just remembering things. I met someone else who always managed to stay cool. Like you.'

'Who? I thought I was the only ice queen in Malaya.'

'A man, not a woman. He was called Adil. I met him going upcountry. Didn't know what to make of him at first.'

There was a flicker of something in Cicely's

face. 'Ice-king, then?'

'He saved a woman's life. On the train. It stuck with me.'

Cicely stroked her emerald necklace. 'Sounds like a decent type. Native, of course. With a name like that.'

Lydia nodded. 'She was going to jump. He reached out and pulled her back in. And he was kind to me. For no reason. Just kind.'

'Why was he going north?'

'Something to see to, he said — '

'Do you like this?' Cicely interrupted, patting the necklace. 'Isn't it gorgeous? Ralph gave it to me last night. Guilt money.'

'He's unfaithful?'

Cicely shrugged. 'Constantly. Chinese girls.'

Jack's relationship with Lili came to mind. 'More than once?'

'Are you calling me a liar, darling?'

Lydia shook her head. 'How do you bear it?'

'Don't be so damned earnest, sweetheart. It happens all the time and I give as good as I get.'

Lydia recalled Alec gossiping about Cicely's bedroom exploits, a scornful look in his eyes.

'At least, with Ralph it's girls. Unlike those in high places. Keep it under your hat, but it's Harriet I feel sorry for.'

Lydia's mouth fell open.

'Come on, Lyddy. Everything's for sale in this damned country. Especially now we're on our way out.'

'End of an era?'

'More like end of the empire, darling.' Cicely rolled her eyes and laughed.

Lydia studied Cicely's chiselled cheekbones, her painted lips, the sleek blonde hair. Did nothing get to her?

'Alec may have been many things, but at least he wasn't like Ralph and George,' she said.

'Alec wasn't a saint.' Cicely brushed a speck of dust from her skirt, and, with a flicker of amusement, stared at Lydia.

Lydia's mouth fell open. 'You're saying he tried it on?'

Cicely nodded.

'With you?'

Cicely snorted. 'Who else?'

Lydia attempted to laugh it off, but, thrown off balance, she got up, opened the French windows, then stepped on to a balcony bordered by pretty iron railings. A mass of noise rose up from the street: bicycle bells, the roar of traffic, the myriad sound of human voices. Chinese, Malay, Indian.

'You're a hopeless romantic, Lydia Cartwright. Now what's next? That's the big question. Have you a photo of the boy?'

Lydia shook her head.

'Well, shut the window and come here. Haven't we got a campaign to plan? I'll phone Harriet right away. And remember, sweetie, if you need money, you've only got to ask.'

Lydia nodded. 'Thank you. I'll have to get a job eventually, but for now I've got enough to get by.'

She noticed Cicely was watching her.

'I didn't . . . you know. With Alec.'

But whatever Cicely might say, Lydia wondered if the offer of money was prompted by guilt, and felt quite shaken that she'd never even had a clue.

30

Outside the tall grey walls of the nursing home, an icy January wind pinched my cheeks. At nearly fourteen, Dad said I was old enough now to come on the bus to visit Gran on my own. In my dream last night were Fleur and me, when we were small, playing hide and seek in the park in Malacca. I smiled at the memory of days when I called Fleur a Mealy Worm, and Mum strutted about, pretending she didn't know where we were, and calling our names in an obvious voice. Now where can those girls be? I'm quite sure they were here a minute ago, she'd say. And we'd clutch each other and squeak with excitement.

I peeked through a large window, its frame peeling. Not, I hoped, a warning sign. Inside it looked as I expected, worn chairs placed around the edges of the room, like lonely little islands.

I was shown into a room overlooking the back garden, its windows draped in thin floral fabric, and where I sat stiffly on a high backed, wooden chair. I watched the hands of a wall clock move slowly. How awful to live surrounded by the musty smell of old age, watching your life tick on, with nothing to eat but semolina pudding.

When a young, pink-cheeked attendant showed Gran in, I blinked the wetness from my eyes. Gran had always been small, but it hurt to see her so frail. Shoulders stooped, and looking down, it seemed as if she couldn't trust her own feet. And they'd given her a square haircut, with an odd side fringe that didn't look right.

She looked up and her deep blue eyes lit up. 'Oh, Emma ducks. You're like a ray of sunshine.' She lifted trembly fingers to where a vein throbbed in her neck.

I hugged her carefully, and led her to a brown nylon sofa. The attendant promised tea and biscuits. While Gran settled back into the cushions, I felt strained, my hopes fading that she might be able to help me.

'It's my hip, dear. Not so steady on my pins now. But never mind that. How long are you home for?'

At least she remembered I wasn't living at home. 'Not long, Gran. It's the end of the Christmas holidays now. Has Dad been to see you lately?'

'I'm afraid I can't really remember. I think he came with that woman.'

'Veronica?'

'That's the one. Poor woman. She wanted a family you know. They came with her brother. Objectionable man.'

I bit my lip and looked at the floor, my crime uppermost in my mind.

'Don't worry, dear, I don't blame you for sticking a knife in his neck. Given half a chance I'd do the same.'

'Gran! You are terrible. And anyway it was a dart.' We both guffawed, and the strain dissolved.

She patted my knee, and went to tidy the strings of her apron, but it was just out of habit, as she didn't even wear one now. 'He's gone

255

away abroad again. Never did like the man.'

With no chance to speak to Veronica yet, I hadn't heard the news about Mr Oliver. I let out a huge breath, and couldn't hide how relieved I was.

Gran sighed pointedly when tea arrived. It was far too hot for me, but she gulped it noisily. She liked her tea scorching, just like Dad. I watched her munch the digestive biscuit. Crumbs fell on her chest and showered her skirt, but apart from being messy, she seemed okay, her memory not so very bad.

'Always digestives, even though it's cream biscuits I like,' she grumbled, then stopped, as if trying to rescue a memory. 'There's something I wanted to tell you, ducks.'

I looked up.

'Yes,' she said. 'Something.'

My thoughts went straight to my mother. Could this be about what had happened to Mum? But Gran drew her brows together and shook her head. In any case, I was pretty sure she didn't know what had happened to Mum. Nobody knew.

'No, it's gone.'

'Never mind, Gran. If it's important, it'll come back.'

'That's just what your dear mother used to say. But I'm afraid I can't count on things coming back any more. At least not when I need them to.'

Gran placed a heavily veined hand on my arm and studied my face. 'How is it there, dear? Really. At school.'

I shrugged in an attempt to look indifferent,

and spoke in a breezy tone of voice. 'It's okay. But Gran I wanted to ask you something. About my dad, and who's paying my fees.'

'Oh, ducks . . . ' Gran's lips trembled as she looked at me, but then, just as I thought she was going to tell me, she turned and looked blankly at the window. 'The garden's a bit grey today. But it'll come to life soon.'

I watched a tear slide down her left cheek. 'I miss your granddad,' she said. 'Every day I think of him. Grumpy old sod.'

I patted her hand. 'He wasn't grumpy, Gran. Only with Dad.'

'They rubbed each other up the wrong way, ducks. Always did. Didn't help that the blighter left me when your dad was just a kid.'

'Really? I didn't know that. Is that what made Dad grumpy?'

She pursed her lips. 'All over now.'

'You forgave him?'

'Of course. That's what you do with people you love.'

'Was Dad grumpy before?'

'When, dear?'

'When he was young. When he was a pilot.'

'Pilot, ducks? Oh no. He was never that.'

'In the war, Gran. Mum said.'

She frowned. 'Your Dad was never a pilot. Ground crew, that's what he was. And very proud I was too.'

I kept quiet. At the bottom of the garden the wind was swishing branches about. Gran's shoulders drooped, and the sad look on her worn face really hit me. Impossible to know if she was right, or if it was her memory again. Poor Gran. She was like a dry leaf, still hanging on, but about to be blown away.

'Now what was it you wanted to know?' she said.

'The fees?' I tried one more time.

A burst of sunlight streamed across the floor, and a watchful look came into her eyes.

'Look,' she said, squinting as the light fell on her face. 'It's clearing up. Though mind you, wrap up, it'll still be a bit nippy.' She shook her head. I felt she had understood, but it wasn't fair to force her.

31

Unused to such high heels, Lydia clattered up the steps of Harriet Parrott's colonial home. Today, not even tight shoes could wipe the smile from her face. She smoothed down the new red skirt. Cotton sateen. Cicely's choice. The slim pencil shape fitted perfectly, moving against her legs and hips as she climbed the steps, and together with a crisp white blouse, her hair newly styled, she felt smarter than she had in months. She glanced back at the noisy street, and took a sharp breath.

In a small library, the walls, newly painted the colour of blue-green glass, gave an impression of cool, though not entirely successfully, as beneath the three-bladed fan the humidity remained. A shame, she thought. The day had started off so fresh, but now, through the window, she saw the garden looked flat, colour and depth already stolen by the sun.

While she waited for Harriet, two Siamese kittens padded across the gleaming oak floor, and rubbed against her bare legs. Harriet would know who to approach, would talk to the right people. She leant down to stroke the kittens, but looked up, surprised to hear George trumpet down the corridor, then stand in the doorway, cracking his knuckles.

'Harriet is out, I'm afraid. Have to make do with me. Drink?'

She shook her head, and sat on the edge of a narrow teak chair, her bag beside her on the floor. 'I thought she was expecting me.'

'Anything I can help you with?' he said, as he mixed his drink.

She paused for a moment. 'To be blunt, I'm here because I need help to find out why Jack was killed.'

He leant towards her, his salt and pepper hair receding now. He was waving a whisky and soda in a meaty hand.

'But you already know, my dear. The communist insurgents. There's no more reason than that.' He gave her a commiserating look.

'Someone set it up.'

'My dear, I don't think it's possible to find out. I understand. It's a normal reaction to want to know. But these people are here today and gone tomorrow. And now, with Malaya on the brink of independence, who knows what chaos is coming our way? Be glad to retire, that's for sure.' He walked to the drinks cabinet. 'Sure you won't have that drink? Sounds like you need one.'

She fanned herself with her hand and paused, aware of her heart pounding. It was embarrassing to have to say it out loud. 'George, there's something else. A Chinese woman Jack was involved with. I think she could provide a lead.'

'Chinese, you say. Sounds like a touch of the green-eyed monster.'

'Exactly what I thought.'

'No. I meant you, my dear.'

He smiled, then opened the window wide, though no breeze relieved the stale heavy air.

Somewhere else in the house, a telephone was left unanswered. She felt sweat at the nape of her neck, reached down to her bag, and fumbled for a tissue. She looked up to see him staring at her.

He was not an attractive man, with large ears, a pug nose, and small eyes swallowed by bushy brows and fat red cheeks. He cleared his throat.

'Always had you down as a bit of a butterfly. Didn't see you as the jealous type.'

There was an awkward silence, broken only by the high-pitched drone of a mosquito. Lydia wiped the back of her hand across her brow and ignored his comment, unsure if he was trying to needle her, or if he was merely insensitive.

'Her name is Lili and I think she may have betrayed Jack.'

'I can put out the word, while I still can.'

'I was hoping for more.'

He looked her up and down and gave a snort of approval. 'You're in good shape. Bit thin, but young enough to start again. Why not let it go, my dear?'

She shook her head in disbelief. 'How could you say such a thing? I've lost my husband, my children and now Jack.'

'You're not supposed to feel insulted. You're supposed to feel flattered.'

She saw a smile flicker across his face, followed by a suggestively raised eyebrow. She gritted her teeth. The man was insufferable, but she needed his help. She ploughed on.

'I know what you said before, but has it been possible to compile a definitive . . . you know, of people killed in the fire. When Jack asked you said it was impossible. But I wondered — '

He squared his shoulders and narrowed his eyes. 'After all this time? Even back then nobody knew who exactly had been there that night. The girls and Alec for sure, and his entire department. Other than that is just conjecture.'

'Are you sure?'

'I hope you're not suggesting I'd lie to you?'

She suppressed the stab of irritation. 'Not at all, but couldn't you phone the department.'

He shrugged. 'If you insist, but I fear it's a wild-goose chase. People are getting themselves killed all the time, what with one thing or another.'

'You mentioned you'd start the process for obtaining the death certificates.'

'Oh my dear, didn't I say? I do apologise. The woman dealing with all that went off to have a baby. Left everything in a dreadful state. I'm afraid we may well have to begin all over again. I'll chase it up now.'

While he made the call in his office, she turned things over. A man in his position. Did he know more than he'd said?

He came back into the room and lit a cigarette drawn from a silver and ivory case. She looked up expectantly.

'Sorry. No list, though someone will start afresh on applying for the death certificates. But take my advice. Put the past to bed.' He spoke carefully, his tone flat.

She sighed. 'Well, at least give me your word that there's nothing more you can do to help me find Jack's killer.'

He came across to sit beside her, legs spread wide, one hand rubbing his knee. She shifted slightly. He reeked of whisky and sweat, and, sitting too close, placed a damp hand on her thigh.

'You're a very attractive woman, Lydia.'

She found it hard to breathe. Outside there was a burst of rain, followed by a weak sun, but it wasn't enough to alter the humidity in the room.

'No point chasing about in this heat. Like I said, my dear, I'll put the word about and we should know soon enough if there are any leads.'

She squeezed her eyes shut. 'There is one more thing.'

'Oh?'

'A little boy I was looking after. He disappeared.'

She saw the sweat on the back of his thick red neck as he strode over to a filing cabinet.

'Should be something in here. Missing persons. His name?'

'Maznan Chang.'

He frowned. 'European?'

'Mixed race, Chinese, Malay and something else.'

He slammed the cabinet drawer shut. 'In that case I can't help. We only record missing whites here.'

She stood up, felt the heat like a blanket, couldn't breathe for it, her skin flushed and prickly.

'Nice seeing you, my dear,' he said, 'but my advice is leave all this. It's all change now in

Malaya. Get on with your life. No point digging around.'

She watched him loosen his collar; saw beads of sweat appear on his brow. He wiped it with a crumpled handkerchief and paced the room. 'Too bloody hot,' he said. Then, hands behind his back, turned to face her, a muscle twitching in his jaw.

George's risky sexual exploits, though largely disbelieved, might still be useful. She straightened her back. After Cicely's revelations, could she use the information to twist his arm?

'I hear you like Singapore, used to speak of it with affection, so Alec said. Go back there. Get a job in admin with one of the expanding companies. I could put in a word. With your looks, shouldn't be hard. Tobacco maybe.'

There was a silence. Instinct told her he'd withheld something, though she had no idea what. Suddenly making up her mind, she took a step towards him.

'George, there are things I know about you. Things you'd prefer to remain behind closed doors.'

His eyes narrowed to slits. 'That's uncharitable. Personally I wouldn't flog a dead horse. And I wouldn't tangle with me, dear. Bringing back the past can be unhealthy. With your nerves the way they are, a little holiday would be the thing. Kuala Terengganu. What do you say? Palm trees, white sands, a bit of a breeze? I can arrange it.'

She shook her head, marvelling at his complete dismissal of her threat.

'No? Then there's nothing more to say. Always a pleasure.' He held out his hand, and called the boy.

The door clicked behind her. She blinked in the sudden brightness, then hurried off, heels clicking furiously. Just before she turned the corner, she stood to catch her breath, looked round at the dusty street and stood thinking. Maybe George was right. Maybe she did need to simply get on with her life. Nothing would bring Jack back, and if George wouldn't help find Maz or Lili, who could? She heard his door close again, glanced back over her shoulder, and spun round. A tall angular man stood on the pavement, backlit by the harsh, mid-morning sun. She couldn't see his face but the long legs, the upright posture, the shaved head, instantly suggested Adil.

She turned away for a moment, unsure, felt herself redden. Should she approach him, say hello? Maybe just wave, to see if he'd come over to her. She very much wanted to see Adil again, but felt shaky after the encounter with George. She quickly thought it through. A friend right now was exactly what she needed. She spun round, but the man had gone. Perhaps it hadn't been him at all, but if not, this was the second time she'd mistaken someone else for him. Once when they left the resettlement village, and now here too.

32

I was down in the dumps about Granny, and though it was a beautiful day, there was still a chill. It was April now, and the first person I saw, after a weekend at home, was Sister Ruth. She was kind of hovering in the hall, and, with a furtive look over her shoulder, she clutched hold of my arm, then led me back outside.

'I have some information,' she said, squinting in the sunlight, and glancing across the cracked and clumpy winter-damaged grounds. 'Promise you didn't get it from me.'

Taken aback, I nodded.

She flushed bright pink. 'Meet me in the garden after lunch, behind the rhododendrons, down by the woods.'

It cheered me up. Sister Ruth was straight as a die. All this 'meet me in the library with a candlestick' wasn't her at all. But it was the sort of thing I loved.

After lunch I found the place and waited for Sister Ruth, wondering what demanded such secrecy. A couple of girls ran past without noticing me. It was a good spot for a meeting. The rhododendrons hid me from passing nosy parkers, and I even dodged Susan, which made me feel mean.

Sister Ruth padded up, carrying a large wicker basket, and we picked our way down to the woods. I hadn't been there since the night I spent alone. Today they looked innocent, shady, but with light patches where the sun shone through the new leaves.

'Why the secrecy? And what's the basket for?'

'I'll explain. The basket's a ruse. I thought it made me look purposeful.'

I grinned at her.

'How was your weekend at home?' she asked, looking over her shoulder, head swivelling like a sherbet lolly on a stick.

'Fine.'

She nodded. 'Emma, what do you know about your mother? Lydia, isn't it?'

I pulled a face. 'That's a peculiar question.'

'I mean what do you know about her birth?'

I scuffed my heels in the dead leaves and gravel on the ground. 'Not much. She was born in a convent and the nuns brought her up.'

'She never spoke of her own mother.'

'No. She only ever mentioned one of the sisters.'

'Was the sister's name Patricia?'

I thought for a moment. 'I think it might have been.'

She held me at arm's length, then glanced back at the school buildings. 'Listen to me, Emma. On retreat this Easter, I met someone who knew Sister Patricia. Her name's Brenda, and she was in the same convent as Sister Patricia for five years. St Joseph's. Sadly Sister Patricia's dead now.'

'How do you know it was the same Sister Patricia?'

'She said that before Sister Patricia died, she'd

267

opened her heart and told her about a baby they'd named Lydia. Apparently she was present when the child was born.'

Sister Ruth tilted her head and gave me an encouraging nod. I heard my mother's voice in my ear, as if she was talking only to me. Overwhelmed by how much I still missed my mum, I felt cold, despite the sun.

I shook myself out of it. 'But who was she? The woman who gave birth. Did she die?'

Sister Ruth shook her head. 'Brenda could only draw the first name out of the old sister, but from what she said, I don't think the woman died.'

'So?'

She gave me another smile and squeezed my hand. 'Sister Patricia gave Brenda a painting. A miniature of the young woman who gave birth. I thought you should have it, though by rights I should really hand it in to the head to give to your father.'

I stared deep into the woods, where a trail of bluebells came to life in a shaft of sunlight.

Ruth shaded her eyes to look at me. 'Let's sit on the bench.'

She reached inside the folds of her habit and brought out a small painting. 'Sister Patricia kept it all these years. Look, there are some initials in the bottom right hand corner.'

The hair was fairer, almost strawberry blonde, but my heart flipped over as I looked at my own mother's eyes gazing out. Exactly the same hazel, flecked with blue and green, arched eyebrows, one fractionally higher than the other, the same oval shaped face, and same wide mouth. It sounds strange, but the picture brought back the scent of my mum. I could smell her skin and hair. See her standing in our old garden, a wave of butterflies, as big as birds, flying by, and the smell of tobacco smoke from Dad's pipe where he sat reading *The Straits Times*.

'Lydia's mother begged Sister Patricia to take care of the picture, and only give it to your mother on her eighteenth birthday. Well, your mother ran off when she was seventeen, and Sister Patricia never saw her again.'

I snorted. 'That's ridiculous. Couldn't she have tried to trace her?'

Sister Ruth shook her head. 'She wanted to, but the mother superior at the time said it was better to leave well enough alone.'

'Surely the right thing would have been to find my mother. Or at least to try.'

'She probably thought it *was* right at the time.'

I looked away. The bluebells were in shadow now, and despite the fine start, a line of grey clouds spread across the sky. I shook my head and stabbed my shoe in the slimy mud surrounding the bench, making zigzag patterns with the toe.

'What was the date of the birth?'

'The sixth of August nineteen twenty-four.'

The date made me catch my breath. 'The sixth of August is my mother's birthday. And she was born in nineteen twenty-four.'

Sister Ruth touched my cheek.

'What was the woman's name?' I asked.

She grinned. 'This is the best bit. It was

Emma, but I'm afraid she didn't know the surname.'

Could she really be talking about my mum's mother? The woman my mum had never even known. I thought it over. A nun called Patricia, a baby called Lydia, with exactly the same birth date as my mum, and the woman's name was Emma too. Mum always said I was named after her own mother. I was almost certain that I was holding a picture of my grandmother in my hand. The grandmother who, up until now, I had known nothing about.

Though everyone thought my mum was dead, I had never believed it, and now I wanted so much for Mum to see this picture of the woman I hoped was her mother. I didn't want to go back inside, and have to do lessons, with this picture fizzing in my head. But the bell went, so I had no choice.

'Thank you, Sister Ruth.' I kissed her on the cheek, and ran back across the grass and into the building.

In the dorm, before I went to class, I looked at the picture again. The woman did look so like Mum. I prayed that my mother was still alive, and as I did, I tasted sugared hibiscus flowers, heard the nightjar tok-tok birds, and the buzz of giant honey bees. Most of all I heard the sound of snakes slithering in the long grass behind our house.

Everyone said Malaya was a dangerous place, though it wasn't danger that I remembered.

I remembered how beautiful it was in the evening, when the sky shone like gold, and behind the dark hills, the jungle waited. We were there when we had the crash and Mummy lost one of her lizard earrings with emerald eyes. I remembered, because it happened on our way home from a wedding. It was the day after Mum and Dad had a row, and the atmosphere was horrible.

And then we came to England.

I thought over my day. I'd been feeling down in the dumps, but now my heart thumped with hope. If I was lucky, and if she was still alive, I might find my grandmother. Who could ever have imagined that? I snatched one last look at the picture. There were initials in the right hand corner. C.L.P. in black paint. My first task must be to find out who the artist was.

33

In the market, Lydia heard footsteps coming up hard behind her. Still unused to Malacca's backstreets, she was doing her best to familiarise herself. Today she was in the outskirts of the Chinese quarter, hoping someone might provide a lead to Lili's whereabouts. Her hair was frizzing in the damp, and she stopped outside a pawnshop to smooth it. As she peered in the window, she noticed a shadowy reflection among the cheap necklaces and pearls. She straightened her skirt.

'Lydia.'

She spun round and there he was. In Western clothes, dark trousers, cream short-sleeved shirt, a gold chain glinting at his neck. He walked towards her, taking his time, head shaven and brown. He held out a hand.

She paused to search his face and gave him an uncertain smile. 'Are you following me, Adil?'

'Come with me. It will be worth your while.'

She frowned. The sun, reaching its height, beat down on her and she felt a flush of colour inch up her neck. He indicated the direction, and she let him lead her to a narrow alley, where the drone of traffic was less. He stopped outside a small coffee shop, with a blue and gold Arabic sign above the door.

Inside, they perched on uncomfortable stools in the far corner of the steamy bar, keeping their distance from the mah-jong players hunched up at the other end. He smiled at her. She acknowledged it, then picked up a copy of *The Straits Times* someone had left behind.

'Are you surprised George didn't help you?' he asked.

She looked up at his unlined forehead, took in the two strong lines that ran from the sides of a long nose to his full mouth.

'What?'

He bent his head to one side, looked her straight in the face, then poured sweet aromatic coffee from an engraved brass pot, before speaking slowly. 'I think we both know what I mean.'

She avoided his scrutiny. 'How do you know George?'

Adil shrugged.

'Well, in answer to your question, he didn't help, and no, I suppose I wasn't surprised. What's it to you?'

He gave her a keen look.

Sun streamed through the single window, throwing a patch of white light on to the bar. She circled her temples with her fingertips to relieve the pressure, sensed his awareness of her too revealing neckline, the skin breaking out into familiar blotches. She'd never get used to the humidity.

For a moment neither spoke.

Adil scratched his chin and gave her a sympathetic smile. 'I'm sorry about your friend. I know words are inadequate.'

She let out a slow breath.

'It will get better,' he said.

Her heart flipped over as Fleur and Emma's faces flashed back, and she tried not to feel irritated.

'Of course, you already know. I'm so sorry.'

'Don't be kind to me . . . Anyway how did you hear about Jack, or the girls for that matter?'

He shrugged. 'These things get around.'

She didn't want to think of Jack now, but a Pat Boone song came on the wireless. It was a favourite of Jack's, and an image of the first time she met him rushed into her mind. She shook her head.

'Here's the deal,' Adil was saying. 'No negotiation. Will you trust me?'

She rubbed away the moisture from her hairline, then drained the remainder of her coffee. She wanted to ask for his help, but could she trust him? She wasn't sure, though he'd been kind to her before. She felt hot and clumsy. A burst of sound from a lorry as it dropped its load in the street startled her, and the ruby red glass slipped from her hand.

'Oh, Lord! Sorry.'

After the barman cleared up the splinters of glass, Adil looked serious. 'Why exactly did you visit George?' he asked.

'Not that it's any of your business but it was to ask questions. I got no answers. He insinuated I should take a break, for my nerves.'

'Maybe he was right,' Adil said with a half smile, and continued speaking with a touch of amusement in his voice. 'Paddling upstream, birds circling up above, mangroves all around.

There's a lot to see. For instance, did you know mangrove trees grow their roots partly above the ground?'

Her eyes narrowed. 'You didn't mention the mosquitoes or the sweltering heat.'

He grinned. 'No, I suppose I didn't. You'd have to watch out for the blue coral snake too. Highly venomous.'

'Well, thanks for the sermon, but now tell me what you were doing at George's place. I thought I saw you outside, the day I was there.'

'I work for him. Well, sometimes. Mainly I — '

She burst in. 'You work for George! Then why on earth should I trust you?'

'Well, I used to work for him. Not any longer.'

Taken aback, her eyes widened. 'You're lying.'

He shook his head. 'I'm sorry you think that. I'll tell you the story. But let's get out of here.'

They got up and stood face to face. She felt light-headed. He realised and put out a hand to steady her, his eyes warm. Why hadn't she remembered that warmth? Had she simply forgotten because he wasn't white? He cupped his hand under her elbow and steered her through the narrow alley.

'What about the park?' he said. 'Fresh air.'

On the way they passed through a pulsating world of Chinese shops. With precision he eased her past curtains of dried fish hanging across an alley. By the time they reached the park the crowds were sparse, and they strolled along a path between leafy trees, where black tree rats bolted up the trunks, to disappear in branches high above. At a quiet spot overlooking a small pond, and surrounded by pink hibiscus, she sat on the bench he indicated, the new shoes pinching her toes.

'It signifies peace,' he said, pointing at the hibiscus. 'Peace and bravery.'

The sun was not much visible and, behind advancing clouds, a body of rain sat poised to fall over the city. She watched a peacock strut among the wild poppies, a feathered fantasy of bluey-green, and gold, where the remaining patch of sunlight lit its tail.

'You smile,' he said. 'But that's not a happy face.'

Feeling hot and sticky, she kicked off her court shoes and rotated her ankles. A prickly silence stretched between them.

She turned towards him. 'You still haven't said how you can help.'

'I overheard a conversation he was having about the boy. Maznan.'

'You mean George did know? I knew it. Patronising bastard. I'm sorry but I don't like him.' She slumped back on the bench, pressing fingers to her temples. 'Why did he lie?'

His face was glum. 'There are things I can't say.'

'Adil, if you know, please tell me.'

She held her breath while he paused for a moment before speaking.

'I was waiting in the hall. He was on the phone in the office, but the door was open. I don't know where the boy is yet, but there's every reason to believe he is alive.'

Lydia pressed a palm to her heart and exhaled

in relief. 'That means so much to me. Thank you.'

A group of schoolgirls, in Emma and Fleur's old school uniform of dark blue pinafores, crossed her line of sight. They dug each other in the ribs and giggled, then turned to stare at her and Adil. Her vision blurred and she closed her eyes. The feeling passed over and a light breeze from the pond broke through the heavy air.

He looked on, oblivious to their stares. 'I'll do what I can. Whatever I can to help. Once again I'm so very sorry about your friend Jack and your children. I know what it is to lose someone you love, but I do need you to trust me.'

She couldn't catch her breath. Adil took her hand and squeezed it in a friendly way, as if to convince her of his good intentions. A green crested lizard ran right over her toes.

'Did you see them?' she said. 'Those girls.'

'It helps to develop selective vision.'

She enjoyed the brief sensation of his cool hands on her bare skin. After a moment she moved away.

'Sorry,' he said, his shoulders hunched. 'Didn't mean to overstep the mark.'

She shook her head and glanced up. A gloomy sky now, the first tepid drops of rain as big as Emma's fist. She forced herself to think of something else.

'What work did you do for George?'

'Mainly undercover operations.'

She thought he looked uncomfortable. 'Go on.'

'I can't really say. There's a lot of corruption. The locals call Europeans the red-haired devil, you know. I sometimes think they're right.'

She stood. Alec had told her that too. Sorry to be leaving, she touched his arm. 'We'd better get going before the rain.'

He smiled back.

Her first impressions, all that time ago, had been wrong. He had seemed cold and distant, but then turned out to be kind. Now she sensed this was a man who felt deeply. She saw it in his eyes.

'How do I get in touch with you?'

'Don't worry, I'll find you,' he said.

She was shocked by how much she hoped he would.

34

I sat in the lounge flicking the pages of an exercise book. I wasn't really working. It was too nice a day, sunny and warm, bright rays of light coming in through two sash windows. I pushed one up to let air in, and looked out. The school grounds were covered with spring flowers, and the grass was bright green. Rebecca, waiting in there too, glowered, despite the lovely day.

Veronica was late. Her letter had said she wished to see me. Though I still didn't know if I could trust her, I could hardly refuse. I patted my satchel. Inside was the miniature I carried everywhere.

A short, red-faced woman, in a bright yellow suit, bustled into the room and waved some papers in Rebecca's face.

'Oh, here you are. You've kept your new foster parents waiting, girl. And let me tell you, you'd better make a better fist of fitting in this time.' She spoke in a strident voice, indifferent to who else might be listening. She turned on her heels, swaying her large yellow bottom as she went.

Rebecca slid from her seat, chin in the air. As she passed me she hissed sideways, 'I'll kill you if you tell.'

I smiled. I wouldn't tell anyone, but at least I had proof she was a foster child, and not the daughter of wealthy parents living abroad. I was leaning back against the wall, enjoying the thought and feeling the sun on my face, when I heard the click clack of high heels cross the floor.

Veronica looked tall and smart in an English sort of way. Low key that is. Not snazzy or exciting like Mum, but okay. Navy blue fitted jacket, and a flared skirt in the same colour that swished as she moved. On her head, a little round hat. White.

She saw me looking at it and patted it. 'Pill box. Do you like it? It's the latest.'

I nodded and her eyes sparkled. She held out a white-gloved hand. 'Emma dear. How are you?'

'Fine,' I muttered, and found I'd turned into a grunting fool, especially as on a day exit you still had to wear school uniform, including a stupid panama hat. I felt like a clot.

* * *

We sat on floral padded seats, in the restaurant of a big store in town, on a sort of balcony that overlooked the shop below. I felt out of place, but this was intended to be a treat, so I put my nose in the air, and looked at windows heavily draped with fringed red velvet curtains. The tapestries on the walls were romantic; the one behind us showed St George riding a golden charger, surrounded by bluebells. At intervals along the balcony were five tall lamps, with blue and gold striped tasselled lampshades.

'Memories Are Made of This' was playing in the background. I doubted that very much, and thought of the shiny memories of my mother. I kept them safe in my heart, like Mum stored her best silks in the heart of her enormous Chinese linen chest. The waitress brought us a gilded cake stand, and the china, when it came, was white with pink rosebuds round the edge of the saucer and the cup. Veronica fiddled with her cup and saucer, and talked nervously about school and kept asking how was I feeling.

I was halfway down a Knickerbocker Glory when I discovered why.

'Your father and I have fixed the date,' she said in a level tone, as if trying to make it sound as ordinary as *Would you like another cup of tea?*

She was blushing furiously, her cheeks bright pink. I sat with ice-cream oozing from the corners of my mouth, and glowered.

'I wanted to tell you myself,' she stammered, and looked at me, her blue eyes matching the shadow on the lids. I stared at her eyelids. How did they make eye shadow so shimmery?

'Emma?'

I wiped my mouth with the side of my hand holding the spoon, and as I did, accidentally tipped a spoonful of chocolate ice-cream on the carpet. It was blue with pink in the middle and ran through the whole store. I couldn't believe I was thinking about carpet at a time like this and glared at her.

'What about my mother?' I said, unable to keep my voice from rising.

She sighed, with such a look of sadness on her face, I thought she was going to cry.

'I'm sorry, I really am. But your mother's gone, Emma. I hoped you might accept that by now.'

I pulled my hat down, and hung my head, as a lump formed in my throat. There wasn't any way I accepted my mother was dead, though I could see that Dad and Veronica suited each other. Something about her made him feel safe, in a way that Mum never had.

'I love your father, Emma.'

I wanted to shout out loud, *And I love my mother*. And she's only missing. I bit my lip and choked on the words. Sunlight shone on the bright white tablecloth, and all the sounds in the shop merged into a loud hum.

She gave me a big smile. 'Isn't it better for you and Fleur to have a stepmother than no mother at all?'

'Fleur,' I snorted.

The conversation paused. I tried to spoon up melted ice-cream as she looked down at her hands folded neatly in her lap. A baby at the next table made a high-pitched whining noise, and in the distance a car honked its horn again and again. I wanted to scream shut up at them.

'What did you expect to happen, Emma?' she said after a while. 'Your father isn't old and neither am I. It's a second chance at happiness for both of us. Would you deny us that?'

She reached out and tried to take my hand. I snatched it away, stared past the white tablecloth, the melting ice-cream, her, and then looked down at the people shopping in the hall below. I wanted to be alone and out of the stuffy department store, but it was too far to walk back to school, and I didn't have any money for the bus.

I pursed my lips and watched her. She was

fidgeting with her gloves, pulling the fingers out, then pushing them back again. She carried on looking down as she spoke, with a little catch in her throat. 'I allowed myself the hope that you might like me a little.'

There was a silence as I thought about it. I didn't mind her, as it happened, but I didn't want a stepmother.

'I'd like to be your friend. I can't replace your mother. But I can make things a little easier with your father.'

I looked up.

'He's no saint and he can be a bit hard on you.'

'That's an understatement,' I said, with a faint smile.

She pulled a face and tilted her head. 'I know what you mean. But if you let me, I can be on your side. I don't have to tell your father everything.'

I looked at her, still unsure, but an idea was forming.

She looked around for a bit. 'He doesn't really like England you know. Sometimes I think he'd rather go back to Malaya.'

I brightened up, pictured the squirrels, the peacock pheasants, the bats. 'Really?'

'Well, I don't actually think he will. It's nostalgia mainly.'

I felt deflated. Going back to Malaya was my dream. First I'd visit our old house and hide under it like I used to, then I'd lie in the long grass, without a thought for the snakes. Then I'd look for Mum.

Veronica looked at me. 'Emma, are you okay?'

'I miss my mum,' I said, feeling my eyes grow wet.

She reached for my hand again. This time I let her.

'I know it must be awful for you. But what if we were to become allies?'

There was a long silence. I looked out of the window for a time, watching workmen climb up the scaffolding on the building opposite, my thoughts conflicted. She didn't prod or push or chatter on, just waited for me to answer. It was touching because it showed she was not at all like Dad, who never listened. In the end that was what decided it.

'Could you help me with something? Dad mustn't know.' Even as I said the words, I noticed a tight feeling in my stomach. If she told Dad, I'd be in trouble, but if I didn't ask her, who else could help? Sister Ruth had done all she could.

'As long as it's not illegal,' she said.

I reached into my satchel for the painting. I held it to my chest for a moment, still uncertain, feeling my heart bang against it. Then looked up at her eyes. She looked so honest, her kindness real, it was hard to believe she'd betray me. I turned the painting round and held it out for her to see.

She took it, stared, looked up, studied my face, and then down at the painting again. 'Surely it can't be. The clothes are too old fashioned.'

'No. It's not my mother. It's my grandmother.'

She smiled. 'She's beautiful. Alec never

mentioned another grandmother. Only your granny. This isn't her.'

'She's my mum's mother. That's the thing . . . I need your help to find her.'

'And your father mustn't know?'

I held my breath, hoping I'd made the right decision. It was a gamble. If she told Dad, he'd take it away, and then it would be even harder to trace her.

'Okay,' she said at last. 'It'll be our little project. Can I ask why your father mustn't know?'

'Until I know where my grandmother is, or at least until I know a bit more about her, I don't want Dad to interfere.'

'We must make plans then,' she said, entering into the spirit of it. 'Confidentially, of course.'

'Would you be able to find out who the artist is? His initials are in the corner and the date. C.L.P. Nineteen twenty-three. The year before my mother was born.'

'I go up to London quite frequently to see Freddy, my solicitor. He's staying in my flat at the moment, and as all the museums and art galleries are close by, it can't be too difficult.'

My ears tingled. This might be my chance to casually ask. 'So your solicitor isn't Johnson, Price & Co. of Kidderminster?'

'No, my love.'

'And you haven't got another solicitor?'

'Freddy's the only solicitor I've ever needed. And a good friend too. I've known him since he was at university in Birmingham, and before his first placement in Worcester. Now, of course, he's quite the London hotshot. Why do you ask?'

'No reason.'

She nodded. 'Funny question though.'

She went to pay the bill and I went to find the lavatory. I decided then that I'd write to Mr Johnson, throw myself on his mercy and beg him to tell me.

In the ladies' powder room, I waited in the queue for a moment or two and felt a tugging pain at the base of my belly. When a cubicle became vacant and I sat on the seat, I found out why. The bleeding wasn't heavy but had stained my knickers. For a moment tears pricked my lids, and I sat feeling awfully sorry for myself. But when I heard exasperated sighs coming from the waiting women, I wiped my eyes, then stuffed some folded sheets of toilet paper inside my pants. I twisted round to check there was no blood on the back of my skirt, opened the door and walked past the queue with my eyes down. I was mortified. The toilet paper was the stiff kind that rustled slightly as I walked.

Veronica stood at the exit and must have seen something was wrong.

'What is it, Emma? You look like you've seen a ghost.'

I pulled a face. 'Not a ghost.'

'What then?'

If I didn't want blood all over my skirt, and her car seat too, I had to say. I swallowed hard, and managed to speak in a small voice. 'I've started. You know, I've come on.'

'Oh. Oh, I see.' She blushed. 'Is it the first time?'

I nodded miserably.

'Have you got what you need?'

I shook my head.

'Oh, darling, come on, back to the ladies' with you. There's a machine there.'

'I saw it, but I didn't have any money.'

'Not a problem.' She paused and lowered her voice. 'I don't suppose you've even got a sanitary belt?'

I shook my head, feeling myself turn beetroot and wanting the floor to open up.

'First we'll get a towel from the machine here. They come with safety pins, so that'll have to do. At least it'll get you back to school.'

I felt my eyes water again and brushed the tears away with my knuckles.

'Then we'll go to Timothy Whites, get you a belt and some decent supplies for later.'

I didn't feel more grown up, as I'd expected to. Quite the opposite. It made me feel small and lonely, and grateful as I was to Veronica, I really wished that Mum was there.

When she dropped me off, I climbed out of the car and held the door open for a moment.

'Thanks, Veronica.'

She smiled. 'You're welcome.'

'By the way, the wedding, you didn't say when?'

'In the school summer holidays so you can both come. We're going to Cornwall for a week afterwards.'

'Who'll look after me and Fleur?'

'I hope my brother will be back on leave, in which case he'll do it.' She lifted her hand to wave, but must have seen my face fall.

'Is it Sidney?' she said.

I bit my lip, mumbled something, and avoided her eyes.

'If you're worried about the dart, he's quite forgiven you.'

I shook my head.

'What then?'

I couldn't speak, fled inside, and hoped something would happen to Mr Oliver. Something really horrible. Again, I felt his creeping fingers on me, and it made my hands go clammy, and my heart pound. I never wanted to see him again as long as I lived. But if I did see him, and if it happened again, I made up my mind that I would tell.

35

She lay on her bed at Cicely's, watching sunset turn the sky purple. As a breeze from the fan cooled her bare skin, day became night, and when the stars and moon came out, she thought of Jack. She felt him against her, as clear as if he were there, his large hand splayed across her stomach, the soapy coal tar smell still lingering on his skin.

She let her mind drift. A woman in blue came out of the ocean, moving gracefully, hair shining pale gold, even though it was night. When Lydia tried to reach her, the vision evaporated, and she was left with squabbling gibbons swinging from branches. She woke, weeping uncontrollably, to find Cicely sitting by her bed.

'Come down. For drinks.'

'How long have you been there?'

'Not long. Did you hear what I said?'

Lydia wiped her eyes and covered herself with a sheet.

★　★　★

In Cicely's elegant sitting room, decorated in subtle creams and palest ice blue, Ralph mixed them each a G and T, clinking in the ice and swirling it round. Lydia, perched on the delicately gilded French chair, felt awkward.

'You've lost weight,' Ralph said with a grin. 'Suits you.'

She lowered her eyes, thinking of Jack. 'It wasn't intentional.'

'Ralph darling,' Cicely purred, 'a manipulative look on her face. 'Come and sit down. We need your help . . . Lydia needs your help.'

He didn't seem to notice the look, but puffed out his cheeks and plumped down next to his wife.

She smiled at him. 'We don't know why, but we think George Parrott is hiding something. It may have been to do with Jack, or the whereabouts of a child called Maznan Chang.'

She turned to Lydia for confirmation.

'He was very prickly when I asked to see the list of people who died in the fire,' Lydia added. 'Said it was well-nigh impossible.'

Ralph frowned. 'Probably true.'

Cicely, watchful and self-assured, patted him on the thigh. A spot of red appeared on both his cheeks.

'I know, darling. But, Ralph, we wondered if you'd heard anything on the grapevine.'

Lydia stared out through open curtains into the darkness, surprised by how well Cicely and her husband got on. Despite all the hints Cicely had dropped, there was an ease between them. And, as if they had a pact, he didn't seem to mind the cupboard love one bit.

He shook his head. 'All the talk was, Alec got caught up in the fire when they moved out of the offices in Ipoh and . . . well you know the rest. A new influx at the rest house, overcrowding, nothing on paper, records burnt. Remains unidentifiable. So no complete list. Sorry, Lydia.'

He gave her a sympathetic smile.

'Well, Lydia thinks George does know something.'

He raised his eyebrows in surprise. 'About the fire?'

'No . . . ' Lydia said. 'Well, maybe. It might be about the boy, or even about Jack and Lili.'

'Lili?'

Lydia's breath caught. 'She used to be Jack's lover. I think she had something to do with his murder.'

There was an embarrassed silence.

Cicely raised her brows. 'How intriguing, darling. Why didn't you say?'

Lydia shrugged.

Cicely turned to Ralph, kissed his forehead and ran a frosted pink fingernail down one cheek. 'Could you get into George's office on the quiet? As his ADO I mean.'

He shifted uncomfortably in his seat. 'And do what? It could take a while . . . '

'But will you do it?' Cicely interrupted. 'Check out his office I mean?'

Lydia's heart lifted when he nodded, but as he started to question her, there was a loud rap at the door. It was late. He and Cicely exchanged looks.

'Not expecting anyone?' he asked, as he left the room.

Lydia watched Cicely fiddle with her necklace, seeming lost in thought. She thought of Jack again, and the row of frangipani trees that edged the graveyard where he lay. There was a sound of voices in the hall, and when Ralph came back in, his face was pale.

He looked from one to the other. 'I'm afraid

the task is quite impossible now. It seems George Parrott has shot himself.'

★ ★ ★

Late afternoon. Outside, the wall of sound almost knocked her over. She glimpsed him waiting on the corner of Cicely's street, and couldn't pretend she hadn't seen. As she got closer, he raised his eyebrows, and nodded at her with a look of quiet determination.

She shook her head. 'Well, I guess I've not got much choice then.'

He came across to her. 'Here,' he said, offering his arm.

She shook him off. 'I'm perfectly capable of walking on my own.'

'Suit yourself. Now let's get out of here.'

She looked at him, alarmed.

He grinned and his solemn face softened. 'You look very nice today, Lydia.'

This was the most personal Adil had been, and she realised she rather liked it. She suppressed her smile by looking up at the blazing sky, and stepped straight into the path of a rickshaw. He pulled her back, looking closely at her face. 'Why are you asking for trouble?'

'I feel nauseous. It's the heat . . . Why not come in and meet Cicely.'

He shook his head. 'Not a good idea.'

Lydia frowned. 'You don't even know her.'

'On the contrary. I work with her.'

Lydia drew back. 'But you said you do undercover stuff.'

'I do.'

'And not for George Parrott any more.'

'You've heard then.'

She nodded. 'But Cicely?'

'What about my flat? We can put our heads together there.'

She glanced back at Cicely's house. The rules were changing fast. She wanted to go with him, felt she ought not; but somehow she needed to trust this man.

He smiled. 'Just for a while?'

At the taxi rank on the main road, next to an open-fronted shop bursting with exotic birds, an Indian snake charmer sat on the pavement blowing a wooden whistle. She stopped.

'So Cicely is . . . '

He nodded. 'Of course, I can't actually say.'

Lydia sighed. That explains Cicely's cool, she thought, the way nothing ever gets to her.

'I live on the other side of the Chinese quarter. You'll like it. Great places to eat. But I'm forgetting you lived in a colonial house on the outskirts. Not so many rats there.'

She shrugged. 'I still had to check the toilet for snakes and spiders, and there are rats everywhere!'

He laughed.

★ ★ ★

He lived in the Street of the Three Dragons, close to the crumbling red light district. Though it was a peeling old building, it retained a faded chic, its arched windows and pale slatted shutters covered with the red, lantern-like flowers of coral vine. It had seen better days but it wasn't a bad address. Upstairs, she settled herself in a rattan chair by the window, and leant back against a black silk cushion. He brought her a Singapore gin sling.

With gin gradually flooding her veins, she watched the movement of the ocean in the distance, and felt like throwing caution to the wind. A faint breeze made her cheeks tingle. Strains of eastern music and oriental voices leaked up from the street, but at least up here she was away from the smell. The room itself was uncluttered and elegant, a bit like Adil, she thought, with a smoked glass vase placed on a teak coffee table, and ripe rambutans in a bowl. More dark cushions lay scattered on a diamond patterned rug that covered a section of the polished floor. In one corner, decorative dried grasses fluttered as the ceiling fan began to pick up speed. She narrowed her eyes as she looked at him.

'Why were you waiting for me?'

His face was thoughtful as he lit a bronze incense burner, but he didn't reply. Then he went to his room to change, leaving the door slightly ajar. The sound of a piano drifted up from the flat below. South American music. She imagined dancing a tango with him or a sultry rumba, her in sequins, him in a tuxedo. As she looked out at the building opposite, a stunning Chinese ancestral home, the evening sky rapidly turned inky blue, pinpoints of sparkling light standing out in the water beyond.

He came back through wearing a long-sleeved, freshly laundered turquoise shirt. Against it, the dark skin of his face, neck and hands shone. His was a different kind of masculinity. Athletic, lean, powerful.

She flashed him a curious look. 'Who are you?'

He grinned. 'I told you. A friend.'

She struggled with her feelings, wasn't sure, yet she wanted to believe him.

★ ★ ★

They were to eat at a tiny Chinese restaurant a couple of streets from his flat. To get to it they passed the Cheng Hoon Temple. Its red pillars were coated in black Chinese script, the rafters painted with lions and tigers, and the roof dipped in the middle to curve upwards to a point at both ends. To Lydia it felt very foreign.

'It's my favourite place,' Adil said, at the restaurant, smiling broadly and scanning the menu. The red glow from a dozen lights, hung from a central beam, provided the only light, though a burst of brighter light and a wave of hot steam blew in from the kitchen each time the waiter passed.

'The walnut chicken is good and so is the saffron rice. How about a starter of shark's fin soup?'

'You choose. I'm too tired to think.'

While he sipped chilled water, he poured her a Tiger beer. She gulped noisily and held out her glass for more.

'Careful,' he said. 'It's stronger than you think.'

'For Christ's sake, I'm not a child,' she snapped. 'You're as bad as my husband . . . I mean as bad as he was when he was alive.'

He frowned.

She knew she shouldn't say it but couldn't help herself. 'It's what we whites do, you know. Get plastered.'

Tendons appeared in his neck and there was a sharp look on his face. 'If that's what it takes, Lydia, but don't we have plans to make?'

Still sullen, she gazed at him.

When he looked her straight in the face, it seemed he could see right through her. 'I'm sorry,' she said. 'I shouldn't have said that.'

He smiled. 'Don't lose heart, not now you've come this far.'

'It's just that I feel so damn tired.'

'Are you ill?'

She shook her head. 'No. Let's make plans.'

'Good. Well, first, I hope to locate the boy.'

'You reckon you will?'

He thought for a minute. 'I will. Like Cicely, I have many contacts.'

She was surprised at how sure he sounded. She tilted her head and looked at him. 'A lot of things seem so odd.'

She thought he avoided her eyes by turning to the waiter and ordering for them both in rapid Chinese. While he was looking away, she studied the angles of his face.

'There's more than work between you and Cicely, isn't there?' It was just a hunch, but she could tell by the faint flush in his cheeks that she'd hit on something.

'You're mistaken.' He didn't meet her eyes.

It hung between them, this unspoken thing.

She sighed, blowing out her cheeks, then looked at Adil, smelt a trace of lemon spice and cardamom. He was decent. Good. She felt sure of it. His face was trustworthy, that was the only word for it.

'Have you ever been married?'

His lips tightened. 'No. Now can we just concentrate on the matter in hand.'

Stung by the rebuke in his voice, and her own lack of sensitivity, she muttered an apology.

He sighed. 'It doesn't matter.'

There was a slight pause. 'Where do you come from? It's hard to tell.'

'I'm really not in the mood for an interrogation.'

She pulled a funny face, as if she were one of the children, and he relented.

'Okay. I'm part Malayan, part Portuguese, with a dab of Sumatran and some Chinese somewhere. Probably descended from pirates. Does that satisfy you?'

She smiled. 'Exotic.'

He let his stony expression go and Lydia felt happier.

'I'll go to Singapore or Johore,' she said. 'See if I can find a lead.'

'You can't just stray from place to place. You need to rest.'

'I can't. I'm going to have to get a job.'

He spread his arms wide. 'Lydia, you've got guts, but you must recharge your batteries, or you'll end up ill. You look exhausted.'

297

The thought of finding Maz tugged at her. 'Okay, but what will you do?'

'Well, as I said, first the child, and then the girl you spoke about.'

'Lili.'

'There isn't much to go on. But someone will know. Someone always does.'

She scratched her head and yawned. He was right. She needed rest.

'I have a contact, an ex-colleague of George's. I'll see what he can do. We'll take it from there.' He looked at his watch. 'Look, it's late. We can look for a taxi if you like, but you're welcome to stay at mine tonight. It's okay, no need to look so worried. I'll sleep on the sofa.'

His eyes were amused, but it wasn't worry he'd seen on her face.

'Thanks,' she managed to say. 'I'll stay.'

36

I woke at dawn, skin prickling, the blanket tangled round my legs. I sat up, and pulled out the letter from Veronica. I knew it by heart, but held it at an angle to catch the light and read the words again.

My dearest Emma, she wrote,

On my last visit to London I discovered the name of the painter. Charles Lloyd Patterson. Unfortunately the gentleman has passed on, but I have his old address, where a small gallery of his work is kept for public viewing. I took the liberty of writing, on your behalf, to ask if we might pay a call. Yesterday the keeper wrote back.

If you agree, I shall collect you very early for your next exeat, and we'll go to Cheltenham. That's where the house is. Afterwards I thought a trip to the Gaumont cinema, if that's agreeable.

By the way, I need to take you for a fitting for your bridesmaid's dress, while we're there. I hope you don't mind yellow. Fleur has already had hers.

With fondest best wishes,
Veronica

It was too early to get dressed so I lay back, listening to the sounds of the sleeping girls and the first birdsong of the morning. More than once I heard Rebecca cry out in her sleep, and thin snores came from dark corners of the dorm. Though it was early May, it was windy, and whistles ran round the building, sending a draught to slip under our door.

As soon as the bell rang, I was up and dressed. I skipped breakfast, rushed into the office to collect my slip, and raced from the building, wind whipping the hair into my eyes. Veronica waited, bright eyed and upright in her Morris Minor. She looked very smart in black ski-pants and a tight yellow sweater.

'Excited?' she said with a grin.

'You bet.'

We drove through a pretty village and then through Kidderminster. I envied the grubby faced kids playing cricket and yelling at each other in the street, and opened the window to listen to them. Then we passed more kids swinging from rafters in a bombed-out church. To me, it seemed that boys had a particular kind of freedom that I did not.

An hour later, on the edge of Cheltenham, we passed rows of simple houses, their gardens strung with washing lines, and lined with tiny vegetable plots and smelly pigsties. There, apart from the kids, the streets were narrow and empty, but further on it changed to leafy avenues, and sweeping regency buildings. In the centre it was very noisy, with cars, bicycles and pedestrians.

Veronica parked and we walked past the Gaumont cinema, where bunting stretched right across the street, and a huge poster advertised the new John Mills film, *The Dambusters*.

'I know Birmingham's closer but I love Cheltenham,' she said, with a broad grin. 'After London, it's my favourite place.'

'Where will you live? I mean with Dad.'

'In the village. Your father isn't keen on London. Though I still have my old flat there. It's a crumbly old place in Wandsworth. I really should sell it or let it out, but it's so handy when I go up to town. I'll take you there sometime.'

She stopped and grinned at me. 'Here we are. Remind me before we go to get a pound of cheese and some sliced ham at Victoria Stores.'

★ ★ ★

We walked up the stone steps of a moderately sized town house in a small terrace. I looked back over my shoulder at the trees spaced all along on both sides of the road, their roots lifting the pavements.

The woman who answered the bell looked about sixty, with white hair piled randomly on top of her head, very pale skin, gold specs and a look of importance in her grey eyes. Though when I glanced at her feet, the fluffy pink mules didn't quite match. In fact, I could just imagine the rollers in her hair, partly covered by a paisley headscarf, while she smoked on the doorstep of one of the houses we saw on our way into town.

She held out her hand. 'Bonnie Butcher. Do

301

come into the back drawing room. You can ask whatever you like there. It used to be Mr Patterson's favourite room. Mine now, of course.'

I didn't know who she was. It crossed my mind she might have been the painter's wife, but the genteelly disguised accent, and the image I first had of her, told me she was not.

'It's a lovely house,' Veronica remarked.

'Do make yourself comfortable while I fetch the tea. Would you like cake? I'm afraid I have to charge for cake and admission.'

Veronica nodded politely, as my stomach growled from lack of breakfast.

I looked round the room. There were knick-knacks on every surface, and the wallpaper was fussy, patterned with yellow willow trees and exotic blue birds. The sofa was upholstered in plush green velvet, and studded in a diamond pattern, and three gold-shaded standard lamps lit the room, their tasselled edges shifting slightly with the movement of air. I leant forward, pressing my palms down on the velvet pile of the sofa.

Bonnie Butcher came back with a delicate tray and placed it on a small round table between us.

'Help yourself to cake.'

There were two kinds. I went for a slice of chocolate layer cake, but groaned inwardly when I noticed two clear prints where my clammy palms had flattened the velvet pile of the sofa. Transferring the cake to my other hand, I carefully rubbed one of the marks, only making it worse. I shifted uncomfortably in my seat, and hoped she hadn't noticed.

A stretch of silence passed, with only the clink of teacups, and me trying to chew as quietly as I could. The lady drank her tea with a little finger raised in the air and kept glancing at me. When she'd finished, she patted her lips with a paper napkin, and took a breath.

'Now, you wish to find out the name of somebody who sat for the artist. Is that correct?'

'Yes. In the nineteen twenties. I have the picture here.'

Veronica took the miniature from me and passed it to the woman.

She nodded. 'Oh, yes. I can help you there.'

'Oh, please,' I burst out.

She raised an eyebrow.

I plastered what I hoped was a trustworthy smile across my face and explained. 'You see she might be a relative.'

I don't know if what I said upset her, but she frowned, and with narrowed eyes looked cagey for a moment. I held my breath and crossed my fingers behind my back.

'I know this woman,' she said, after a long pause. 'There are two more of her. You'd better follow me.'

I rose from the sofa with as much poise as I could, and she led us up a sweeping staircase to a room with big windows. They stretched from floor to ceiling, and overlooked a garden with tall trees swaying in the wind. Though it wasn't cold, a fire blazed in an ornate, open fireplace.

Portraits of varying sizes covered the walls. Old faces, young faces, ugly faces, beautiful faces; their eyes followed you wherever you looked. On the wall opposite the windows, a painting of a middle-aged gentleman with a beard and a moody-looking face hung beside two other pictures of portly men.

'This is the gallery,' she said proudly. She pointed a finger past my shoulder. 'And that woman is the one in your painting. Emma Rothwell.'

I spun round. The face was luminous, her cheeks soft, her face oval, and proud arched eyebrows framed hazel eyes, though flecks the colour of deep water took them somewhere between blue and green. She looked even more like my mother than in the miniature I held in my hand. I sucked in my breath. Veronica nodded and smiled, but I felt a burst of heat. The room spun and I stepped back against a table.

I must have gone dizzy, because the next thing I knew, I was leaning back on a big squishy sofa with Veronica bending over me. Bonnie Butcher had left the room.

'Are you all right?' Veronica said, looking worried.

'It's the heat.'

She reached out a hand.

I held it and the words came out in a rush. 'My mother's maiden name was Rothwell. She never thought it was a real name. She thought it was just a name the nuns gave her.'

'All right,' she said. 'Now we know what we have to do. Let's find out if Emma Rothwell is still alive.'

I nodded and said a little prayer. Please God

let her be alive, and please let us find her. We went downstairs, Veronica holding me by the elbow. At the bottom Bonnie Butcher handed us a little catalogue.

'Of course, none of it's for sale. He left the place to me you know, for my lifetime, that is. I just have to keep it going as a gallery.' She paused. 'If you're interested, I can show you the rest of the house.'

I grabbed the opportunity, my mind spinning with thoughts of Emma Rothwell. Who she was, what she was doing there, how she knew the painter. I hoped Bonnie Butcher could tell me more.

Downstairs was very old fashioned, just three rooms with uneven flagstone floors, and small high windows that you could only see out of if you went on tiptoe. The two at the back looked out on a yard. She saw me balancing.

'We keep the coal out there and, of course, the original WC is there too.'

In the narrow front room an old black hob with a copper pan took up half the wall, with a mangle and Belfast sink on the other side. From the ceiling a wide contraption hung, with wheels and rope: a kind of pulley, I guessed, for drying clothes

'He liked things kept the way they used to be,' she said.

Upstairs her eyes darted about as she showed us his studio, a high, north facing room, with a larger than usual window. She stroked the objects as we went round, as if by touch alone she could assure their continued presence.

Everything seemed to be intact, as if the artist had just popped out. Tubes of oil paint, brushes, even a lingering trace of turps mingled with the smell of Ibcol disinfectant. There wasn't a speck of dust anywhere, though I didn't imagine it was like that when he worked there. Bonnie Butcher prefers it this way, I thought. Easier to clean a dead artist's studio.

'She would have sat there for her portrait,' she said.

I looked at the faded chair in the window. That chair. Emma Rothwell sat in that chair when she wasn't much older than me.

'Can I?' I asked.

She nodded, and I sat to look out on an old-fashioned garden, with a square lawn, hedges down the sides, and tangled ivy climbing over the wooden fence at the back. In front of that were tall poplars. My grandmother must have stared at those same trees, in all sorts of moods, listened to the blackbirds chirrup, heard voices from the other gardens. For a moment I couldn't have felt more alone. The sky was sullen and dull, but maybe she looked out when sunlight threw a pattern on the grass beneath the trees. Or maybe it was winter, and the lawn and hedges would have been white with snow.

So close to her, I felt myself slip back into the past. I wondered if she wore scent, and what it smelt like. I wanted to hear her story, yet I, who could tell stories from morning until night, couldn't think of a single reason she would abandon her baby in the way she had.

I heard a transistor radio playing in one of the

gardens. *Housewives' Choice*. Doris Day was singing '*Que sera, sera*', one of Mum's favourite songs. It brought me back to the present.

'Did you know Mr Patterson for long?' I asked.

'All my life. He never married, though he was a handsome man. I was his housekeeper. He made his name as a war painter, you know. First World War of course.'

I didn't know. There only seemed to be portraits on display.

'The war pictures all sold, every one. After the war he turned to portraits, though they didn't do as well. I met her, you know, Emma Rothwell.' She gave me a funny look. 'With the light on your face like that, you have a look of her.'

My heart was pounding as I asked the next question. 'What happened to her?'

'Oh, I wouldn't know about that. I only saw them when they sat, dear. And it was a long time ago.'

★   ★   ★

We didn't go to the park to see the boating, or to see a film, but Veronica took me to the Belle View Hotel for lunch, and then we went shopping. I couldn't believe it when she let me choose some black ski-pants just like hers, a dark blue duffle coat that I'd wanted for ages, and a little tight-fitting powder blue jumper. I was so happy I could have cried. She told me her hair was permed and asked if I wanted mine done. I laughed and pointed at my wild curls, but I said

I'd like it cut, and she took me to her own hairdresser. While my hair fell on the floor, 'Sweet Sixteen' played on the radio. Veronica took out a slim silver cigarette case and lit up, and I really wished I *was* sixteen. I came away with a short pixie cut and felt very grown up. We forgot the cheese and ham, though, sadly, not the yellow bridesmaid's dress.

★ ★ ★

Taller now, Fleur was growing up too. The puppy fat was gone, and her once blonde hair, now light brown, was in a ponytail. When she came into my room dressed up in some old clothes of Granny's — she'd pinned up a long black skirt at the back and wore a floral blouse — I saw her as if for the first time, and realised Fleur was very pretty. Little snub nose and dimpled chin. The boys that wanted a girl who hung on their every word, while they pretended to be tough, would be after her. Unlike me. I was too opinionated to be attractive to most boys.

'Do you want to play dressing up?' she said. 'We could do one of your stories, like we used to.'

'Why would I want to do that? It's kids' stuff.'

She looked at me strangely.

'Why are you looking at me like that?' I snapped.

'Nothing. It's just your hair. You're different, Em, you never play any more.'

'In case you haven't noticed, I'm not here most of the time.'

She looked at me with tears in her eyes. 'But even when you are you don't.'

'Don't be silly. Anyway it's nothing to do with you.'

This wasn't strictly true, because what was on my mind was everything to do with me and her, but if I told her, she'd give the game away.

I left the room to find Veronica. Father was at home all the time, and though he'd accepted a job in Birmingham, an admin job at a hotel chain, he hadn't started yet. He was glued to the television, watching the news, so I motioned to Veronica to come outside.

It was growing dark in the garden, and mist rising across the field made the beech tree look ghostly. I had a flash of our garden in Malacca, and felt sad about that one, as well as this one. Granddad's pride and joy. Once there had been gooseberry bushes, a lilac tree, raspberry canes in one corner, and a gnarled crab apple at the back. And all along the wire fence, he had grown prize marrows and cabbages.

The mist turned to fine rain as soon as Veronica came out.

'I've been thinking about Emma Rothwell,' she said, putting up a hand to protect her hair.

'Me too.'

'If she's alive, and if I can find an address, let's visit her together.'

'It's a big if . . .'

She patted me on the shoulder and went in. I'd wanted to know if I could trust her, and now I really felt I could. Was it wrong? Would Mum be cross that her rival was helping me? I shook my head. In my heart I knew Veronica was not Mum's rival, knew too that my mother did not love my father.

In Malaya, when the moon lit the balcony, I used to hide, listen to the adults talk and watch the foxes fly between the trees. When I told Billy foxes could fly, he called me a liar and ignored me for a week. I knew all about Mum's love affair with Jack, though she didn't know I did. Once, when Jack stayed the night, I slipped round the outside balcony and peered through the open window at their sleeping bodies, the thin sheet hardly even covering them. I didn't know what to do. I was angry, wanted to rush in there and push him out. Dad should have been there, not him. But then Mum smiled in her sleep, and I crept away. For days I kept looking at her and wondering what to do, but the thing was, everything went on as normal. The world didn't end, at least not then.

37

The sour smell of her own sweat woke her, followed by the shrill ring of the phone. She wiped the damp from her hairline, tripped over her clothes, and sat at the end of the bed nursing her ankle. It was late. Bright sun had already burnt off the morning mist and she was wondering why she'd stayed. She knew, of course, but tried to convince herself it was because she felt deceived by Cicely, who'd never hinted at the nature of her work, nor even that she had a job at all. And after all, if that was the case, what more hadn't she said?

There was a sound of knocking. She stumbled from the room, rubbed the sleep from her eyes, grabbed Adil's bathrobe and opened the door.

Cicely stood on the mat, serene and coordinated, in a dove grey, silk shift dress, and red, patent-leather strap sandals. She held a large holdall, had a contrite smile on her face, and smelt of her usual expensive scent. Someone less like a spy it was hard to imagine, unless, of course, you took into account her incomparable ability to maintain her cool.

'What on earth?' Lydia said.

'Sorry to interrupt, darling. Had no choice.' Cicely put her foot in the doorway.

Lydia raised a hand to block her. 'I know, Cicely. About your work.'

Cicely's eyes widened. She cocked her head

311

and shrugged. 'Then you'll know the doormat is not the place to discuss it. Here, I brought you some clothes.'

'How did you know I was here?'

'Oh, darling, don't be silly. Of course I knew.'

Lydia allowed her to pass and trailed after her into the flat. Cicely positioned herself in front of the window. Then her wide-eyed stare swept over Lydia. 'I see you've taken my advice.'

Lydia glanced down at Adil's black silk robe. In the night, when a dream of Lili shocked her into waking, she'd padded to the bathroom, heard his slow regular breathing as she passed. A full moon had cast a silver light across his forehead and cheekbones, throwing the hollows of his face into greater darkness. He stirred in his sleep, and she'd hurried back to bed.

'It's not what you think.'

'I believe you. Thousands wouldn't,' Cicely said. 'Though I have to agree, he's utterly delectable.' She raised her eyebrows and gave Lydia a grin. 'However, just a little tip, darling, stay away from God's gift. He's dangerous. But then you like bad boys don't you, darling? So much better in the sack. Where is he anyway?'

'Did he tell you I was here?'

Cicely shrugged

Lydia looked away. 'I've no idea where he is.'

'Well, come over here and listen to what I've heard.'

Lydia stood where she was, hands on hips. 'Hang on a minute. You haven't explained why you never told me about your job. Or that you work with Adil. In fact, when I mentioned his name, you didn't even tell me you knew him.'

'There's more than one Adil, darling, though even Ralph doesn't know the half of it. I told you men never know what's really going on.'

'I'm beginning to believe you.'

She stared past Cicely at the typical blue-skied Malacca morning. Where was Adil? He'd promised to call on a colleague of George's, but hadn't mentioned how long he'd be gone. She crossed to the refrigerator and took out a beer.

Cicely lit a cigarette, blonde hair neatly tucked behind one ear. 'Something rather extraordinary has happened,' she said. 'Promise not to be upset.'

There was a subtle shift in atmosphere.

'It's about Lili.'

Lydia tensed.

There was a glint of amusement in Cicely's eyes. 'She's been picked up by the harbour police. You know they have to keep a watch out for subversive suspects on the fishing boats. Though it's more likely the communists are smuggling across the Straits of Johore, not here. Anyway, Lili's been implicated in Jack's murder. I thought you'd want to know — shall I go on?'

Lydia inhaled sharply and gave a curt nod.

Cicely told the whole story, and when she'd finished, she walked towards the door. 'Well, I'll let you get on. Come back to the house when you get tired of lover boy.'

★ ★ ★

Lydia sat on the sofa and leant back. According to Cicely, a chance remark from a harbour master had alerted the police, and Lili was picked up wandering the docks. She declared she was ruined, and claimed Jack had raped her. She insisted she'd only wanted to pay him back. Lydia gulped down the beer to rid herself of the bitter taste. With the image of Lili's perfume bottle in her mind, Lydia knew it was lies. The girl's duplicity left her breathless. She clenched her fists, the anger growing so intense she had to sit to stop herself from smashing something. Lili had been perfectly willing. Jealousy caused Jack's death, nothing more. George had been right about that. She hung her head and covered her eyes, desperate to wipe the image of Jack's blood from her mind.

When brought in and challenged, Lili had admitted her involvement with the insurgents, maintaining that she'd run away to be free of Jack. Crushed and dispirited, she'd hidden in the only place he couldn't find her. The jungle. When the communists picked her up, she had persuaded Maznan's mother that her son was in danger. So they ransacked Jack's house, and came away with food, but no money, but the important thing was, they'd found a way in, and the next day Maz was taken.

Lydia remembered Lili's slender waist and back, the long black hair stretching all the way down to tight, high buttocks. She imagined Jack sleeping with her, night after night. She imagined Lili cry out, and saw them lie together afterwards, Jack smoking, hands behind his head, blue eyes gazing at the ceiling in the way he did. Even now she felt the sting of jealousy. For a

314

moment she thought of Alec, and their old life together. The way she used to come out of the bathroom, intentionally dropping her towel on the floor, and completely naked, raise her arms in front of him to tie up her hair. He wouldn't even notice her there. It was the price she'd had to pay to be somebody, and for ignoring the early presentiments of disaster.

She wanted to blame Lili, but couldn't get away from the thought that if she hadn't turned up at the plantation, none of this would have happened. Lili would be happy in her role as Jack's mistress and Jack would still be alive. Instead, some months after Maz was taken, on a line crackling with interference, speaking in a gruff imitation of Bert, one of the insurgents had made that fateful call to Jack.

Lydia pushed herself up and paced about Adil's apartment. She picked things up, looked at his books, tried to work out what the place revealed. She took a large illustrated text on Monet from shelves stuffed with records and books, mainly philosophical works and books on art, and flicked through it. In Adil's absence, she thought about him too much. On the coffee table, a few neat models brought to life the animals of the jungle, and on the walls, large, heavily layered abstracts were interspersed with black and white photos of people.

Adil had left no indication of when he'd be back and didn't call, so she made a light meal of toast and tinned sardines. The bread tasted stale and the tin of sardines was the only thing she found at the back of a cupboard, his fridge mainly containing soft drinks and a few bottled beers.

She thought of going back to Cicely's house but wanted to see Adil again, so she sat in the window and watched the people passing by, noting how they dressed, the way they moved. When she dozed off, hair-swinging visions of Lili tormented her.

★　★　★

When Adil turned up after midnight, he found her sitting in the dark, paralysed with guilt, her face ashen.

'Lydia?'

For a moment, she barely noticed him sit beside her. He took her hand and gently stroked her cheek. A dull rumble of traffic and the sound of a piano came from the street. She covered her face with her hands, then, feeling his breath on her neck, she cried.

He held her very close, their breathing in tune, but a blast of noise in the street broke up the moment.

He coughed, and she pulled away, feeling a little foolish. 'Who painted the pictures?' she asked, avoiding his eyes.

There was a pause.

'Someone I used to know,' he said at length. He seemed to be studying her face in the half-light. 'I'm sorry it took so long. I have to tell you my news.'

Her feelings under control, she looked at him. 'Is it good? Your news?'

'I hope so . . . '

38

Veronica popped into my room to say she was off. I really wanted to talk to her before she went, but considered for a moment. If the school found out how I'd rifled through the files, more than a year before, I'd be in big trouble.

I took a breath, crossed my fingers, and smiled at her. Then I explained how I'd found out a solicitor was paying my fees.

'So I wrote to him, but he said they couldn't divulge the name, client confidentiality or something.'

I felt slightly nervous when she looked a bit dismayed.

'I won't tell your father, Emma,' she said, 'if that's what you're worried about. It's not that. It's just I thought *he* was paying.'

'I thought it was Dad too, but Gran says he's broke.'

She tilted her head to one side, narrowed her eyes and began to smile. 'You thought it was me, didn't you?'

I reddened.

'That was the reason for the grilling you gave me that time, wasn't it? About Freddy, my solicitor. I thought it was strange, your sudden interest in my legal concerns.'

I pulled a face.

'Well, darling, it really isn't me. But next time

I see Freddy, I'll ask if there is a way he can find out.'

'Thanks.'

She gave my shoulder a squeeze and left.

★ ★ ★

Half an hour later I went out, humming. My collar up, I stared at the pavement as I walked, trying to get to one hundred without walking on a crack and disturbing the frighteners who hid in there.

I liked the quiet of the May half term holiday. It was nice in a way, not knowing what would happen next, even though nothing much ever did. At school everything happened to a timetable, even down to when you brushed your teeth or went to the loo, and heaven help you if you hadn't done a number two, because then they'd dose you with cod liver oil.

Between the tall trees lining the road, the wind was blowing wildly. I was counting, and didn't see him approach from the shadows, only glanced up because there was the smell of smoky bacon coming from a house nearby.

'Emma,' he said, and made to walk past.

I caught his eye, and saw, behind him, the morning clouds were black and broken, with silver light in the gaps between.

'Billy! Sorry, I didn't see you.'

I was close enough to smell the shampoo he must have used. Peppermint. And close enough to see the way his frayed shirt collar stuck up at the back.

'Thought you were ignoring me.' He looked at the ground, and the tips of his ears turned red.

'Don't be daft. It's just I was miles away.'

He shuffled from foot to foot. 'How's school?'

A moment from the past returned to embarrass me. The memory of undressing in front of him. He might have had the same thought, because his whole face turned red. In the uncomfortable silence, he laughed. 'Fancy a trip to the barn?' he said, though his voice sounded unnatural. 'For old times' sake.'

As we stood face to face, I reckoned he just said it for something to say, and I didn't know what to say. I hadn't seen this tall gangly boy for ages, but suddenly the devil inside me piped up, and I agreed.

My feet moved somehow, and we made off in the direction of the barn, neither of us speaking. The sun came out brighter, and from the field behind the trees a smell of cow dung drifted our way. Each blade of grass was emerald, backlit like in a film, and the sky turned yellow between the dark clouds. As we walked, every noise seemed emphasised, the birds, the wind, our footsteps clunking and shuffling, not walking in time. In the distance an occasional car beeped its horn. I was buzzing all over, so much so that I had pins and needles in my toes.

He was still shabby, but when the sun touched his face, from the corner of my eye I saw there was something sweet too. He sloped rather than walked, hands in his pockets, dark blond hair falling over his eyes. And he'd grown into his teeth. In fact they looked white and sparkly. He

319

said he went to the grammar school.

'How is it?' I asked.

'Yeah. Good.' He paused and touched my arm. 'Em.'

Something fierce about the look of his face made me blush, and the gap between us suddenly shrank.

'Sorry about before. You know . . . I had no choice.'

My heart flipped over. He was referring to the day he'd been forced into telling them where I was hiding. 'Don't be daft, Billy,' I said. 'That was zillions ago. Forget it.'

We walked on, chatting a bit more easily, though the feeling of awkwardness hung on a bit. At the barn he stopped at the bottom of the ladder, stared at his feet, then looked at me with eyes shining like mirrors, and a strange expression on his face.

'You're really beautiful, Em,' he said. He half smiled but looked self-conscious.

At once I knew why we were there, and it wasn't for old times' sake. I didn't care. He called me beautiful and in that moment, more than anything, I wanted to be.

We avoided the rotten boards and sat with a gap between us, our legs dangling over the edge. He leant across as if to kiss me. I moved the wrong way and his lips caught the side of my nose. He turned scarlet but I giggled and shuffled up close. He kissed me again and this time it was in the right place. He put an arm round me and I leant up against him. He was warm, really warm, but a voice in my head repeated words I'd overheard my father say to Mum.

'Blood will out, Lydia. Emma is uncontrollable. She'll follow in your footsteps — *and* your mother's — if she remains out of control.'

He'd slammed the door, but I stayed glued to the spot. What was it my mother had done, and exactly where would blood come out?

Before Billy and I left the barn we lay on our backs holding hands. We didn't do anything more after the one kiss. He smelt of cigarettes and though he no longer wanted to be a magician, he still had magic in his hands. I knew because when he squeezed mine, the tingle spread to my chest. It was like being in another world, safe and out of the way.

★   ★   ★

Back at school again, and it was Saturday. I sat in the hall outside the office, waiting to pick up my letters. The odd job man appeared with a ladder and chucked me a toffee. I watched two nuns pass by, heads together, looking serious. Three girls came by and one of them winked: Rebecca. We seemed to have reached a truce of kinds.

The black and white hall floor had chips round the edges of the tiles, and dirt impacted in deep scratches. The walls were dull brown, and a houseplant took up one corner of the hall, a spindly rubber plant, grown too tall, missing half of its lower leaves. Nothing like the rubber trees of Malaya.

Once, Father took me up in a helicopter, early.

As the light came up, I looked down on our house and the school, and saw the mist that lay above the rocky boulders in the river. Then we flew above rubber plantations and the jungle. From above, the land looked dense and frightening. Father said the spirit of the jungle had a voice, a Chinese voice. I thought he was talking about real spirits, and laughed. He didn't explain he was referring to terrorists.

My mum and dad were so different. An image of my mother's wide smile appeared, full of life. Dad never laughed as much as her. I tried to remember what she was wearing the last time I saw her, when she drove us to school. I remembered getting out of the car and us waving as we ran backwards. But that's all I could remember. My eyes grew damp. It upset me that I was losing my memories.

The secretary came out of her office and stood in the doorway, a clutch of envelopes in her hand.

'Penny for them,' she said with a smile.

I stood up, feeling defensive, as if she could see into my heart. She reached across, holding an envelope by the tips of manicured fingernails, lacquered in sugar pink. I slipped it into my pocket, and went to the bench in the middle of the shrubbery. With the summer holidays approaching, I would get a chance to talk to Dad. He worked in Birmingham now, smartly dressed and travelling long distances.

I felt in my pocket for his letter and ripped it open. They were usually brief and today's was no different, except for a fact tucked away at the bottom. I hugged myself when I read that Mr Oliver was ill.

Just the thought of the wedding made my heart lurch. My fantasy was that if Veronica found Emma Rothwell, alive and well, we'd go to stay with her after the wedding. I didn't consider she might not want us with her, or might refuse to accept us as her grandchildren, or might not even be our grandmother.

I went to the quiet room to write more of my latest venture. Lose myself in a story.

It was a large airy space with high up windows, so you couldn't look out, and where we sat our dreaded end of year exams. Supervised by a rota of sixth form monitors on Saturdays, anyone who felt inclined could go there to get on with what they wanted. Talk was forbidden, so it became my only opportunity to write uninterrupted. Most girls avoided it like the plague; I guarded it jealously. I wanted to work on my current story, a melodrama in which my new heroine, Claris de la Costa, was locked in the suffering caused by her evil grandfather. Sinking into the silence around me, I needed to come to a swift conclusion. Something that would have the reader gasp, open-mouthed with surprise, at my wit. But I kept losing the thread, so relieved by the contents of Dad's letter that I couldn't concentrate. I crossed my fingers and made a wish that Mr Oliver would stay ill for a very long time. In fact, for ever.

39

The decaying hospital, once a palatial District Officer's residence, had been taken over by Japanese during the war, and used as a prison. The sombre building, halfway up the hill, now a place to house the mentally ill, was entered through an intricately carved wooden door. Inside, Lydia shrank from the stench. With no natural light and a series of locked doors spaced round an octagonal hallway, it wasn't hard to imagine the screams of torture victims. She flinched at the thought of how much pain must have been absorbed into those walls.

With fists clenched, and a stern face, Adil walked over to the office. There was no trace of the previous evening's gentleness. At the desk he flashed his ID. A reluctant guard nodded, then opened one of the doors and led them through the length of the building. From the floor above came the sound of misery: a peal of unnatural laughter, soft persistent weeping, a sudden low pitched sob. Just as they became accustomed to the gloom, the guard opened another door, indicating they should enter.

'Press the bell when you want to leave.' The man grunted and slammed the door.

Lydia heard the key turn in the lock and looked about her. It was a drab little room, from which all colour had drained away. A stink of urine and disinfectant came from a covered bucket in one corner, and there was the sound of water from an underground stream flowing beneath the floor. With the damp, the smells of the jungle leaked through. Lydia's stomach turned over.

Lili sat on a metal chair. Ragged and changed beyond recognition, her formerly luminous complexion grey, her slim frame emaciated, the beautiful long hair roughly shorn. She raised a face dotted with mosquito bites, and lined with rage.

'Are they mistreating you?' Lydia asked, appalled.

The girl got up, spun round and hurled her chair at Lydia. It clattered against the wall, before landing on the floor, missing her target. She launched herself at Lydia. Adil caught her arm and forced her back. Eyes darting between them, she struggled, scratching and clawing at Adil's face, and beating his chest. When she eventually grew limp, he let her go.

'She stole him from me.' She hissed the words and narrowed her eyes, a thin smile twisting her features. 'Only I knew what Jack really liked.'

Pulling up her skirt, she turned round with her back to them, and made a rotating movement with her naked arse.

Lydia recoiled, suppressing the urge to retch.

'I only persuaded his mother the child was in danger. In return for helping her get Maznan back, they said . . . ' She paused and hung her head. 'I did not want them to kill him.'

'Go on,' Adil said coldly.

Lili winced. 'They agreed to bring Jack for me.'

Lydia's hand went to her mouth.

'No! Not to kill him. If I helped them get Maznan, they would take Jack away. From you. White bitch. Not kill him.' She pointed at Lydia, then leant her skeletal body against the wall and slumped to the floor.

Adil went across to her, lifted her by the arms, placed her chair the right way up and sat her down on it. 'Do you want a glass of water?'

She shrank back, and stifled a sob. A silence fell. Lydia looked at the dim square of light at the barred window. She wanted to blame the girl, but this wasn't her fault. An image etched on the back of her eyes surfaced once again. Jack lying in the dust, his blood congealing.

After the girls died, she'd hoped her love for Jack would be the road to salvation. That together they'd give each other what both longed for. Instead she brought death to him and insanity to Lili. No one had been saved. She felt dizzy in the stagnant air. There was no salvation in this hellish country, only the certainty of heat, sweat and violence.

Adil motioned Lydia towards the door.

'What happened to Maznan's mother? Have they got her?' Lydia asked him.

'I never meant for him to die,' Lili sobbed. 'I loved him.'

Adil pressed the bell. 'I'll tell you afterwards.'

'I painted the wall of the temple,' the girl said, in a sing-song tone, staring at Lydia with a dangerous edge to her black eyes.

Lydia caught Adil's eye. He shrugged.

'I painted four dragons, galloping in the sky.

But I painted their pupils in. It was big mistake. They flew away.' She laughed bitterly and spat on the filthy floor.

Adil glanced back at her.

She put one finger to her mouth and gave him a fierce look. 'Shhh! Just one remained. The one with a blank eye . . . ' She trailed off, still staring at him.

They left the room and were shown out of the back entrance. Relieved to be out in fresh air, Lydia closed her eyes and breathed freely. Adil was already moving off.

'You said you'd tell me about Maz's mother,' she said, catching up.

'Maz's mother became one of the girls who collects subscriptions. Dressed up as a tapper, in dark blue with a black headscarf.'

Lydia frowned.

'She collected subscriptions for the people on the inside. She got access that way. To the insiders, and at the same time to the workers on the plantation.'

'And how did Lili end up here?'

He shrugged. 'After she was picked up by harbour police they decided she was deranged.'

Beneath a pink sky they walked on to a once beautiful mosaic floor, now pockmarked, and surrounded by white hibiscus grown ten feet high. It gave on to rambling overgrown gardens, where fragments of sound rose from the town below. A flock of birds swooped by, and in a distant part of the grounds, she heard a door swing in a sudden breeze. She looked towards the sound.

'It's a summerhouse. Would you like to see?'

He walked with purpose to a crumbling pavilion. The house itself was hidden in a small grove, and surrounded by half a dozen tall trees, their branches leaning in to form a patterned canopy. Chattering monkeys raced up the trunks, to swing, one handed, from the top. Flowers of intense rose pink, with dark wrinkled leaves, fought their way through the windows, and the broken glass was tinted gold as the sun sank behind the mountain.

The door was warped, but with a determined push from Adil's shoulder, it gave way. Within, all that remained was a wooden bench and a couple of shabby rattan armchairs.

'I used to come here you know. In the beginning, George got me a job as a waiter. Those dazzling pre-war social extravaganzas. It's where I first met Cicely, laden with necklaces and bangles halfway up her arms, all bought from the spice market. Nineteen, penniless, and reckless.'

Lydia stared him in the eye. He was showing the strain.

'Of course it wasn't like this then. It was a scene set for love. Harriet Parrott saw to that. Silk cushions, scented candles, incense, flowers.' He spat into the dust.

Goose bumps came up on her skin. 'What is Cicely to you?'

He cleared his throat. 'I told you we worked together.'

'That's all?'

A brief silence followed. At the back of her

mind something wasn't right and she realised she didn't quite believe him.

He ran a hand across his smooth head. 'She's a dangerous woman.' There was a pause as he looked about. 'Come on. Let's go. I hate this place.'

'Is it just the place?' She tried to meet his eye, but he snorted and avoided contact. She watched him carefully, his face in profile now. 'I'm right aren't I? There is something else?'

'I didn't realise it showed.'

'Why?'

'You sure you want to know?'

She nodded, but had become used to searching for clues and felt a twinge of fear. If he was about to fill in the gaps, she wasn't sure if she really wanted to see the whole picture.

His voice was distant as he began to speak, and she was reminded of how he had seemed when they first met. She'd almost forgotten that cool haughty man, and watched as he turned his back on her.

'A jeep full of Japanese soldiers took my mother to a place very like this. This and other buildings like it. Mainly they wanted underage Chinese girls, but even though she was older, she still had a freshness about her and an air of fragility, so they gave her to the young green boys who treated her brutally. She was lucky to live. Most were kicked to death, or had their throats slit.'

Lydia looked through the broken glass in the window at the darkening sky. She closed her eyes and concentrated on his voice.

'They put her in a tank of cold water up to her neck. She had to stand for forty-eight hours or drown. How she survived . . . '

He paused, and she opened her eyes. He seemed somewhere else, and the shrug of hopelessness he gave, palms held uppermost, twisted her heart.

'They kept her for six months. Then one day they threw her out on to the street, naked, stinking of faeces and vomit, and covered in sores from where they put out cigarettes on her flesh.'

He pulled at a rope of dark leaves that twisted through a broken window. Picked a large, intensely pink rose, brought it to his nose, then let it drop to the ground. Very deliberately, he placed his heel on it and ground it into the dirt.

'As I said, she was lucky, if you can call it that. Many were forced to dig their own graves, then buried alive. She never recovered. Not really. Later, in her greatest hour of need, I . . . '

He hesitated.

'I was just too busy. The last time I saw her, she barely recognised me. Can you imagine how that feels, Lydia? I will never forgive myself. Never.'

Lydia sat completely still, the air between them thickening. As his words sank home, she felt for the first time the pain in them, the inaccessible place he kept hidden.

'I'm so sorry, Adil.'

He shrugged. 'That was the world then.'

'Do many Japanese remain?'

'All I know is, very few bastards were born.

330

They had a habit of killing the women they raped. I know all men are capable of cruelty, but because of my mother . . . '

'Adil.'

He clenched his fists. 'The war here ended in the middle of August, following the dropping of the bomb on Hiroshima. Thank God for it!'

She gulped, shocked by his words.

He lit a cigarette.

'I didn't know you smoked,' she said, wanting to help, but not knowing how.

'Only sometimes.'

'What will happen to Lili?'

'She'll get better. They'll let her out. She might get a chance to work in one of the troupes of actors. Or she'll turn to prostitution.'

'And Maznan's mother?'

'Come on,' he said. 'I think we've had enough. I'll tell you on the way.'

They left the summerhouse and passed back through the lonely gardens. A flat, black Malayan night descended with the rapidity of a curtain, and a depth of blackness like no other. She kept close to Adil. She didn't want to stumble in the dark, but she didn't actually touch him either.

'In the end Maznan's mother came out. She'll be in detention by now with her son.'

'Maz will be all right?'

'I think so.'

'Won't she be a target for the terrorists?'

He shrugged. 'Hopefully not. More and more are surrendering.'

'Why?'

'There's suffering on the inside. It'll be over

soon. Since Templer took over in nineteen fifty-two, it's only been a matter of time.'

Lydia knew. Alec said Templer was a tough, hands on Commissioner, who, along with the Psychological Warfare Department, used every trick to counter terrorism.

'His idea, was it, the acting troupes and film vans?' she asked.

Adil nodded. 'It's working at last.'

Only the tip of his cigarette lit their way, and in the darkness she lost her balance. She tipped forward, her heel caught in a crack in the hard ground. He reached out a hand to break her fall, but when she examined the shoe, she felt the high heel hanging uselessly. She pulled it right off. Now she had no option but to lean on him as she hobbled towards the entrance where they'd parked.

'So Maz is with his mother?' she asked, once they reached the tarmac.

'I told you I'd find someone who knew. That was the tip-off I had yesterday, but I wanted us to see Lili to confirm her involvement.'

★ ★ ★

That night it was her turn on the sofa. She padded into the kitchenette, mixed herself a large gin and quietly pulled up the blinds. A full moon slipped from between the clouds to silver an expanse of water, punctuated by dark sampans. She examined her nails, filed, clean, lacquered, prettier than when she lived with Jack. Oh, Jack, she thought, can I have forgotten you so soon? Only when the gin tingled in her blood and she felt light-headed could she relax.

Now she knew the truth about Jack's death, and what had happened to Maz, what was there to keep her here? After all, that's what she'd come to find out. And as for Adil, she couldn't allow herself to get closer. Apart from the fact he wasn't white, it was far too soon, and Jack still cast a long shadow.

She thought of Adil and scanned the horizon in the dark, tried not to imagine him asleep in the next room. She felt the war inside her. Her mistrust and her need. Who is he? she thought. He'd done all he said he would, but none the less, she was sure he'd withheld something.

40

The bus rumbled along the rugged shoreline of the Malacca Straits. Tiny fishing vessels dotted the water, and on the distant headland, Lydia spotted the lone ruin of a Dutch fort. She slid open the window to sniff wild orchids tumbling over wide spreading fig trees, their scent mingling with the hot salty air. White metallic sunlight suddenly blazed on the water. Blinded, she drew her head back in, and looked ahead instead, where the clouds spun out in a fan.

She longed for a sense of elation, a chance of hope, or, at the very least, some courage to face the future. She thought she'd become used to it, but when they picked up speed across the causeway between Johore and Singapore, her heart caught with memories of being there with her daughters. She felt the full weight of the loss bear down on her. How would she ever endure this?

Once in Singapore, the bus followed Connaught Drive, the sweeping road that paralleled the harbour, before stopping beside the Cenotaph, at the edge of Raffles Square.

As soon as the bus disappeared from view, she looked eastward and out to sea, and managed to resist a descent into sorrow. She squared her shoulders, and without even a glance towards the arched verandas of Tanglin Road, she ignored the tree-shaded boulevards of the European quarter. She turned her face up to the sun — it'd be fine. For her, like many others, that life was gone; instead, she made her way back along Victoria harbour, and the busy wide river that sliced the city in two.

A group of Englishmen in white hats, shorts, and long socks smiled as she walked past. She nodded in acknowledgement, carried on until her case grew heavy, then stopped to take in the old-fashioned trading vessels loading and unloading. Surprised to see them still there, she threw back her head, and laughed at the chaos. She began to feel better, watching cars and rickshaws ignoring the turbaned Indian traffic cops, and streams of people crossing the streets, kamikaze style. Singapore hadn't changed.

She hopped on another bus. As she got closer to Chinatown, Chinese music blasted from ornate buildings, and washing hung like flags from poles thrust haphazardly from every apartment. Singapore. Crossroads of the East. Isn't that what people said? The cheapest shopping centre in the whole world.

Most of the cheap hotels were cathouses, and she was lucky to find the Welcome Retreat, a tall thin building on three floors, with the unexpected odour of wood wax on every level. She clattered up the narrow staircase, dragging her bag to one of the three rooms at the top, which shared a bathroom.

In there, she struggled with the metal catch on the window. She wanted it open to let in air. It wasn't the Oceanview Hotel, but at least it was clean, and though the room was musty, it didn't stink of rancid fat, or cheap perfume. She took in the shabby furniture, then counted her dollars, for now still decorated with the portrait of the queen. With so little left, and needing a job, Singapore was the right place to be. Then maybe, with enough cash, she might get back to England: make a real new start.

Outside, a car's tyres squealed. On the floor below, a door banged. There was something else. Strained whispers from the room next to hers; a couple having a tense argument. She sat on the edge of the bed, trying not to listen. Time crawled as she wandered round the little hotel room, wanting something else to do. She told herself this was a decision she had to make. She couldn't rely on Adil for ever, and, in any case, it was time to be independent. Strong. She thought of his powerful face, remembered his breath on the nape of her neck when she'd cried.

The room reminded her of the dormitory at the top of a winding back staircase at the convent. Three of them had shared. She hadn't come very far, she thought, as she lay on the bed and closed her eyes. She tried to remember the person she'd been, but the girl she saw in her mind's eye seemed like another person, someone from another life altogether.

She saw herself just before her sixteenth birthday. The war had already begun. It had been summer, a sunny day with a totally blue sky, and she was expecting a visitor. Hair, fiery then, and wilder, like Emma's, and Sister Patricia, hands on hips insisting she have it cut. She'd been the only girl left, the only one with nowhere to go in the holidays.

She remembered waiting on the bench in front of the convent. Eleven o'clock came and went. They brought her lemonade, and an hour later, fish paste sandwiches. She couldn't eat and threw them on the ground for the birds. She leapt at the sound of every passing vehicle but didn't leave the spot. Sister Patricia gave her a copy of *The Family from One End Street* to read, but the words wouldn't lie still on the page.

Her visitor never came.

Lydia rubbed her eyes. The past hurt. That painful need for love. More than anything it was that. She thought of how much *she'd* loved her children and how little her own mother could have wanted her. She thought of Em and the last fancy dress competition at the club. Emma had gone as a clown. It was not the costume that won it, but Em turning a double somersault as she passed the judges' desk. The dismayed expression on her face when she dented her hat had made them laugh, and she bagged first prize on the strength of it. She smiled at the memory of Fleur's love of pretty dresses, and the terrible time when she'd had pneumonia and taken so long to recover.

She remembered standing in front of the ocean at Terengganu with Alec in 1946, six months after the war in the east ended. Malaya had been torn apart by the Japanese invasion, but they had stood, arms entwined, eating brazils and drinking coconut juice from a freshly cut shell. It had been a short break before his first tour began. Emma was just three and Fleur was on the way. She thought of the salty smell of the ocean, and when they kept the window open, the seductive scent of wild jasmine at night. How the scent had mingled with the smell of Pimms, and the heat from their bodies. How after they'd made love, she'd asked him to tell her more about his childhood. Ordinary, he said, except that his father disappeared for a while when he was a kid, but that's what inspired him to go places.

She sighed. Things had changed. All of that was gone and with so little of Jack's money left, she had to stop thinking and get a job. That's what it boiled down to.

* * *

The first job she found was in Singapore's largest department store, a marble pillared place of scented counters and whispered calm, where well-heeled customers were attended by overly courteous staff.

But on her floor, household goods, it was noisy. No calm. No perfume. A hundred cleaning products were lined up in meticulous rows, the lurid bottles dusted daily. Kettles were polished, kitchen utensils kept pristine.

To Lydia, the platform where she demonstrated the use of newfangled pressure cookers was a little theatre. It paid quite well, and she liked it, just as long as she didn't blow one of the darn things up. Required to begin a demonstration every hour, whether or not there was a crowd, she sat on a high stool on the platform overlooking the store, her long legs crossed.

338

From there she gazed out through the large window to watch her past walk by. European women, hair freshly set, meeting for cocktails at Raffles, and the church, surrounded by palms, where English children were instructed not to run by heavily accented Chinese amahs. It was amazing that, with an end in sight, and after so much had been destroyed by war, it all still went on.

*   *   *

On the day she found her second job, it filled her with hope. This was something she could do, and do well. Thrilled by her own daring, she slipped through an archway into a tented arcade of patterned silk, where fans gently moved the air, and clouds of voile floated like butterflies. Crammed into shelves that stretched from floor to ceiling, dragons, birds and pagodas on shiny taffeta fought for space with rich brocades. Her mind alight with plans, she ran up a couple of dresses on a machine borrowed from a Chinese waitress.

*   *   *

Though the job kept her busy, and she enjoyed the feel of the fabrics as she turned them into sequinned evening dresses, the feeling of excitement soon passed. Three months later, August 1957, with Malayan independence about to go through, and more than two and a half years since her girls had died, Lydia ended the song to scant applause. Singapore hadn't exactly lost its shine, but tonight was Tuesday. And slow. Tonight, they wanted to fill their stomachs with booze and fried chicken.

Sister Patricia used to say she should do something with her voice. She hadn't envisaged singing in the Traveller's Inn at the Oceanview hotel. More appropriate would have been musical theatre or a choir. But when the manager turned out to be a portly man she and Alec had known years before, all he'd asked was could she sing.

She took a cold beer from the barman, smoothed down her skirt and went to sit by the window. She liked to watch the lights sparkle, loved the sound of water as it lapped the jetty posts, couldn't resist the night time scents of cinnamon and ginger, and the fishy salty smell of the sea.

The manager approached her, with a grin. 'Pink gin at the bar for you.' He indicated a spot at the end of the long shiny bar.

People often bought her a drink at the end of her set. She felt a flash of despondency, but stood and forced herself to move. It was either that, or allow life to destroy her.

'Who's the guy?' she asked. It was dark at the end and as the bar curved round a corner she couldn't see more than a shape.

He shrugged. 'Search me. Have a good night. I'm off for an early one.'

Lydia walked across. Two pink gins and a couple of double whiskys were lined up side by side.

A voice came out of the shadows, all breezy civility. 'Glad you could join me.'

'Cicely!'

'How are you, darling?' Cicely held out an arm, glossy red nails and silver bangles shining, but her words were slurred.

Lydia took a step back.

'No, don't run off. Stay and have a drink. For old times' sake.' She pulled a stool up for Lydia and patted it.

'You're drunk.'

'A teeny bit.'

Lydia sat. Unusual for Cicely to lose her cool. 'Why are you here?'

Cicely smiled. 'I stay here when I'm in Singapore. Can't bear Raffles.' She waved her hands. A mix of Chanel and sweat wafted about. 'All those fuddy-duddies banging on about how it was before the war. What a joy to find you.'

'You didn't come to find me, then?'

'No, but now that I have . . . I must tell you, Adil's been looking for you.'

Lydia downed her drink quickly and enjoyed the sensation of gin burning her throat. She stared at Cicely, and imagined his lips as he spoke her name. 'Let me get this straight. Did he send you?'

Cicely shrugged. 'Darling, don't be so suspicious. Why would he do that? Anyway, I already told you, I didn't come to find you.'

'What does he want?'

'Search me. He seemed to think he had something to tell you. You know Adil. Mystery man. He refused to say.' Cicely twirled her glass and rocked on her stool. 'Something I've often wanted to ask, darling. Did you ever love Alec? You seemed so unsuited. Such a little man.'

A storm went off in her head. 'For heaven's sake, Cicely, he's dead.'

Cicely pouted. 'Don't be a crosspatch.'

Lydia's heart was suddenly heavy. The previously hidden thoughts about why she'd married him in the first place rose up. She sighed. 'Okay. I thought I loved him. You persuade yourself, don't you? He was handsome in a quiet way and I needed what he offered.'

'Maybe he was more sensitive than you think.'

'What?'

'He believed you never loved him. Cried on my shoulder afterwards. Men don't advertise that they're not so hot in the sack, do they?' She grinned.

Mild shock ran through Lydia. 'Afterwards? You said you didn't . . . '

'I lied. Let's have more drinks.' And she waved some dollars at the barman.

Lydia narrowed her eyes. Cicely didn't seem to have a stab of conscience, and chatted light-heartedly of the latest Malacca news. Lydia was on her fourth gin by the time they got to the subject of Jack.

'You loved *him* though?' Cicely said, then continued with a look of guarded friendliness. 'It seems we share a similar taste in men, doesn't it?'

Lydia frowned. 'Not Jack! You didn't . . . ' Her voice trailed off.

'No, but it wasn't from lack of trying. He only

had eyes for the voluptuous Lydia Cartwright.' She gulped a mouthful. 'A bit skinnier now, mind you. But go on. Tell me. I'm dying to know. What was he like?'

They stared at each other.

'But I was forgetting, darling. You're one of those women who can't live without love.'

Lydia sighed. 'That isn't true, and not that it's any of your business, but at first we couldn't keep our hands off each other, then we got caught up emotionally, and shouldn't have. I was married with kids, and then, after the fire, he was so wonderful — '

She didn't declare her most hidden thought, that though she had loved him dearly, and he her, there was a chance that marriage to Jack might have ended up being no more than the dream of recreating a lost family. A substitute. How sad it would have been if the passion had died, and they'd discovered, after all, there was nothing more.

'I understand. So that leads us to Adil, unless you've got a few more hidden away. Oh, do confess, darling. I'd love to think of your life littered with discarded men . . . or women.' She growled and gave Lydia a look from under her lashes.

Lydia shook her head.

'Well?' Cicely said. 'Where does my ex fit into the scheme of things?'

'Pardon?'

'Darling, it's all right, he's all yours if you want him.'

Lydia flushed, but whatever Cicely said, she'd

seen the look of alarm in her friend's eyes.

'You mean naughty Adil didn't tell. Yes, sweetie, the gorgeous Adil and I.'

'When?'

'I met him soon after the war, when I was only in my teens, and before it all kicked off.' She ran a hand over her breasts. 'Darling, it's okay. If anyone can certify how scrumptious he is, it's me.'

'You make him sound like dinner.'

'Well, isn't he a bit of a dish, sweetie? A mouth-watering dessert, say. Or perhaps that was Jack.'

She pouted, then bit her lip and bent across to Lydia. She flicked a speck of nothing from Lydia's shoulder, licked her finger and slowly ran it down Lydia's neck to her cleavage. Lydia froze and Cicely took her chance, pulled Lydia to her and kissed her firmly on the lips.

For a moment Lydia didn't react. She had never been kissed by a woman before, never even imagined it. She blinked rapidly, came to with a start, then shook Cicely off and held her at arm's length.

'You're drunk.'

'Don't say you didn't find that just the littlest bit enjoyable. You are luscious, Lydia dear, and I want to go to bed with you. I'm staying here. So it's awfully convenient, isn't it. What do you say?'

There was a silence.

'Just one night, darling?'

Lydia shook her head and began to laugh.

Cicely's face spasmed, then she smiled brightly. 'Is it so funny?'

Lydia shook her head again. Cicely, used to attracting the stares of men and women alike, suddenly looked pitiable, an aging, melting ice queen. There was another long silence as Lydia raked her fingers through her hair. What was the source of Cicely's misery? She looked at her friend closely, at the slightly flaring nostrils, her painted lips and the gorgeous topaz eyes.

'I loved him you know. Adil. The only one I ever have. Something in his eyes. And, oh my, what a body!' Cicely declared. 'But don't underestimate Adil. He's a dangerous man.'

'Funny, that's what he said about you. Come on.' Lydia seized her arm. 'I'm putting you to bed. On your own.'

Outside the wind was getting up and Lydia felt the cool air as she bundled Cicely into the lift. She heard a mumble and decided to ignore it, but Cicely repeated the words.

'What was that?' Lydia asked, not really expecting clarity.

'George paid Adil to get you to stop off at Jack's, you know, paid him to delay your arrival at Ipoh.'

She decided to put it down to Cicely's drunken rambling, but that night dreamt her teeth were crumbling. As soon as they were rebuilt they began to crumble again, as soft as chalk. It left her feeling as if she was no longer walking on solid ground.

41

Billy and I saw each other a lot at the start of the
summer holidays. It was a good way to put
the forthcoming wedding to the back of my
mind, and he was fun. We sloped about the
village, or met at the bus stop with other local
kids, or hung about at the old Thomas Telford
Bridge to see what came down with the river.
Mostly it was debris, though once a dead sheep
dipped and plunged on its way past. Of course
Billy and I were waiting for the day a body
appeared, all puffed up and crinkled.

We were in the bus shelter keeping out of the
rain when Billy gave me a nudge and said, 'Em.
Why don't we go to the barn again?' He
shrugged. 'Only if you want.'

It was as if he read my mind. With a big grin,
he looked me straight in the face. Then, he
combed his great shock of dark blond hair back
with his hand, and turned bright red. He made a
roll-up, I reckoned to cover his embarrassment,
and offered it to me. Though he fancied himself
a James Dean look alike, he was really a sweet
young man, calm, and very kind. I refused the
roll-up.

On our way there, I kept thinking of the
moment he had kissed me before. Every time I
tried to think of something else, I came back to
his lips. The way they were warm but not wet.
The way the shiver went down my neck when he

346

said I was beautiful. The way I felt like a child, but grown up too.

I was nearly fifteen, well fourteen and a half, almost, and quite well developed, and I reckoned the heroines in my stories needed some sexual adventures to keep things realistic. Though I hadn't fallen in love with Billy myself, there was something cute about him, and lots of the village girls were after him. Apart from how embarrassing it'd be to take off my clothes, I thought it was time, even if I did regard him as more of a mate.

The barn was due to be demolished by developers who wanted flats in its place, so this was our last chance. We scrambled up the ladder, me first. I slipped, and he gave my bottom a shove to heave me up, leaving his hand there as I climbed. I was only wearing a thin cotton skirt and it felt hot and strange to have his hand on me like that, and the warmth made me tingle.

Up there, it smelt of mould and damp and musty straw. It scratched my skin, the straw, made me itch, and I felt thin and gawky, despite my newly acquired chest. You couldn't see much from up there, just a strip of green where the field stretched into the distance.

When he kissed me, his lips were cool and moist, not wet or sloppy, though they smelt slightly of tobacco. He told me he really liked me, speaking with a bit of a local accent, which added to his appeal. I muttered I liked him too, and thrilled by the feel of his hands on my body, I felt miles away from my normal life. It became a bit of a blur. He pressed his body so close I felt as if my own heart thumped inside of him, and as he slid his hand between my thighs, I felt hot and an electric flutter passed through me.

I stopped thinking, surprised when my body automatically knew what to do when he lay on top of me, in just a pair of white Y-fronts. Though we both wanted to, we didn't go all the way, but held each other really tight. Something definitely did happen though, because we moved about, bumping on the uneven floorboards, until he shook a couple of times, and said, oh my God into my neck.

While he put his tongue in my ear, I looked past his head to the roof of the barn. The rafters were black and rotten, and the underside of the roof was mouldy green. Where some of the slates were missing, you could see little squares of pale sky. I noticed it had stopped raining and a fresh new sun had appeared.

'Sorry,' I said, when I saw him frown at my distant expression.

'Doesn't matter,' he shrugged, but I could see that he was hurt.

'I'd better go. I'm meeting Veronica at the library.'

I didn't want to make things worse, so I said there was always next time.

He turned to look at me with a big grin. 'Really?'

'When are they pulling down the barn?'

'End of the holidays.'

'Well then.'

★ ★ ★

The reading room was in the basement, with a strong smell of varnished wood and yellow light from angled table lamps. I had an idea for a story set on the continent, and wanted to research European history. While I waited for Veronica, I put Billy to the back of my mind, and laid out several heavy books on the table, glad that I almost had the place to myself.

Glued to the history, I failed to hear her footsteps, so when she spoke my name, I jumped.

'Sorry, sweetie. Didn't mean to startle you.'

I started to pack up. 'Do you want to go now?'

She dumped her shopping and pulled up a chair next to me. 'To be honest, I'm so hot, I'd just like to sit for a moment. My poor feet!'

I glanced at her stilettos and grinned.

'I know. I know. Anyway what are you reading?'

I shoved the open book across to her and she peered at the page. She lifted her head.

'Oh dear, it's a bit dry, isn't it?'

I grinned.

'By the way I told you I'd ask my solicitor friend, Freddy, if there was a way to discover the identity of a client. Well, I saw him last week. As you know he's staying in my flat in Wandsworth.'

I looked up hopefully. 'Did he suggest anything?'

'Unfortunately not. He said no solicitor can risk breaking client confidentiality.'

I shrugged. 'That's what I thought.'

'He did remember the firm though. His first placement was with a rival solicitor in Worcester, but he and a chap at Johnson, Price & Co. had to work together for a while. On the transfer of land deeds apparently.'

I gave her a nod, piled up the books, and began to feel hungry. She took the hint, collected her bags, and we walked to the door together.

'He did say he'd look into it for me, but not to hold out much hope.'

★   ★   ★

After dropping me at our house, Veronica went straight on to her cottage, but came back later on looking like she'd been crying. She told us she'd received a telegram from abroad, a summons from her brother. He was really sick now and the wedding would have to be postponed. Fleur and I went outside to wave her off. Veronica didn't look too happy to be going, but kissed us both goodbye, and went home to pack before going to nurse Mr Oliver in Africa. I stared after Veronica, and Fleur started skipping. Trouble was, I liked Veronica and without her help, I had no idea how to search for Emma Rothwell on my own. So far Veronica had found nothing.

'Everyone leaves,' Fleur said.

'Veronica will be back.'

Fleur began a skipping rhyme.

*'Cuddly bear, Cuddly bear, turn around.
Cuddly bear, Cuddly bear, touch the ground.'*

She was brilliant at skipping, the best in her class, and could do all the movements in time, without breaking the rhythm. As she concentrated on turning around and touching the ground, I thought she'd stopped listening, but then she said, 'Will Gran ever come back home?'

I shook my head.

'Cuddly bear, Cuddly bear, show your shoe.'

'Let's remember the good things,' I said.

There was only the sound of Fleur skipping through the rhyme once more.

I joined in on the last line and we shouted it out together.

'Cuddly bear, Cuddly bear, that will do!'

She stood still for a moment. 'I liked Gran's apple pie.'

'Yes,' I said. 'Let's remember Granny's dinners.'

She started skipping again.

'Cottage pie for breakfast, cottage pie for tea,
Cottage pie for every meal will be the end of
me!'

'What about liver and onions?' I said.

'Ugh!'

'Roast pork on Sunday.'

'Fish pie on Saturday.'

Tears came and I couldn't get my breath. Oh, Granny, I thought, I'm so sorry you can't be here. And I was sad, not just because she was in the home, but because it brought back to me how things can be going along as normal, and then suddenly end.

Fleur dropped her rope, came over and touched my cheek. 'Never mind, Em. You've still got me.'

I looked in her eyes. I did still have her. She smiled and I thought that perhaps, one day, when we'd both grown up, we might be real friends. I wanted to talk about what I'd done with Billy, but she was too young, so I kept the secret to myself.

I stared out at the dog rose trailing over the front hedge and thought about Billy. I wasn't sure if I'd really enjoyed what we did. While I was with him, I still had my writer's hat on, imagining what feelings would be stirring Claris. It made it much more acceptable to think of her in my place.

I couldn't tell Billy I didn't love him. I liked him a lot and didn't want to hurt his feelings. But I always felt safer with stories, and while Claris benefitted from my tender experiences, I had to be more careful than ever to hide my sensationalist scribbling. Dad would kill me if he saw it. What I really enjoyed was sitting by the willow tree on Coal Quay steps, and dangling my legs in the river with Billy, watching the dragonflies and feeling like a kid.

42

An intense smell of cooking, sweat, and patchouli reached her where she stood perspiring in a doorway in the Street of the Three Dragons. The green paint of the building was still peeling and the place seemed seedier than before. She kept her eyes on his door. Before leaving Singapore, she'd slipped into a silky cheongsam, slit high at the side. Too suggestive. She took it off. Tried a simple cotton blouse and crisp skirt. Too dull. In the end she'd plumped for a shift dress in sea green; understated and fitted, it made the most of her hair and eyes. She drew on her eyeliner like a Chinese girl and applied bright lipstick, then she pulled herself together, and stowed away her feelings.

She didn't want to loiter like a streetwalker, but made the decision to show herself only if she saw him at the door. It would be as if fate had taken a hand. If he didn't appear, she'd get the next bus back, and he'd never know.

A woman settled in the shadows of an alleyway nearby, a thin boy squatting beside her. She cradled an infant in her arms and with deep sorrowful eyes cried out for food in Malay. '*Makan. Makan,*' she said, and pointed at the little boy's mouth, her palm held out.

Lydia felt helpless. What could she do, other than give money and hope that it would be spent on food? But a furtive glance at the baby and

Lydia caught her breath; the infant's stiff grey face suggested it was too late for food.

She dipped in her purse for some coins, and in doing so, almost missed him. Startled, she heard her name called, realised it was he who'd seen *her*, as he'd started to walk off down the street.

He stepped across the crowded street and grinned at her, sable eyes full of curiosity. 'I take it you're coming over,' he said. 'It's been quite a few months, hasn't it?'

'Have you been keeping track of me?'

He shrugged and offered his hand.

A dusty gust blew grit in eyes that began to water badly. 'I hate the wind,' she said.

'Ah. So you've been touched by the wind demon too.'

She wiped her eyes with a tissue.

He looked at her face and laughed. 'Oh dear. I don't usually make women cry.'

'So I've heard.'

He raised his eyebrows. 'My guess is you've been talking to Cicely.'

She bit the loose skin at the side of her thumbnail, and felt the heat rise to her face.

'You have black smudges. Here let me.' He took the tissue from her and she looked at the ground as he wiped them away.

She muttered her thanks.

'Seems like I've got some explaining to do. How about we get inside first? You look like you need a cold drink.'

Upstairs the blinds were down. He left them like that, turned on a couple of lamps, and a ceiling fan jerkily moved the sticky air about. It was another humid day, in desperate need of a downpour to clear the air.

'I'm sorry to call unexpectedly. I don't want to inconvenience you.'

'How British of you, Lydia, but since you ask, you're not inconveniencing me at all.' He smiled and with a questioning look, held up a large orange.

'You remembered.'

He sliced the orange, then squeezed it, and a lime, into a tall glass. The citrus scent filled the air.

'You lied to me.'

'Could we call it an omission?'

She wasn't there to quarrel. 'Call it what you like. Why didn't you tell me?'

'About Cicely?' He shook his head. 'I'm sorry. I wanted to. Nearly did, the day we went to see Lili, but the truth is — well it's complicated.'

She stared at her feet, glad she'd painted her toenails, but avoiding exactly what that meant.

'I have a question for you as well. Why did you run off like that without a word?'

She sighed. 'That was complicated too.'

There was a silence while he added soda water and ice to the glass.

'Did George pay you to see that I didn't get to Ipoh too quickly?'

'Ah.'

'You don't deny it?'

He held out his arms wide in a gesture of surrender, then passed her the glass. 'George was my boss, and the sad truth is that I didn't know you then.'

'And when you did?'

'When I did — you left.' He looked her in the eye and smiled a slow smile.

She drained the glass. She'd come for answers, but couldn't hide the fact that now she was here, she felt more alive than all the time she'd been in Singapore, where, though she'd tried to deny it, her thoughts kept returning to him.

'Look, George asked me to follow you, delay you where I could. How I did it was up to me.'

'But why?'

He shrugged.

'And what about the bus? It doesn't make sense.'

'I knew it would take the same route as you were taking. It was only a matter of time before you ran out of petrol.'

'But there *was* petrol.'

He tilted his head 'Not too hard to drain it off and tamper with the gauge, while Suyin brought Maz to you.'

'I can't believe it. I thought it was cats outside.' She considered for a moment. 'What if the driver hadn't let me on the bus?'

'I'd have persuaded him.'

'What about the ambush?'

'No. Even I don't have control of the terrorists, though I knew one of the perpetrators. He'd been arrested some time before and was feeding us information.'

'But not about the ambush.'

He shook his head.

'But this is crazy.' She paused for a moment. 'You didn't say why George asked you to delay me.'

'I don't know. That's the truth.'

She looked at his high wide cheekbones, the deep-set slanted eyes, the long nose and full lips, and noticed something vulnerable. This wasn't how it was meant to be. She wanted to feel cross with him, but believed he was telling the truth.

He took her hand. 'Look, after I followed you on the journey to Ipoh, and delivered you to Jack, I came back and did some investigating. I wasn't happy. As I said, George wouldn't say why he wanted me to delay you, and I already had clues that he was involved in something unsavoury. There's a suggestion of fraud and possibly arms dealing. I wondered if he needed Alec to take care of some business before you joined him up in Ipoh, and that was why he wanted me to delay you. It was just a guess, of course. George once had strong connections with the Singapore underworld, smuggling, Chinese triads, that sort of thing. Mostly before the war.'

She shook her head and withdrew her hand.

'I missed you. I mean it, Lydia.'

Lydia's thoughts spun. She had missed him too, but nothing seemed to make sense, and there was still a question she needed to ask.

'Why did you and Cecily split up?'

His eyes went muddy. 'She was ashamed of me, my background. When my father died we had no money. Not only am I not white, but my mother had joined the oldest profession. Cicely is a snob. She found out.'

There was a pause.

He turned to face the window, his back to her.

'It might be hard to understand now, but I was young, influenced by her. It was slow and poisonous, until in the end I was too ashamed of my mother to visit her. I let her die alone.'

'I'm sorry,' she said.

'She asked for me, but I delayed. By the time I arrived she was dead. Now, the shame . . . ' He looked at his feet.

She watched his chest rise and fall, and immediately felt the impossibility of saying anything that wasn't trite.

He looked up. 'It's something I have to live with.'

As they sank into silence, Lydia wondered how to react. She didn't want to pry, or cause him further pain.

'How did you get to where you are now?' she eventually asked, feeling it was better to change the subject.

'I owe it to George Parrott.'

She raised her brows.

'He was a client of my mother's, in the days when we lived in the shanty town down by the docks. He offered me a way out. The job as a waiter was just the start. After that I worked for him. He took me under his wing.'

'I see.'

He came to sit beside her. 'I'm sorry I wasn't honest with you about my past. And now here it is, sneaking up and spoiling the present.'

'Isn't it guilt that does that?' she said, but the talk had made her uneasy.

He gave her a glum smile. 'Or fear. Don't you want to disown anything in your past?'

'It's not that simple,' she said, thinking of her own mistakes, and seeing in her mind's eye the zoo where she used to take the girls, and sometimes met Jack.

'So where are we now, Lydia?' His voice was quiet.

She inclined her head. His mood had caught her unawares.

'Everything comes back to George Parrott. I hate it. Nobody's the way they seem.'

'The day you visited him, the day you spotted me, I was in the room next door, waiting. After all he'd done for me, it wasn't easy to tell him I was on to him. We quarrelled.'

'You're not saying that's why he shot himself?'

Adil gave a wry smile. 'Not while I was there.'

Lydia felt a spasm in her chest. How had she got caught up in this? She stood up. 'So who do you work for now?'

His eyes clouded. 'The police. I thought you knew.'

'Okay. Just one more question.'

'Fire ahead.'

'Did you love her?' she asked as casually as she could.

He cleared his throat. 'She was difficult to love.'

'But you did?'

He nodded.

★   ★   ★

When they went out that evening, the sky was pink. Seconds later, night rolled down a curtain of black. Starless, moonless. Fast. Soon the stars would come. From the alleyways they heard shouts, laughter, the desolate howl of a dog, and the stink of privies, which were never far away. It still felt deeply foreign to her. A low wail came from a building behind her, more a lament than a cry. She tried to remember the incantation the gardener taught the children, to keep the demons of night and darkness at bay. At times like this, Malaya seemed impossible. An impenetrable world of myth and magic, a place where colonial officialdom fought Chinese rebellion, where falsehood was rife, and having a white skin made you a red-haired devil.

She stood still, but under the blackness, the heat was building up. In hope of finding a breeze, they headed for the docks. But there, the sailing boats were still; further out, the scattered pinpoints of light from fishing boats split up the dark. There was no breeze at all. Irritable patches appeared on her neck. She rubbed her skin, and then noticed a Chinese medicine man selling ointment and herbal remedies from a makeshift stall. She looked at Adil for confirmation. He shook his head.

'Another cold drink,' he said, and pulled her through an archway.

They headed for a corner table at the back of the smoky bar, where a radio was playing slow music, and two or three couples danced beneath the ceiling fan. She watched green lizards dart across plain grey walls. A bare electric bulb drew enormous whirring moths that slammed into it over and over, so that they crisped and fell to the floor. He ordered iced beer for her, flavoured with cardamom.

'Would you like to dance, Lydia?'

She opened her mouth, then closed it without speaking.

He held out a hand. 'Come.'

Their drinks arrived. She sipped hers for a moment, then took his hand.

'Cicely said you wanted to tell me something,' she said as he placed a hand in the small of her back and they started to move together.

'No.'

'She said you were looking for me.'

'Certainly I hoped you'd come back, you must know that, but I wasn't looking. If you wanted to come, it would be because you decided. I didn't say anything to her. Haven't even seen her.'

She felt the tingle of his breath on her neck, forced herself to concentrate on his words, and decided to believe him. She closed her eyes for a second before she spoke again.

'Are you sure you don't know why George paid you to delay my journey to Ipoh?'

'I really don't know. At least not yet.'

She looked into his eyes. 'Is there any reason I should trust you?'

'I think I might be able to find a way to persuade you,' he said, with a gentle smile, and led her back to the table. She noticed his hands, strong, well shaped, with a few dark hairs curling just above his wrists.

From across the bar a man watched them through sinister puffy eyes. Adil walked over to speak, waving his hands as he spoke. He had the advantage of speaking most of the vernacular languages of Malaya, though Lydia only caught the odd phrase. He slipped the man a couple of dollars. An image of Jack came back to her, bent over the table, reading in the light of a single lamp. She squeezed her eyes shut to block out the past and turned her face to Adil.

He smiled as he walked back. 'Just getting the information we need for tomorrow.'

She felt confused. He felt foreign to her, unknowable.

Back into the night, an oily expanse of cloud was moving quickly.

'It'll be cooler now,' he said.

He was right. All round them, shop signs flapped, litter picked up and drifted, and the boats had started to bob in the water. With the wind came air, and though she could breathe more freely, she felt constricted by troubling emotions. They hurried back as an increasingly livid sky delivered the first few drops of warm rain.

43

The grass smelt of cat poo, and thistles and dandelions had spread over Granddad's once pretty borders. The air was full of the smells of late summer. Father heaved out the old lawn mower, examined its rusty blades, shrugged and abandoned it. He went off somewhere, shoulders drooping, and, more to the point, his clothes dishevelled. He must be missing Veronica, I thought. I felt lonely too. Fleur was quieter than ever and Billy was busy helping his dad.

I was imagining the house at the end of the sea, where my next heroine would live. American, white clapboard, and surrounded by water. I'd just got her to the ocean's edge, when I heard a voice.

'Hello. Anyone there?'

She sounded different, and her voice caught in the way it does when you're trying to hide your real feelings. I looked up to see her come round the side of the house. She looked awful, her usually flawless skin red and blotchy, and her hair untidy. I pulled up a garden chair and Veronica slid into it. Shoulders shaking, she dug in her bag for a Kleenex.

For a moment neither of us spoke. She gulped, then made a bottled-up hiccupping noise. Embarrassed by this display of unlikely emotion, I stared. For a moment I hoped Mr Oliver had died, then erased the bad thought.

'I thought you were in Africa.'

She looked up. 'It's Sidney,' she said and started to really cry. I bit my lip, looked at her eyes and saw the panic there. She gulped again and her face twisted. Veronica usually showed a happy face to the world, calm and in control. It was awful to see her like this. In the end she blew her nose and managed to stop the tears.

'He wasn't ill at all. He's been arrested.'

I remained completely still, not even blinking, not daring to ask, but knowing all the same.

'For . . . ' She trailed off.

There was a controlled silence, on both our parts. She looked at me, blue eyes watering, and my heart thumped.

'For molesting a child,' she managed to say, so quietly I almost didn't catch it. She let out a slow breath and wiped her eyes. 'There, I've said it. I'm sorry. I wanted to see Alec.'

'He's out.' I hung my head.

'Emma?'

I shook my head: couldn't look up.

'Emma.' She put a hand on my arm. 'Now, dear, I very much want you to tell me the truth.'

I shook my head again, this time with my hands over my ears. I didn't want her to touch me, didn't want to hear. I felt like a malu-malu plant, wanted to fold right up, conceal myself, so nobody could ever touch me.

She leant over, took my hands from my ears and lifted my chin. I knew from her white face, Veronica had guessed.

'Is that why you stabbed him?' she asked, in the tiniest voice.

I nodded and folded my arms across my middle.

'Oh no. Please, not you, sweetheart. What did he do?'

I stood up abruptly, wanting to keep it all inside. Nothing would make me say the words. Nothing.

'Why didn't you tell us?'

The garden swayed. The tree at the bottom of the garden shook. I spun round. Felt trapped. Heat exploded in my head and I couldn't get out. My voice seemed to disappear. If I spoke, the terrible words would stick to my lips. Then anything might fall from my mouth. All the secrets I'd been guarding would fall on the floor in front of my dad. All the poisonous things I thought about him, and about what had happened to Mum, all the sinful things I'd done with Billy. All my plans. Everything would come out of me.

'Nobody would believe me,' I managed to say.

'You didn't give us a chance.'

I took a step back. 'He made me feel dirty.'

I turned on my heels, ran up to the bathroom, locked the door behind me, sat on the floor and sobbed. When I stopped crying, I looked at my swollen eyes in the mirror. All the pain of losing my mum was there. And the dread I'd never again see the person I loved more than anyone. I hadn't been able to tell her about Mr Oliver. Hadn't been able to ask her what to do. I thought I'd locked the pain away, but could everybody see it in my eyes? I filled the sink, sloshed water back and forth, then splashed my eyes and sat on the floor with my knees drawn up, arms wrapped round. I held on tight to keep myself together.

Voices rose from the bottom of the stairs. Dad, back again, and talking to Veronica. I couldn't hear what she said, except for a loud sob, followed by my father's voice, soothing and gentle. A side to my father I could never find.

The voices went on for a few minutes, then I heard footsteps on the stairs. Veronica I hoped. Not Dad.

'Emma?'

It was her, but the words still stuck in my throat, and my heart jumped so much I could hardly breathe.

She tapped on the door. 'Emma dear, I'm so sorry. I'll do anything I can.'

A rush of anger drove me up and I threw open the door. I hurled the words at her. 'You knew. You must have known all along.'

She stepped back as if I'd hit her, shook her head and clutched the banister rail behind her.

'No, I swear. I promise.'

I saw the shock in her eyes and heard Dad approach. We stood squashed on the little landing at the top of the stairs, just outside the bathroom door. I wanted to run, but when I looked at his moist eyes and stricken face, I stayed put. Nobody moved or spoke. I looked past my father at the flocked wallpaper. Pink roses, sprinkled with blue forget-me-nots. Granny's choice. I felt a lump grow in my throat. The silence deepened. The whole world seemed to stop its business. Then he held out his arms to me and with a gulp I went to him. For the first time that I could remember he held me, and gently stroked my hair.

'Forgive me, child.'

We stayed like that for several minutes. In the end I sniffed, wiped my face and pulled away. After that he didn't know how to look at me. I took a breath and reached out a hand to him. He frowned at it, as if he didn't understand the gesture. He looked thin and worn suddenly. I let out my breath slowly.

Veronica put her arm round me and led me downstairs, where Fleur sat white faced at the kitchen table.

'It's all right now, isn't it?' she said, in a small voice.

44

They woke at dawn and left to the rattle of shopkeepers pulling up metal blinds and throwing their doors open to the day. The mist lay heavily over the water, giving rise to a pale morning, with wispy clouds stretched right across a surprisingly washed out sky. Out of town the trees were buried in shadow.

Lydia shut her eyes and the image emerged, always the same. A woman in a pale blue dress, with dark blue cornflowers at the hem and neck. But something was different. This time the woman turned and spoke. Lydia couldn't see her face but felt her hands, as soft as a child's, and heard the words 'Tell her I came.' That was all.

She opened her eyes, not realising she'd been asleep. By the time they reached a resettlement village, the sun was so bright it bleached the colour from the day.

It was an uneasy time among colonial administrators. Malaya had, at the end of August, achieved independence from Britain. Lydia had seen the new ten-dollar notes, the queen replaced by a farmer and buffalo ploughing a paddy field. A few British Civil servants, like Ralph, were retained to keep the administrative arrangements running smoothly. Others had gone. The new prime minister was setting up an Inspectorate General of Police with responsibility for internal security, though some British police stayed put. Lydia didn't know how much it would affect her life, but was aware of feeling less comfortable in the streets. Eyes followed her where none had before, and she began to hold her handbag tighter.

Adil looked sideways at her, his slanting eyes intense. 'What do you see when you close your eyes?'

'Memories. Images. You know. Things I want to remember. Sometimes things I want to forget.'

'Do you want to know what I see?' He paused and grinned at her. 'Well, perhaps not.'

She smiled. 'Tell me.'

'I see a woman who doesn't realise how strong she is.'

'I don't know. Sometimes it all feels too much.'

'Don't lose heart. You've come so far.' He made a wide sweeping gesture. 'After all you've been through, you're still out in the world. Still doing your best.'

His words brought tears to her eyes.

'How are you really, Lydia? I can't always tell.'

She shrugged.

'You have good days and bad days, right?'

'I suppose so.'

'Well, I hope this will be a good day. There's someone I think you'll be happy to see.'

She noticed he carried a brown paper parcel. 'What's in there?'

He tapped the side of his nose.

With a gesture of authority, flashing his ID, he led her through security at the gate of the village. The smell of exhaust fumes met them, as an armoured car, packed with Malay police holding submachine guns, drove in.

He saw her look. 'Some women got picked up for . . . well, they call it cohabiting with terrorists, though of course they don't live with them at all, and now the police are using them to set traps. See that lorry. Full of women and SEPs. Surrendered enemy personnel.'

'Why do they surrender?'

'The ordeal of life on the inside. Here they get housing, food, and medical aid.'

She scanned the huts. 'I went to a new village with Jack once. This seems less grim.'

'They were only intended to be temporary, but they're a bit cleaner now and there's piped water.'

Lydia watched as the lorry started to drive round, its sides draped with canvas.

'There are slits in the canvas. Can you see?'

She nodded. A couple of Malay policewomen walked alongside it, dressed in khaki with silver badges on the front.

'The men and women inside will be made to point out anyone who is connected with the rebels.'

People shuffled by in a wavering line, waiting to be scrutinised. They seemed calm, even if one or two sets of sullen eyes followed her.

'Some of them don't look too happy,' she said.

Adil shrugged. 'Despite Independence there are still Chinese rebels in the jungle. These villages are run by the Malays now, and people get ownership of a little land. That helps.'

The night's cloudburst had long passed over and the heat was blistering. Despite appearing cleaner, deeper into the village, thin cats slid along alleys, where the smell of pig manure and rotting fruit made Lydia reel. She heard the harsh cry of a caged bird, smelt the chilli-pepper and tamarind as they passed women tending fires, and the sickly smell of Chinese cigarettes from small groups of men packed together.

They turned into an alley, stepped over banana skins and pineapple peel, passed a flow of people coming and going, and at the end, where it opened into a little clearing, they stopped. Two children with glossy black hair, a boy and a girl, were playing in thick layers of dust, rolling stones, to see which went the furthest.

The girl looked towards the interruption with an indignant shout. The skinny, long-limbed boy followed suit, but then his mouth fell open and he halted for a moment, before jumping up and charging over.

'Mrs Lydia!'

He stopped just before her, suddenly shy. She held out her arms to him. 'Maz! You don't know how pleased I am to see you.' She pulled him to her, hugged him, then examined his face. He looked well, eyes bursting with intelligence. 'You've grown, Maznan.'

They stared at each other.

'Yes, Mem,' he said.

She scanned the little clearing. 'Where's your mother?'

He looked downcast. 'Mem, I am staying with Auntie again. My mother has gone.'

'This is for you,' Adil said, holding out the parcel.

His eyes wide, the child took it. 'Really? For me?'

Adil nodded.

Maz sat on the ground to tear open the wrapping. First, a curled skipping rope fell out, then a shiny blue ball rolled in the dust.

'I need to speak with Mem now,' Adil said.

The boy nodded, passed the rope to the girl, and with a shout began to dribble the ball around the clearing.

Adil took Lydia's arm and stepped a few yards back. Broken clouds were massing overhead once more and the wind began to rattle a nearby metal roof.

'I wanted you to see that he was safe.'

'Okay.'

'And explain why he was given to you to take north.'

Lydia stood completely still.

'Maz was brought to you by his aunt, Suyin, on the orders of George Parrott. It was hoped that when the child's mother heard of his disappearance, it would force her out.'

She blinked rapidly, shocked to the core.

'Let me explain — '

She interrupted him. 'Of course, you knew I was with Suyin when you drained the petrol. I hadn't thought about why you'd known she was there.'

There was a shout from inside a hut. When a woman came out, Adil moved forward, prepared to intervene, but she shook her fist and threw the shiny blue ball into the clearing. Adil ran for it, but Maz got there first and kicked it to the girl, who dribbled it down the alley. Maz was left with the skipping rope and a frown on his face.

Lydia picked up the rope. 'Look, it's easy. You'll soon get the hang of it.' She showed him how, then went back to listen to Adil.

'So,' she said, 'let me get this clear. You're saying that George used *me* to draw Maz's mother out of the jungle?'

'His mother knew too much, and had become associated with one of the top rebel leaders. George Parrott wanted to stop her.'

'Giving government information away you mean?'

He nodded. 'She worked in Alec's office for six months, but left when she fell pregnant.'

'Why did she join the rebels?'

'Her brother-in-law was a comrade living on the inside. He was shot during a failed ambush attempt on a road train. His body was brought into town as a warning to others. Maznan's mother saw him lying in the mud, riddled with bullet holes, and that's when she vowed to get even. Maz saw too. The man was his uncle.'

'The poor child,' she said. 'He told me he loved his uncle but he was gone. Never said why.'

'She left her sister to care for Maz. With three children of her own, a baby on the way and her husband dead, the sister eventually baulked.'

'Another mouth to feed.'

'Exactly. Maznan's mother sent word to her sister, telling her to go to the child's father for money.'

'Why did she need to send her sister?'

'Once she'd spent time on the inside, which

she had, she couldn't risk being seen herself.' Adil was silent, heavy eyebrows furrowed. He stared at the ground for some minutes before looking up again.

Lydia watched the child's attempts to master the skipping rope. It was clear he'd never owned a skipping rope before, and even though the rope kept tangling, he didn't give up. So much had gone wrong for him, yet he had the sweetest nature, and it never seemed to alter.

Adil explained he hadn't agreed Lydia should take the boy. He had argued with George. Said it was dangerous and might not even work.

'And George paid you to make sure I broke my journey at Jack's.'

'That was the only part of the plan that seemed sensible. You'd be safer with Jack taking care of the rest of the journey. And, of course, Maz's mother might have come out into the open there, which again would have been safer for you than if it had happened somewhere on the road. We were confident Jack would take you to Ipoh himself. In the meantime, Bert knew of the plan and was on the watch for Maznan's mother.' He stopped suddenly and held her arm. 'Look, Lydia, I'm sorry I didn't tell you everything.'

He looked sincere, his eyes full of regret, but she shrugged. Every time she thought there were no more secrets, there was something more.

'Then the fire?'

'Turned all the plans upside down.'

'Did Jack know about all this?'

'No.'

Lydia tried to read his eyes. 'You said you didn't know why George wanted to delay my arrival at Ipoh?'

'I don't.'

'He wasn't anything to do with the fire?'

Adil shook his head.

'So who took Maz from Jack's house? Was it his mother?'

'With the help of insiders and Lili.'

'But I thought Maz and his mother were together in detention.'

He shook his head. 'That was meant to happen.' He paused and shrugged. 'Best laid plans — '

'Look!' Maz shouted, interrupting them. 'I can do it.'

They both turned to see he'd finally mastered the skipping technique.

'You clever little thing,' she said, then ran to him and picked him up. But she couldn't help her breath catching at the memory of Fleur's skipping rhymes.

Along with his cousin, they took Maz for a sticky cake. Lydia grinned at the sight of jam spreading round his mouth. She ordered two more, but as she sat back down, Adil indicated the blackening sky. With a tiny burst of red at its centre it looked ominous.

'We'd better get back. This one's a real storm.'

She bent to kiss Maznan's cheek. 'I'll see you again. I promise.'

As they headed off, Lydia waved to the children and Maz carried on waving until they were out of sight.

'Why promise what you cannot know you'll keep?' Adil said.

Sheeting rain exploded in the dust, sending trails of wet dirt running up Lydia's bare legs. She ran to the car, too confused to speak.

Once in the car neither of them could have been heard if they'd spoken. The rain was so loud it even drowned out the thunder. Though she'd been elated to see Maz, Adil's revelation had darkened the occasion for her. He focussed on driving, and where the road surface was obliterated by red mud, the car slid repeatedly. Rain blurred the view and no other headlights came their way. She took a deep breath, tucked the hair behind her ears, and held her hands tightly together in her lap. Outside, wind bent two-hundred-foot tualang trees almost horizontal. At the edge of town, it ripped off attap-leaf roofs and lifted tin shacks as if they were toys. There was not a flicker of light anywhere.

The storm was brief but intense. Instead of a normal sunset, the sky turned a strange orange-brown. In the face of so much destruction, Lydia's perspective gradually restored itself, and by the time they reached Adil's flat, she was calm. She'd been used by George, it was as simple as that, and Adil had been an unwilling part of it. But the question now was whether he'd told her everything.

Upstairs, she watched him pick up a copy of The Straits Times and flick through. He hesitated then folded the paper to show her.

'There's to be a memorial, Lydia. For those people lost or killed during the Emergency.' He paused to see her reaction. 'Will you go? I'll come if it helps.'

Lydia shook her head and handed the paper back. She didn't want sympathy or condolences, genuine or otherwise.

She looked down on the mismatched houses and shops changing colour in the orange light, and at the glowing Chinese mansion opposite. A steady hum rose from the street now that the rain had passed.

'Tell me about George,' she said, as he made them some coffee.

'Newspaper and governmental records were pretty much destroyed by the Japanese, but I got hold of some old press cuttings. Before the war there had been a whiff of scandal, nothing concrete.'

'Didn't you trust George?'

'I had my reasons not to.'

'Yet you worked for him?'

'I had very mixed feelings. Put it that way. Just before the Japanese invasion, the Parrotts managed to get out. They went to Australia, taking Cicely with them, and all traces of wrongdoing disappeared in the post-war chaos.'

'But you carried on digging?'

'Exactly.'

She felt a stab of weariness in the pause.

'Look, enough of all this,' he said. 'I don't like to see you look so sad.'

She shook her head. 'I'm not. It's just lonely sometimes. Without them I mean.'

'I understand.' He thought for a moment. 'Maybe we need some diversion. Let's go out, see a film or something?'

She held her breath as a moment from the past tugged at her memory. One of the times she and Alec had taken the girls out. It might be nice to go once more. It would be as if she was watching just for them.

'What about the Chinese circus?' she said, and breathed deeply.

'If you prefer.'

She'd be happy to go with Adil. There were fewer associations, and like a snake rising to the charmer's whistle, she was drawn to him. Whether he'd told her everything or not, she felt she had no choice. This was not the physical passion she'd had with Jack, nor the security that Alec had once seemed to provide. She didn't yet have a name for it.

'I'm glad I met you in an ambush,' she said, as she picked up her bag.

He frowned. 'You'd recommend it, would you?'

'No. It's just that I met Alec and Jack at parties. Look at what happened.'

Adil was exotic, intense, like Malaya itself. She walked over and put a hand on his shoulder, felt the muscles tense beneath her touch, smelt the scent of rain still on his hair. He wrapped his arms round her, smiled, and she realised each time he did, she felt as if the door was opening a little wider.

'You're not angry?'

She shook her head. 'Not any more.'

Who cared about class or colour now? She looked back at herself, caught a glimpse of the woman she'd once been. The one who cared about fancy dress parties, drinks at the tennis club, playing bridge and getting plastered. And despite her doubts, all that mattered now was standing with Adil, and looking out at the full moon casting shadows through a break in the clouds.

45

A smell of burning drifted through my open window. I'd lost the thread trying to tell the story of our arrival in England, and found myself writing about Billy and me. I wanted to experience things so I could write more realistically, yet the words were dull and the draw of the bonfire was enough to pull me away.

I was wearing holey shorts and an old shirt, and hadn't bothered to brush my hair. My pixie cut had grown wild during the summer holidays, and the colour had brightened to a flaming orange. Dad insisted I go to the hairdresser, but I wanted to look like Bertha Mason in *Jane Eyre*, my all time favourite book. I was different from other girls, though I'd seen them with their stiff hairstyles and even stiffer clothes, looking all the same. It must be Malaya that made me different, I decided, as I loped off down the stairs.

Outside, plumes of smoke rose from the fire, and at first I didn't see who was poking it with a long stick. When I got close enough for the smoke to make my eyes sting, I saw Billy look up. He'd heard the crunch of my footsteps above the crackles. We stared at each other, listening to the sound of neighbours' gossip behind the fence. He was the first to break the awkward silence.

'I thought everyone was out,' he said, and swung round to the fire again. 'Haven't seen you lately, Emma.'

380

'You were working with your dad.'

'Just for one week, Em.'

I stared at my feet. 'Everyone is out. I didn't feel like going.'

He turned and took a step towards me. 'I called round the other day. Saw your dad. Fleur said she'd tell you, but you never came round.'

I kept my eyes on the debris that Dad had been threatening to clear for weeks.

He shrugged. 'Have I done something wrong?'

I shook my head. 'No, of course, not . . . How are you?'

He didn't speak, just sighed.

'What are you doing?'

'Isn't that obvious?' he said. 'Don't worry. I didn't just march up here and decide to light a fire. If that's what's bothering you . . . ' He trailed off.

'No, of course.'

He prodded the fire. 'Your dad's paying me to do some gardening. Get the place under control in the next couple of months, before winter. He wants it to sell quickly.'

I gaped at him.

'Didn't he say?'

I shook my head and listened to the crackling fire, the droning insects, the breeze. All the sounds and smells of early autumn were already there, and now, with a new school year coming up fast, Dad was planning to sell.

'Aren't you going to offer me a coffee?'

I felt I couldn't refuse. In the days when we made go-karts out of old crates, we used to be able to say anything to each other, but now we were no longer just friends and I felt tongue tied. He was cagey with me and I knew it was my fault.

'If you like,' I said.

While I made the coffee, Billy hung about the small kitchen, looking out of place. He pulled out a bag of Smiths crisps from his back pocket, and sprinkled the salt from the little twist of paper. He offered me the bag but I shook my head.

'We'll have it in my room,' I said, and placed two mugs on a tray with a couple of custard creams, then headed for the stairs. Half way up I hesitated, hoping he wouldn't take going to my room as a sign.

The smell of smoke from his clothes came up with us. We sat on the bed about a foot apart talking about nothing, in the way you do when one of you has something important to say, but doesn't know how to begin. The only sounds came from Billy crunching the crisps.

He put down his mug and shifted closer. 'Do you fancy coming down the music shop. There's a new record I'm after. We could listen together in the booth. One headphone each.'

Before I could reply, he pushed the blond hair from his forehead and kissed me.

I tasted the salt on his lips and pulled away. As I did, I saw his jaw clench.

'What's wrong, Em?' he said. 'You liked it before. Are you turning square or what?'

I sighed. 'Billy, I can't.'

I couldn't think of what to say. I looked about the room and then at the floor. I saw my notebook had fallen on the carpet beneath my desk. Billy noticed it at the same time, and must have seen the anxiety in my eyes, because he picked it up. I tried to snatch it, but his eyes slid across the page. He held it out of my reach and his face grew rigid. After a while he read aloud.

I need experience to write well; flights of imagination only take me so far. And when it comes to sex, surely nothing beats the real thing. After the first effort, I'm unsure and unsettled, but I begin to see the wealth of experience Billy offers me. What a perfect opportunity to give my characters depth.

I hung my head, and chewed the inside of my cheek.

'Well. Aren't you going to say anything?' He practically choked on his words and stood up abruptly. 'Bloody hell. How could you, Emma?'

I shook my head, wanting to hide my red face, but I managed to look at him. 'I'm sorry.'

'Is that all it was? A chance to give your characters depth.' He spat out the words.

'No,' I mumbled. 'I enjoyed it.' But I couldn't make it sound like it was true.

He sat at the end of the bed, looking cut to the bone. Please don't let him cry, I thought. My motives were complicated and not even clear to me, so how could I explain them to him? Boys didn't understand how you could really wish for something to happen, but when it did, you found you didn't want it after all. Mostly they supported their football club and went to matches with their dad. Billy did all that too, but he was different from the others, or so I thought.

'Billy,' I started off, in an attempt to defend myself, though the way he looked at me, so mistrustful, almost silenced me. 'I want to be a writer, so in a way everything I do has two levels.'

He looked steadily at me, hurt showing in his eyes. 'That's not the way it works, Em.'

'What do you mean?'

'You need to live your life for the sake of living it. Write about it later. You can't live your life just to write. It won't work, Em.'

'But can't I do both?'

He shrugged. 'You used me, Emma, and made me think you really liked me.'

'I did . . . I do.'

He sniffed, and shook his head with a more distant expression, as if he'd made a decision. 'You can't treat people like that. It was dishonest.'

He stood up straight and went to the window.

'Better make the bonfire safe. I'll see myself out.'

He had such an openly hostile expression on his face, I couldn't hold back the tears.

'Your tears won't work on me, Em. Never had you down as a calculating bitch. Tell your dad to find another gardener.'

After he left, I stood at the window. He patted the fire until it was only smouldering, and I watched him leave the garden and walk out of my life with his head held high.

I looked at my face in the mirror: at turquoise

eyes rimmed with red, and blotchy pale skin. More like Bertha Mason than ever, and scarcely a dazzling beauty. Billy was my one true friend when I came home from school, and I'd made him hate me. I felt ashamed and didn't know how I could ever make things right again. I didn't like myself and felt out of my depth, as if by dipping my toe into something grown up, I'd stirred up feelings I couldn't handle. And it wasn't as if what I'd written was even true. I did like being with Billy. I just wasn't ready for things to go any further and I was too stupid to say.

I needed to do something to make myself feel better, take myself in hand, make a fruit jelly or a blancmange for Fleur, clean up the kitchen for Dad. It wasn't much and it wouldn't make me a good person, but it might make me feel not quite so bad. Every time I thought about Billy, I had to wipe my eyes. I couldn't bear that I'd hurt him. Most of all I wondered how long it would take to sell a house, and whether I'd have time to make my peace with him before it was too late.

46

The memorial service was to be held in the park. Lydia, breathing lightly and full of nervous energy, drummed her fingers on the windowsill. Who was it who said that staying alive in Malaya was like trying to stay alive on swampland? If you struggled it swallowed you; if you hung on you died from heat and dehydration. Was it something Alec used to say? Or Jack? She closed her eyes. The dark green hell of Malaya still terrified her, yet the beauty of it had crept under her skin: the firewalkers, the snake charmers, the villages hidden away, the mists over the jungle.

She let her coffee grow cold as she stared out of the window at wind blowing litter and dust about. She had once needed Alec, Jack too. Times had changed. She'd changed. She checked her watch. It was time to leave and she'd decided to go alone. And when it was over, she'd have to find herself another job, and an apartment of her own, but it would be in Malacca, not Singapore. She wanted to be nearby but could hardly stay at Adil's for ever.

★　★　★

In the park, Lydia stood apart from women dressed in subdued colours, and gathering in knots of three or four. They fanned themselves with wide-brimmed straw hats, heads close together, and behind their hands they spoke in whispers. The men had already congregated around Ralph, who strutted in a stiff linen suit, then signalled for silence.

As a senior administrator in the new Malaya, he began an impassioned speech about the sacrifice of lives lost to terrorist atrocity throughout the years of the Emergency. He glanced in Lydia's direction but she avoided his eyes. She didn't want to be there, but as this was the final link in the chain since the night when insurgents set fire to the rest house, she owed Emma and Fleur her presence. After the speeches, she nodded at people she knew, moving swiftly past their guarded looks of sympathy, not caring to hear the platitudes that made her feel so hot and angry. She sidestepped Cicely, and shook hands only with Ralph. She had no need of condolence.

Relieved that the ceremony had passed without incident, she was headed for the exit when Cicely approached with a determined look. Lydia guessed there'd be no escape.

'I know you may not want to talk to me even a teeny bit, but there is someone you absolutely have to meet. No arguments, darling.'

Lydia sighed. 'For God's sake Cicely, don't you ever give up?'

Cicely ignored her, and taking hold of an elbow, marched her across to a tall, blonde woman, who stood alone, smoking a cigarette. Cicely rattled through the introductions. The woman's name was Clara and she was American. She and her sister had been in Malaya since the war and had both worked for the British Administration. They'd come in search of her sister's husband, who went missing in the war, and then both had stayed. Sadly, the woman's twin sister was one of the secretaries who had been living at the rest home at the time of the fire. After the introductions, with a farewell sweep of her arm, Cicely slipped away.

'You live here?' Clara asked, in a west coast drawl, looking closely at Lydia.

'Here now. I was in Singapore.'

'Cigarette?'

Lydia shook her head. 'I don't want to be rude but . . . '

The woman held up her hand. 'I'll get to the point. Do you have pictures of your daughters?'

Lydia took a breath. 'Yes, but I don't see . . . '

'Please. It will only take a minute.'

She removed her locket and held out the images of her girls.

The woman studied them, then looked up. 'And you say your girls were there on the night of the fire.'

'The records were all destroyed, but yes.'

Clara paused while she examined the locket again. 'I was there the night of the fire.'

'You must have seen them then.' Lydia bit her lip.

There was a long pause.

Was this why Cicely had introduced them? So she could talk to someone who'd been there, someone who could bring her a little closer to her daughters, let her into their last days. She found her voice. 'How were they? Did they seem happy?'

Clara hesitated. 'Thing is. I don't recognise them. I — ' She stopped suddenly.

Lydia stared over her head and frowned. The sounds in the park grew louder. Insects hummed, traffic accelerated, and as the steady drone of voices wrapped itself round her, she wanted to be somewhere else.

'I'm sorry,' she said, holding out her hand for the locket. 'I can't do this. I have to go.'

Clara looked at the photos again, shook her head and handed the locket back. 'A family with two girls was staying before the fire happened, but they moved into a house a week before. There were a couple of other kids.'

Lydia stopped in her tracks. 'Girls?'

'Just two boys.'

There was a long pause. Lydia placed a hand on her heart. 'Can you be sure the family with girls had moved?'

The woman smiled. 'Absolutely. Even though it was pretty wild that night. My sister had lived there for three months, but quite a few people moved in straight after the warning that the offices in Ipoh were under threat. Luckily the place had been fairly empty up until then.'

This was crazy. The ground beneath her feet was shifting. 'No other girls at all?'

Clara shook her head.

'Tell me about the family with girls.'

'There was the man . . . two daughters.' She paused and appeared to be remembering.

Lydia folded her arms across her chest, felt her throat thicken, more nervous than she'd ever been.

The woman's eyes lit up. 'I remember. The wife was heavily pregnant. That's why they left, to be in their own home before the baby came. Like my sister, they'd been at the rest house two or three months. Oh, yeah, the husband was as big as she was. I remember thinking she wasn't the only one eating for two.'

Lydia thought of Alec, skinny as a rake. 'So there were no other girls?'

'It was way past midnight when I left. I signed the book and noticed the last arrivals were at six, just a middle-aged couple, no kids. The party wound up, everyone drunk, sleeping on camp beds in the recreation room. The porter locked up after me.'

She paused.

'Please go on.'

'The terrorists surrounded the entire building with accelerants you know, blocked the exits. With so much wood it went up in moments. It was the last time I saw my sister.' She sighed, but didn't lower her eyes.

Lydia touched her arm in sympathy. 'So my girls could only have been there if they arrived in the middle of that night.'

'Nobody ever arrived by night. There was a strict curfew and it was far too risky. I was only able to leave because I had a lift in a police car. They reckon the fire started about one or two a.m.'

'If they were there, they'd have already been there for a couple of weeks anyway,' Lydia said, remembering George telling her how they'd gone ahead to the rest house. And that was

390

before she left Malacca. 'You'd be bound to have seen them.'

'I saw my sister every day for three months, and apart from the family who'd already moved on, there were no other girls during that time. We used to talk about who was staying there.'

'In that case — ' Lydia's legs went to jelly. She reached out her hands and Clara took them, held them firm, but Lydia couldn't finish her sentence, the lump in her throat preventing words.

Clara's face became very serious. 'I know it's a shock, but I'm absolutely sure your daughters were nowhere near the rest house the night of the fire.'

Lydia closed her eyes and felt the breath sucked right out of her. Her heart was roaring in her ears, distorting the sounds in the park as they melted into the background. Clara hugged her, patting her shoulder as she did. Lydia tried to catch her breath again, drew back, kissed the woman on the cheek. The woman smiled.

'Thank you. You'll never know how grateful I am,' Lydia managed to say and walked off into Malacca, her mind shooting off in a million directions.

In the town, babies cried, men shouted their wares, and women gossiped as they walked arm in arm. Yet she didn't register the distinct noises of the world: the rickshaw bells, the kids playing in the gutters, the music floating down from open windows. She only heard blood pounding in her ears as she fought her way through the current of pedestrians, arms held out, ready to clasp her daughters to her, ready to feel their heartbeats thump. Their heartbeats! Their soft living flesh. In her mind her children's voices surged and faded. She saw Emma sitting at her desk in Malacca, writing in her journal and smiling in that intense way she had. And so practical, even when Fleur fell in the storm ditch. Dear sweet Fleur.

Whenever the memories came, she felt her eyes smart and had to wipe away the tears. To think that all this time they'd been alive. So accustomed to thinking they were dead, it was impossible to grasp that they were not — that they *might* not be. They'd always kept their place in her heart, but it was a place that had hurt too much. And she was so used to thinking each day was a step further away from them, that she could not comprehend the turnaround, and that now, every day might be a step closer. She dug a nail into her flesh. This wasn't a dream. She was wideawake and getting wet in fine silvery rain.

When the wind got up she thought of Emma, who at the age of three had whirled round on a blowy day and asked in a loud voice, 'Where does the wind come from, Mummy?' Lydia told her it came from a giant's breath. Emma looked at her with narrowed eyes, head on one side. 'Don't be silly, Mummy. There's no such thing as giants.'

When it sank in, she wanted to stand in the street and shout. Give vent to an explosion of joy that set blood pounding through her heart and tears to spill unrestrained. She felt unhinged and ecstatic at the same time, transported to a place where nothing was the way it had been, where life was changed beyond anything she could ever have imagined. A place where your children died and were alive again. Only at the very beginning could she have believed such a thing. When she would wake after dreaming and for one heartbreaking moment believe they were still alive. When the smell of fire in her head had sparked madness in her mind. But now that it had happened, had really happened, she wanted to see Adil. Needed him to convince her it was real.

Only when the town darkened and lanterns were lit did she let herself into his apartment. Her hands shook as she made herself a coffee. If they were alive, as Clara seemed certain, where were they, and what had Alec been up to all this time? It didn't make sense. Why would he take her daughters and just vanish? It couldn't have been about Jack. She'd promised it was over and had been certain Alec accepted that. She longed for the sadness to come to an end, and now it might, it really might. But there was an undercurrent to her joy. What if Clara was mistaken? Or if she was right, what if she never found Emma and Fleur?

She put the coffee down, unable to drink. Was Alec somewhere in Malaya? Somewhere across this seething jungle-cloaked land.

Adil's building, creaking and squeaking, seemed as restless as her. She opened a window and occupied her mind by watching an old woman shuffle along the narrow sidewalk opposite. But the room began to close in, her skin prickled and her head started to thump. She sat on the floor, knees against her chest and looked out at three stripes of pink cloud that lay across the sky. She thought of the brightly coloured Malayan birds, the shiny fish, the glittering insects. Were her children still somewhere here? Somewhere in Malaya? A zigzag of gold appeared in a space between the clouds and she took it as a sign. They were. She felt sure they were. She stood up. Stared in the mirror. Saw the fear and excitement, placed a palm to her heart, and took several deep breaths.

Adil will know what to do, she thought, and waited, calmer now.

An hour or so later, she turned her head as the door clicked open. He came across to sit beside her. He held her hand and allowed her to sob. When she tried to speak, her voice was muffled by tears that would not stop. But when she finally finished telling him, she looked in his eyes and saw herself reflected there.

'This is very good news,' he said.

'It's wonderful news.'

She sniffed once or twice and couldn't keep from grinning. Then, though she was thirsty and her eyes were raw from crying, the tears turned to unstoppable laughter.

He pulled her closer to him. 'I will do whatever it takes to help you find them,' he said.

'What would I do without you?'

'You'd find a way, but you don't have to. We will succeed. That's a promise.'

He lowered his head and kissed her on the lips for the first time.

When he sat with his arms around her, the loneliness that she'd felt for so long dissolved. With a pounding heart, she realised it had been replaced by a sensation of belonging, and for the first time since the terrible day when she believed her girls had died, she felt safe.

47

She began the next day full of hope, though tired from lack of sleep. Once Adil voiced doubt that they were still in Malaya, she didn't know what to think. He was certain they'd have heard something; she wasn't so sure. She watched the merchant ships load up from huge warehouses: rubber, wood, silk. And further out to sea, distant liners slid like great white whales. Had one of those carried her girls? On her way to the shipping office on the busy wharf, she pictured their life on a liner. The excitement, the shivery thrill at night when lights flickered on the water, and the fishy smell of the ocean followed you about as water thumped the depths of the ship.

But at the shipping office, there was no record of Alec boarding a ship with two girls. The sweat grew cold on her skin. No ship bound for Australia, Borneo, England, or anywhere else. Afterwards, she walked slowly back along the dockside, and held back her tears. Not even the low-slung Sumatran boats that rocked in white tipped waves could raise a smile.

She called at the offices of *The Straits Times* where a journalist waited to interview her for the woman's page. Telephones rang, typewriters clattered, and the radio was turned up too loud. A group of chain-smoking men with nicotine-stained fingers whistled and stared openly at her

396

legs. She felt their eyes on her back, but held her head high, hope returning a little. It was a long shot, but if Adil was wrong and the girls *were* still in Malaya, someone's memory might be jogged. A woman who believes her kids are dead finds out they're alive, but doesn't know where they are; our female readers will love that, the journalist said, and lit another cigarette.

Afterwards Lydia stopped off to send a telegram. She stood in the queue for half an hour, feeling the familiar prickling in her neck and chest. Alec had always insisted that whatever happened, nothing would entice him back to England, and although he was not in contact with his parents, could there be a chance they might know where he was? Alec's father refused point blank to have a phone installed, though she checked with International Directories just in case. But no, so a telegram or letter it had to be and a telegram was faster. She thought of addressing it to Alec's parents, but on a sudden hunch addressed it to Emma, at their house. Her heart flipped over at the thought of Emma reading it.

★   ★   ★

It was Adil's idea to drive up to the reservoir to catch the sea turning sapphire. He'd just come off the phone after talking to the police in England and Australia. It was a humid evening and Lydia repeatedly wiped the sweat from her brow as they walked to the car.

'So what did they actually say?' she asked.

'They said without proof Alec was actually in the country in the first place, how could he be missing?'

'What about a criminal investigation?'

'They can only investigate a crime committed in their country. The British police did at least suggest writing to the Inland Revenue, or to the Ministry of Pensions and National Insurance.'

'I'll do that the moment we get back, catch the first post tomorrow.'

'I can turn round if you want?'

She hesitated. 'Now, or in a few hours, it won't make any difference. Let's go on.'

'We won't be long. I just thought it might do you good.'

'I know.' She paused. 'I could just go straight to England. Try Alec's parents' house. After all, you don't think they're in Malaya.'

'I don't, but you said yourself he'd never go back there. Why go chasing halfway round the world for nothing. It'll cost a fortune and they could be anywhere. Let's see if we can uncover something concrete first.'

'Maybe a private eye?'

He pulled a face. 'In my experience they're a dishonest lot. Take your cash and leave you high and dry. But it might be worth contacting Somerset House in England. If he has remarried there'll be a record of the marriage certificate.'

'What about Interpol?' she said.

He smiled. 'Unlikely. I'll write to the Interpol General Secretariat if you like, but they're more concerned with organised crime.'

Lydia sighed, and on the fast road, lost herself

in the rhythm of the car, composing letters in her head.

She was jolted from her thoughts when Adil veered off the main road and curved on to a twisting mountain road. Near the top he parked. The wind came in fresh off the sea, and in scented evening air they followed the remains of a path choked with ferns. He helped her round huge boulders, and when his hand touched hers she was aware of something she couldn't explain, a sense of fate. *Yuanfen* the Chinese called it, a kind of binding force. Lydia couldn't yet say if they were destined to be together, but at the very least he'd helped her acknowledge her own strength. Mauve light filtered across the tips of the mountain, throwing the hollows into darkness. He looked at her and smiled. The protective veneer gone, he was opening up to her, and the warmth she'd first glimpsed on the day they caught the train together was now plain to see.

'Look,' he said, taking a step away. 'Over there. That's the Parrotts' house.'

'It looks so close.'

'As the crow flies, but by road considerably further.'

They carried on past waterfalls and rock pools. At the very top, she looked down the hillside. Tiny dots of light began to appear, like a necklace of fairy lights strung across the valley. Past the land at the western point, where the sky edged into the ocean, a band of pale lilac vanished in an explosion of orange and gold. She spun on her heels, caught the vast surface of the reservoir turn red, and let out a slow whistle. Then she turned back to see the sky fast disappearing into the ocean, with only the twists of tiny purple boats marking the harbour.

Adil looked at the darkening sky. 'We'd better get back. The weather's worsening.'

'Thanks for this. It's wonderful.'

An expression of something she couldn't name spread across his face. When she touched his hand, she felt she'd known all along, but wanted him to say the words. He didn't speak, but came to stand in front of her, slipped down the straps of her dress, and put his hands on her shoulders. She tilted her head and reached up to touch his face.

Neither of them spoke.

'Maybe now is not the time,' he said. He slid back the straps and glanced up at the sky again.

'Wouldn't it be wonderful if, just for once, life could be free of complication?'

He laughed. 'Maybe, but my guess is we'd all be terribly bored.'

'After what I've been through, I'll settle for a slice of boredom, thanks.'

He grinned, took her hand, and they raced to the car, stumbling over the boulders and laughing, as they attempted to beat the rain and the dark.

By the time they reached Harriet's house, fat drops of rain were splattering on the ground. They stood in the porch to escape a soaking, but a mature creeping fig, attached to the upper wall of the building, had spread under the glass roof and was dripping on to their hair and faces.

When Harriet's narrow-hipped boy opened up, he frowned and gave them a suspicious look. Adil convinced him to lead them into the large hall, but the boy remained guarded. After a few minutes voices reached them, and Harriet appeared in the doorway, dressed in an acid yellow kimono. Harriet's bright orange lipstick had spread to her teeth and ran up in lines from her top lip. Her eyes flicked from face to face, clearly not pleased to see them, broad cheeks flushed. The rubies at her neck glinted, almost lost between the folds of flesh.

Was she drunk or just being cagey, Lydia wondered.

'I thought I might have seen you before now,' Harriet said.

Adil nodded.

'Well, let's sit down, for heaven's sake.'

When Lydia studied Harriet's face, she thought her aged since their previous encounter. Her roots were showing white, her eyelids drooped at the corners, and she'd gained an even heavier layer of fat. It might be George's death, or just the strain of maintaining an outworn colonial life.

'You're looking at me strangely, dear. Don't you like what you see?' Harriet spoke with an edge Lydia hadn't heard before.

Lydia muttered something meaningless.

'As we are here,' Adil began, looking steadily at Harriet.

'As you are here,' she cut in. 'Let's not mince words. I imagine you'd like to know the truth about George?'

Adil sat stony faced on the edge of his chair, his eyes unwavering.

There was a prickly silence in the room.

Harriet laughed unnaturally. 'If only George hadn't been tempted again. You came so very close to the truth, Adil, but by the time your officers arrived, we'd destroyed every scrap of evidence.'

'The fraud?' Lydia said.

'Arms dealing, my dear. Alec knew, of course, was part of it to some extent. George refused to say exactly. But that's the reason George helped Alec get away. False passports, false trail for you, my dear. I'm so sorry.'

'False passports? False trail? Hang on. That means he *must* have taken the girls abroad.'

A hot panicky feeling engulfed her. She turned to Adil. He nodded. She wanted to speak but had to make do with taking deep breaths until the panic passed.

While Lydia struggled, Harriet cleared her throat and looked away.

Lydia managed to regain her voice. 'I don't understand. Why did Alec have to get away so desperately? It couldn't just have been about me and Jack, surely.'

'That played a part I think. Never underestimate a man's pride, my dear.'

Lydia glared at her. 'Oh, come on. He took my children.'

'Nevertheless . . . but you're right of course. George got greedy. Used government funds. That's where Alec came in I think. Financial admin.'

Lydia felt her heart pause. 'Are you claiming

they were in it together?'

Harriet shrugged. 'I'm afraid I don't know to what extent.'

'Well, I've called Alec a lot of things in my time, but I never thought him dishonest.'

'Oh, you don't need to worry — '

'Worry? About Alec? That's the last thing I'm doing right now!'

'Well, anyway, there's nothing left to prove it, except one, rather incriminating document.' Harriet looked at Adil, with questioning brows.

He shook his head.

'Then it's as I expected, Alec has it, and he's hardly likely to give himself away is he?'

'What name?' Adil interjected and gave Lydia a subtle warning look to keep quiet. 'What name did he travel under?'

Harriet shook her head. 'I'm sorry I don't recall.'

Lydia felt sceptical and must have shown it in her face.

'It is the truth,' Harriet said. 'I only heard it the once. Something rather similar to his own. Believe me, I was unaware until just before George died.'

'So what happened?' Adil asked.

'When we burnt everything, we found the document was missing. George didn't know if it was you, Adil, or Alec, who had it. Either way George couldn't let the shame tarnish his name if the truth got out. A man in his position. That was when he confessed everything to me.'

Harriet stared at the floor, then lifted her face to them, feigning a smile that didn't reach the eyes.

Lydia took a sharp breath in and pressed her lips together to control her anger. It ran through her mind that Harriet might know more than she was letting on.

'If I hadn't found out my children were alive, would you ever have told me, or would you have gone on letting me think them dead?'

'My dear, I did tell you in my own way. I discovered Clara and it was me who asked Cicely to introduce you.'

'But how could you do that to me? How could you be so cruel? When I found them gone it was you I came to.'

'I promise I really didn't know then.'

'Maybe not then, but you have known for months.'

'I'm truly sorry. I had to find a way to let you know that didn't incriminate my husband. For all his faults I loved him, even after I found out what he'd done to you.'

There was a pause. Lydia stood, and feeling her heart pound, took a few steps away before turning on Harriet. 'Jesus Christ, this is unbelievable! You're telling me the reason George delayed my arrival in Ipoh was to give Alec a head start? That he lied to me about everything?'

Harriet nodded.

'And you let me think my children were dead.'

'I am sorry. It was so nearly different.'

'What do you mean?'

'From what George said, I think the travel arrangements took longer to organise than he'd expected.'

Lydia's hand flew to her mouth. 'Dear God. I

404

can hardly bear it. You mean I must have only just missed them.'

Harriet cleared her throat again but didn't speak.

'But why was all this necessary? Couldn't Alec just have taken me with him?'

Harriet sighed. 'You know why. He thought you were with Jack.'

Lydia felt her head explode. 'What the hell would have happened if there hadn't been a fire? What would have happened when I turned up in Ipoh and discovered Alec wasn't there?'

'I imagine he'd have planned another false trail for you,' Harriet said.

'And in the end?'

Guilt darkened Harriet's features. 'I'm sorry.'

The only sound was rain beating in the courtyard and then a sudden burst of thunder. Lydia felt her jaw tighten.

'Do you have any idea what it did to me? Do you know that when I thought they were dead, it was as if a part of me ceased to exist?'

Harriet took a deep breath and stared at the floor.

'No, I don't suppose you do. You never had children, did you?' Lydia's voice began to crack. That she had been so hoodwinked, so deceived. It beggared belief. While she calmed herself, she heard Adil's voice break the silence.

'Will you stay on here?' he asked Harriet. 'I mean, since Independence so much has changed.'

'Oh, I think so,' Harriet said, her voice sounding brighter. 'Where would I go? That's the sadness of old age. What you've got is what you've got. No more second chances. I'm not complaining. I've always known about George's sordid pastimes. I could put up with that, funnily enough. But not the dealing.'

Lydia stared at her. 'I imagine not.'

There was another brief silence then Harriet smiled faintly. 'I like Malaya. Can't imagine going back to Surrey. Well, life and death are inseparable here, aren't they? They are everywhere, of course, but here you know it. Your friend Jack. He knew.'

Lydia flinched.

'Russian roulette. You know the way it goes. Of course it was before he met you. I think the futility of life after the war caused his depression. Meeting you broke him of it, but it was just a matter of time with his type . . . ' Harriet trailed off.

'Look, I've heard enough,' Lydia said. 'Jack's dead now and I don't see the point of rehashing the past. I think we'd better go now. Don't you, Adil?'

Harriet ignored her. 'We only left Malaya once — during the war. Nineteen forty-one. George's doing, not long before the first air raid by the Japs on Singapore.'

As Harriet drifted back, Lydia and Adil exchanged looks. Still angry, she mouthed a question at him. What do we do now? He gave a subtle head shake. Outside the rain continued to pound the ground, sounding like machine gunfire. She felt trapped, wanted to leave, and felt if she stayed a minute longer she'd lose all self-control.

'I owe George my life,' Harriet said. 'When

Malaya fell in forty-two, old friends died. Life. It's all swings and roundabouts. You'll see.'

'Can we just please stop this. Now.' Lydia felt her voice rise. 'I'd rather not look back.'

'You're right, my dear, and I hope we can draw a curtain over George's unfortunate dealings too.' Harriet looked at Adil.

He met her eyes but gave nothing away. Lydia needed time to think. As Adil and Harriet talked a little longer, she focussed on a vase of startling pink roses on a side table in front of the window, their sickly sweet fragrance reaching her from there.

'You'll stay the night,' Harriet was saying. 'Twin beds all right? There are other rooms, of course, but none of the beds are made up. The storm's simply too ferocious to drive back now.'

'Maybe,' Adil said, glancing at Lydia for confirmation.

She looked at the rain and shrugged.

Harriet indicated which door they should take, and as they left the room, Lydia turned back over her shoulder. 'I wonder. Do you have airmail note paper and a pen I could use?'

'Writing paper? Of course, I'll have it sent to your room.'

⋆ ⋆ ⋆

In the small guestroom at the back of the house, Lydia left the window slightly ajar and turned off the overhead light. A small table lamp cast a muted light in one corner of the room. Adil came across to where she stood beside one of the

407

beds. He paused, stepped back a little so that he could study her face.

'Are you all right?' he asked.

'Bloody furious actually.'

The shock of hearing Harriet's confession had left her with a sense of unreality, compounded by the fact that now, here she was, alone with Adil in a bedroom at Harriet's house. Everything was happening so fast, and she was unnerved by the strength of, first, the anger she'd felt, and now the explosion that was going on in her.

'Let's lie on one of the beds together,' he said. 'Just until you feel better.'

Both on their backs, they lay fully clothed on top of the counterpane, fingers laced together. She turned sideways towards him, rested one hand on his thigh, and looked at the reflection of lamp light shining in his eyes. He squeezed her hand. Thoughts floated in and out of her mind as she went over everything Harriet had said.

'Calmer now?' he asked, after a while.

'Yes.'

Suddenly shy, she touched his face, and something passed between them. Very slowly, he rolled over, loosened his shirt, then resting on one elbow, reached across and slid open the zip at the side of her dress. He seemed to wait. She slipped her hand inside his shirt, felt the cool of his skin as she ran her palm up the length of his back.

'Let's get into bed properly,' she said.

'You're sure?'

'I'm sure. Now for heaven's sake, get that shirt off!'

He raised his eyes upwards and grinned. She

gazed at him for a moment, then tilted her head back and laughed. He pushed the hair behind her ears, and sat up properly to remove his shirt. She slipped her dress up and over her head, then dived under the covers, her legs tangling in the sheets. He kicked the bedclothes off and on to the floor. She took a slow breath and closed her eyes.

There had been a time when Lydia believed she'd never feel peace again. Even though she looked the same, life had aged her, stolen her innocence, and replaced it with knowledge she'd never asked for. It had set her apart, but in that space, she'd also found Adil. She opened her eyes, blinked, and smiled at him.

Their love making was the kind that comes from a very slow burn, the sense of disbelief combining with a hitherto unknown thrill. Adil was gentle, completely in tune with her, so much so that at times she felt so breathless she could hardly breathe at all.

Afterwards he pulled up a sheet from the floor and covered their naked bodies. She curled into him in the cramped single bed. He kissed her on both eyelids, then, one of the lucky ones, fell asleep instantly, snoring softly. She took comfort in the intimacy. By moonlight, she watched him smile in his sleep, his snores merging with the sound of rainwater splashing from the roof. Not wanting to leave him, but unable to sleep and feeling overwhelmed by the events of the day, she untangled her limbs and decided to write her letters.

After she'd written to the Inland Revenue, the

Ministry of Pensions, and Somerset House, she extinguished the light and made herself comfortable between the cool sheets of the second twin bed. Adil would obtain the necessary addresses in the morning. She stretched out a hand to touch the other bed and feel the warmth of him. In the simple relief of night, when words and actions were over for the day, her body lay still, but not her mind.

The night had unfolded unexpectedly and her thoughts continued to revolve. It was unbearable that they still didn't know where Emma and Fleur were. She pictured them, felt their hands in hers, and considered why no proof of their journey had been found. If Alec was still here in Malaya, surely someone would know something, especially with Adil's contacts. But there was no record of them anywhere, and what was a false passport for, if not for travelling abroad? She thought again of Alec's parents, but she was certain Alec would never go back there. How many times had he said how much he hated it? She wondered if he'd got hold of a different car and driven up through Thailand. Yet Adil had made sure all the border controls were checked.

But to send her off on a false trail? To cause her such utter grief. And for George to have deceived her in the way he did. She shook her head. The affair with Jack must have hurt Alec more than she knew. By the time dawn was rising and narrow bands of red had spread across the sky, the sound of weeping reached her from another open window. Harriet, she thought, and with heavy eyelids, finally fell asleep.

48

It was the autumn half term, 1957. I pictured our first February in England, back in 1955, when we'd just arrived. I started to write about the shock of frosts that iced our bedroom windows, and the novelty of coal smoke that hung in the air as we walked home from school. But it brought back too many memories of leaving my mum.

Veronica popped her head round the door. She and Dad were still not married, thanks to the delay caused by her visit to Africa.

She came across, put an arm round me and looked over my shoulder. 'A new story?'

'Nothing really.'

'Look, Emma, I'm in an awful rush, but I just dropped by to tell you there's some exciting news.'

I looked up, my skin starting to tingle. 'Has someone found Mum?'

Her face fell a little as she sat on the bed. 'No, sorry, darling. We've been over that, and you must know it isn't going to happen. But I promise you will be pleased.'

At the same time as that, Fleur clattered into my room, shutting the door behind her.

I swung round and gave her a cross look, annoyed at the interruption. 'We were talking, Fleur.'

'Guess what?' Fleur said, ignoring me. She

couldn't keep still, eyes shining and cheeks bright pink. 'You didn't see it, did you?'

'See what?'

She sat on my bed, next to Veronica, and bounced. 'I saw the boy deliver it. He was ever so smart. In a navy blue uniform with red piping and a pillbox cap too. He whistled at me.'

'Fleur, what on earth are you jabbering on about?' Veronica said, as she picked up her bag.

'The telegram. It had Em's name on it. Dad took it.'

'Was this just now?' I said.

'A little while ago. It looked foreign. Dad took it upstairs.'

Despite everything, Fleur's loyalty remained firmly with Dad, so it was odd she was telling me this. She frowned and looked at the floor. 'I thought he was going to give it to you. But then you didn't say anything. I wanted to know what it was. Are you sure he didn't give it to you?'

I shook my head. Since the day he hugged me, we'd kept away from each other, both of us too embarrassed to speak of what had passed.

'Don't say I told,' Fleur pleaded, her eyes huge.

'Well, how else can I ask him?'

She pulled a face.

Veronica nodded to me. 'I think you'd better ask him. But look, I really have to be off. I'll see you tomorrow, Emma. Okay?'

I nodded but I was furious with Fleur. Now I'd have to wait until the next day to find out Veronica's news.

'Aren't you having any lunch?' Fleur said.

Veronica shook her head.

412

After she'd gone, Fleur and I went downstairs.

Dad was in the kitchen heating Campbell's cream of chicken soup. It was Fleur's favourite, though I preferred Gran's homemade split pea. I swallowed the lump that came whenever I thought of Gran, and folded my arms.

'Can I have the telegram please?' I said, trying to sound calm.

He looked at me, his face severe. I stood my ground.

'The one addressed to me.'

His shoulders sagged. 'I only wanted to protect you.'

I stared at him. 'But, Dad, it was addressed to me. Fleur saw it.'

Fleur sat with her eyes glued to the Formica tabletop. As if the pictures of saucepans, carrots, and casserole dishes were completely absorbing.

I thought of something else. 'Why didn't you tell us you planned to sell the house? Billy told me.'

'You know it's been on the cards,' he said, his back to me as he stirred the soup.

I felt my skin prickle, but controlled my temper. 'No, Dad, I don't know. I don't know anything, because you don't tell me.'

The room went silent, but for the soup bubbling on the stove, and his wooden spoon stirring and scraping the bottom of the pan.

'And anyway I don't want to move.'

He whirled round to face me. 'That decision is not up to you.'

I held out my hand. 'Please can I have the telegram?'

'Fleur is mistaken. The telegram was not for you.'

I saw Fleur's mouth fall open in surprise. To her, Dad could do no wrong.

'Well, what was it then?'

'You have overstepped the mark, Emma. The telegram was no concern of yours.'

Then the air sort of went out of him and he looked at the floor. 'Serve your soup. I'll be back in a minute.'

The new venetian blinds were down in the kitchen, just slices of light lit the gloomy room. I served up and we ate our soup in silence.

When Dad didn't come back, Fleur went to turn cartwheels outside, and I tiptoed up to his room. He wasn't there. No sign of the telegram either. I couldn't understand why he didn't show it to me, if only to prove it wasn't mine. It had to be something about Mum. It had to be. I saw my reflection in his dressing table mirror, a pale face with dark circles under the eyes. Outside, a flock of starlings whistled as they spun across the sky then flew out towards the village.

I felt uneasy. Heard the hiss of the jungle snakes. Softly they came through the long grass. I shook myself out of it. This was England. No snakes. No jungle.

In my bedroom, Veronica had scribbled a message on my notepad.

Town Hall, tomorrow, ten o'clock sharp. See you there, and bring your letter from Johnson, Price & Co. x

49

At last, after several weeks, the article was published, but with no reply to the telegram she'd sent Emma, and nothing on the passenger lists, Lydia's spirits remained in turmoil. At the post office, she requested an airmail sticker, folded the article in four, and slipped it into a large brown envelope. With an aching head, she wiped her brow, then flipped open her diary, and searched for the address. She didn't believe he'd gone to England, nor that he'd informed his parents of his whereabouts, but she had to try.

Somerset House had written back with a kind letter, but had no marriage to report. The Inland Revenue in England had not been at liberty to divulge information, and so far, there'd been no reply from the Ministry of Pensions. Adil had even driven to the new British High Commission, in Kuala Lumpur. While housed in a stunning building, with multiple pillared verandas and a leafy garden, the systems were in disarray. Come back in a couple of months, they'd said. She and Adil agreed to work through each country, systematically, until something turned up. But letters, even airmail, took an age, so what was she going to do for cash? Her savings from Singapore would only last another month or two, with enough for one long trip besides, but any more than that, and she'd be looking for a job again, this time in Malacca.

Back at Adil's, she took a sip of bitter black coffee, and glanced uneasily at the street hawkers. The hum of city life melded in an indistinguishable noise. Chinese, Indian. The strains of jangly Malay music. A single movement opposite drew her eyes. In the shadow of a doorway she saw a woman stare up, her eyes narrowed against the light.

Lydia stared back and the woman beckoned. She blinked. The woman in the doorway wore a pale blue dress, blue flowers at the hem — surely not — it couldn't be. She felt dizzy and rubbed her temple. Side effects from the Chinese pills Adil had given her for her headache? She picked up her bag and slipped down the stairs, noticing an envelope on the mat and stuffing it in her bag on her way out. Outside, the heat hit her like a wall. She swivelled to check the street, packed with rickshaws and traders. The woman had gone. She turned to go back in, but then caught a flash of pale blue skirt at the street corner. The woman beckoned again, and Lydia couldn't help herself. She followed, sweat beginning to drip beneath her dress.

The woman continued deep into the maze of streets that crawled down to the old Chinese quarter by the docks. The sounds around her clashed. Bells rang, dogs barked, and birds sang in cages. A pack of feral children chased thin Malays on bicycles. She stepped back. The Malays escaped, but amid a mass of noise and fingering, the kids hemmed her in. She panicked, heart pounding. The woman in blue heard, turned, and yelled in standard Chinese. The children melted away.

At the juncture where torn posters of acrobats fought for attention with propaganda leaflets pasted by the old British Administration, the streets narrowed, and she blundered into strings of washing hanging right across. She hesitated. Fear of assault closed her throat. The woman remained a few steps ahead, slipped across a bridge and turned to summon Lydia with a quick gesture. It was midday, and from the open door of one building came the aroma of chilli and crispy duck, from another tamarind and coriander.

At close quarters, the houses were narrow and squashed. Lydia clung to her bag, pressed it hard into her chest. Her head spun with the noise. She'd reckoned without the crowds of people and found it hard to breathe, but she wiped her forehead with her hand and picked up her pace. The woman was too far ahead to see clearly, but still Lydia went after each flash of blue, further into the depths of the quarter. Once the people thinned out, she sped past herbalists, jewellers, and the shops selling paper goods for burning at the graves in the Chinese Cemetery. In one window she glimpsed a paper guitar, a pagoda, a tiny paper sampan.

On one of the narrow bridges that crossed the canals she stopped for a moment to get her breath, and looking down, caught sight of minnows flashing by in glittering silver shoals. She had no idea where she was, hadn't seen any cabs for ages and she realised she'd never find her way back. But then she saw the woman standing near the edge of an open sewer.

The smell was sickening, and now that she had a chance to look properly, it was obvious the woman wasn't well. Her skin was pallid, her body too thin. A spark of dislike fired in the woman's eyes as she waited, then she spun round and threw open a pair of dragon gates on to the dock itself. She took a few steps to the left, turned into a narrow passageway, and stopped at one of the shabby tin huts at the water's edge.

The woman went in and squatted on a worn rush mat. Lydia followed and looked for a chair. There was none. The dismal room smelt of cheap scent and rotting pineapple, and the ceiling was black with flies. But for a dented paraffin lamp at one end, and a pair of trousers hanging from a nail, it was bare. Mat-covered wooden planks formed a bed that wobbled when Lydia perched on the edge. As she grew accustomed to the gloom, she focussed on the woman's face and saw that, though her appearance was shabby, her manner declared her to be proud.

When the woman spoke again, her words were deliberately slow.

'You do not recognise me?'

Lydia shook her head. 'Should I?'

The woman gave her an exasperated look and spat on the ground. 'No. Your sort never does.'

'My sort?'

'Spoilt white woman sort. *Mem*.' She spoke the last word scornfully.

Lydia was taken aback by the open enmity. 'What do you want?'

The woman narrowed her eyes. 'Did you read it?'

Lydia frowned.

'You did not read it?'

Lydia thought for a moment, then reached into her bag. 'You mean this?'

The woman nodded as Lydia pulled the envelope apart, and a slip of paper floated to the floor. She reached down and picked up a cheque. She couldn't read the name, but someone had received a cheque from Alec worth several hundred dollars.

She was puzzled.

'My price for silence,' the woman said, without removing her eyes from Lydia.

'Your silence?'

'You cannot be that stupid.'

Lydia bristled. 'I have no idea what this is for.' She studied the cheque. Dated three weeks before Alec had vanished, it obviously hadn't been cashed. She turned it over. Nothing on the back.

'Your husband paid me to keep my mouth shut. Gave me that cheque.' She spat on the ground. 'What use is a cheque to me? I told him. Cash. No cheque. So he turned up with cash, demanded I give the cheque back. I told him I threw it away.'

'He believed you?'

'I do not know, but what could he do? It is my insurance policy.' The woman laughed, but it was a bitter laugh that didn't reach her eyes.

'I don't know what you're talking about.'

'Not what — who!'

Lydia frowned.

'Maznan. My silence. Never to say who his father is.'

She stared hard at the woman. Could it be true? She took in the compacted dirt floor, the rough wooden walls, the flies on the ceiling. Surely Alec hadn't come here. It was unthinkable.

The woman stared with a satisfied smile, and then nodded her head.

'Let me get my mind round this,' Lydia said. 'You're surely not telling me that Maznan is Alec's child?'

'Ah. She understands. But that is just the first part.'

Lydia suspected a demand for money, but none came.

'Take Maznan to his father.'

Surprised, Lydia shook her head. 'I have no idea where Alec is . . . and isn't Maz happy in the village?'

'Resettlement village!' The woman snorted. 'Without money my sister will not keep him. I have no money and I am sick. Soon I will be dead.'

'Why should I believe that Maz is Alec's son?'

The woman pulled out a small pile of photos from a pouch at her waist and handed them to Lydia. Every one showed Alec naked with this woman, each shot more compromising than the one before.

'He didn't know these were being taken?'

The woman smiled. 'Of course not.'

'But why?'

'Insurance policy. I told you before.'

She shook her head. 'What a way to live!'

'We cannot all have your comfortable life, Mem.'

Lydia flicked through the remaining pictures. Four showed Alec holding a small boy on his lap, the child cuddled up to him, with one arm curled round Alec's neck.

'Very cosy.' She spoke more confidently than she felt. 'This doesn't prove anything.'

She threw them back at the waiting woman and watched them flutter to the floor. The woman carefully returned them to her pouch.

'What about Maznan's grandparents? Wouldn't they want to look after him?'

'Too old,' the woman said.

'Even if I believed you, why should I help?'

The woman considered her words. 'It is not for me. It is for Maznan.'

'What about Jack? Nobody helped him.'

'I stopped them from killing you too. They wanted to.'

The woman could be lying. Where was the proof? The cheque might have been for something else, and the child might not even be Maz. She hesitated. No, that wasn't true. In one of the shots it had been clear the child was Maznan, and Alec would never let an unknown mixed race child snuggle up close.

The woman folded her arms across her chest. 'Did you never think about his pale eyes, almost blue?'

Lydia held her breath, completely shaken. My God, the deception was bad, but a child he had simply abandoned. That was far worse.

'So that was why I was the perfect person to accompany the child,' she said. 'Keep it in the family, so to speak.'

There was a pause, as Lydia rubbed her temples, the pain there beginning to throb. She thought of Alec's sneer when she'd told him about Jack. Yet he had slept with Cicely, and if this was true, had a son by his driver's daughter. Another unwelcome thought occurred; had Adil known about this but hadn't said? Was that why he had discouraged her from taking the child, when they first spoke on their way to Ipoh?

She then thought back to when she had first met Maz. 'He was injured when your sister brought him to me. Why was that?'

The woman smiled, 'Just an accident, but it helped you to decide.'

There was a noise at the entrance. An elderly woman with white hairs growing from her chin, pushed a child into the room, smiled toothlessly, and left.

Lydia stood. 'Maz!'

His mother got up, put her arm round the boy and took a step forward, the sneer gone. 'So will you take him?'

Lydia was struck by the sadness in the woman's eyes.

'But he's your son.'

'I cannot give him a life. Your husband can.'

Lydia felt torn. She was very fond of Maz, but this was crazy. She recalled Adil saying Maz's mother would end up dead, and then what would happen to the child?

With a grin Maz came across and put his hand in hers. Lydia knew when she was beaten and smiled back.

The woman led them out through the maze of alleyways and back to Adil's district. Lydia felt she was juggling with life, hoping she'd find the place where Alec had taken her girls. And now that fate had thrust Maz into her care for a second time, she had to find Alec, for the boy's sake too.

The woman kissed Maz on the forehead, and handed Lydia a folded scrap of tissue thin paper. 'You need this for the passport.'

Lydia opened it out. My God, she thought, it's his birth certificate. In the space where it requested father's name, Alec Cartwright was clearly printed. Why on earth hadn't the woman shown it to her at the start?

As they walked away, Lydia thought of the poverty she'd seen. Remembered how her old gardener scraped together his living. How he scared the girls with stories of spirits, snakes that swallowed small children alive, and witches who only came out at midnight, in search of people to capture. Emma raced in once, breathlessly telling a tale of a frog-faced demon that killed a Siamese cat in the back garden.

Fleur insisted they needed a demon catcher, and Lydia came up with using an old doll. They dressed her in white, and stationed her outside the children's window. The next day, the gardener appeared with a rag doll made by his wife. So then they had two, and of course he wanted money, and she'd felt tricked.

But life was hard, not just in the new resettlement villages, but in the outside world too. And now she'd seen at close quarters the way people were forced to live, she saw how they had to do anything to make a dollar. Truth was, the gardener had been quite creative.

Maz chattered happily, despite leaving his mother. He was too young to really understand the finality of what had happened. She squeezed his hand, and before they turned the corner into Adil's street, she turned back to catch a glimpse of blue skirt disappearing into the crowd. How odd, she thought, if the woman hadn't worn blue, I might never have followed.

50

It was Friday, the last day of the autumn half term holiday. At the town hall, where Veronica had asked to meet me, she requested the electoral register. In her left hand she held my old letter from Mr Johnson and flapped it at me.

'See, Emma,' she said, and pointed at a reference code in the top right hand corner.

I read it out. 'E C-Mb/0557/002.'

'Okay. The first part, E C-Mb. Those are initials.'

'And the rest?'

'0557 means the fifth month of nineteen fifty-seven. And 002 refers to the numbers of letters sent that month, concerning the owner of a particular file. In this case who E C-Mb is.'

'I get that. So?'

'Well, it confirms the news I didn't get a chance to tell you yesterday.'

'But you said there wasn't much hope.'

'There really wasn't. But a few weeks ago when I was up in town, I treated Freddy to a good lunch and begged him to intercede on your behalf.'

I was puzzled and pulled a face.

Veronica held up a hand. 'It will come clear. He decided to ask Johnson, Price & Co. if they'd be prepared to contact their client and explain your interest. Mr Johnson had received your letter, of course, so already knew about you.'

'And did Mr Johnson contact the client?'

'Well, he was reluctant at first, but Freddy is very persuasive, and in the end he agreed. The idea was to see if there was any chance she might allow disclosure.'

My heart thumped. 'She?'

Veronica nodded. 'Well, she considered it, and eventually agreed. Miss E. Cooper-Montbéliard. That's who it is. Such an unusual name, isn't it? Look at the reference again.'

I glanced down. 'Oh.'

She grinned. 'Exactly!'

'C-Mb stands for Cooper-Montbéliard.'

She nodded. 'Yes, the clue was there all along, though it would have been impossible to figure out.'

'So now we check the electoral register. Make sure the address Freddy was given is correct.'

'But it's the last day of the holiday,' I wailed. 'There's only tomorrow, then I'm going back to school on Sunday afternoon.'

She patted me on the arm. 'But you can write, can't you?'

★　★　★

The next day, after I had written my letter, I sat down with one of my stories while I waited for the rain to stop. I was having trouble with my main character. The hero, a tall man of Spanish extraction, who went by the name of Pedro Gonzalez Montes, was in the process of climbing up a ladder to rescue Claris from her evil grandfather. As he approached the top, the ladder slipped and he fell, not dead, but blinded and permanently disabled — no use as a hero at all. Unless he was Mr Rochester.

Writing wasn't as easy as I thought when I was younger. My characters used to do what I told them, now they fell from ladders, made unexpected announcements and generally misbehaved. With a disgusted snort, I abandoned Claris to lie on blood-encrusted sheets, with the sound of rats scuttling behind a thin partition wall.

It had turned into a drizzly autumn day with lumpy clouds full of moisture, the kind that isn't wet enough for an umbrella, but you get damp all the same. After I posted the letter, and as I neared the gate on my way back, Fleur darted from the house, and bumped straight into me, cheeks wet with tears. I put an arm round her, held her against my chest, and patted her back until she stopped crying.

'Come on, let's go down the road a bit, then you can tell me what's wrong,' I said.

She looked up at me, red eyed, then glanced back over her shoulder at the front door. She gave me a nod and between gulps managed to say, 'I heard them fight.'

I asked her what about, but she couldn't speak for stuttering. It might have been funny, except she was deadly serious. We walked slowly down the lane and I waited for her to squeeze all her tears out.

She tried again. 'It was awful, Emma,' she said, but stopped and rubbed her eyes. 'It came in the post after you went out. Veronica and me were sitting at the kitchen table when Daddy came in with a large brown envelope. When he opened it, a newspaper fell out and slipped on to the floor. *The Straits Times*. I saw it.'

She started to cry again. So far none of it made sense.

'Veronica picked it up . . . I saw it, Em. A picture of Mummy and us, when we were younger. Veronica went white, absolutely white. It had a big headline. Daddy tried to snatch it, but she stood up and read out loud.'

I bit my lip hard.

'I was so scared.' She stared at me with huge shiny eyes, and tears ran down the side of her nose. I patted her back again.

'Mummy isn't dead. She didn't abandon us. She isn't even missing.'

She'd spoken in such a small voice, I wasn't even sure I'd heard her right. 'If this is a joke, Fleur, it's not funny.'

'It isn't, Em. It isn't. She's looking for us. She doesn't know where we are. She thought we were dead, and then she found out we weren't, and now she's looking for us.'

I took a sharp breath. I was so hot, I thought my head would burst. The bare trees lurched and pitched, the still air came to life, and the world turned upside down. Dozens of questions fought for space but none of the answers made any sense.

'She's still in Malaya. Daddy sent me to my room, but I carried on listening from the hall.'

I had to sit down on the kerb to stop the road from spinning. 'Maybe it was an old paper,' I

428

managed to suggest, but my tongue had doubled in size and the words came out funny.

'Veronica read out the date. It was recent. Why did he say she'd abandoned us?'

I leant over and put my head between my knees. Fleur sat down beside me and took hold of my hand.

'Veronica started to cry. I heard Daddy say things quietly, but she wouldn't stop crying and calling him names. She was shouting about how he wanted to make a *bigamist* of her, and how could he do such an evil thing. And what about the girls.' She paused for a moment. 'Em, what is a bigamist?'

I screwed up my eyes. 'Oh, Mealy. It's someone who marries two people.'

'But then it wouldn't be Veronica who was one of those.'

'No. It would be Daddy.'

Even though I hadn't believed him about Mum, to have it confirmed like this . . . I actually felt winded, as if someone had come along and thumped me in the back.

'You never believed it, did you?'

I shook my head.

'I'm sorry, Em. I'm sorry for being mean to you about Mummy. I wanted to be a bridesmaid.'

'Oh, Mealy!' I pulled her to me and clung on, both of us trembling. I heard a car drive past, but didn't care what they must have thought. After a bit, I closed my eyes on the grey day, took a few breaths, then pulled her up. We turned round and headed for whatever waited for us at home. I

429

was certain now that the telegram had been something to do with Mum, maybe had even come from her.

Veronica passed by in her Morris Minor, her face so red from crying, I don't think I ever saw anyone look so upset. I lifted my hand and attempted a smile, but she didn't see me.

I had never got over the ache of separation, and now I wanted to yell so all the world would know my mum was alive, but back home, the sound of bangs and thumps in the kitchen made us hurry upstairs. Fleur held on to my hand and begged to come to my room.

'Em, what do you remember about Mummy?'

'Lots of things.'

'Tell me.'

'Her hair. The way she pinned it up and the way she was always singing in the morning.'

'The park. She took us to the park.'

'Yes, and the zoo. Mum loved the lions.'

She looked down and gulped. 'I can't remember that.'

'Don't cry, Fleur.'

'I think I remember the tigers. Didn't Mummy love us, Em?'

I put my arm round her and turned her face towards me. 'Is that what you've been thinking all this time? That she didn't love us?'

Fleur nodded.

'Listen to me. She loved us more than anything. More than anything in the whole world.'

I felt like seizing hold of my father and shaking him till his teeth fell out, but forced myself to stay calm while we waited to see what he'd do. I read one of my stories to Fleur, not the one with the slippery ladder, but an earlier one where Claris joined an acting troupe in a bid to run away from her captor. Reading helped calm my mind, but all the time, a part of me was wondering how I'd handle Father. We'd just got to the point where Claris found the key to her salvation, when he came in and stood with hands on hips, feet wide apart.

'Why are you looking at me like that?' he said.

He'd spoken defiantly, but I guessed he was bluffing.

'I know how this looks, but I did it for the best.'

Fleur stared at the carpet, and I looked over the top of her head to stare at him directly. 'What's going to happen now?' I asked, as levelly as possible, while resentment simmered inside of me.

He didn't hesitate. 'We're moving. That's what.'

Fleur and I looked at each other in disbelief. He couldn't. Surely he couldn't. Fleur gave me a little nod, to show she was backing me up, and I decided to stand up to Dad.

'But, Daddy, what about Mum?' I asked, still trying to remain polite. 'How will she find us if we move?'

'Are you doubting me, Emma?'

I was, of course I was, but his look silenced me. I swallowed and tried to control my temper.

'Good. I'm glad to see you're both being sensible.'

I don't know if it was the look of relief on his face that sparked it, as if yet again he'd somehow got the better of me, but I lost the struggle to hold back. Something broke and the words Mum used came back to me. I stood up straight, stepped forward and jabbed a finger at him.

'You fucking bastard. You absolute fucking bastard.'

Fleur's mouth fell open, and in the second before he raised his hand to me, I stared straight into his eyes. Both of us froze. I waited for him to breathe, and when he did, his face was red and his Adam's apple jumped up and down. I heard Fleur say in a small voice, 'Daddy, don't.'

His face fell and he seemed to sag. 'I'm sorry. Oh God,' he said. He swivelled round and left the room, leaving the door open.

Fleur and I stared at each other, both of us shocked that I dared say those words, and shocked by our father's response. I had almost felt pity when he crumpled.

'Why did he do it, Em?'

For once I was completely lost for words, but I couldn't let it go. 'I don't know but I'm going to find out.'

No longer scared if he flew into a rage, I found him outside in Granddad's old greenhouse. Veronica had attempted to keep it going, but all that remained were a few tomato plants with just a sprinkling of dead tomatoes, and one cucumber plant. Veronica was proud of that, slicing the bitter fruit into our corned beef sandwiches, though Fleur and I always slipped out the cucumber and dumped it when she wasn't looking. Poor Veronica.

He didn't acknowledge me when I opened the

door, but walked right past to the bonfire, staring straight ahead. A wisp of smoke rose from the heap but there were no flames I could see.

'Dad,' I called after him. 'Isn't it a bit damp?'

He turned a sad face to me, his control shattered. I never saw my father like that before. With a lump in my throat where I stopped myself from crying, I could hardly speak. He looked old and frightened, and I felt the ground shift beneath my feet.

'Daddy, why did you tell us Mum abandoned us, and that she was presumed dead?' I asked in a gentler tone of voice.

Thin blue smoke spiralled up. He shook his head and mumbled something about not enough air. With a long metal bar he poked and lifted the leaves to let some in. A cloud of darker smoke appeared, and for a moment I felt I was hallucinating and that none of this was real.

'It's what I thought,' he said, still not looking at me. 'It needs air.'

'Dad, why didn't Mum come to England with us?'

He took a couple of steps round the other side of the fire and looked through the smoke at me with pink eyes. 'There are grown-up things you don't understand, Emma. That you'll be able to understand when you're older.'

'I'm not a child any more,' I said, raising my eyebrows as Mum used to do.

He saw it and there was silence. A kamikaze blackbird flew over the bonfire inches from the top.

'I kissed Billy, you know, properly.'

'Oh God,' he said softly. 'Just like her mother.'

'Daddy, I want George Parrott's address. I have to know where Mum is.'

He looked at me then, looked at me properly. 'George Parrott won't be any use to you.' He reached inside his jacket pocket, pulled out his wallet, and unfolded a newspaper cutting. I read the words through twice and realised it was true. Mr Parrott was dead.

In the silence that followed, I was tempted to let it cover everything up, make believe we were a normal family, act as if I was outside with a dad who really loved me, and my mum was in the kitchen getting our dinner. He tried to talk normally for a bit, as if there wasn't a wall between us. Said he couldn't consider a return to Malaya to find Mum, because the *For Sale* sign was up, and we had to be here to show people round. Maybe a trip to Malaya when I was older, he suggested, as if that would pacify me.

'Can I see the article about Mum? I could write to the person who interviewed her. They might be able to tell us where she is.'

He pointed as the bonfire finally burst into flame and smoke spread all round the garden.

I ran to extract a blackened corner of newsprint, tears spilling as I dropped it and the fragments fell to the ground.

He came to put an arm around me. 'Really it's better, Emma, if you forget her. It was that man she went to. That's who she wanted. Not me.'

I went rigid.

'Not *us*, I mean.'

I pushed him away, and felt my cheeks puff

434

out. I couldn't decide if he really had wanted to protect me from disappointment, or whether he was covering up.

'Better for who? For me, or for you?'

His face was flushed and I could smell the odour of his armpits as he reached out to me again. He looked lonely, as if he didn't know where he really belonged. But it was too late.

'Come on,' he said. 'You're upset. Let's bandage that hand.'

'You're right. I am upset . . . I hate you.'

His face stiffened. 'Emma, listen to me.'

'No, I don't believe you. And I don't believe you about the telegram. Mum sent it. I know she did, and I will never give up looking for her. Never.'

I turned and fled. Mum was looking for us. As I ran I felt the touch of her, smelt her perfume. My mouth felt dry and I thought I was going to be sick. All that mattered was finding Mum, and even if she had gone to Jack, I didn't care. She was my mother and I loved her.

As I escaped down the lane, I saw smoke rise from where the village houses began, and where Billy lived. A lump came in my throat again, and when we bumped into each other in the village, I managed to say how sorry I was. I burst into tears and in the short embarrassed silence that followed, he looked at me with narrowed eyes. I fiddled with my hair as I waited for him to speak, then he kissed me on the forehead, got out a hankie to wipe my tears, and smiled.

'Don't worry, it's clean. Come on, Em, let's just forget it.'

'Friends then?'

'Friends,' he said, with a wink.

I told him about the article in *The Straits Times*.

'And now Dad's burnt it, I can't do anything. Look, my hand's all red where I tried to pull it out of the fire.'

'My mum will put something on that.'

I nodded.

He looked at me with a funny expression and grinned. 'You are an idiot, Emma.'

I frowned. 'I've already said I'm sorry I was mean. I thought it was all right now.'

'No, not that. Don't you see?'

I shook my head.

'Emma, there is a way. Come on. Let's go to mine. I'll tell you while we walk.'

51

On their way to Adil's flat, Lydia and Maz were loaded up with bags of food. Adil came into sight, back from a long trip to the shipping offices in Singapore, where he'd been checking every single passenger list for the past three years, including sensitive ones. This time with official authorisation. Out of breath, and red cheeked, he grasped Lydia's shoulder with one hand, held Maz with the other, then bent over to catch his breath.

She stared at him, saw the excitement in his eyes, and felt her heart skip a beat. 'Slow down,' she ordered. 'Take your time.'

He took a breath then carried on. 'A man answering Alec's description was seen.'

'In Malaya? Do you mean in Malaya?'

He held up a hand to stop her. 'Was seen — boarding a cargo ship bound for England, with two young girls, at about the right time. One of the clerks in the office remembered. Said it stuck in his mind because you didn't often see a man travelling alone with children.'

Lydia stood absolutely still, suspended in the moment.

'Originally, I'd had all passenger lines double-checked, but I missed the obvious — the cargo ships that sail from Singapore. The ones that take just a few passengers. So I got approval to check the cargo lists for the whole of that year.'

'And?'

'Well, there was no mention of Alec Cartwright.'

Her face fell, but he quickly put a hand on her arm. 'No. Listen.' He held her away from him with both arms. 'You remember Harriet said it was a similar name. Less difficult to falsify . . . '

She felt light-headed, hardly dared to breathe. Could this really be it?

'I checked all the names beginning with C with no luck. But an Alec Wainwright, with two daughters, was listed on a cargo ship bound for Liverpool from Singapore.'

'Oh God! Wainwright instead of Cartwright. Only three letters to alter.'

'Exactly.'

'Alec swore he'd never go back to England. Are you sure?'

'One of the girls was eight and the other eleven. And they are listed as Fleur and Emma. It really was them, Lydia. It really was.'

She put a hand to her heart. She'd been angry with him for keeping the circumstances of Maznan's birth from her. Now she didn't care. The children were in England and she would find them.

'Thank you, Adil. Oh, thank you.'

She kissed him on the cheek, and then they grinned at each other, while Maz gave a little yelp and did a funny little dance on the pavement.

She burst out laughing. This was an impossible dream come true. She'd kept the children alive in her mind. Not *kept* exactly. As time went on, she had no need to try, they simply invaded her thoughts. Even when she still believed they were dead, they had lived inside her, sunny little people with light in their eyes. An image came now of Fleur, sitting cross-legged beneath the wide canopy of a banyan tree, blue eyes shiny, feet hidden beneath a carpet of pink fruit. With the sound of a hundred birds chirping above her, and with a wistful look in her eyes, she'd said, 'Mummy, what does snow look like?'

And now, after everything, it was beginning to appear that her little girl might already know the answer to that.

52

Gran's wallpaper, with its pictures of chickens and pigs in yellow and light brown, was long gone, and now the walls, painted a sunny egg yolk colour, looked modern. We were sitting at the kitchen table waiting for lunch. Fleur and me. The Christmas holiday was almost over and it was the start of the New Year 1958, and my heart was light. This was the year I hoped to see my mum again. Last half term holiday, the day Veronica and I found out at the town hall that the address was correct, I had written to Miss E. Cooper-Montbéliard, of Kingsland Hall.

In my letter, I'd explained who I was, and requested that she reply to me at home, but not until the Christmas holidays. But now I had an awful thought. What if she didn't know when the holidays ended, and what if the letter arrived after I'd gone back to school? Nothing more had been said about the newspaper article, and Dad had recovered his usual self-control. I'd written to *The Straits Times*, of course. I didn't need the name of the journalist, but wrote directly to the editor, as Billy suggested. He was right. I was an idiot not to think of it myself. So far, no reply.

At last we'd had a phone installed. Dad had written to Veronica to tell her the number, but nobody called for three days. When it rang, while we were listening to *The Goon Show* on the radio in the kitchen, we all jumped, and Dad marched out to the hall. I turned the radio down and heard him sound really sorry, a different father altogether. Afterwards, he came to tell us Veronica was coming over. Fleur clapped her hands and I grinned.

Before the newspaper article arrived, and we found out Mum was not missing, there'd been no trace of Emma Rothwell. Though Veronica had done her best, I'd felt disappointed. Now, happy to be seeing Veronica again, at least I'd be able to talk to her about how to find my mum. I hoped so much we'd have more luck with that.

Since before Christmas, the post had been all over the place, arriving erratically, twice a day. Each day I rushed to get it before Dad. It was still the holidays, but I'd soon be starting a new term at school. Today the post came during lunch. Dad started to tip his chair back.

'It's okay. I'll get it,' I said, scrambling up and racing to the hall.

'Expecting something, Emma?' Dad called out from the kitchen.

'No, nothing,' I said, and slipped the envelope into my knickers. 'Just wondered if there were any late Christmas cards.'

Lunch was slow. It might seem odd that after all that had happened, life went back to normal. That nothing changed. But that's what happened. Dad's cooking remained as ropey as ever, today bubble and squeak with corned beef. It wedged in my throat and I found it hard to swallow.

Lunch over, I raced upstairs and into the bathroom, locked the door, leant my back

441

against it, and let out a long slow breath. Then I opened the envelope.

Dear Emma, I read.

I wasn't surprised to receive your letter, as after giving the matter considerable thought, I had decided to allow my solicitor to divulge my name, I would be pleased to meet you. I was hoping tea tomorrow, Saturday, here at Kingsland, if that's acceptable? Before you return to school. If this is inconvenient, there's no need to inform me. I shall be here, in any case, as I always have tea at four. Just drop me a line to suggest an alternative date, if this doesn't suit.

Yours most sincerely,
Emmeline Cooper-Montbéliard

Excellent. I was going to meet E C-Mb at Kingsland Hall, four o'clock tomorrow. It was my chance to find out who she was, and why she was paying my school fees. I slid the letter safely under my mattress, and decided that when Veronica arrived for tea, I'd beg her to drive me there.

★ ★ ★

The next afternoon, Veronica turned up again on the dot of three. Snow had transformed our garden, iced the front hedge and hidden the lawn, and outside our front door a spider's web hung frozen solid. I loved to watch spiders slowly build their web, thread by thread. I wondered what happened to them. Did they freeze too?

Dad looked surprised to see Veronica again so soon, but he hadn't heard us whispering when she left the day before. Hadn't seen her kiss me on the cheek and tell me how much she'd missed me. Good old Veronica. She made an excuse to Dad about having my feet measured for new shoes. I'm not sure if he completely swallowed it, but he was hardly in a position to object.

We passed through narrow Kidderminster streets, bordered by dirty red brick houses, and soon were out in open land, where snow had blanketed the fields. Despite icy roads, we made good progress, and before long arrived at a pair of tall cast iron gates hanging wide open.

At the end of a gravel driveway, lined on both sides by enormous bare-branched lime trees, Kingsland Hall rose up tall and smart. It wasn't the sombre mansion I'd expected, not a stately home, or even a hall, but more of a comfortable sized manor. It was a pinkish-red brick building, with no pillars or columns, and judging by the windows, it had three floors. I stared at one in a row of several ground floor windows, where a woman pressed her cheek against a pane and looked out. She didn't turn away when she saw me, so I stuck out my chin, hoping to look responsible.

My breath rose in white puffs as we walked up a short flight of steps. Veronica rang the old-fashioned bell. The solid oak door, embellished with carved acorns at the corners, and flying cherubs across the top, opened. Though I felt nervous, I put a smile on my face and peered over the shoulder of a middle-aged man.

In the wood-panelled hall, my enthusiasm fizzled out. Gold-framed oil paintings, and heavy furniture piped with twisted ormolu lined the walls. The pictures were of stern looking gentlemen with bristling whiskers, and demure ladies with white bosoms. Above the panelling, the walls were painted dark green. If this is a charity, I thought, I'll be so embarrassed. I watched the hands of a grandfather clock inch forward, and heard a different bell.

The same man came back across the hall and invited us to follow him. We went into a long sitting room, with three tall windows overlooking the front garden and driveway. It was in one of these that I'd seen the woman. In contrast to the hall, the room was very light, and she sat close to a roaring fire in the biggest hearth I'd ever seen.

She was tall and thin, wore a pale blue suit with frilly white blouse, and had completely white hair cut in a short modern style. With an intense look she asked us to sit.

'Now that we've sorted out the formalities,' she said, 'let's have some tea.'

Her assistant gave a nod and the door closed heavily behind him.

Her eyes slid to my face and I shifted in my seat. The phone rang. I thought she answered it reluctantly, but it gave me a chance to look round. There was a sweet perfume in the air, as well as the smell of wood burning in the fire. The walls were covered in pale silky fabric, the floor with oriental rugs, and the windowsills were dotted with shiny wooden animals.

The call ended, and with a friendly look she turned to us. 'I see you like my little animals. They're African.'

I smiled uncertainly.

'I'm glad you've come. I gather you want to know why I'm paying for your education.'

Finding a way to behave in the grand atmosphere of the room was awkward, but I managed to nod and found my voice. 'Yes please.'

She sighed, as if weighed down by something. Veronica and I exchanged looks.

After a few moments the woman spoke again. 'When my assistant told me he'd heard of your father's return, without your mother, I was puzzled.'

'How did he find out?' Veronica asked.

'Local gossip. In these country places it doesn't take much to set tongues wagging.'

I frowned. 'But why did it matter to you?'

There was a brief pause.

'I think Emma would like to understand your interest in her family,' Veronica said.

The woman's voice shook slightly. 'I'm afraid there is only one way to say this. I hope you won't hate me when I tell you.'

'No,' I muttered, not understanding.

The room went quiet, but I heard church bells in the distance, a car engine roared, and the wind began to get up.

'You see the truth is,' the woman continued. 'Lydia Cartwright is my daughter.'

I gulped and put out a hand to Veronica

'Then you are — ' Veronica's voice trailed off.

'Yes — I am Emmeline Cooper-Montbéliard, Emma's grandmother.'

I struggled from the chair and stood, hoping my legs weren't about to buckle. 'You can't be. My mother's mother was called Emma Rothwell.'

She nodded. 'That's correct. Rothwell was my great aunt's maiden name. She died many years ago with no descendants. As that branch of the family had long come to an end, I took the name on for the duration of my confinement, and simply shortened my Christian name to Emma.'

I studied her closely, took out my little portrait, handed it to her and watched. I attempted to speak, but my mouth was so dry I couldn't say a word.

'Yes that was once me,' was all she said, and gave the picture back. But then she bent forward, arms folded across her chest.

I sat down again. I felt as if a hand was squeezing my throat and it became even harder to speak.

She looked up. 'My solicitor made discreet enquiries, found out exactly where you were all living, and that was when we discovered Lydia definitely was not with you, nor was she living at your old home in Malacca.'

'Our old house?' I said, finding my voice.

'Yes. I'd known where Alec's parents' house was, of course, as my solicitor had kept me informed of Lydia's whereabouts, even before she went to Malaya. I contacted your father, and when I told him who I was, he and I met. This was important to me, you understand. Given that she seemed to have disappeared, I couldn't remain quiet. Of course, your father didn't know who I was, and was quite shocked to find out.'

He never said a word to us, I thought.

'He told me that your mother had abandoned you and your little sister, and that was why you'd all come back to England without her. After what had happened to her as a child, I found it utterly unbelievable that she would abandon her own children.'

'I never believed it either,' I said, swallowing rapidly. 'Never.'

'Anyway, your father and I came to an agreement. He was experiencing some financial difficulties, so in return for me paying your bills, *he* would help me locate your mother's whereabouts. It was fortunate I approached him at the time he was considering schools for you. He insisted the arrangement had to be secret, and though I very much wanted to meet you and your sister, he forbade it at that time. He said it would be too unsettling. Well, I didn't know you, so I had to accept his view.'

'What did he find out?' Veronica asked.

'Nothing of any use, just that she was missing.'

'That's what he told us, missing, presumed dead,' I added.

'Well, I thought it was nonsense, so I carried out my own investigation. At first I didn't get anywhere, but recently I found out the address of a friend of hers through a Malay newspaper article, and sent a telegram to her.'

The woman stared at the floor.

The newspaper article. From being cold, the room was suddenly stifling. I gripped the edges of the chair and leant forward, still looking at her, my body tense. She put a hand to her neck and fumbled for something. Just under her frilly collar, a silver lizard with emerald eyes was attached to a chain.

'So far I've had no reply.'

I felt my heart speed up and had to force myself to breathe slowly.

'Please tell me about your mother, Emma,' she said in a small voice. Her hands trembled and she seemed to find it hard to keep her voice steady.

'What did you say?'

'Your mother.'

I felt as if I was walking backwards down a long corridor. I must have gone pale, because I heard Veronica tell me to put my head between my knees.

After a while I looked up. 'My mother has lizards . . . They gave her the earrings. It's all she had.'

'Yes, they were mine.' There was a short pause. 'I want to say, the person I was is not the person I am today. We change. Life changes us.'

From the corner of my eye, I saw Veronica nod.

'I was forced to give her up and wasn't allowed to see her. It was a terrible wrench, but I was in disgrace. You can't imagine the shame I'd brought on my family.'

I looked at her face, at the fine lines and delicate skin, and at the deeper wrinkles on her forehead. I almost couldn't bear it when I saw the pain in her eyes.

'It was nineteen twenty-four and my parents forbade all contact, though I did persuade one of the nuns to let me meet Lydia, just the once. They were going on a day trip to the seaside, Weston-super-Mare. I met them there, and we watched a sand sculpture of a lion being built. I still think of it as the happiest day of my life. I even remember what I wore. A dress with bright blue flowers all along the hem. There was one other time, many years later . . . but that visit was prevented.'

I glanced out at the wind rolling snow about the lawn. I felt heartbreak for my mum and for this woman who had abandoned her, but also rage for my mother's lonely childhood. I longed so much to feel my mother's arms, that the tears spilled over. I brushed them away with the back of my hand.

'When I said goodbye to her, I left a part of my heart behind,' the woman said. 'They never allowed me to see her again. I had given up all rights, and they said it would upset her too much. Things were so different then, you see.'

'And the father?' Veronica spoke softly.

I turned to see how the woman would react. Her chin wobbled and I thought she was going to cry. She turned her back to us, put on another log and poked about until flames appeared. By the time she turned back, her face was composed.

'Charles Lloyd Patterson, the painter . . . you mustn't blame him, he didn't know, and I couldn't take Lydia. It was impossible back then.

With no money, no support of any kind, I did as my parents told me.'

'How did it happen?' Veronica asked.

I wanted to know too, but was startled by her bluntness.

My grandmother, for that is what she was, stood and started to pace up and down in front of the fire, rubbing her hands over and over. 'My parents commissioned Charles to paint my portrait. It took us both by surprise — we fell in love. I was very young. He was not.'

'And after the birth.'

'I wanted to come home, but my father bought me a flat in London instead. I think it broke his heart. I got a cataloguing job at the British Museum, didn't come back until my father's death, left London and came to live here, and then Mother died five years ago.'

'And the painter?'

'I never saw Charles again. He knew nothing of Lydia.'

'We saw two paintings of you,' I said. 'When you were young.'

She stopped pacing and gazed at me. 'You've been there?'

I nodded. I wanted to be angry with her, but found I couldn't. There was a long pause. Neither Veronica nor I was able to speak.

'And you? Do you judge me harshly?' she asked. Her features twisted slightly, and I caught a flash of fear in her otherwise still face.

I wound the tangles of my hair round my fingers. Something in her stirred up such pity. To be forced to give up a baby like that. I tried to judge her, but could not. 'No,' I whispered.

Her face lit up and she held out her arms. Without a moment's hesitation I went to her, smelt a trace of perfume on her skin. She kissed my cheek, the lightest kiss you could imagine.

Veronica watched, her eyes full, and I came back to sit beside her.

'And Alec. How did you know he was Lydia's husband?'

'Come, let me show you.'

Emmeline led us from the room and along a narrow corridor to the back of the house. She took a key from round her neck and unlocked a door into a room, where thin sunlight was softened by the snowy sky.

The walls were covered. Pictures of two babies, two little girls, a beautiful woman with flaming hair, and newspaper cuttings, were all pinned to a large corkboard. I took a step forward. My mother's wedding. The announcement of my birth. My father's short letter telling of my mother's disappearance. Articles about Malaya, depicting its beauty, and the terror that stalked its jungles.

The blood drained from my face. I could hardly breathe. Images flooded my mind. Half remembered incidents, outings, moods, and on our way to the sea, the sun shining on orange roofed bungalows. Most of all, the smell of lemongrass, and my mother's perfume.

'So you know everything about us,' I said, turning to her. 'About Fleur and me and about Mum.'

She shook her head. 'Not everything. I still

451

don't know where your mother is. As I said, I followed her progress as far as it went, via my solicitor, who had kept me informed throughout her life. I knew of her marriage, and that she hadn't returned to England with the rest of you. I instructed him to conduct a search using whatever means it might take.'

She put a hand to her throat and held it there.

'Please go on,' I said.

'Sometime later, when we picked up a trail, I went abroad to discover more. I hoped to visit Malaya, but didn't get further than Australia. Ill health, you see.'

'We must find her,' I said quietly.

She looked at me steadily. 'We shall, and I hope you, Veronica, will assist us.'

Veronica nodded.

Emmeline showed us to the door and I held her hand. It was cold as ice. Over her shoulder I saw the oil paintings again and wondered if they were my ancestors.

'Why didn't you tell her who you were after she grew up, after you came to live back here?' I asked.

'I always intended to. But the longer I left it . . . ' Her voice trailed off. 'Well, events conspired to prevent me. There was the war, and they went out to Malaya so suddenly. I'm sorry.'

'So when the solicitor asked if you'd be prepared to let it be known that you were paying my fees, why did you agree now?'

'I wanted very much to meet you and your sister, and as I'd had no success looking for Lydia with Alec's help, I felt it was time to reveal my interest in you both, whatever your father might say.'

She paused.

I saw her distress and kissed her on the cheek. It too was cold.

'Come back in February, at half term, and I'll see what can be found out by then,' she said. 'And if we have to go to Malaya to find her, we'll jolly well go together.'

I grinned as I waved, and Veronica and I walked out into the winter landscape, where the sky had turned thin and milky, and though it was freezing cold, my heart was on fire. I knew now who was paying my school fees, though that hardly seemed to matter at all. What mattered was that I had found Emma Rothwell. I had found my grandmother.

I wondered if Veronica was asking herself why Father withheld the truth. I knew I was.

'What shall we do about Dad?' I asked.

'Maybe it's best to keep this from your father, until we know more about the whereabouts of your mother.'

'But he wants to sell the house.'

'Don't worry. I'll work out a way to slow that down. I'll pick you up at half term and we'll go back to see your grandmother together.'

'Do you still love him after this?' I asked.

She nodded. 'Love isn't simple, and I know it's hard to understand, but I think I do. He's a complex man and he needs me.'

She was right; it was hard to understand.

53

When she couldn't sleep for excitement, Lydia took two sleeping pills, left over from when she believed her daughters had perished in the fire. She slept well and woke splayed across his bed. The sun, slanting through the bedroom shutters, striped the room with bands of light, and she thought of how it had felt when Adil lay there with her. Her mind was full of him in the morning when she woke, but at night when she went to sleep, and throughout the day, she thought only of her daughters.

She heard voices coming from the living room, dragged herself up and stumbled to the door.

Cicely lifted a perfectly made-up face. 'Hello, darling. Heavy night?' She laughed pointedly and pulled a face at Adil. 'Feel like joining us for coffee?'

Lydia felt awkward. Cicely always knew how to rattle her. She frowned and went to stand at the window, to avoid the teasing in Cicely's eyes. She stared at her own hands, as if wholly absorbed by her new red nail varnish, then looked out of the window. It was unusually blowy. Unsure how to be, she watched as the wind made puffy white clouds fly about, but suddenly remembered that she owed Cicely her thanks, if nothing more.

She spun round. 'I never thanked you for introducing me to Clara. If I hadn't met her, well, it doesn't bear thinking about.'

'No need for thanks, darling.'

Lydia looked at Cicely's face in the harsh sunlight and felt sorry for her. It seemed as if the fan of lines around her eyes had deepened, and she looked her age.

'Better be off now. Good luck, darling.' Cicely laughed, tilting her head at Adil. 'Enjoy!' She lifted a brow and with a quick flick of her bangled wrist was gone.

Lydia pulled a face.

Adil winked at her. He was dressed in burgundy and blue and the colours accentuated the brown of his eyes. 'Don't let her get to you.'

Maz, peeling a satsuma, spun round on his stool and an orangey fragrance filled the room

'What did she want, other than wanting to embarrass me?'

He shook his head and held up an envelope. 'You're too easily embarrassed. But it was this. She came with this.'

Lydia blinked. 'Who's it from?'

He shrugged and passed the telegram over with unconcealed curiosity.

She read it and frowned.

'So?'

'I don't understand. A woman is asking for details of my whereabouts.'

'Who is she?'

'Her name's Cooper-Montbéliard. She says it's on behalf of my family. There's a P.O. box number in Worcestershire for a reply.'

'Why did she send it to Cicely?'

'Search me. But what does she mean?' She

glanced down. *'On behalf of my family.* She must mean Emma and Fleur.'

There was a moment of silence. She read it several times before glancing up again. He held out his arms to her. She went to him, buried her head in his chest. Maz jumped on to the coffee table, squealing and flapping his hands.

'Maz, you'll break it.' Adil held out a hand, and the boy scrambled down. 'And tidy up the camp bed, for goodness sake.'

'What are we waiting for?' Lydia said, pulling away. She scribbled the P.O. box number on a scrap of paper.

'Do you know this woman?'

She shrugged and held up her hands. 'I don't care. I'm sending a reply today.'

'Will you go immediately? To England I mean.'

She nodded and a pulse throbbed at her temple. She wanted to touch him again, feel his heart thump as she lay her head against his chest. But the sound of her daughters' voices drew her back.

'Has anyone ever told you, you have the most extraordinary eyes?' he said, with a grin.

'I thought you'd never notice,' she said, head tilted to one side. She laughed, but there was a tremor in it. She'd been told she was beautiful before, but with Adil it meant more.

In the silence, nobody moved at first. Her feelings for him had grown slowly, and with them, the strange sensation that whatever she felt, he felt too. Her chest constricted. Unable to breathe, she kept her back to him and busied herself with the washing up. Torn at the thought of leaving him, there were things she needed to say, yet the words just wouldn't come.

Maz spun round and round, back on the stool again, and she heard Adil talking to him.

'I have to speak,' she said suddenly, in a voice choked with tears.

They stood facing each other across the room. Adil listened with absolute stillness, as if his whole body was absorbed by her.

'I failed my husband, failed my daughters.'

'If you did, you didn't do it all on your own.'

'Maybe not. But I do need to do this alone. See my daughters again. I'm sorry. I mean — '

He took a step towards her. She'd hoped his feelings for her were as real as her own, that she hadn't simply convinced herself that he cared. Now a flood of emotion caught in her throat, and she waved him away with the dishcloth.

'I have to put my children first,' she said. 'If I'd done that from the start, none of this would have happened . . . Whatever do you see in me?'

'I see the woman I want to be with.'

There was a short silence. Even Maz ceased spinning on the kitchen stool.

'Knowing everything about me, Jack, the girls, you still say that?'

He came across, put an arm round her waist and kissed her lightly on the forehead. 'Lydia. Put the dishcloth down. Go and get dressed.'

She gazed at him, gripped by the look she saw on his face. He cared.

★ ★ ★

457

After going to the shipping office, and back at the flat again, Adil was relaxed and smiling.

'You're sure you don't need me to come?' he said.

Her heart felt like it was trying to jump from her chest, as she smiled and blinked the tears away. 'I already have my little travelling companion.'

Maz looked up and grinned. 'I am going on a ship.'

'Thank God the Suez Canal is unblocked,' Adil said. 'Would've taken you a month otherwise.'

She hadn't thought of that. Thank goodness too for Maz's birth certificate. With it, Adil had managed to secure the necessary travel documentation, and it left just enough time, before the sailing, for a reply to come from England. She hoped it'd tell her exactly where to go.

'You'll like going on a big ship won't you, sweetheart,' she said, and ruffled the boy's hair. 'Don't worry, I'll look after you.'

She glanced over Adil's shoulder at the sea mist and the clouds spreading over the ocean. She turned from the view, took in his high cheekbones and wide set eyes, then watched his loose limbed walk, as he started to move about the room.

'I'm sorry,' she said in a quiet voice.

His face was still as he ran a palm over his head. She waited for something more, a subtle shift in his expression perhaps, or maybe she waited to understand herself a little more. She hardly knew. But then, besides the familiar lines of his face, there was something. A slight movement in his eyes, a deep warmth as he smiled, hardly noticeable, but enough to show her his feelings were real. And knowing it gave her permission to breathe more freely, as if the tight knot of pain had started to come undone in her. She smiled, picked up a box of sugared dates, and went to the window. Maz and Adil came over, and the three of them ate the dates, watching gulls riding in the suddenly cloudless sky.

'No more regrets,' he said.

'None at all.'

'You'll write? Let me know. Soon.'

'Very soon.'

The sweet scent of melons rose from the street, and a burst of birdsong outside the window made her glance out again. In a funny way she'd be sad to leave Malaya.

'Thank you,' she said, her mouth suddenly dry.

He leant down, and she held his face in her hands. She kissed both eyelids. 'You've always been what you said you were — a true friend. But you are far more than that. I don't know how you did it, but you made me see myself clearly.'

'I will be here when you're ready,' he said. 'One word from you and I'll be on the next boat. We can decide what to do as soon as you're settled. Nothing will change that.'

She nodded and put a finger to her lips. This was a new grown-up kind of love. There was a certainty that needed no explanation. Something

Emma once said came back to her. When a couple she and Alec had known well in Malacca separated, Emma had put her head to one side, and said, very sadly, 'It's because they're not with their *proper* people.'

Reminded of it now, Lydia grinned.

'What's so funny?' Adil asked.

'You. You are my *proper* person. I hope you won't mind the cold in England?'

He laughed. 'I'm tough, Lydia.'

She couldn't picture her life without him now. The future rose up before her and in every place she saw herself, he was there too, and even if she'd wanted to, she couldn't paint him out. It was going to be all right. They would see each other again and it wouldn't be long. The sun appeared through the clouds, the air cleared and that was it. She closed her eyes and smiled inwardly, feeling intensely light. Over at the edge of the shore, a woman in a pale blue dress waved. At the back of her mind, the ghost who hovered over her life faded, and Lydia turned towards the future. God willing, she was about to see her daughters again. Life had given her a second chance, and that was what mattered now.

54

At the eagerly longed for start of half term, Veronica was due to collect me to go back to Kingsland Hall. It was a cold day, so early that a white mist still lay over the grounds. I found her parked at the side of the school, where the harsh weather had cracked the wall.

It was only when I got into the car that I realised something was wrong. I asked her what, but she barely looked at me, and when I wanted to know if we were going straight to Kingsland Hall, she half turned towards me with a sad little smile on her face.

'Sorry no. We have to go straight back.'

'What's happened?'

'Your father knows.'

I frowned.

'He knows we deceived him, that I took you to Kingsland Hall without telling him. He's furious. Says I've been disloyal.'

'How can he say that, after what he did!'

Veronica gave a little shake of her head and looked close to tears.

'How did he find out?'

'He overheard me on the phone to your grandmother, last night, talking about the tickets.'

She'd spoken in a matter of fact tone of voice, but I knew immediately what that meant. Despite her mood she smiled. It was magic. I couldn't believe it. I hugged myself, tingling with excitement. Tickets to go to Malaya!

'You know, don't you, that after your grand-mother saw your mother's newspaper article, she got hold of an address for her friend, Cicely. From the journalist who wrote the article, apparently.'

'I remember Cicely.' I'd had no reply myself from the editor, but was overjoyed my grandmother had been more successful.

'She sent Cicely a telegram, but didn't receive anything back, so now she's going to send an airmail letter, saying you'll both be going out to Malaya.'

I had an awful thought. 'What if he tries to stop me from going?'

'Then your grandmother will go alone,' she said. 'Anyway, that's why we're going straight back. He's in a foul mood and I want to see if I can talk him round. We need to sort you out a new passport, and I can't do it without his help. I don't want to give him too much time to brood.'

Back home the atmosphere was stiff. Fleur was at a school friend's for the day and night, and I was in my room with the door ajar. Dad's voice reached me from below, and though I couldn't make out all the words, I could tell by the tone of his voice that he was being difficult.

Eventually she came upstairs, pink-eyed, and even paler than usual. 'We're going out. I've persuaded him to take a drive over to the Cotswolds to have lunch in Chipping Campden. Will you be okay?'

I answered with a grin.

As long as I had my grandmother, what could Dad do? My grandmother. I said the words over again, and pinched myself. Though I worried whether she'd cope with Malaya's harsh climate, and there was still the matter of a passport to sort out.

The afternoon passed slowly. I was feeling quietly hopeful, dreaming of the heat of Malaya, when I heard a sound outside. I frowned. Had Fleur come back early? I went downstairs, and glanced out of the kitchen window at a low sun, shining behind the bare beech tree at the bottom of the garden. It was nearly dusk and someone was there. I opened the back door.

'You'll write about all this one day,' Billy said, as he came through, then kissed me on the cheek.

I wasn't so sure. I'd written very little since I abandoned Claris to her fate. 'About what?'

'About the wind flying through your hair, Em. I've got my dad's motorbike. Where do you want to go?'

★ ★ ★

On our way to Kingsland Hall, I glanced at the river, black and cold, and remembered when I'd dangled my legs in the water with Billy. As we rode up the long drive, a new moon came out above the house. I let out a long slow breath. New moon. New life.

At the door, we were met by my grandmother's assistant. 'She's not here,' he said, with a troubled look.

My heart jumped. 'Where then?'

'Your grandmother is in hospital. I'm very sorry.'

I turned to Billy. 'Can you take me there? Please, Billy.'

The assistant put out a hand. 'I'm afraid she's seriously ill. With all the excitement, I knew something like this would happen. I've just spoken to the matron. They won't let anyone see her until tomorrow morning.'

'Billy?'

'Come on, Em. We'll go in the morning. Like he says.'

★ ★ ★

Legs like jelly, I stood at the desk. The receptionist directed us to the top floor of the main wing. Though it was early, the hospital was wide-awake, and a strong smell of ether followed us everywhere. Porters pushed trolleys, and we had to avoid white-coated doctors, huddled together and speaking softly. I pushed open a swing door into a noisy ward. Everyone seemed to be running, a phone rang continuously, and frail voices called out for help. The sign above the door said *Acute Observation*. They were serving breakfast, so I stepped back, and straight into a plump nurse.

'This isn't visiting time,' she said, with a frown. 'We're strict on that.'

'Please. I've come to see my grandmother. Miss Cooper-Montbéliard.'

She deliberated, then led us out of the main door and down a corridor. She stopped outside a

464

room, with a red light glowing overhead, and looked at me.

'It's the only single occupancy room on this floor. You can go in, but don't excite her. She's very ill.'

I took a deep breath. 'Will you wait, Billy?'

He nodded and I pushed open the door and peered in. The curtains were closed and the light was low. A bottle of Lucozade, still in its orange cellophane wrapper, a tin of Ovaltine, and an unopened box of Black Magic chocolates sat on the metal bedside cupboard. At first I couldn't see her, her white face and white hair vanishing into the pillows and sheets. It seemed as if no one was there; only a gentle whistle told me I wasn't alone. I listened to her breath, then moved closer and sat on a hard, straight-backed chair beside her bed.

She was connected to a drip on a stand. I leant back in the chair and closed my eyes. I'd never wished for anything so much before. I pleaded with God to make her better, to keep her alive so that my mum could know her. I knew going to Malaya was out of the question now, but that didn't matter, I just wanted her to live. It would be too unfair to find her, then lose her so soon. I brushed away the tears but they kept on coming.

After a while she opened her eyes, and I caught a strange look on her face, but she didn't seem to recognise me and closed them again. A nurse came in with a concerned look, nodded to me and left. I sat for hours, my bottom going numb on the hard wooden chair. Billy brought me hot chocolate and a bun, and then went back down to the canteen to wait.

A doctor came.

'Will she be okay?' I asked, my shoulders tense.

He cleared his throat. 'She has pneumonia.' His voice was flat and unemotional.

'She's my grandmother. Please tell me.'

He seemed to consider for a moment. 'Look, it's hard to say. She's asthmatic and this is a serious complication. We're watching her closely. You can wait here, but it's better if you go down to the canteen.'

'I'll wait.'

He opened the curtain fully then turned on his heels.

I blinked in the sudden daylight. The window overlooked a car park, and I looked down at the people coming and going, with all their own sorrows and fears. Then I pulled the chair close to her and shut my eyes, thinking of all that had happened in the last three years. I left Malaya as a kid, and now, listening to my grandmother breathe, realised how far I'd come. I sat like that for ages, staring at the grey lino floor and thinking.

Her voice startled me.

'Emma?' she said.

My breath caught — I saw her eyes, full of life, completely conscious.

'You're going to be okay.'

She smiled and spoke breathlessly. 'Listen, child. I've made a new will. My solicitor has it, and my assistant knows what to do. If anything happens to me, it's all yours and Fleur's, when you both come of age.'

'But nothing is — '

She held up a shaking hand. 'In the meantime, I've arranged it that until then a trust can access anything either of you might need. You'll both be able to live at the house, as soon as you're old enough, if that's what you wish. I'm so looking forward to meeting my other granddaughter.'

'And my mother?'

'Yes. If she forgives me. I planned to come to your school, then this happened. I wanted to surprise you with tickets for Malaya, but now.' She let out a breath and gave a slight shrug.

I took hold of her hand. 'What's going to happen about Mum? Shall we write to her friend again?'

'I already have. It takes a little while, even with airmail, but I should hear something before too long. Of course, this Cecily woman may not know where Lydia is, but it's somewhere to start. My assistant has cancelled the tickets, by the way. But when I'm better, we'll still go.'

My heart raced, and when I laid my cheek on her bedcover, she stroked my hair.

'Don't worry, sweetheart, you will see her again. You'll have such a lot to tell each other.'

I looked up. 'And you.'

'Me too.' She closed her eyes.

I gulped. A lump grew in my throat. I felt her pulse.

'Don't you worry,' she said, eyes open again. 'I'm just tired. I'll be up and about before you know it. So much to live for now. So much more than I deserve.'

467

My throat was parched and I couldn't speak. She was going to be okay. And one day we would all live together at Kingsland Hall.

The high ceilings and polished wooden staircase flashed into my mind. Could it be possible? Not for a moment in my wildest stories could I have imagined this. I felt so happy I wanted to leap up and down, yet at the same time, a voice was whispering — *Why hasn't Cecily replied to your grandmother's telegram? What if your mother doesn't want you any more?* I shook my head to make it go away. I couldn't breathe for wanting my mum and longing to see her. It was unthinkable that we might fail.

55

At Liverpool docks, people stood in restless groups, the pale day a blissful contrast to the dark clouds and tropical storms of Malaya. Men smelling of machine oil, and wearing caps and greasy blue overalls, struggled with heavy ropes and chains. A layer of soot lay on the ground, yet behind the bustle and dirt, there was tranquillity in the Englishness. She hardly dared think of her daughters, and the three long years since she'd last seen them. The time she thought they were dead, she remembered like a dream.

She'd been surprised when another telegram from Miss Cooper-Montbéliard hadn't arrived. She had counted on having an address to go to, but had decided to try Alec's parents anyway. She held Maz's hand tight, felt the thrill of anticipation, and imagined the rolling green meadows that lay ahead. A few people stared when she tilted her face, arms stretched out wide, palms upwards, damp settling on her skin.

★　★　★

The taxi drew up slowly. She instructed the driver to park nearby and asked him to wait.

She patted the boy on the head. 'Maz, stay in the car. I won't be long.'

From a distance, Alec's parents' house looked exactly the same. Close up, though, she saw a garden gone wild. Something wasn't right. Alec's father wouldn't let it get like this. She noticed a *For Sale* sign lying abandoned on overgrown grass by the front hedge. Her heart sank.

She looked about. Next door but one, a neighbour was raking the lawn. She walked over and coughed. The man looked up.

'I'm so sorry to disturb you,' she said. 'I'm looking for Eric Cartwright and his wife. I don't suppose you can tell me where they are?'

The man stood up and rubbed his back. He cupped a hand behind his ear. 'What's that, dear?'

'I was after Eric Cartwright,' she said in a louder voice.

'Oh no, they're gone,' he said, shaking his head. 'Sorry, dear.' He picked up his rake and ambled back to his garage door.

'Do you know where they've gone?' she called after him, but he didn't hear and closed the door.

★   ★   ★

At the telegraph desk in the post office, she spoke to a grey-haired woman behind a metal grille. When the woman stared openly at Maz, Lydia held his hand even tighter, and smiled what she hoped was a convincing smile.

'I received a telegram from a Miss Cooper-Montbéliard. The address was a P.O. box. I sent one back to her, and was expecting to hear from her again, but I didn't.'

'What's your P.O. box?' the woman said.

470

'No, I haven't got a P.O. box.'

'But you just said you were waiting to hear.'

'I'm sorry there's been some confusion. What I need is the home address of the person who sent me a telegram from a P.O. box.' She dug in her bag, fished out a sheet of paper. 'Look, here's the number. I wrote it down.'

The woman pursed her lips. 'Oh no. We never give out addresses. That's the whole point of a P.O. box.'

'But this is really important.'

The woman bristled. 'It always is, dear. Now, if that's all.'

Lydia shook her head. She hadn't come all this way to be brushed off. 'No, it isn't all. Look, this is the number. Can you at least check to see if another telegram was sent to me. Mrs Lydia Cartwright.'

'Well, I can do that.' The woman paused, glanced at the number, and frowned.

'Are you sure that's the correct number?'

Lydia nodded.

'Haven't you got the original telegram?'

Lydia searched her bag, feeling more and more agitated. Surely she couldn't have left the telegram in Adil's flat? She remembered writing down the number on a sheet of paper, leaving the telegram in a safe place so as not to lose it, and taking the piece of paper to the telegraph office. The same piece of paper she now had.

'I'm sorry, dear. That isn't one of our numbers. We cover a wide area but none of ours begins with seven five. I wish you good day.'

Lydia turned on her heels and held herself

471

together. She racked her brain trying to remember. She must have brought it with her. She remembered packing a bag for herself and one for Maz, but she could not remember picking up the telegram again. Could not remember slipping it into her bag. How could she have been so careless? In her haste, she must have made an error jotting down the number, and then in the whirlwind of excitement, left the actual telegram behind.

It was clear Miss Cooper-Montbéliard could never have received her reply.

She stood with Maz in the high street and her spirits plummeted. What now? This wasn't going at all the way she planned, and the fear that, after everything, she might not find her girls caused such pain in her chest she almost forgot to take in breath.

'I am cold, Mem,' Maz said, teeth chattering.

She pulled him into her own looped mohair coat. 'You poor little thing. I'd forgotten about the cold. We need to buy you a thicker coat.'

★ ★ ★

Once they'd got him a nice warm duffle coat, they sat in a café out of the cold. Maz watched, full of questions.

'Where are we going now?' he said.

'I'm just thinking about that.'

He stared through steamy windows at passers-by. Muffled in scarves and woolly hats, they couldn't have looked more different from the people he'd been used to.

'Is it always so cold?'

'Not in the summer.'

'Is it hot, like Malaya, in the summer?'

'No, darling.'

She grinned, suddenly realising what to do. Of course, the estate agent. She jumped up right away and held out her hand to the boy.

★ ★ ★

Maz stuffed his hands into the pockets of his navy coat, and sat in the taxi, a little way from the house.

'Sorry, sweetie,' she said. 'Just wait a minute.'

They were back at Alec's parents' place, the wind now blowing the long grass about. She found a pencil and scrap of paper in her bag, opened the gate and bent over the *For Sale* sign, by the hedge. She carefully copied the name, address, and phone number of the estate agent, unaware of a car pulling up.

A man called out. 'It's about blasted time. You'd better hammer it in properly this time. No wonder we haven't had any luck.'

Lydia instantly recognised the voice. She stood up straight, wiped her damp hands on her coat, and turned to face him.

He stared and took a step back. 'Lydia!'

There was a prolonged silence.

Of all the feelings she could have felt, she was surprised by a twinge of pity. He looked drained, as if life had taken him and shaken the stuffing out. Dressed in a dark overcoat, short hair thinning, eyes circled with blue shadows, he looked a great deal older. Over at his car, a young girl stared out of the window. Lydia's heart thumped wildly, and her eyes widened as the girl climbed from the Morris Oxford and stood on the road beside it.

This wasn't her blonde, baby daughter, with her hair in a parting and a bow at the side. This Fleur had light brown hair, in one long plait at the back of her head, and she wore glasses.

'Fleur?' she said.

A knot formed in Lydia's throat. She stood in the front garden trying to speak again, but nothing came. The moment went on. She opened the gate and began to walk, unable to see clearly through the tears. She stopped. The girl hadn't moved. Lydia held out her arms.

'Fleur, it's Mummy. Don't you recognise me?'

Lydia brushed away her tears. A tall blonde woman, wearing a grey suit, stood at the other side of the car. She came round, whispered something in Fleur's ear, patted her on the shoulder, and gave her a little push towards Lydia. Fleur took a few steps forward, like a clockwork doll. Lydia moved too. They stared at each other, Fleur silent and white-faced. By the time Lydia knelt in front of her daughter, her throat was choked. She couldn't speak, could barely breathe.

She smelt Fleur's soft soapy hair, raised a hand, almost touched it.

Fleur turned back to the blonde woman for confirmation. The woman nodded, but Fleur didn't move. Confused, Lydia looked over at the woman too. She nodded again.

Lydia and her daughter remained a foot apart,

not touching. Then Fleur leant very slightly towards her mother. Taking her cue, Lydia gently stroked her daughter's hair.

'Look at you. Your hair's so long. So lovely.'

She wrapped her arms around her daughter. She'd imagined this moment so many times, hugged her phantom daughters in her dreams, searched for the light in their eyes. But this was real. Her daughter, more precious than life itself, had been given back.

'Well, we can't stand out here in the cold. You'd better come in,' Alec interrupted.

Lydia stayed where she was.

'Lydia?' he said.

She held on to Fleur's hand, stood up, and looked him straight in the face. 'Where have your parents gone?'

'They haven't gone anywhere.'

'The neighbour said they'd gone.'

'I'm so sorry. Eric's dead, Alec's mother is in a nursing home,' the blonde woman said. She stepped forward and held out her hand. 'I'm Veronica.'

Lydia shook her hand, but it was her daughters that dominated her mind, and she scanned the street.

'Where's Emma?'

Alec nodded at a spot fifty yards beyond them. A tall girl was climbing down from the back of a motorbike. Lydia watched her remove a helmet and shake her hair, then stand on tiptoes to kiss a boy on the cheek.

'He parks down there so we don't see,' Veronica said. 'Though, of course, we know.'

The girl turned round. Lydia saw her stand completely still. A tall girl in modern clothes. Three-quarter-length trousers, despite the cold, ankle boots and a short haircut. Lydia kissed Fleur on the forehead, Veronica put a comforting hand on the girl's shoulder, and then Lydia ran towards the tall girl. She slipped on the grass. Stopped. The girl hadn't moved. Was this grown-up girl her daughter? The girl who dressed in a clown's costume, and came racing out of school screeching, *Mummy?*

Emma appeared to sway.

Lydia went to her and held her by the shoulders.

Emma's chin trembled. 'Mummy?'

She examined Emma's grown-up face, saw the turquoise eyes fill with tears.

'Oh, my darling girl, I was so scared I wouldn't find you.'

'I left you a letter, Mummy. I told you where we were going.'

With a sharp intake of breath, Lydia twisted her head to glance at Alec, but continued holding Emma's shoulders. Alec looked at his feet.

'When I came home, the house was empty and you were gone. I didn't find a letter.' She paused, gulped back tears, saw the depth of pain in her daughter's eyes.

She felt everyone watching. Not just Alec, Fleur and Veronica but the eyes of the entire world seemed to watch.

'Oh, Mummy,' Emma whispered.

Lydia wrapped her daughter in her arms, felt

Em's heart thump against her chest. Never in a lifetime could she have imagined anything as precious as this. Em began to sob, and she wiped her daughter's tears with her fingers.

When they separated they stared, looked for tiny changes, a line here, a change of contour, a filling out, a thinning down.

Emma stepped back. 'You have more silver threads in your hair. You look different.'

'You too.'

Emma blushed, and tried to speak between another bout of sobs. Lydia patted her back, watched her chest rise and fall with each breath. Fleur joined them, and her two daughters stood side by side. Lydia stared at them, so proud she thought her heart might burst.

'You are both so beautiful.'

Fleur smiled sweetly and Em turned red.

Alec and Veronica stood a little way off.

'She's nice,' Fleur said softly in Lydia's ear. 'She forgave him, even though Dad wanted to make a bigamist of her.'

Did he indeed, Lydia thought. She took a few steps towards Alec, holding on to her daughters' hands.

'I think we'd better go inside,' he said again.

'Yes, please do come in,' Veronica added. 'I'll make some tea and you can talk in private.'

For a moment nobody moved, then the teenage boy began to back away. 'This is family stuff. I'll see you later, Em.'

'Billy can come in too, can't he?' Emma said.

'Perhaps not. There are things we need to talk about,' Lydia said. 'Why not go in with Veronica and Fleur, while I speak with your father for a moment.'

Fleur shot a questioning look at Veronica who smiled her approval.

While Fleur and Veronica went through the gate, and Emma kissed the boy goodbye, Lydia and Alec locked eyes.

Away from the others, his face twisted. 'I loved you, Lydia. All that nonsense about a sick friend. You ruddy well left me.'

'I chose you.'

He stared at her. 'You stopped choosing me a long time ago. It was the girls you chose.'

She examined his face, noticed a razor cut on his chin, a worn edge to the collar of his shirt. Not so immaculate now. But when she looked in his eyes, it was in the hope of finding a trace of the man she once loved.

In the uncertain silence, Alec folded his arms across his chest.

Emma, having left her young man, headed over towards Fleur and Veronica, who were now at the front door. Lydia heard footsteps and a small voice calling from the direction of the taxi.

'Mrs Lydia. Mem?'

She spun round to see Maz run towards her.

'Oh my lord, I'd forgotten. She took hold of the little boy's hand, squeezed it, then turned to her daughters. 'Girls, please come over here before we go in.'

Fleur went across to join Emma.

Lydia patted Maznan on the back. 'Maz,' she said. 'It's time to say hello to your half sisters.'

Lydia saw Emma turn white. She shook her

head. 'No, darling, he's not my son.' She looked at Alec who was staring at Maz.

There was a long silence.

Lydia noticed the wind get up again, heard the rustle in the grass. The last few years flashed through her mind. The grief. The heartache he'd caused. Nothing he could do would put that right. Except maybe this one thing.

Alec held her eyes for a moment, then, hearing Veronica's sharp intake of breath, twisted round and attempted a smile. She shook her head, stepped back against the front door. He looked at the waiting girls, and finally returned to Maznan Chang.

The little boy grinned in recognition.

Everyone watched as he bent to pick up the child.

The little boy hugged him, and beamed at Lydia.

'Mem, my mother said never to tell. This is my papa.'

Fleur gulped and Emma put a comforting hand on her shoulder. Veronica unlocked the front door.

'I think I've heard enough,' she said, in a stiff voice. 'I suggest we all go inside. I don't pretend to understand any of this, but it's clear there's quite some explaining to do.'

Epilogue

1958: Three months later, England

Three years I lived without my mother. Now, when we talk about the lost years, we put on brave faces, and say at least it made us stronger.

Mum watches us constantly, can't allow a moment's inattention. In a locket round her neck, she has a photo of me and one of Fleur, never takes it off, except in the bath. When I look at my picture, I see a kid with an observant face, a lopsided grin, and a smear on the end of her nose. Hard to remember who I was then, but sometimes I feel I can stare myself back into the past, make it live again. And there we'd be, Mum, Fleur and me, and it would still be only 1955, and none of this would ever have happened.

When we went into Dad's house that first day Mum got back, I'd never seen her so angry. In front of us all, she threatened Dad with the police: for crimes of fraud and abduction, she said. Fleur burst into tears and Veronica, white-faced, managed to calm her down. Dad said she had no evidence, but Mum refused to let us stay the night with him. I think he was bluffing about the evidence thing, because in return for Mum not going to the police, he let us go to a hotel with her. Fleur took some persuading, mainly by Veronica, but the boy and I were excited. Mum has permanent custody of

Fleur and me, and Maz chose to live with us. The truth is, Mum's heart wasn't in a police investigation. We've been through enough, she told me afterwards, and it would be awful for Fleur if our father went to prison.

We don't let Fleur or Maz see the anger we both still feel when they go to stay with Dad some weekends. I can't forgive Dad for what he did, and neither can Mum. She is coldly polite with him when he drops Fleur and Maz back. I get the feeling he wants to talk, but she doesn't. The saddest thing is Veronica left the day we all got back together. It's been three months and nobody has seen her since. Perhaps Maz was the final straw? Anyway, Dad's lonely, and maybe that's punishment enough.

After Mum met her own mother for the first time, she came back to the hotel with red-rimmed eyes, but also with a big smile and the keys to Kingsland in her hand.

I watch her lay the fire in my grandmother's big sitting room, twisting the newspaper, adding the pinecones and the kindling. She's still beautiful, in a way more so, but less shiny, and her hair, held up in a large tortoiseshell clip, no longer tumbles down. It's already May, but Mum's cold.

She gets up from kneeling by the fire, her cheeks red, and sees us waiting there.

'Mum, this is Billy. You saw him at Dad's.'

'I remember. Hello, Billy. I won't shake hands.' She wipes her dirty hands on a rag.

'Billy's group is playing at the Mecca Ballroom, in Birmingham. On Saturday.'

'Oh?'

'We're only a support but it's a great opportunity,' Billy says.

'I'm sure.'

'Anyway, Mum, thing is, Billy's asked me to go with him.'

'Not on the motorbike, Mrs Cartwright. She'll come in the van with me.'

'Oh, I don't think so,' Mum says, and starts towards the kitchen, where Fleur's baking a cake. 'She's far too young.'

'Mum!'

'Emma?'

We stare at each other motionless. This isn't the first time she's forgotten. I pull a face. 'Mum, I'm *fifteen*.'

She looks at me with expressionless eyes, as if she's trying to remember something, then nods her head and her eyes grow damp. 'So you are.'

'So can I go?'

'Well, even fifteen is quite young.'

'My dad's driving the van if that helps,' Billy adds.

'Okay, I give in. As long as she's not back too late.'

Billy and I grin at each other, as Mum goes to help Fleur. I'm so excited I jump up and down like a child of ten.

'I thought you were *fifteen*,' he says, imitating my tone of voice, and looking me straight in the face.

I thump him.

★ ★ ★

Nothing can lessen these days of hope. It's great to be young, to be going to the Mecca Ballroom with Billy, and to have my mother back. The invisible thread, one end attached to my mother's heart, and the other to mine, never did break. I always knew it wouldn't. And more than anything, more than the discovery of my grandmother, more than living at Kingsland Hall, that's what's precious.

Only if I lie spread-eagled on the floor do I travel back to when I was eleven. I close my eyes and I'm lying on my tummy again, counting the holes in the floorboards of our bedroom in Malacca. Malaya is such a long time ago and so far away, but I'll always remember the clouds that looked like puffs of sherbet lemon, and the ribbons of scent that wound round the trees at the bottom of the garden.

No matter where life will take me, and even if one day I no longer hear the sounds, deep down Malaya will always be there, beating at the heart of me. It was where I was a child, before I knew that life could go so badly wrong. And it's where the smell of lemongrass will stay with me for ever, that and the sound of my mum singing in the morning, a bird of paradise flower clashing with her auburn hair.

Author's Note

The Separation is a work of fiction, set against the background of the Emergency that took place in Malaya during the 1950s. While the characters are imaginary, and no resemblance to any person living or dead is intended, there are resonances and echoes from my own childhood spent in Malaya at that time.

Parts of the novel were inspired by family stories; I did, for example, stumble into a waxworks museum as my character Emma does, and I saw exactly what she sees, and my mother did indeed sing at a hotel in Singapore. Among other memories, I recall swimming in a natural plunge pool on a rubber plantation in the Johore area, guns piled high on the hall table when the rubber planters came into town for a party, and the colour and noise of Chinatown where I was taken by my Chinese amah, Ah Moi. I remember the houses on stilts, the lizards that left their tails behind, and so much more of the smells, sounds and sights of Malaya.

My mother's memories, her memoirs, and her wonderful photograph albums were the inspiration for many of the locations in the book, particularly Jack's plantation, Harriet Parrott's house, Cicely's house and the Mental Hospital. YouTube provided brilliant footage of old colonial interiors, useful details of daily life on a plantation, and also gave me insight into domestic life in Singapore and Malacca. The Colonial Film catalogue produced a wealth of moving images about the British Empire.

My father worked in the development and restoration of postal systems and we moved eight times in as many years. He didn't talk much about his work, but he loved Malaya and his memories left me with a lasting impression of his life there, and were partly responsible for the way I formed my picture of the jungle, the Malay villages and the resettlement camps.

As well as the Internet, Amazon and Google gave me access to a world of books, blogs and memoirs. I am grateful to them all for so many facts about the country that was Malaya, and in particular Malacca, where I was born. I feel lucky to have been born in such an extraordinary place, and at such an extraordinary time. I'm certain its influence remains with me. Much of Malacca, as it is in the novel, was based on memory, so any errors are down to my own hazy version of the past. I felt I wanted to keep that quality as I described it, and resisted visiting modern-day Melaka for that reason. I have kept the spellings of places in Malaya as they were during the 1950s.

The story of Lydia, Alec, Emma and Fleur is not, however, my own family's story. We were never separated, but all came back to England together on the kind of ship Emma sails on, though our journey was in 1957, when the Suez Canal was still blocked. The ship scene is based very much on my own memories of finding my sea legs in a storm during that journey.

The ghost stories and tales that Emma remembers were inspired partly by stories I found on the Internet, and partly from the following books:

1. *Malay Magic* by Walter Skeat (Macmillan, London, 1900).
2. *Shaman, Saiva and Sufi* by R. O. Winstedt (first published in Singapore, 1925; reprinted by Forgotten Books, 2007).
3. *The Book of Chinese Beliefs* by Frena Bloomfield (Arrow Books, London, 1983).

For Lydia, facing what she has to, I drew on my own experience of being a parent coping with the death of a child. It is something that never really goes away. So finally, I'd like to include a poem here, written by my then brother-in-law. Of all the wonderfully kind cards and letters I received at the time, these words still have the power to bring a lump to my throat. I hope that some of the words in this novel might do the same.

To Dinah, on the death of her son

Next time we see you coming,
like a one-legged man,
we shall all be looking
for the limb that is not there.

With our smiles
half-way to his laughter,
next time we see you coming
we shall be watching for his grin.

But when we hear you talking —
proud, like a one-legged man,
refusing to stumble —
it is we who shall limp with your pain,

and there will be only peace
when we notice
quietly gathering round your chair —
our one-legged man —
ready to catch you
when, as you must, you fall,

there will be only peace
when we notice
quietly gathering round your chair
the fourteen shadows
of the sunlight of his years.

Dick Holdsworth, 1985

Acknowledgements

I'd like very much to thank the following people whose help has been invaluable in bringing this book to publication. My old friend, the author Gillian White, for her generous encouragement right from the start. Vanessa Neuling for reading the first drafts and for her perceptive and clever feedback. My agent, Caroline Hardman of Hardman & Swainson, for taking the book on with such enthusiasm and commitment, and for her expert advice. To all the team at Viking/Penguin, especially publishing director Venetia Butterfield, and my editor Elspeth Sinclair, who have both been fantastic. Nicole Wotherspoon for sharing her memories of living in Malaya in the 1950s, and for her recollections of life in an English boarding school. Sophie Endersby for information about inheritance law at that time, and for what to do about death certificates when the bodies are missing. My mother for her memories and photograph albums. And my lovely supportive family, young and old, especially my long-suffering husband, Richard, who always believed in the book and who enjoyed helping me with the research. Thank you all.